MANHATTAN STATE OF MIND

An Opposites Attract
Office Romance

Rosa Lucas

PROLOGUE

Lucy

I sit up in my chair, putting on my game face.

It's that time of year again at Quinn & Wolfe: performance reviews. When managers morph into grumpy trolls, and we minions scramble to cram a month's worth of work into a single week, all in a futile attempt to prove our worth. It's our white-collar *Hunger Games* but with more paperwork and no Hemsworths.

Helen from HR slides a stack of papers to my boss, Andy. He inhales deeply, eyeing the pile as if it holds the weight of the world's woes. "Let's get this over with, shall we?"

Flipping through the papers, he glares at Helen. "Why's it so much longer than last year?"

She meets his scowl with a polished smile. "We've included a comprehensive assessment of soft skills—communication, teamwork, collaboration." She punctuates her words with a triumphant pen tap against his file. "It's all in there, Andy."

"Jesus fucking Christ," he mutters under his breath.

It's not often I agree with Angry Andy.

He sighs again, settles on the first page, and clears his throat noisily as Helen slides a copy my way.

"Productivity, excellent. Problem-solving skills, excellent..." He flips the page with the enthusiasm of a man forced to read a dishwasher manual. "Flexibility, excellent."

As he yammers on, my attention drifts to the view outside—the Empire State Building. It's easy to forget I'm hovering forty floors above reality when I'm elbows deep in wireframes and screen designs.

"Your designs are exceptional," he drones. Funny, that doesn't *sound* like a compliment.

Still, it's hard to argue with "exceptional." I blush, basking in the ego stroke. This is it. Come on, Andy, spit it out already. *Lucy, you're promoted to Lead Graphic Designer. Congratulations.*

About freaking time.

"Teamwork..." Andy looks up from the paperwork. "Good, although stop covering for Matty when he sneaks out for a three-hour lunch."

"I don't—"

"I have eyes, Lucy, and they aren't just for show."

Right. I squirm in my seat. No more all-you-can-eat Turkish buffet for Matty.

Andy skims the rest of the form as if trying to beat a speed-reading record. "Attendance." He flicks a glance my way. "Actually, you're too early for meetings. Like a dog waiting by the door for its owner. It's off-putting."

I stare at him, stunned. Helen looks like she's ready to disappear under the table.

Too early for meetings? Is that even a thing? Before I can mentally give him the finger, he's already plowed on.

"Time management, great. Everything's done ahead of time, in fact"—he flips the page and gives me a look that could be a smirk or a facial tic—"Steve from marketing dubbed you 'Wonder Woman' for your swift work on the blog design."

I nod in stoic agreement, face carefully blank. "Just doing my job."

Wonder Woman, my ass. More like a chronic workaholic.

To buy more time, some people claim jobs will take five days when really, they take two. Take my work buddy Matty as a prime example. Me? I'm the opposite. I'll stay up all night to perfect a task, then breezily claim I knocked it out in a couple of hours.

"All right, let's wrap this up." He slams his pen down, turning to Helen. "Are we good?"

Hang on a second.

"Andy," Helen interjects, "You skipped section 15.8."

"Ah, for fu—" He lets out an exasperated sigh, shooting her a look of utter contempt.

"Health and safety. Do you need any adjustments to your workspace? Ergonomic chair, ergonomic mouse, etcetera." His hand does a lazy dance in the air. "Look, just read through the list yourself, will you?"

"We've got some new desk models with built-in footrests," Helen chimes in. "Take your pick."

"Umm, Andy," I say slowly. "Can you just go back to what you were saying before all the ergonomic stuff?"

Grunting, he flips back a page. "Time management—"

"No, not that," I cut in, leaning forward with my hands on the table, maybe to strangle him. "About my design output. What about the promotion?"

"What promotion?"

My eyes bug out. "*My* promotion?"

The one you've been dangling over my head for six months to get me to pick up yet more responsibility around here without extra pay, you jerk?

"Oh, right. No promotion this round." He gives a casual shrug, shoveling his paperwork toward poor Helen as if she's some sort of human filing cabinet. "We'll revisit next year, yeah?"

No, no, a thousand times NO.

This cannot be happening. There's absolutely no way I'll be able to walk out of this office and face Matty, Taylor, and the rest of the design team without that promotion.

Keep it together. Don't turn on the waterworks. I swear, if a single tear trickles down my face, I'm throwing myself out the window.

"Andy," I say, attempting to keep my voice steady. "I've worked my butt off this year. You even said my designs were excellent."

"Yeah, it doesn't matter how excellent your designs are."

I blink at him, flabbergasted. "It doesn't?"

"You're AWOL at networking events, you make rare guest appearances at company parties, and you couldn't pick our senior executives out of a police lineup," he rattles off, shaking his head. "Come promotion time, you're practically a ghost."

"I network!"

He arches a skeptical brow. "Name one time."

"Fine."

Think fast.

"The design convention four months ago!" I let out a whoosh of air in relief. That counts, right?

He sighs. "You spent the night hoarding chicken wings in the corner while the rest of the team was bent over backward to schmooze the Quinns and Wolfe."

My mouth gapes. What a complete and utter... I knew Andy wasn't exactly a hearts and flowers sort of boss, but I genuinely thought he appreciated a good work ethic.

"I hadn't eaten lunch that day," I mutter, sinking lower into my chair. "I was finishing up a project for you."

I'm awarded a dismissive grunt in response.

I glance over at Helen, who's nodding at me like one of those dashboard bobblehead dolls in a power suit.

I take a breath, summoning what's left of my dignity. "Listen. I get that networking matters. But I work hard, and I think my designs speak for themselves."

I'm no good at small talk, handshakes, and sucking up to the elite of our corporate world. I'm a designer, not a friggin' politician.

"That's why you're a great Senior Graphic Designer."

I slump, deflated. "But I thought I was Wonder Woman."

Did those words seriously just tumble out of my mouth?

"Luuuucy," Helen drags out. "Andy's right. Fitting into the culture of Quinn & Wolfe is key. Our door is always open if you want to talk."

My eyes meet hers. "We're talking now, aren't we?"

Andy's stomach decides to join the conversation with a monstrous growl. "We'll revisit next quarter. Let's wrap this up."

Andy's already on his feet. He's done.

I'm floored. Outside the glass monstrosity, the window cleaner gives me a cheeky wink. I'm half-tempted to hitch a ride down with him.

"Do reach out to us if you need anything, Lucy," Helen coos.

Reach out? Is she after a group cuddle?

"Wait, Andy, I..." The words catch in my throat, a lump of disappointment weighing me down. Getting overlooked for the promotion is a low blow, particularly after I've slaved away for Quinn & Wolfe's IT team for an eternity. It stings, not making it to the top tier. "What can I do to fix this?"

There's a loud knock on the door. Laura, our admin support, practically falls into the room.

"Reception called," she pants, desperately clawing for breath. "He's early. Wolfe's on his way!"

"Goddammit!" Andy bellows, creating a mini spit shower on the table. "He wasn't supposed to be here until three! Out, Lucy! Move it!"

"But..." I stand, frozen in place, as Andy quickly lifts his arm to sniff his armpit, grimaces at what he finds, and then readjusts his tie with a frantic urgency.

Should I throw myself at his feet, begging him not to leave?

He bulldozes past me, striding toward the open office floor plan.

I follow him out like a dejected puppy, my spirit crushed. Why can't I just design? I don't want to play these corporate games.

"Clean up your desks, people!" Andy's shout slices through the office. "He's early! He's coming up NOW!"

The pit in my stomach tightens. There's no way I'll get Andy's ear now, not with the Big Bad Wolf making an early appearance to blow our office down.

JP Wolfe: co-founder of the monolithic Quinn

& Wolfe Hotel Group and one of the wealthiest men in America.

I've met him once before at a company event. Our encounter lasted an excruciatingly awkward twenty seconds—just long enough for him to rake his eyes over me and deliver his signature scowl that wordlessly stated, "Not. Impressed."

The guy is one scary son of a bitch.

Now we're on the brink of launching a new innovation project, which always comes with a partner chaperone from the board of directors, and we've drawn the short straw—we get the wolf himself this time.

I plaster on a smile, taking in the pandemonium unfolding around me. My usually chill colleagues are frantically tidying up as if the hounds of hell are at their heels. I suppose one is. The foosball table sits abandoned, balls everywhere.

Matty, usually indifferent, is cleaning his desk, a first since his hiring, while Mona is under her desk, applying lipstick like her life depends on it. One desk over, Taylor strategically arranges her design trophies for maximum visibility.

Dwayne, meanwhile, remains in his own world, oblivious to the frenzy, headphones firmly in place.

"Matty, for the love of all that's unholy, lose the Lucky Charms! This ain't a damn café!" Andy barks, hands on his head, wet patches under his arms beyond repair. "This is the most prestigious hotel group in the United States, or did that slip your mind!?"

Fair enough. Matty's desk is a mess, full of paper stacks, countless spent pens, and more cereal boxes than a supermarket aisle. The cleaning crew hates him.

Defeated, I slump down at my pristine desk, watching Matty's futile attempt to jam a cereal box into his already overstuffed drawer.

"Dwayne!" Andy strides over to him, snapping his fingers in front of his face. "Look alive. Are you even alive?" He throws his hands up in despair. "God, give me strength, people."

Wendy, in her fluster, drops a soda can.

"Clean that up!" Andy yells as he marches off to annihilate the developers. "We're supposed to make a good impression here! He already thinks this department is the Wild fucking West."

How do I make a good impression on Wolfe? The man isn't affectionately known throughout the company as the Big Bad Wolf because he enjoys cuddling in a furry onesie. No, it's because we're his little pigs, and every now and then, he takes one of us from our homes and devours us alive.

A quick check of my getup—worn-out jeans, a plaid shirt that screams "vintage" in all the wrong ways, plus sneakers begging for retirement. I might as well be auditioning for a spot on a lumberjack team.

Maybe I have slipped into a bit of a rut. But I received the Design Dynamo of the Month Award five times this year—shouldn't that count for something compared to schmoozing and dressing corporate?

Matty pauses his frantic drawer-stuffing long enough to grin at me. "Are we looking at Quinn & Wolfe's new Lead Graphic Designer?"

The team suddenly falls quiet, their cleaning fervor taking a back seat as ears prick up. Dwayne swivels in his chair to face me.

"Not this time!" I squeak out in a high-pitched, overly cheery voice.

Matty stares at me in disbelief. "You're kidding, right?"

I paste on a fake smile. "Nope, not kidding."

"Sorry, Lucy," some of the team chime in, along with other murmurs of condolences.

Matty crosses his arms and frowns at me. "Luc —"

"Let's save this conversation for later, okay?"

I cut him off, my teeth clenched, throwing him a meaningful look that screams *Not in front of Taylor*.

But it's too late—her sharp eyes are on me.

"Luceee," she coos, clasping her hands in feigned sympathy. "You poor thing. You didn't get promoted? That's just so sad."

My hackles rise to unprecedented heights. Taylor got promoted this morning, and I've been contemplating sticking chopsticks in my ears just to drown out her relentless bragging.

"Well," she purrs, "at least we have one Lead. Don't worry, your voice will be heard through me." She sighs as if bearing a tremendous cross.

"Missed a spot with your award-polishing, princess," Matty retorts.

"And your awards are where?" She glares at him, chin high, eyes blazing. "Oh, that's right, they're non-existent because you set the bar for yourself so low, yet you *still* fail to reach it."

"I don't need little wooden plaques to validate my self-worth." He leans over and lifts an award. "The Design Excellence Award, eh? Do you sleep better clutching this?"

Her jaw tightens, and she snatches it back. "Mr. Wolfe will probably only want to speak with the leads," she shoots, aiming at me.

Bitch.

Before Andy can explode, I toss an empty soda bottle from Matty's desk. "So, how'd your review go?"

"Angry Andy said I've lost an unusual number of grandfathers... Sixteen in four years. Helen even had a damn spreadsheet tracking them all." He smirks. "All I told them was Grandma was real busy in her twilight years."

Chuckling, I collect scattered papers. Matty's brazen attempts to skive off work have become office legend.

Then, the double doors swing open.

Straightening, I *feel* the room's energy shift, chatter dissolving into a tense silence.

There he stands—the Big Bad Wolf, towering well over six feet tall. His athletic build strains against the fabric, broad shoulders, and muscular chest filling out the jacket flawlessly. His piercing brown eyes match his cropped dark brown hair. Dark stubble accentuates his strong jaw.

He's dressed in trousers and a crisp white shirt, open at the collar, no tie. The white shirt contrasts strikingly with his tanned skin and navy suit. A gaze that could melt steel and probably panties.

With his intense stare trained on us, he looks every bit the hot hitman zeroing in on his next mark.

Us.

He's indisputably the sexiest, most unapproachable man I've ever encountered.

Good Lord. Everything about the guy screams raw masculinity. I couldn't pull my eyes away from him if I were paid to.

Wolfe heads up the casinos and clubs, while the Quinn brothers run the hotels. Together they seem to own every brick in America.

Okay, slight exaggeration, but they are loaded.

Andy scurries over to him like a puppy rushing to get a pat. "Sir. Welcome! Welcome to the design floor. Mr. Wolfe, it's an absolute honor to have you here." Wow, dial it down, dude. The team collectively cringes. "This is where the magic happens. Team, on your feet so Mr. Wolfe can get a look at all of you!"

Wolfe levels Andy with a look so fierce his eyes seem like black holes. I swear, for a second, I glimpse a hint of sharp, predatory teeth.

We rise as one, ready to be inspected.

"He'll be asking us to curtsy next," Matty mutters, not as under his breath as he thinks.

I step on his foot hard to shut him up.

"I'm sure you're aware why I'm here," Wolfe says coolly, his intense gaze scanning the room.

"We initiate Project Tangra in less than two weeks. Unless you've been living under a rock in Central Park, you know this is an important venture for the business."

No kidding. Tangra's been the buzzword for a month. We're rolling out the "ultimate cashless casino" experience. The aim is to make every Quinn & Wolfe casino across America completely cash-free.

Place your bets, collect your winnings, all with a simple tap on your phone—you're in the game. No more clunky chips, no queuing at ATMs, no cash transactions slowing down the thrill of the gamble. It's like a high roller's dream come true. A dream where you have no idea how much you've spent until the harsh light of day. Just how Wolfe likes it.

All of our projects are named after stars because, as they put it, we're "reaching for the stars." It's cheesy as hell. Thankfully, Tangra's name is more digestible than its predecessor, Xamidimura. That star was a nightmare to spell correctly in every damn email.

His penetrating gaze sweeps over us—over the developers, Dwayne, Taylor, Wendy, me. And then, it stops. I feel my pulse pick up speed under his scrutiny.

Why has it stopped?

I offer a tentative smile which he doesn't return, waiting for him to move on.

He doesn't.

My knees nearly buckle.

He seems to be examining me, his frown deepening by the second.

Shit.

What did I do?

Is there something foul smeared across my face?

My pulse spikes. No wonder they say never to stare down a wolf.

Only when I glance down do I realize the source of his wrath.

All bodily functions cease. Breathing. Blinking. Blood flow.

In my hands, I'm clutching Matty's ridiculous caricature of a wolf in a suit, complete with an oversized tail and teeth.

Matty, you utter fuckwit. Why are you so talented at caricatures? This could not be a more perfect likeness of Wolfe than if he'd sat for it himself.

You've got to be kidding me. The squiggles. Oh God, I didn't even notice the squiggles. Is that...? Yep.

That's definitely a cock and balls. Some smart-ass has added a big veiny cock with a rather impressive head.

With a look of sheer horror, I attempt to hide the incriminating sketch from Wolfe's unflinching gaze, failing miserably.

The room plummets into a tense silence.

I'm about five seconds from wetting my pants. I attempt speech but only manage a silent O of panic.

Andy's face turns a shade of white that matches his shirt. "Ahhh, Mr. Wolfe, that's just—"

Wolfe silences Andy's rambling with a raised palm. "You know," he says, his voice taking on a dark edge. "I've got my finger on the pulse of every artery in this company. Sales. Accounts. Hotel staff. Marketing. Security. I know everything and everyone that moves through this company. Every single dollar. Every single person. And yet, there's always this one department that thinks it can play by its own rules."

His piercing gaze latches onto me. "The IT department."

I stand frozen, trapped in a silent scream, my heart having a party in my body that I'm not invited to.

"You're the joker in my otherwise flawless deck," he sneers.

Those predatory eyes are still trained on me. Does he mean the entire IT department or just me? *I'm the joker?*

"It's time I had a closer look." *Closer* sounds like it might involve a chainsaw.

Beside him, Andy mimics Wolfe's ramrod posture in a desperate bid to match his towering aura. The result is less alpha wolf, more skittish Chihuahua. Andy looks ready to wet his pants too.

"Ah, sir," he squeaks out, his voice in stark contrast to Wolfe's deep baritone. "We abide by the rule book! You won't find a more company-minded, er, committed team than us, sir." Without pausing for a breath, he bulldozes on, "There's no need to think of us as the black sheep! We embrace the company culture here, Mr. Wolfe! Or should I say, JP, sir? Can I call you JP, JP?"

Mr. Wolfe—or JP—glares at Andy in a way that suggests imminent job termination.

"I'll be the judge of that. Seems like I've let the tech playground run wild for too long. It's time I get a little more acquainted." His predatory gaze returns to me, and I feel my fight-or-flight response kick in. "You. And who might you be?"

"Lucy," Andy jumps in, his panicked eyes sending a clear SOS: *Girl, you better pull your shit together.*

Anxiety swells up, threatening to choke me. I'm not a creature you can put on the spot. Being the sole focus of Wolfe's unwavering attention may be some employees' fantasy.

But not mine.

And certainly not like this.

"Um, hello! Yes, I'm Lucy," I stammer, hitting all my least favorite activities at once—self-introduction, impromptu speech, and being caught red-handed with a caricatured voodoo doll of the boss.

"I, uh, I'm a Senior Graphic Designer here. I worked on the Xamidimura project. And, um, comic books... they're my thing," I blurt out. "That's what inspired the, um, wolfy artwork."

The deafening, prolonged silence stretches out, amplifying my embarrassment to unprecedented heights.

Smooth move, Lucy, real smooth.

"The *artwork* you're unsuccessfully hiding behind your back?" he growls.

I meekly place the sketch back on my desk with a strained smile. "Not anymore."

A smothered giggle sneaks out from Taylor. "That's right. Lucy even dresses up as the Hulk!"

"She-Hulk," I correct her instantly, not thinking it through. Is the window cleaner's cart still hanging outside for a quick escape?

I glance over to see her smirking and hate her a little bit more.

My comic book collection might have been a lousy cover-up attempt, but it's also a sacred truth. Going to Comic Con with my dad every year since I was four is one of the few precious memories I have left of him.

"Is that so." Wolfe's expression remains unreadable, his deep brown eyes are practically black as they bore into me.

I bite my lip and look away, distraught.

I've fucked up with a capital F. I've landed myself in the same bumbling idiot category as Andy. In Wolfe's eyes, I'm a dirty doodling, She-Hulk wannabe. And I didn't even doodle the damn cartoon.

"Steve Reynolds calls her Wonder Woman," Matty chimes in, giving my arm a supportive pat.

My head rolls into my neck. *Shut up, Matty.*

"A pleasure, Lucy," Mr. Wolfe says with a glint in his eye, making it clear I'm anything but.

"Okay!" Andy attempts to clap his hands together but misses the mark, smacking himself in the chest instead. "Shall we keep the ball rolling, Mr. Wolfe? Introduce the rest of the team?"

"You have two minutes."

They think my day consists of shuffling buttons and pondering the philosophical question "should the button be blue or green?"

Scanning the room, Taylor looks like she's seen a ghost, Dwayne's frowning like he's decrypting the *Da Vinci Code*, but Andy? Andy's nodding, ready to take on this mission impossible.

A Lead Designer would step up, speak out, tell the arrogant suit his demands can't dictate timelines without consultation. It's not some sliding scale where he gets to pick and choose the finish line.

Except, I'm not a Lead Designer. And the suit in question signs my paychecks. And he's caught me with a scathing caricature of himself.

"Fantastic!" Andy claps his hands in a jittery motion and rocks back on his heels.

Our eyes widen as our fate is sealed. No one's going to dare question him or voice any disagreement.

Then he's leaving. Thank you, God.

But just as he's about to turn, he stops and stares at me again.

"It's Lucy, right?" he practically growls.

I nod, throat tightening. "Y-yes, sir."

Those brown eyes bore into mine. "Consider this your one and only free pass, Lucy. I don't tolerate disrespect. Cross me again, and you'll be fired on the spot."

ONE

One Year Later: Present Day

JP

I used to believe love was a distraction. An inconvenience. Love was for the weak-hearted, those still stuck in the pitiful illusion of the quintessential American dream, the white picket fence, and the two-and-a-half kids. It didn't align with my game plan.

But then, it caught me off guard.

I found love lurking in the most unlikely corner of my empire. The IT department, of all the damn places.

It's like an addiction, something I never imagined I'd be susceptible to. Something that chips away at my armor. Something that makes me vulnerable. Something that gnaws at me until I start to crave it, the sweetness, the warmth, the... fuck... love.

Then, true to form, I ended up sabotaging it all. I screwed it up. I took that delicate thing and wrecked it because that's what I do.

Damn it, even a wolf can bleed.

TWO

Lucy

As a kid, there was this giant, snow-white dog named Buddy who lived down my street. Every day, like clockwork, I'd poke my arm through the fence just to give Buddy a rub, and his deep, amber eyes felt like they understood my childish chatter.

One day, it all changed.

I heard a shout and ran to the window to see a van across the street. Buddy's human was hysterical. I watched, frozen, as Buddy was muscled into a cage by two burly men. His head forcefully jerked against the bars in protest as they restrained his neck with a pole. He thrashed and snarled, clearly expressing his disapproval.

My dad wrapped his arms around me as we watched the van carry Buddy away.

Where had all the fury come from? In a blink, our neighborhood marshmallow had morphed into a raging beast. I can still hear his pained howls ringing in my ears. It sounded as though something precious had been taken from him.

Every so often, I get flashbacks of poking my little arm through that fence, but instead of seeing Buddy letting me stroke him, I see the snarling face and bared teeth ready to chomp on my arm.

Somewhere in the far-off distance, there's a beeping sound—like an alarm clock from hell. It won't quit. And in my mind's eye, I can hear Buddy's grumbling growl as I reach my arm into the danger zone.

I can't help myself. His intense amber eyes lock onto mine just as his teeth sink into my flesh.

Jesus, that's real pain.

I try to yank my arm back, but he clamps down even harder, stealing the groan that's building in my throat.

"Urghhhhh."

I'm pretty sure that the guttural sound is mine.

But it's more than my arm that hurts; it's my head. It pounds like I've been flattened by a truck, and the giant tires are still rolling over me.

Buddy's eyes are like lasers boring into mine. Can't he tell how much he's hurting me? They seem to morph right before my eyes, shifting from liquid gold to a deeply human shade of brown.

Those brown eyes bore into mine, their

intensity bringing more pain than any physical wound ever could. I want to look away, to hide, but the vice-like grip of his stare leaves me paralyzed, consumed by an emotional pain so raw it's unbearable.

Then, as if a light switch has been flipped, his eyes return to their regular golden shade, only now they're glaring like high-beam headlights.

I squint against the brightness. Wait, are my eyes even open?

No, this is just a nightmare. I'm safely tucked away in my Manhattan apartment. Not revisiting my Jersey childhood with Buddy trying to gnaw my arm off.

Even with my eyelids squeezed shut, the light filtering in is too much.

The beeping sound is getting harsher and more grating.

How hungover am I, exactly? A couple of glasses of wine isn't nearly enough to justify this brutal headache and trippy dream. Matty and I hit the bar last night to mope about my lack of promotion and discuss the whole Wolfe fiasco.

Oh... shit. Wolfe. I'll probably hear today if he wants me pulled from the project. That's why I feel so bad; I'm sick with nerves. At least he didn't fire me on the spot.

I roll my tongue around my mouth, picking up a bitter, medicine-like aftertaste. Probably the preemptive Advil I popped last night.

Well, that was a total fail.

Something feels off.

I can sense it, even with my eyes still shut. I stretch out my arms, and my fingers don't graze the familiar cotton sheets of my bed. These sheets are cool and silky.

I take a deep breath. The air smells foreign too —like disinfectant mixed with a hint of lavender and floral undertones.

My God, did I hook up with some old guy last night? Bits and pieces from yesterday trickle back: Matty and me at the bar, the impromptu jazz club detour... then nothing.

Blinking slowly, I take a moment to connect the dots that the obnoxious beeping isn't just some cruel trick my brain is playing; it's originating from near my bed. My phone?

Have I overslept?

Wait, what day is it even?

Bracing myself, I force open my eyes and...

My heart slams against my chest. The fuck is this place?

This isn't my bedroom. This isn't some random dude's room, either. This is a hospital room. A ridiculously swanky one at that.

I lift my head a smidge, instantly regretting it as a wave of pain crashes into my brain.

What fresh hell is this? How did I end up here?

Don't freak out.

Do not freak the fuck out.

Breathe. Just breathe.

Everything's gonna be just fine.

Testing the waters, I wiggle my toes and fingers to check that all my bits and pieces are in their rightful places and functioning. There's an IV line burrowed into my arm. It feels itchy and tickly.

I lightly trace my face with my thumb—nose, eyes, cheeks—no missing parts. I don't *feel* like I've been Frankensteined together, but there's something tight around my head—must be a bandage.

Ouch. A tender spot throbs on my forehead when I touch it—there's probably a bruise there, so I must have whacked my head on something. But where? Did I fall out of bed?

I need a mirror. I need a nurse. Stat.

I survey my surroundings without moving too much. The walls are painted with soft pastel colors, serene blues and grays. Someone put effort into designing this room. It looks like a Pinterest board. Flower-packed vases crowd the bedside tables, partially blocking the expansive window view. I can just about make out the Quinn & Wolfe building in the distance. At least that's familiar.

Oh God, I need to know what's going on. How did I end up here from my bed?

"Hello?" I croak, peering at the open doorway. "Helllloooo?"

Nothing.

There's a call button by the bed. I fumble to press it, the IV line dragging at my skin. "Hell-ooo?"

A nurse breezes in. "Lucy." He flashes me a bright smile as he nears the bed. "You're awake. How are you feeling?"

"Confused." I try to haul myself up against the pillows, wincing as my head pulses. "What happened? Why am I here?"

His smile slips for a second, but he plasters it back on quickly. "You can't recall how you ended up here?"

I shake my head weakly.

"You've got a concussion, honey. Don't worry, it's normal to feel disoriented, especially after waking up. You've been in and out of consciousness for the last few days since your accident."

I gape at him. "My accident?"

"You slipped down a set of stairs at the Platinum Plaza Hotel. Hit your head pretty bad," he says, searching my face for any spark of recollection.

The Platinum Plaza Hotel? That's one of the Quinn & Wolfe hotels in SoHo. What the hell is this guy talking about? Did I sleepwalk out of my bed, take a swan dive out the window, and roll ten miles downtown or something?

My brows scrunch up, struggling to make sense of it all. "No, there's been a mistake."

Oh my God, this explains it. They've mixed up my identity. It's a chart switch-up.

I give the room another once-over, estimating what this suite would set me back at one of the Quinn & Wolfe hotels. It's enormous, and I've never seen a plush four-seater sofa in a hospital room before.

I'm screwed. I can't afford this.

"The accident must have happened at my apartment in Washington Heights. Maybe the chart is wrong?"

His brows lift, but he stays silent.

"What hospital is this?" I ask, feeling the panic bubble up again as he checks the IV in my arm.

"Royal Heights Hospital on Seventh."

Christ, it's a celebrity hospital.

He smiles. "You're in the best hands in New York."

And the most expensive hands. Hope my work insurance covers it.

His eyes shift to the chart clipped next to my bed. "Yup. You were admitted three nights ago following an accident at the Plaza."

"That makes no sense. That's all the way downtown."

He squints at the clipboard. "Lucy Walsh from East Hanover, twenty-seven years old."

"That's me... Except for the age part, I'm twenty-six. I don't turn twenty-seven until the summer." I tell him my birthday.

He stares at me as if I'm an idiot. "So you're twenty-seven."

He's the idiot. "No," I repeat, stretching out each word. "I'm twenty-six. Like I said, I turn twenty-seven next summer."

He glances at the clipboard again, then back at me, looking slightly rattled. "Okay, no problem, Lucy. The doctor will be in soon. Just... stay put, okay?"

With an IV drip in my arm, where does he think I plan on going?

"Hey, is my mom here?" I call after him weakly, but he's already out the door. The hallway fills with hushed whispers. Lots of them.

"Hello, Lucy." A brunette lady in a white coat saunters in. "I'm Doctor Ramirez."

"Doctor." I breathe a sigh of relief. "There's a mix-up on my chart. Can you tell me what happened? How did I end up here?"

She gives me the same incorrect account as the nurse. Fell down stairs. Plaza hotel. Three nights ago. Apparently, she saw me come in with her own eyes.

For a swanky hospital, it's a bit unnerving that they can't keep track of basic details. What are they pumping into me through this IV? What if it's meant for a different Lucy?

"I think you've got someone else's chart," I say, trying to hide my frustration. "Last night, I had a few drinks in midtown and went home. I must have... fallen down the stairs or something." That sounds plausible.

Doctor Ramirez studies me as she stands at the side of the bed. "Lucy, I'm going to ask you a few questions that may seem strange." She pauses. "Can you tell me what day it is today?"

My mouth opens, but nothing comes out. A tight knot forms in my stomach as I connect the dots from the last forty-eight hours: drinks with Matty, that horrible meeting with Wolfe, and the no promo news. "Thursday," I say, my voice weak. "Yesterday was Wednesday."

"It's actually Sunday, but you don't need to worry," she replies soothingly. "You've been on medication for the bad bump on your head. Trauma often makes your memory foggy."

I blink anxiously. *I've lost four days?* This is some twisted state of mind.

Keep calm. It's okay.

"Just one more question. Try to relax. Can you tell me what month and year it is?"

I stare at her, taken aback. I'm beginning to worry about the patient care level in this fancy hospital. I quickly reel off the answer.

Dr. Ramirez hums like she's debating something before asking her next question.

I gulp nervously. Do they think something's wrong with my brain?

She proceeds to grill me like a weird bar quiz—who's our local Senator? Can you tell me the names of your family members? What's your mom's name? Can you tell me the last few events you remember?

"Okay," she finally says, resting her hand on the bed railing. "We need to run some more tests. We'll pencil you in for an electroencephalogram and a PET scan this morning."

She pauses.

I look at her with wide eyes; it's never good when a doctor pauses.

"Lucy, it appears that you have a form of retrograde amnesia brought on by the trauma to your head."

I swallow hard and nod. "I've completely blanked on the last four days."

"It's more complicated than that," she says slowly. "We'll need to assess the extent of your condition, but it appears you're missing memories from the past year."

"A year?" I scoff, a laugh erupting so abruptly that I feel a brief spray from my nose. "Christ, no way. I remember everything from the past year. It's just these past few days that are foggy."

"I'm afraid you're mistaken, Lucy," she says gently. "The inconsistencies in your memories hint at retrograde amnesia." As she reveals the actual month and year, I stop breathing. "Once we've run our tests, we'll know for sure."

She smiles at me as if this news should cheer me up.

"What?" I screech, bolting upright in bed. "No." I shake my head. "That's not possible."

That's a whole year in the future.

Unless...

I gulp for air. "Have I been in a coma?"

I've been out cold for a whole freakin' year?

"No, you were admitted three days ago," she explains. "Retrograde amnesia refers to the inability to access memories. You've lived through the past year; it's just that your mind isn't able to retrieve those memories at the moment."

The year she stated circles endlessly in my mind without making any sense.

"So you're saying we've somehow fast-forwarded in time?"

She gives me a look, the kind one reserves for explaining complex things to a child. "No." The year echoes in the room again as she repeats it.

Stop saying that, I silently scream at her.

I brace myself, waiting for the punchline of this sick joke.

When the punchline never comes, my chest tightens as the awful truth crashes into me like a tsunami: I've lost an entire fucking year?

I can't breathe. Dr. Ramirez becomes a blob as the edges of my vision blur.

It's okay. Just focus on breathing. They'll be able to fix me.

"Will this electro... electro feeling scan... gram... fix me? Will it reboot me so I get my memories back?" I squawk, not capable of keeping a steady tone. "Turn me off and on again?"

To stop myself from screaming with hysteria, I laugh instead.

She indulges me with a sympathetic smile. "We'll determine a treatment plan after testing. We don't know the extent of your memory loss yet. We're still in the early stages here. Just try not to worry too much for now."

Easy for her to say; she remembers yesterday.

"We'll be with you every step of the way."

"I don't think I can afford you to be with me every step," I mumble, my mind racing with thoughts of astronomical hospital bills. "Am I really twenty-seven?" I ask in a tiny voice.

She responds with a gentle nod.

None of this makes any sense.

Yesterday was last year? The drinks with Matty, the meeting with Wolfe, the carrot cake I had before lunch, the meeting with Andy and his growly stomach—it all happened one year ago?

My heart hammers so hard in my chest I feel sick. I'm suffocating. My head's spinning more now than when I first woke up.

I gawk at Dr. Ramirez, who seems unfazed by my meltdown. I suppose for her, it's just another day at the office.

"I missed a whole year of my twenties?"

The tightness in my throat intensifies. I'm sweating, but I'm freezing.

"Did I miss Comic Con?" My voice squeaks out an octave higher.

"Just focus on your breathing, Lucy. Deep, slow breaths," Dr. Ramirez instructs, resting her hand on my wrist.

"But… what have I been doing all this time?" My eyes are as big as saucers as I stare at her.

She smiles reassuringly. "We'll help you figure that out."

Deep breath in, deep breath out. Maybe, if I close my eyes and nap, this nightmare will be over when I wake up.

THREE

Lucy

It's not.

I squint my eyes open, wondering how much time has passed. I'm still in the seven-star hospital bed. The sunlight filtering in is more subdued now, so it must be later in the day.

Or, knowing my luck, I've missed another fucking year.

My headache has dulled to a faint vibration, but fatigue's ready to drag me back under. I blindly reach for the water glass on the bedside table and nearly send it flying, along with some flimsy papers.

Curiosity piqued, I pick one up—it's all about retrograde amnesia. There's a disgustingly cheerful couple plastered on the front page, announcing: "You may not remember the past, but the future looks fabulous."

Is that supposed to be comforting? We're

talking amnesia here, not a Bahamian cruise.

I pull a face, or at least I give it a shot. I'm on enough drugs to sedate a whale, so even face movements are hard.

"Lucy." A nurse steps into the room. "You're awake."

"Hey," I croak, water dribbling from my chin, having missed my mouth entirely. "How long was I out this time?"

"Only a few hours," she says as she comes closer to the side of my bed. "I need to take some blood tests. By the way, I'm Katie."

"Sure, Katie." I muster up a weak grin. A flutter of unease has me asking her to confirm the year, in case I've somehow lost or gained more time.

"That's it." She smiles back sympathetically. "Don't worry, the doctor will be in shortly to talk to you about the next steps, now that you're awake. You're in the best care here. Dr. Ramirez is a rockstar in the world of head trauma medicine."

"I'm so drowsy," I moan, lifting my arm a couple of inches off the bed. "Everything feels heavy and sluggish, like I'm swimming in syrup."

"That's the pain meds. We're tapering you off those." She swabs some antiseptic onto a cotton bud and gently applies it to my skin before fastening a band around my arm. My arm clenches as the blood flow slows down.

"Is my mom here? Does she know?"

"She'll be back soon, she dashed out to grab a bite. She flew in from England this morning. Brace yourself, sharp scratch coming now."

"From *England*? But she wasn't in England." Mom wasn't visiting Aunt Meg. I avert my eyes, feeling the prick of the needle piercing my skin. "She shouldn't be... I don't remember," I whimper.

"Try not to worry, Lucy. You're on a high dose of medication. You've had some friends drop by too."

Must be Priya and Libby. Maybe Matty? They'll jog my memory. A few stories from them and it'll all come flooding back.

Hopefully, I've won the lottery. That could explain why I'm holed up in this swanky hospital.

"Hey, do you know where my phone is?"

"I don't think you came in with one. You must have lost it. Your belongings are all in the locker— you have your purse and driver's license though."

"But I don't drive."

"You must have learned." She smiles at me as she places a cotton ball over the puncture wound. "All done."

She moves away to record my info while I stare at the ceiling.

43

Maybe not having my phone at this point is a blessing. Am I really ready to have my past unveiled via a screen?

The cocktail of drugs numbing my senses is the only thing stopping me from losing my shit. Questions race through my head like wildfire.

What the hell's been happening in my life?

Is everyone alive?

Any catastrophes I should know about?

What if my resentment toward Taylor turned me into some nutjob, and I went all *The Shining* on her?

There's a whole year's worth of changes to process. A year's worth of front-page news, a year's worth of life's merry-go-round, a year's worth of heartaches and headaches and goodbyes.

Changes that I'm sure I dealt with in real time but now they'll all hit me simultaneously head-on.

I can't go there yet.

Katie leans over my bed. "Are you all right?"

It's then that I realize the loud wailing noise is coming from me. "Er... yeah, sorry," I say, trying to appease her. "Just a little overwhelmed."

She pats my hand. "Of course. It's understandable."

There's no way she could understand.

How could I erase an entire year of my life? The

idea of being a stranger to my own life story sends chills down my spine.

"Hey, Katie?" I ask, realizing I don't know what the 27-year-old me looks like. "Can I see a mirror, please?"

"Of course." She hunts through the drawers and hands me one.

I take a deep breath and brace myself. A woman with wide, frightened eyes stares back.

Oh man, I look like the girl from *The Exorcist*.

My dark, usually wavy hair is a wild mess and deep creases are etched across my cheeks. The bandage is gone, but stitches line my forehead. I hope the scar isn't too big.

My usually light olive skin is ghostly white.

On closer inspection, things look different. Did I get bangs? Looks like it could pass for an edgy haircut when not covered in grease. Huh.

I've definitely done something cool with my eyebrows. They're all angular and dramatic. I look permanently surprised.

It's me, but it's not me. This other woman looking back at me has lived a year of my life that I know nothing about.

"Time for your scans, Lucy," Katie tells me cheerily. "The nursing assistants are here to take you down to level four."

My tired eyes stare blankly back at me through the mirror. They droop as exhaustion pulls me under...

◆ ◆ ◆

When I open them again, I'm met with a familiar face.

"Mom," I try to shout, but it comes out a squeak as I prop myself up on the pillows.

"Oh, Lucy." Mom's pace quickens, her stern features softening in an all-too-rare display of relief. "Thank God you're awake."

She plants an eager kiss on my cheek, triggering a sudden onslaught of tears from me. After I've sobbed myself dry, I gulp in air and scrub the remnants of snot and tears off my face.

It's dark outside, so a few more hours have passed since my last bout of consciousness.

"I'm so sorry I wasn't here earlier, darling. There was an earlier flight, but it was delayed, and then they canceled it, and then I was put on standby... I managed to catch the earliest flight I could," she spills out in a single breath.

I grapple to keep up with her, which is hard in

my state.

Shockingly, Mom looks a bit of a wreck too. She's wearing her cardigan inside out, and she's not wearing a bra. She never leaves the house without a bra on.

"It's fine. By the way, you have a roller in your hair."

She emits a small gasp, patting her perfectly coiffed hair before extracting the offending roller. "I stuck a few in while you were sleeping."

"What were you doing in England?"

Her eyebrows knot together. "Meg's birthday. You knew that."

"I did?"

"Of course, you did! Oh, darling, you're all mixed up. But you're safe now," she coos as she sits beside the bed. "How are you feeling?"

"Dopey."

Like the time I took the mushrooms in Amsterdam; but I leave that little nugget out.

Hauling myself up into a sitting position, I take a generous swig of water. "I can't remember things. The doctor said I have amnesia."

"They told me. It's beyond me, though. How can you just forget a whole year? They must have misdiagnosed you. You know how these doctors are, making blunders left and right. Just last week,

I read this horrifying story about—"

"Mom," I interrupt before she can go down the rabbit hole of the horrors of medical malpractice. "I don't remember the accident. Do you know why I was at the Plaza Hotel?"

She throws me a disapproving glance. "A work event. Honestly, Lucy, I can't imagine what you were thinking. Drinking excessively and then tripping down the stairs, in public no less."

I freeze. Was I really inebriated at a work event? Why on earth would I do that? How mortifying. Hopefully, none of the big wigs saw my swan dive into humiliation.

"Your dad wouldn't be pleased if he were alive."

I glare at her. That's such a shit thing to say.

"Priya mentioned that your behavior has been rather... strange of late," she adds, an all-knowing look in her eyes.

"Strange how?" I choke out. And why's Priya snitching to Mom?

"She believed it was due to a guy."

"A guy?" I sputter, water droplets launching themselves from my lips onto my chin. "I have a guy?" Where is he then! Why isn't he here mopping my fevered brow with a damp washcloth? "Who is he?"

The cold terror of a significant person in my

life that I can't even recall sends a shudder down my spine.

"You didn't say anything about it to me, so I can only guess it wasn't serious," she says with a dismissive wave. "And really, considering your history, I wouldn't be surprised. You've never had the knack for finding a decent guy to settle down with."

And there it is. The familiar sting of her unsolicited judgment, less than a quarter-hour after her arrival.

But it sounds about right. Likely, it's one of those dating app flings that limped into a three-month stint before inevitably petering out. Either the men are too nice or absolute assholes. Like Goldilocks, I can't find a happy medium.

The hard truth? I've never had a serious relationship. It's a bit embarrassing, really.

Exasperated, I change the subject.

"Mom." I pin her with a look, pulling together as much seriousness as I can muster in my groggy state. "I need you to fill in some gaps for me. Can you recap this past year for me? What have I been doing?"

My question startles her, panic flitting across her face. "Well, uh... you seemed content, I suppose."

I wait for more. Come on, Mom, work with me here.

Looks like I'll have to be more direct.

"I still work for Quinn & Wolfe, right?"

Her face brightens. "Oh, yes, you're still there."

I heave a sigh of relief. So I didn't get fired. That little indiscretion with the cartoon wolf must have blown over. Wolfe likely doesn't even remember me.

"Oh my God, did I get promoted? Am I a Lead?"

The panic returns to her face. "I'm not really sure, Luce. You mentioned something about being a dynamo? Your work talk always flies over my head."

"And what exactly is my job title these days?"

"Uh... designer? You design... things." There's a long pause as I see her brain ticking over. "On the internet!" She finally beams, apparently satisfied with her answer. It's not technically true, but there's no point in correcting her.

This is agonizing. I'll need to ask the girls or Matty for specifics.

I suck in a breath. "Did I sell my apartment? Where am I living now?"

"No, you're still at your place in Washington Heights."

"What? Why didn't I sell?"

She offers a noncommittal shrug. "I'm not sure, Luce. You said you had a change of heart."

God, give me strength. Inwardly I groan, have Mom and I lived on different planets this past year?

Maybe the noisy neighbors moved out, so I didn't have to? At least when I leave the hospital, I'll return to familiar surroundings. And hopefully, my memories will come flooding back, revealing why I didn't sell.

That's what I'm banking on, anyway.

I switch gears again. "All right, can you tell me anything significant about this past year?"

She reflects for a moment before answering, "I got the kitchen all redone. And you've helped me with the garden. We planted delphiniums— they're coming along nicely—and started an herb box." She thinks. "Oh, and your cousin Nora? She's expecting her third. They're hoping for a boy this time."

"Great, Mom," I say, attempting to mask my disappointment.

That's it? That's all the life updates she has for me?

Since Dad passed away, I've tiptoed around her. Anything resembling a real-world problem was neatly swept under the proverbial rug, leaving me to solve it. Instead, she opted to immerse herself in the garden. A silent agreement was reached; Mom would bury her head in her hydrangeas, and I would handle the ugly realities that life tossed our way. Post-funeral, she was more engaged with bugs on her roses than Dad's will. The brunt was mine to bear.

But communication has clearly gone downhill this past year—this is far worse than I imagined. I clearly didn't tell her *anything.*

My heart nearly stops when her hand shoots up to cover her mouth.

"Oh God, Lucy!"

"What?" I demand, pushing myself up from the bed.

"You don't remember."

"Remember what?"

"Mrs. Forry from down the street died."

"Oh, for the love of..." I slump back into the pillows. "I can't even remember who she is."

"She had that dog you liked so much, Buddy."

"Oh yeah... right." Odd, considering my dream, but not really relevant. I'm not heartless, but I haven't seen Mrs. Forry in two decades.

"I'm twenty-seven now," I blurt out, the statement sounding alien to me. "How did I celebrate?"

"Oh! You, Priya, and Libby went to the spa then

had dinner afterward. And you and I had dinner at Captain's Crab in town."

So that's it? Am I the most boring person alive?

"Lucy." Dr. Ramirez knocks before entering the room. "Are you ready to discuss your treatment plan?"

"Is it a magic pill that will bring my memories back?"

She smiles gently. "I wish I had better news, but we must consider all possibilities. We'll provide you with the necessary support if your memories don't return."

Oh my God. I hadn't even considered the possibility that my memories might not come back.

I manage a weak smile because if I don't, I'll cry. And by cry, I mean bawl all over the floor, kicking and screaming.

"Let me guess: the future is fabulous?" I quip, waving the pamphlet at her.

"I can't promise that, but things will become easier, Lucy," Dr. Ramirez says, standing by the bed.

"But some people remember, some don't? Which type am I?"

She hits me with one of those trust-me-I'm-a-doctor smiles. "Unfortunately, the brain isn't that predictable. Each case is unique, and we approach them accordingly."

"But why am I missing a whole year, not just the night at the Plaza?" I question, trying to make sense of this new reality.

"Sometimes, our brain tries to shield us from painful memories. It's a protective mechanism. Maybe there's something from this past year that you're not quite ready to confront yet."

Dread rises up in my chest.

Mom clasps her hands together dramatically, eyeballs aimed at heaven, as if begging for some divine intervention. Helpful as always.

I work on swallowing the emotions lodged in my throat. "I think I could use a top-up on that morphine, doc."

As far as scariest moments in my life go, this ranks high.

Because right beyond that hospital door is a year's worth of change waiting to flatten me the second I step out.

FOUR

JP

Every damn time I think life has settled into a predictable rhythm, it drop-kicks me in the balls. Again.

My steps echo ominously through the corridor of the neurological ward.

I should have been here sooner. All of this—it's on me. I thought I had already done enough damage before the accident. Because evidently, smashing her heart to smithereens wasn't enough. I had to go ahead and have a crack at her body too.

"Mr. Wolfe, you're back," the nurse chirps, falling in step beside me. Her eyes linger a beat too long, irking me. "Can I get you anything?"

I grunt out a terse "no," trying to fend off any idle chit-chat. It's not her I'm pissed at, but Lucy's dicey state has me on a razor's edge, my temper one misstep from boiling over. I feel like a fucking pressure cooker.

Nearing the door to Lucy's room, I grip the handle, when a woman's voice freezes me in my tracks.

"Mr. Wolfe, hold on!"

I stop, turning to see Dr. Ramirez closing the distance. "What's the matter, doctor?" I ask.

She motions for me to follow her. A cold weight of unease settles in my chest as I match her stride.

We halt a bit down the hallway.

"Lucy's condition has changed since this morning," she informs me.

My throat tightens. "I know. She's awake."

"That's not all."

I brace myself, dread pooling in my stomach. "What else?"

She takes a deep breath, looking me straight in the eyes. "Lucy's been diagnosed with retrograde amnesia. It's a memory disorder as a result of her head injury."

I recoil, doubting my hearing for a second. "*Amnesia*? Lucy has amnesia?"

Dr. Ramirez nods. "Yes, her accident impacted her memory."

"All right," I say slowly, crossing my arms as I scrutinize her. "What's the plan to rectify this?"

"Her condition isn't simple or quick to treat.

We're developing a customized recovery plan for her."

"So she's got a fuzzy memory because of the fall? Isn't that expected?" I try to reason, desperate for some semblance of control.

She clears her throat, seeming to grope for the right words. "I'm afraid it's more serious than that."

Jesus Christ. Lucy's got brain damage.

Stay fucking calm.

I fight to keep my voice steady. "Spell it out," I say, my tone low. "Tell me exactly what we're dealing with. What can't she remember?"

Dr. Ramirez meets my gaze steadily. "Based on our initial evaluations, Lucy has lost all memories from this past year."

Everything goes quiet as I process the bombshell she's dropped on me.

"You cannot be fucking serious."

She recoils slightly. "I assure you, Mr. Wolfe, this isn't a matter I would joke about."

Incredulous, I struggle to understand. "A year? Just like that, it's gone? When will she remember?"

"Unfortunately, we can't make promises," she says carefully. "We're initiating a rehabilitation plan, but we cannot guarantee the return of her memories."

Her words slam into me, leaving me leaning against the wall for support. This can't be happening.

"After I've invested a small fortune into this clinic, you're telling me you have no goddamn clue if she'll recover?" My voice echoes down the hospital hallway.

I've garnered an audience in the hallway, but I couldn't care less.

Dr. Ramirez blinks in surprise, her composed mask slipping. "Mr. Wolfe, please understand. Our top neurologists are working on Lucy's case. We're doing everything possible, but there are no surefire guarantees when it comes to the human brain. It's a slow process. Your money can't speed up her recovery."

Her platitudes only incense me further. "No, this is unacceptable. There has to be a plan, a procedure to fix this now."

Her smile is tight. "We can't fix this kind of damage overnight, Mr. Wolfe."

Cursing under my breath, I push my fury down. "Sorry," I grit out. "This is... I'm not handling this well. I need to see her."

"She's confused and disoriented. We're reintroducing familiar faces slowly, with her consent," she explains.

Frustrated, I run a hand through my hair. "Then tell her I'm here."

"I'll let her know. She's with her mom now. Please, wait here," she says, heading toward Lucy's room.

What are a few more minutes in the grand scheme of things? This week's been hell anyway.

I watch as she disappears behind the hospital room door. I stand by it, stuffing my hands in my pockets to hide my clenched fists.

I've never been so nervous in my life. If Lucy hated me before the accident, it'll be tenfold now.

I hear Dr. Ramirez from within the room. "Lucy," she says.

"Hi, doc," comes Lucy's tired reply.

A sharp pain pierces my chest.

"JP is here," Dr. Ramirez says.

An eerie silence follows. Thick and suffocating.

"Who?"

I want to throw open the door but I'm frozen, stunned. What the fuck?

Another pause.

"JP... Wolfe?" Dr. Ramirez questions, uncertainty creeping into her voice.

"JP Wolfe?" Lucy's words come out slurred and sluggish. My hand itches to open the door, but

Lucy's words stop me cold. "Mr. Wooooolfe? Wha... Why's he here?"

Her words hit me harder than any punch. My hand freezes mid-air. What the hell is happening?

"Would you like me to ask him to come back another time?" Dr. Ramirez asks.

"No!" Panic and confusion fill Lucy's foggy voice. "Why's he here? Am I in some kind of trouble?"

Leaning heavily against the cold wall outside her room, I struggle to draw in full breaths. The harsh reality slams into me. To her, I'm back to being Mr. Wolfe.

It took forever to make her see me not just as a corporate shark but as a man who bled when cut, who hurt when wounded, who had vulnerabilities like anyone else. To allow her past my defenses? That was even tougher. But I did it.

She might have mistaken her love for hatred in the heat of recent events, but at least there was passion, there was sentiment.

Now? We're back to square fucking one.

"Who is he, darling?" another female voice, presumably her mother, pipes up.

"He owns the freaking company! The woooolf! But it can't be... can it? Not him."

"It's okay," Dr. Ramirez says soothingly. "I'll let

him know now isn't a good time."

"Oh my God, what if he's here to fire me?" Lucy's panic returns. "I've met him before... sometimes, I think... or was it just once? I don't remember..." She trails off, her voice full of despair. "My head feels funny. All floaty and dopey..."

I clench my fists against the cold wall, my heart hammering like I've been injected with enough adrenaline to take me down.

A feeling of helplessness washes over me, stronger and more powerful than anything I've ever felt. I was ready for anger, for hatred, for resentment. But this... I wasn't prepared for this.

A growl seethes in my chest, a primal sound that echoes in the hushed corridor. Maybe loud enough for them to hear in the hospital room.

"Everything's okay, Lucy," Dr. Ramirez attempts to reassure her.

"I can't see my boss like this. I look like a trainwreck."

"I can fix your hair, Luce," her mom offers.

"No, it's not about my hair. Please just tell him I'm sleeping or something."

The words plunge me into a freefall, a nosedive from the pinnacle of Quinn & Wolfe HQ.

I'm the man she met a year ago. A complete

stranger. The head of her company. The Big Bad Wolf she used to fear. Not the man who cared for her, who loved her, who screwed up royally with her, and who has been paying the price every goddamned day since.

This isn't just bitter resentment. This is worse. This is a void. A black hole.

Lucy's frustrated groan filters through the door. "Oh, fucking hell."

"Language, Luce!"

"I know why he's here—it must be a mix-up with my insurance not covering this hospital! How much does this place cost per night?"

"I don't believe that's why he's here," Dr. Ramirez interjects. "Perhaps he was in the vicinity and thought to visit on behalf of the company. Please try to stay calm."

"Your pal Matty came in to see you earlier, after I arrived," her mom chimes in. "He said he told your team. Does he work with this guy?"

I press both hands to the wall, dragging in ragged breaths.

It's all right. It's temporary. I'll fix this.

"Are you all right, Mr. Wolfe?" The young nurse lingering around taps my bicep.

I clench my jaw and whirl to face her, shooting her a hostile glance. I wish she would fuck off instead of trying to constantly get my attention. "I'm fine," I mutter. "Thank you."

The nurse takes a step back in surprise and quickly scampers away as Dr. Ramirez appears. She gestures for me to follow her down the corridor.

We walk in tense silence, distancing ourselves from Lucy's room until we're out of earshot.

Dr. Ramirez glances up at me, her smile brittle.

"She doesn't remember me," I grind out, my voice a rasp. I rub at my stubble, wrestling for control. "I was ready for her not wanting to see me, but this... she doesn't even remember me. Not in any way that matters."

Dr. Ramirez touches my arm. "She remembers you. But as the man she met a year ago. I'm guessing a few things have changed since then?"

You could say that.

"Correct," I answer, my voice grinding like gravel.

She nods. "I understand this must be difficult."

"So, you're telling me," I begin slowly, "that Lucy has erased our history? That she's scrubbed me from her memory?"

Dr. Ramirez gives me a long, measured look. "Unwillingly, yes."

I take a steadying breath before locking eyes with her.

A pit forms in my stomach. "What's my move here, doc? Do I waltz in there and jolt her memory back into place?"

She recoils slightly, caught off guard. "I can't tell if you're joking, Mr. Wolfe."

"Neither can I," I growl back.

She motions me toward the chairs nearby.

"Your frustration and confusion are completely normal," she tells me as we sit. "But we must be careful not to overwhelm her with the past. Pushing information could create false memories and skew her understanding of things. Your case is complicated, indeed, a rare occurrence —it's not often we encounter a situation where a boyfriend or partner is completely forgotten."

My jaw clenches. I don't think Lucy would call me either of those. Not anymore. I lean my head against the wall. "So Lucy feels nothing for me right now?"

She looks like she's chewing on broken glass when she answers. "If your relationship progressed after the point where her memory ends, then she might not recall any emotions associated with it."

"So that's a fucking no." My voice catches, and I clench my jaw to avoid showing any further emotion.

I stand up and pace, running a hand through my hair. How the hell does this happen? The mind cherry-picks parts of your life to keep and tosses the rest?

This is surreal. It feels like I've walked onto the set of some Hollywood drama. This kind of bullshit isn't supposed to happen in real life.

I stop pacing and face her. "So if Lucy is blocking out painful memories, forcing them back could do more harm than good?"

Her nod confirms my understanding. "Lucy's current distress seems predicated on the relatively minor matter of a forgotten comic convention. With more significant events, it's better to let her mind take control, revealing memories when she's ready. Trying to force her to remember too soon could harm her mental health."

She pauses, her gaze unsettlingly perceptive. "Are there any major incidents that might be unsettling to her?"

Her question sets off a frenzy in my chest.

I clear my throat, my voice breaking the silence. "Lucy and I... we had a complicated relationship, to say the least."

"Go on. It's better for her recovery if we know what we're dealing with here."

The scene plays out in my mind like a well-worn film reel, each frame filled with anger, hurt, and regret. It feels wrong, recounting this private pain to a near stranger. But it's not about me anymore. It's about Lucy. It's always been about her.

"I behaved in ways... ways that I regret deeply."

She watches me, her face neutral. "You had a disagreement."

"Disagreement," I echo, a bitter laugh threatening to escape. "Yeah, you could say it was that."

We didn't just "disagree." I was a monumental prick, and I pushed her away. No, that's too mild. I practically shoved her off a cliff. And then I had the audacity to be surprised when she didn't stick around.

This is me. This is all on me.

FIVE

Lucy

I might as well have been born yesterday.

As we leave the subway, Libby and Priya flank me on either side, like a toddler taking her first steps. The familiar concoction of BO and pee—the perfume of the New York underground—is oddly comforting. If it smelled like Yankee Candles, I might've had a proper freak out.

We're bound for Washington Heights, where my apartment precariously straddles the line between bohemian chic and the less desirable elements of the neighborhood.

Health-obsessed hipsters crunching avocado toast on one side, drug dealers on the other.

After a week at Mom's in New Jersey, I've learned... jack shit, really. Mom isn't a great source of information about my life, it seems. Her idea of therapy wasn't a heartfelt dialogue over steaming cups of cocoa or reminiscing through old photo albums. Instead, she dragged me through the garden center, as we scrutinized begonias, her critical gaze landing on my worn-out jeans more often than not.

My bank statements were more forthcoming. They told me I now have a subscription to an ethical, female-focused porn site and my odd fixation with a single movie I had streamed a staggering seventeen times.

The entire ride from New Jersey, I've been grilling the girls on the gaping black hole of my lost year. Every time I ask something, there's a thirty-second delay, like they're worried my brain might short-circuit if they tell me too much at once. I still have no clue who the mysterious guy I dated was.

"Why wouldn't I tell you guys about him?" I ask, exasperated. Makes not a lick of fucking sense. "Do you think he's a crook or something?"

"I thought he was really ugly, and you were embarrassed," Libby says.

"Well, that's nice."

"You mentioned not expecting it to last," Priya says.

"Great, so that'll be why he hasn't come looking for his amnesiac girlfriend then," I mutter as we cross the street. "Not like I'd know him from

Adam anyway. The hospital is just one big blur. I don't remember seeing you guys. And supposedly my boss Andy stopped by. People just morphed into this nondescript blob."

"We know." Libby laughs. "We were there. It was like you were high on weed gummies all the time."

Priya shoots me a quizzical look. "There's no way you can recover the data from your phone?"

"I'd been lazy about backing it up to the cloud."

"But you're an *IT* person."

I shrug, feeling at a loss. "I don't keep anything important on that thing! My laptop is really my only source of information now, and all it shows is work-related stuff and some chat logs with Matty. It's times like memory loss when I wish I wasn't so anal about my online life. My social media posts are just pics of us, and a single photo from Comic Con. Guess I went alone, right?"

Priya offers a faint smile. "I think so, Luce. Had I known you were going to end up in the hospital, I would have come along, even though after the last time—"

"You'd rather dunk your head in a toilet," I complete her sentence with a nod. "I know, it's okay. It's my thing."

"After that guy in the latex suit started

humping my hip, I was out."

"Elastic Man." I smile ruefully. So last year I went alone. I feel sorry for myself.

Either you're all in for Comic Con or you're out. Priya's more of a feet-on-the-ground gal while I'm a head in the clouds gal. For me, Comic Con's all about the thrill of pretending to be someone else for the day—like a superhero.

"So, a quick recap of my year: no promotion, still living in the same apartment, started a relationship destined to fail, and the only positive thing is that the doctor finally figured out why I got a rash on my elbow."

Priya smiles smoothly. "Tiny, manageable increments. Remember? We don't want to inundate you with a year's worth of memories at once. Doctor's orders."

I side-eye her suspiciously. Does the lack of events indicate my dull life or are the girls holding back?

Priya's poker face is intense. That's why she's a hotshot lawyer. She's not lying; she just knows how not to show her hand.

Right now, I feel like she's got a whole deck up her sleeve.

Libby, on the other hand, looks on the verge of a full-scale verbal vomit. "The pamphlet recommended we feed you bits and pieces of your life," she stutters, practically trembling.

My eyes roll. "The pamphlet called 'Forgotten Memories But Never Forgotten Friends'?"

It was written in a lovely, soothing font that would make any graphic designer proud.

There was an illustration of three people resembling me, Priya, and Libby hugging each other. One was goofy, with big googly blue eyes and brown hair; the second could have been American-Sri Lankan like Priya, and the last had curly blond hair like Libby. Does the swanky clinic personalize the brochures for the patient?

"I bet my plants are all wilted, and my fridge is a science experiment," I grumble, navigating the obstacle course of garbage bins. "The hospital had really nice food. Funny how I remember their menu but can't recall one twenty-seventh of my own life."

Actually, it's not at all funny.

A dickhead cyclist almost mows through us just as we're about to cross the street, and I jump about seven feet in the air. My nerves are frazzled.

Priya pats my arm. "It'll be okay, Luce. Your first therapy session went well, didn't it?"

"Yeah, but I still can't remember anything. On the bright side, they gave me a calendar with daily mindfulness memes."

I stop abruptly in the street, my mouth hanging open. "Are you kidding me?"

I gawk in horror at the fast-food fried chicken joint occupying my beloved Perky Pot Café's spot. "Oh, for the love of—this is the absolute worst."

The girls exchange an anxious look.

"Mm-hmm," Priya says gently. "You started going to another coffee place two blocks away."

"No wonder," I moan, glaring daggers at the smug chicken winking at me. This is an unmitigated disaster.

Libby looks at me intently. "You really don't remember *anything*?"

"Lib, seriously, I'm not doing this for kicks," I grumble, irritated.

They gently guide me away from the chicken.

Libby tries to jog my memory with stories of our weekend in Atlanta, but nothing clicks.

"Okay. One more," she says. "The date where you caught the guy talking to the lobsters in the restaurant tank? Do you remember that one?"

"*What*?" My brow furrows as I grapple with the absurdity. "Nope, nada, niente. But that does sound like typical date material for me."

"Okay, okay, I've got it. You have to remember this. When you had the shits last month and were bedridden for days? You complained about it so much."

"Libby," Priya cuts in. "Knock it off."

I sigh, still traumatized by the chicken, as we trudge along the sidewalk. At least the pizza place is still standing.

Just before we turn onto my street, Priya stops me.

She chews her lip, then clears her throat. "There's been a few more changes. Stay calm, okay?"

She's using her lawyer voice. This can't be good.

I stare at her incredulously, feeling the hairs on my neck prickle. "How can anything be worse than Perky Pot closing?"

"Deep breaths, Luce." Libby suddenly grabs my hands, taking deep breaths and blowing them into my face. "Breathe with me."

I pull away, exasperated. "Christ, Lib, that's not helping."

I look to Priya, the voice of reason, but all I see in her eyes is a deep weariness.

And that's when I know. This is about to get so, so much worse.

SIX

Lucy

I'm hallucinating. It's the only explanation.

New York fades away, all the smells and sounds of the city. All that's left is me and the six-foot inflatable doll in the storefront window. Perfect plastic tits and red lips puckered in an O of perpetual surprise.

She gazes at me from her perch, right where the bakery used to be. Right below my apartment where the smells of warm bread and buttery pastries wafted through my bedroom window every morning.

My mouth drops open, matching her O.

My inflatable neighbor presses her palms to the glass, bright red panties smooshed against a neat stack of cock rings and furry handcuffs. The flamboyant pink wig sits lopsided on her head with a curled fringe dropping seductively over her eye.

"Is that a sex shop under my apartment?" The words whoosh out in a gulp of air. "Where's the bakery? Where's Eddie's Cinnamon Rolls?" My voice fades to a rasp. I spin to face the girls. "Please tell me this is a pop-up, for fuck's sake."

But no one's laughing.

Priya clears her throat, trying to sound calm and lawyerly. "Actually, Luce, it's... more than just a sex shop. It's a... brothel."

I almost choke on my own spit. "Come again?"

"It becomes a brothel at night."

"Oh my God." I look at her like she has two heads. "I feel faint."

Priya grips my shoulders, turning me to face her. "You got through this before. You can do it again. The bakery closed after you listed your place. The brothel moved in shortly after."

"But... but... that can't be legal," I whisper. "Can't I just call the cops?"

Priya shakes her head, smiling sadly. "It's operating under a 'massage parlor' license. There's nothing we can prove unless someone's caught pants down. And it seems some of the local cops might be... patrons." She trails off, shrugging helplessly. "Sorry, Luce."

In horror, I look between the girls and the plastic temptress.

"Sex sells," I say, struggling to swallow. So this is what I'm suppressing. How stupid does my subconscious think I am? Didn't it think I'd notice a full-sized sex doll under my apartment?

"But why didn't I just sell?" I shake my head, bewildered. "Why would I stay here?"

"You didn't choose to stay, Luce," Priya says in a soothing voice. "It was just... crappy timing."

Realization hits me like a ton of dicks. "My apartment's been on the market for a year. It didn't sell because of this."

It takes all my willpower not to blubber as I take in the doll, the cock rings, and a long pink metal rod for God knows what.

Of course it didn't sell. Who'd want to live above this?

As the dam of emotions breaks, the first sob escapes me like a burp. "W-what the hell is happening?" I bawl, as the girls wrap their arms around me in a hug. "I woke up in some messed-up alternate universe. This year is screwed up."

"You'll get past the shock," Priya reassures me, gently wiping my cheek. "There's always a way. You were looking into a company that might be able to help. Nab Your Pad."

"Nab your... What do they do?" My nose drips unattractively as I groan. "How do they work?"

"Ehm, they buy homes for a fraction of the asking price."

"Like, how big of a fraction?" I throw up my hands. "No, don't tell me. I can't handle this now."

I inhale through my nose, reminding myself to breathe. No wonder I wanted to forget. No wonder I woke up looking like the girl from *The Exorcist*. My life needs a fucking exorcism.

I must have launched myself down those Plaza stairs head first, hoping to lobotomize my prefrontal cortex on impact. And the only reason I know it's the prefrontal cortex is because of all the damn hospital pamphlets.

"You used to stay in Vegas a bit with work. You sent poolside pictures." Priya links her arm through mine, smiling warmly. "It's not all bad. Come inside, and we'll get you settled in."

I shake my head in disbelief as I trail behind her toward my front door. "Surely it can't get any worse than this."

Trudging up the stairs behind Priya with Libby in tow, my mind runs rampant. All I need is a nice hot bath with a cup of hot chocolate, some time to think this through, and then everything will be okay again.

This is Manhattan, for God's sake. People want to live here. Of course I'll sell the apartment.

"They can't be that loud when they're having sex downstairs. You don't expect to get much sleep in a city that never sleeps anyway," I mutter more to myself than the girls, trying to convince myself of the situation's bearability.

Maybe being above a brothel can even be a selling point; it might attract sex addicts looking for convenience. The agent can market it that way.

I fumble with my key in the lock. It's stiffer since last year. Nerves take over at the thought of what I may find. What if I've done a full reno and hate it? What if I don't know where anything is?

I shove the door open, dropping my bag.

"It's so good to be—" I cut myself off with a scream as I gawk at the strange guy with the wild beard sprawled on my couch, balancing a pan on his crotch.

He glances up, chewing. "You're back," he mumbles through a full mouth.

"Shit," I hear Priya mutter behind me.

"We totally forgot about Spider," Libby chimes in. "I can't keep up with what you know and don't know. A year goes by so quickly."

Spider?

I'm rooted to the spot, smack dab in the middle of the kitchen. "*You're* my boyfriend?"

As if in slow motion, I watch an avalanche of

oats plunge down his beard.

"No," Priya interjects hastily. "He's your roommate."

"Huh." The bearded guy looks at me, still chewing, flicking oat bits in his beard. "So the memory loss is for real? I thought your friend Matty was high."

I stare in disbelief, hoping he'll vanish with each blink. How did I end up with this random, bearded dude as my roommate? I can't stand sharing my living space.

Priya touches my arm gently. "You needed help with the mortgage."

"You don't think a little warning about this would have been good?" I hiss. "That's a big thing to omit."

She throws her hands up in defeat. "Look, sorry. We were so preoccupied with worrying over how you'd respond to the sex shop that I completely forgot about Spider here."

"It's okay. It's not your fault." I sink onto the bar stool beside the kitchen island, and my gaze falls onto crumbs that I credit this guy for.

"But I always had my mortgage under control." I turn to Priya, aghast. "Always."

"Well, you had a bit of a rough patch, Luce. And unfortunately, Spider was the only one who wasn't put off by all the cock rings downstairs."

My new housemate raises a leg to scratch his backside as he turns his attention to whatever show he's watching. This entire mess is all thanks to the plastic floozy in the window downstairs.

"I'm living with a man I don't know," I murmur, mostly to myself. Then louder to him, "Did you say your name's Spider? Like the bug?"

His fork stops mid-air. "Are you serious?"

"Yes," Priya answers for him, her voice sharp. "This is Spider."

I inhale deeply. I would have preferred an infestation of the actual arachnids over this slob. At least they're tidy.

"How long have you been living here, Spider?" I resent the stupid nickname as soon as it leaves my mouth. How would someone acquire that nickname? Does he have a talent for scaling walls or something?

He sets the saucepan down. "Woman, you gone full psycho?" He shakes his head, muttering, "Half a year."

"Uh-huh. And what do you do?" Judging from the state of the place, he's not a professional de-clutterer.

"I'm a life drawing model."

My eyes widen. That's a job? "Please don't tell

me you do that here!"

"Nah. I go to art studios around the city."

I breathe a small sigh of relief. Small mercies. "Why are you eating out of my saucepan?"

He shrugs. "It's just easier, isn't it?"

"But that's my special saucepan for making jam."

Suppressing the urge to deep clean the whole apartment, including the strange Spider man, I whimper and decide it'll be a task for future Lucy.

I look at Priya, who's already halfway to my bedroom with my bag.

"Let's take you to your bedroom, Luce."

"Okay," I squeak.

"Hey," Spider calls after us. "Don't forget you agreed to lower the rent."

"Give me one item of good news, I beg you," I moan as the girls bundle me into my bedroom. "Do I need to check if there are any dead bodies in the bath?"

I flop onto the bed, relieved that my bedroom looks the same.

"Take some calming breaths," Libby coaxes, settling beside me. "We could draw you a nice warm bath with some aromatherapy salts. And you won't be sharing it with any dead bodies."

"Thanks, Lib, that's sweet. But I need

something stronger than aromatic bubbles right now."

I scan the room, praying for a memory to spark. Zeroing in on my bedside table, I wrench open the drawer.

"Comics?" Priya smirks, eyeing the stash in the drawer. "That's what you keep in your nightstand? I'd die if you saw what's in mine."

"Yeah, no, thank you for that offer." I rummage through the top stack of comics. If she looks closer, she'll see that some of them are erotic graphic novels—my version of porn. And then, there's the mundane: bills, mortgage documents...

I shut the drawer with a loud bang and hoist myself up, giving my room another once-over. Hunting for clues. *Anything.*

Exasperated, I throw open the wardrobe doors and— Woah. I'm now the proud owner of new jeans, sexy shirts, and a killer little black dress.

"Do I... actually wear this?" I question, holding up the dress.

Priya grins. "You wanted to switch things up a bit."

I hum in approval, my fingers brushing over the array of hangers until I stumble upon some shiny black material.

"What the hell's this?" My jaw drops as I unveil

a skintight blue-and-gold leotard. It would look perfectly at home at Comic Con if it weren't for the gaping holes at both boobs and, oh my god, the crotch. It seems I've taken cosplay to new levels.

I choke out a surprised, "Miss Nova," to no one in particular.

"Since when did Miss Nova get a sexy makeover?" Priya smirks. "Wouldn't Superwoman or Wonder Woman be better for bedroom roleplay?"

"Miss Nova is a strong, sassy woman who doesn't shy away from her sexuality," I retort, sick of defending her. "And she can control light particles. She's a classic superheroine role model!" I pause, taking in the racy outfit. "Although, I do have to wonder what possessed me to buy this."

"It seems you don't tell us *everything*, Luce," Libby says. "You're a dark, *dirty* horse."

I don't know what to make of that discovery.

Next up, the underwear drawer. To my surprise, I discover a treasure trove of raunchy lingerie mixed in with the sensible cotton that 26-year-old Lucy wore. Nice.

I grin, touching the silky material. Then my eyes bulge as I lift a pair of sexy black men's briefs. I swivel to the girls, holding them up. "Whose are these?"

And why isn't the owner of these contacting me? Why isn't he worried about me?

Priya raises an eyebrow while Libby shrugs. "Maybe Spider mixed his laundry with yours?"

I inspect the undies, eyes narrowed. Designer. Sexy as hell. Definitely not Spider's.

"If I have a boyfriend, why hasn't he made his grand appearance yet?"

Priya shuffles uneasily, eyeing Libby. "Maybe it's for the best that you've forgotten about this guy. I don't think it ended well. You were a bit... sad."

Sad hangs in the air, giving me a sense of foreboding. Exactly how sad are we talking? Sad as in *Cried into my wine for a week* or sad as in *Considered swan diving the stairs of the Platinum Plaza Hotel*?

Priya and Libby blink at me, offering zero answers, and all I want to do is scream until my lungs give out.

Turns out, I'm learning a lot today.

One: my home is now an episode of *Roommates from Hell*.

Two: my sex life took an interesting turn during my memory sabbatical.

And three: whoever this mystery man is, the one who had me all weepy, he's got some seriously hot briefs.

SEVEN

Lucy

My thoughts are playing a maddening game of hide-and-seek, but I'm going to hunt those elusive little fuckers down.

And where better to start than the office, where I spend most of my days?

Three days of house arrest with Spider was enough. The less said about the rogue toenail clippings lurking in the bathroom, the better.

Every time I step foot into my apartment, Roxy, the life-sized, inflatable reminder of my new life, greets me. Roxy is the name on her packaging.

I mostly wallowed in the strange familiarity of my apartment, barring an aimless foray to the Plaza Hotel, where Libby, in her well-intended yet futile attempts, tried to unlock my memory through reiki.

But unfortunately, all amounted to naught— not a sniff of recollection of ever having been there.

Nestled amid Manhattan's concrete zoo, the Quinn & Wolfe Hotel Group HQ is a staggering, seventy-floor strut of glass, ambition, and ego. A steel point juts out aggressively from the top, like a shiny middle finger to the skyline.

Walking into HQ's reception feels weirdly comforting. Everything's the same—the suits are in their suits, the creatives are in their jeans and I... well, I'm feeling pretty sexy in my silk blouse.

I smooth down the fabric, feeling like Wonder Woman in her power suit. Still in jeans but the blouse gives it a whole new vibe from my usual checkered shirts.

27-year-old Lucy is a teensy bit more sophisticated. I'm the I've-got-an-important-meeting Lucy, not the I-can-devour-an-entire-flock-of-chicken-wings-before-HR-finishes-the-safety-presentation Lucy.

According to my emails and phone marathons with Matty, I've got another shot at a promotion in a few months. Amnesia isn't going to work in my favor, but maybe this style upgrade will get me some brownie points.

The reception area is a flurry of activity as usual. People rush into elevators, eyes glued to their phones as they walk, cursing as they bump into each other.

Everything's the same, but something feels distinctly off.

Me. There's a huge arrow over my head screaming LOOK AT THE WEIRDO!

"Lucy!" Abigail from reception chirps. "You're looking well. Glad you're feeling better!"

I flash her a smile. "Thanks, Abigail."

I'm not sure if I'd agree with her assessment of my current state, given I feel like I've been transported into the fucking future.

I wave goodbye, my mind already sprinting toward my desk. Fitting in with no memory of the last year won't be easy but moping at home wasn't helping. Time to throw myself into work, memory or no memory.

Spotting a few familiar faces, I give a cursory nod and sprint toward the elevators. Quinn & Wolfe is huge, and my social circle here, comparatively tiny. Andy has a point. I've been living in my little bubble, too shy to venture out.

"Hi, beautiful!" A burly security guard saunters over. It takes me a minute to realize he means me.

"Er, hi," I stammer, pasting on a rigid smile as anxiety begins to churn within. Now's my chance to fess up and tell this guy I have no clue who he is.

I subtly read his name tag. "Logan! Hi! Sorry, I

can't stop. I'll see you around."

He winks at me and gives me a thumbs-up. "You'll kill it, Lucy, you always do."

I scoot into the elevator, relieved to find it empty. My nerves are fraying, and I haven't even reached my floor yet.

Just as the elevator is about to close, someone jams their foot in to stop it.

When I look up, JP fucking Wolfe strides in.

You have *got* to be kidding me. Out of all the possible elevator buddies today, he is the last person I want to see—the dark, brooding, and unreasonably intimidating co-owner. I'd rather be locked in with an actual wolf.

This box suddenly feels claustrophobic. Will there be enough oxygen to reach the fortieth floor?

Would it be weird if I sprinted out?

"Morning, Mr. Wolfe," I croak. Flashes of that cartoon fiasco are playing in my head—like it was just yesterday.

Cross me again, and you'll be fired on the spot.

"Lucy," he greets, his voice sending shivers down my spine.

So he remembers my name.

He gazes at me so intensely I'm sure he can see all my cringey little secrets. My cheeks go from zero to flaming in about a nanosecond.

Without a word, he hits the close button.

The door slides open again.

"It's full. Take the next one," he growls at the poor guy who freezes with his foot hanging over the threshold.

"S-s-sorry sir," the guy sputters, retreating so fast he accidentally stomps on the woman behind him.

My eyes are like saucers. "Should I, um, grab the next one too?" I manage, already edging toward the escape route.

His glower hardens, nostrils flaring, eyes smoldering and suddenly, I'm rooted to the spot. My heart's going crazy. Oh God, does he still hate me?

"No." His voice is deep and gravelly and sends my nerves into overdrive.

He hits the close button again, locking us both in our metal box.

We ascend in silence, side by side.

I channel my inner Wonder Woman, staring straight ahead, clinging to my laptop like a lifeline, hyper-aware of his every move—the rise and fall of his chest, the clenching and unclenching of his fists, the impatient sweep of his hand through his hair.

He's a good head taller than me; my nose is

level with his shoulder. He's wearing the same crisp white shirt as the day he threatened to fire me. His sleeves are rolled up, showing off tanned, muscular forearms.

His cologne's intoxicating, all earthy and sexy. It's the kind of scent that fits his whole manly vibe perfectly.

I mentally slap myself, warding off the unwanted thoughts. This, right here, is exactly why I don't do well at rubbing shoulders with the top dogs. Or wolves, in this case. Taylor would use the airtime with him to metaphorically kiss his ass. Others might try their luck flirting with one of America's most eligible bachelors.

Me? I'm fighting the urge to repeatedly faceplant into the doors until they release me.

Even with my eyes glued ahead, I can feel his gaze raking over me, burning into my skin.

Get over yourself. Of course it's not.

"How are you feeling?" His deep voice cuts through the silence, and I nearly jump out of my skin.

Slowly, I pivot to look up at him. Now my mouth is level with his pecs. His jaw clenches as our eyes lock. There's light stubble shading his jaw.

For a fleeting second, I wonder what it would feel like between my legs and the hairs on my arms stand on end. Those hands everywhere, that growl of a voice murmuring in my ear, telling me what a bad girl I am…

Gah. Get a hold of yourself.

"You know about my accident?" I ask, wondering who ratted me out. HR?

He looks angry. "Of course I do."

"I'm starting to feel better, thank you." They really need to crank up the A/C in these elevators. A girl could pass out from the heat.

"Any memories from the past year making their return yet?"

"Uh, still a work in progress, I'm afraid." I rub the back of my neck. This is not good if news of my accident made its way up the corporate ladder.

A crease appears between his eyebrows. "Have you recovered any data? Texts? Photos?"

My eyes widen. "All my work stuff is backed up, sir. Nothing's been lost."

His frown deepens. It could be a headache, or maybe he's just living up to his reputation. The wolf isn't known for being Mr. Congeniality.

"I meant your personal data. Have you managed to recover anything from your phone?"

"Oh. No," I squeak. Why's he even talking to me? He never usually gives me the time of day. At company events, he looks right through me like

I'm not even there. Just the way I like it.

"You don't remember anything from the past year? Nothing?" There's an edge to his voice now. He takes a step closer to me, propping a hand on the elevator's back wall.

This is bad. I don't want to be on the wolf's radar.

Every movement he makes seems deliberate, as if he wants me to notice. Probably a power play to intimidate poor defenseless creatives.

Twentieth floor, come on, move it, already.

Do I lie?

"Not yet, sir, but my treatment plan is in place. I'm sure they'll all come rushing back to me soon!" I chirp.

His nostrils flare again. "That's less than ideal," he replies, staring at me for so long that I start to wonder if I've suddenly grown a third nipple on my head. I subtly run my fingers over my lips and nose—no apparent issues there, though I did have some nosebleeds in the hospital.

His stare doesn't waver and my pulse revs up a notch. What's his deal? Is he seething because I misplaced my memories? It's not like I recklessly slid down the banister at the Plaza, for Christ's sake.

Thirtieth floor. I need out.

Finally, the elevator dings at my floor. The fortieth.

I make a move to leave as the doors slide open.

"Wait, Lucy." Wolfe slams the stop button and the door jerks to a halt. "What did the doctor say?" He pauses. "You've had a check-up recently, I presume?"

Maybe he's concerned I'll botch the project. My anxiety spikes as his finger stays on the stop button.

"She said... she assured me I'll remember everything in no time." My throat tightens. Lying was never my strong suit.

As if on cue, someone on the floor tries to call the elevator. The doors attempt to open, but Wolfe holds them shut, resulting in an annoying ping on repeat.

"Really?" He raises a brow, clearly unconvinced.

"Yup. Absolutely."

The person outside is persistent, little do they know who they're contesting against.

"You don't need to worry, Mr. Wolfe," I say in a rush. "I've read up on everything we did during Phase One—I'm right back up to speed. Are you getting off here too? This is my floor."

He releases another loud breath and this one

definitely turns into a low growl.

I don't wait for a response.

The elevator doors open with a soft whoosh as he releases the button. By now, whoever was trying to get in has given up.

Almost tripping over myself, I hurry out of the elevator and make a dash for freedom.

A loud thud resonates from within the metal box, but I don't dare look back. Here's hoping that's the last encounter I have with the wolf for a *long* while.

My heart might not survive the replay.

EIGHT

Lucy

The office floor is dead, thank God. Barely a soul in yet.

As I make my way to my desk, I get an exhausted nod from a developer who looks like she's been coding all night, living off Red Bull and Taco Bell.

A giant balloon that reads "Get better, Lucy!" floats from my desk, alongside a second featuring a cruelly unflattering image of my face.

My God. It's so distorted that my chin has disappeared entirely, and my cheeks look like I'm having a severe allergic reaction to shellfish. Matty, you're a dead man.

I slump into my chair, tears prickling in my eyes as I scan the get-well cards. At least everything else seems familiar—my trusty blue notebooks, Post-it notes, and pens neatly arranged. I'm more a creature of habit than I realized.

Then I clock something out of place—an action figure perched defiantly atop my monitor. Lev Gleason's Golden Age "Daredevil"; he's clad in his vintage two-tone costume of deep crimson and bold royal blue, complete with his signature dark blue cowl. He seems to fixate on me, even though I can't see his eyes.

Weird. I never take comic memorabilia to work, considering it a touch too fan-girl cringeworthy. Why on earth would I break my own rule?

My gaze wanders around the design team's area. Some things haven't changed at all: the stupid dented crown for team member of the month, Matty's cereal boxes, Taylor's trophies, and the dunce-of-the-day hat for whoever screws up.

Hanging on the wall is Wendy and Matt's attempt to make their knees resemble bums, bringing a small smile to my lips.

There are subtle differences. New schematics and Post-its detailing Project Tangra's second phase pepper the walls. But the remnants of Phase One are still visible. It seems so exciting. Shame I don't remember a minute of it.

I go through the printouts on my desk filled with user journeys and design blueprints, feeling a sense of accomplishment that I don't quite understand. I did these? It's so strange that I can't remember. They're dated two weeks ago.

I'm glad no one's here to see me well up. Why is my brain being such a stubborn asshole?

Enough wallowing. It's time to get to work, even if I have to pretend everything is fine while wrestling with a memory-shaped black hole. All I can do is tread water and hope I don't sink.

I wasn't lying to Wolfe when I said I was up to speed. Sure, I don't remember the blood, sweat, and tears behind these designs. The late nights, stress headaches, and shouting matches over interface details that could make or break Tangra.

But I've got the straight facts right here. The real, concrete results of all our hard work. And it's obvious, I was grinding it out here nonstop. It would explain why my past year has been so uneventful. I must've been living at this desk 24/7. All this, without a promotion.

We got something substantial off the ground for Phase One. Not exactly by Wolfe's stopwatch, but we were close. Atlantic City's smallest casino is now 100 percent cash-free for its high roller games, per Wolfe's vision.

Judging by the timestamps of some emails, we worked our asses off and didn't sleep.

I'm so engrossed in my work that the slow influx of colleagues around nine barely registers on my radar. My stomach churns, dreading any unforeseen changes.

But except for a few new faces, everyone is familiar: Wendy, our junior User Researcher, the two Tonys, the developers, Brody, the graphic designer, and team playboy. No Taylor yet. Matty's late, obviously.

They swarm around my desk, then the questions start.

People don't believe I've lost a year.

Or they don't get it.

"Hey Luce, how are you feeling?"

Followed by: "Shit, so you really did lose your memory? Andy sent an email yesterday."

I feel like I'm a freak show exhibit.

They're skeptical.

I get it; it's unbelievable.

Yes, I lost my memory. No, I don't have a clue what I was up to last week. And sadly, I did not get my memory back overnight like some sort of amnesiac superhero.

I tell them that the doctor said they need to handle me with care.

They nod along, making sympathetic noises

before jumping right into questions about work. It's a good thing I busted my butt preparing. But all the attention makes me anxious, like I'm under a microscope. I put on a fake smile, faking a confidence I don't feel.

"Luce, can you check if my feature matches the design now?"

"Luce, did you sort that copy issue I showed you?"

Posts-its and papers flap in my face. Laptop screens are set down in front of me because people need answers.

Heads peer down at me from all sides, making me feel claustrophobic. Politely demanding I hurry up and remember because I've been out of action for over two weeks, and work's piling up.

"Matty!" I call out when I spot him in the aisle. I need him to act as my human shield from my coworkers.

He takes his seat beside me and gives me a quick hug. "Looks like you're the center of attention."

"Yeah, but not in a good way."

"Listen up, show's over," he announces to everyone still looking at me. Mimicking Andy, he places both hands on his head, his sun-kissed surfer hair now long enough to be pulled back into a ponytail. "There's work to be done here, people."

I flash him a grin. Unless Matty's had a brain transplant, I doubt he's the poster boy for Workaholic of the Year.

"I still can't believe you don't remember the last year," he says as he pours some cereal into a bowl before powering up his laptop. "Do you remember me visiting you in the hospital?"

I shake my head sadly. "No. But thanks anyway."

"Probably for the best, you had drool all down your face."

"Thanks." I scowl at him while he pours yogurt over his cereal.

"So let me get this straight—you've got a sort of time-warping memory thing going on, remembering stuff from a year ago like it happened yesterday?" He furrows his brows, clearly confused. "That's quite a neat trick. So do you remember what you were doing this time last year?"

"Not really. It's like I took a two-week vacation then came back and forgot everything that happened before the trip. The memories are kind of foggy."

"I don't need a vacation for that. I walk out of this office each day and come next morning, I can't remember what I was doing."

I roll my eyes, smiling, and lean over toward his desk. "Hey, what did Andy's email say about me? Hope he didn't say I've lost the plot."

"Nah, it was the opposite." He shrugs and shovels yogurt into his mouth. "Y'know what he's like," he mumbles between mouthfuls. "Basically, you've lost your memory but it's business as usual... oh, and the IT team meeting has been bumped up an hour today. In fact, that was the headlining message."

Typical Andy. "Well, I guess it's good Andy's being blasé. I don't need the entire office gawking at the strange girl with no memory." I pause, chewing on my bottom lip. "I saw Wolfe in the elevator. He was moody as usual but started interrogating me about my memory loss. I think he sees me as a liability or something."

"You must have the worst luck." Matty grimaces. "He's been in a shitty mood all week. Not that anyone would notice the difference. Lucky for us, he's been around less than usual."

"Oh God, I wasn't expecting him to be around at all?" The thought of running into Wolfe again makes my stomach churn.

He jerks his head toward the glass-enclosed corner office. "Sometimes he uses that office when he's here. Usually when he's coming to talk to us about the project."

"Shit." I eye the office warily. I won't feel at ease knowing he could appear at any moment. What's he doing slumming it with us instead of being up with the Quinn brothers on the exec. floor? "What's he been like with us?"

"The cold-hearted bastard we all know and loathe," Matty says wryly. "I may be exaggerating slightly—he's actually softened over the past few months. But, man, when a deadline slips and affects his bottom line, he's brutal."

"I take it I've stayed out of his way?" I ask, hoping against hope that I've somehow remained off his radar since the doodle fiasco. Matty already told me I wasn't axed from the project so that's something. "Have we crossed paths much or not really?"

He sucks air through his teeth. "Weird vibe. He seemed to hate you for a long time. I think it softened a bit to indifference."

"He hates me?" I say in dismay. I get a full-body shiver at this revelation. "I think I liked it better when he had no clue who I was."

"You mouthed off to him once during a meeting. We thought you'd get taken off the project, for sure."

I gape at Matty as my heart nose-dives into my underwear. "I mouthed off to Wolfe? Are you kidding me?"

Matty winces, pushing away his now empty yogurt cup. "Yeah, not your finest hour. We were sure you were done for."

I cradle my head in my hands. This just keeps getting better and better. "What the hell did I say to him?"

He shrugs. "You told him his demands were unrealistic. Which they were, to be fair. You had a point, but wrong time and place."

"Holy shit," I groan. I've been on a one-woman crusade to antagonize the man.

"If it helps, he eased up a bit after that. He seemed to mellow out. We were all silently cheering you on, despite fearing for your job."

"Well, small mercies and all that," I mutter. Although, it doesn't change the fact I now have to share floor space with a boss who loathes my existence. Fan-fucking-tastic.

"Just keep your head down. You know, there's a running joke that he pushed you down the Plaza stairs."

"What?" I choke on my spit, spraying his face.

"I appreciate the gesture, but I had a shower earlier today."

"Sorry. But why? Why the hell is this joke going around?"

"He was there when you fell. He called the ambulance."

I stare at him, appalled. "Did you witness the fall? Anyone else?"

"No, sorry, Luce. I don't know anyone who did."

I must look distraught because he nudges my arm. "Relax. It's a stupid joke. We don't actually think he pushed you."

"This is mortifying," I murmur. "Why did I have to get drunk?"

Matty shrugs. "You seemed upset. When I asked, you blamed your monthly visitor and told me to drop it."

What bullshit.

"Hey, don't worry about it. You have enough to deal with in the present, without digging up the past."

I swallow, nodding, even though the thought of Wolfe witnessing my humiliation is difficult to shake off.

I'm not ready to unpack more of this disaster —my anxiety levels are spiking as it is. Time for a subject change.

"Here, take a look at this..." I pull out the

Daredevil action figure I had stashed under my monitor. "Do you know why I've got this on my desk?"

Matty frowns. "Why are you asking me? You're into all that superhero shit."

"Yeah, but I don't display it at work." I stare at Daredevil in my hands, then glance up—and my stomach plummets.

JP Wolfe is barreling down the aisle, his face an impenetrable mask of steel.

Oh, fuckadoodledoo.

HR Helen attempts to glide alongside him and engage him in conversation, but fails to hold his attention.

No, that's all on me and my stupid Daredevil.

His eyes blaze with such ferocity that everyone on the floor must feel it.

Clearly, he thinks I'm unfit to work, sitting here playing with toys my first day back. I think I just aged in reverse. Compared to him, I feel like a child instead of a 27-year-old woman, and he's only got ten years on me.

In a frenzy, I yank my chair back, smacking my knee in the process. Yowch.

I duck behind my monitor, shoving Daredevil under the desk—but the stupid plastic fool has other plans, rolling onto the floor, right into the path of the oncoming storm.

Cursing under my breath, I plunge to the floor to rescue Daredevil. Wolfe is practically upon me.

"Lucy." His voice rumbles low. I'm imagining it, surely, but—no. That's definitely my name rolling off his lips.

Heart pounding in my chest, I dare to look up at him. We're locked in some bizarre unmoving vortex, eyes fused in an unspoken standoff.

My cheeks swell with a deep flush, my earlobes throbbing from the rush of blood.

I release a gargled, "Hi."

As he begins to lean in, I make a desperate lunge for Daredevil, nabbing him before Wolfe can.

Then, I'm back in my chair quicker than a blink, feigning deep interest in my laptop screen as Wolfe glides past me.

I glance at Matty to gauge his reaction to the weird interaction between Wolfe and me, but he's engrossed in some YouTube video.

What just happened?

My head feels forty shades of fucked up. I'm torn between the fear of Wolfe's wrath and the intoxicating thrill of his unexpected attention.

And I haven't the faintest idea which terrifies me more.

NINE

Lucy

Taylor. The last person I need to see.

She marches in, all business, skirt swishing, hair wrestled into a bun so severe it'd give that porn star—the one Matty was caught ogling on the company desktop—a run for her money.

Over the past year, she's morphed into a new level of power player, her blazer even boasting shoulder pads, reminiscent of the '80s superheroes' costumes.

Instead of sitting, she stands in the aisle. "Boardroom five. Now."

I glance around. Everyone seems unfazed—even Matty doesn't so much as twitch an eyebrow.

She whirls around on her pointed heels, executing a theatrical pirouette, before sashaying off toward boardroom five.

One after another, my colleagues fall into line behind her.

Something's not right here.

Even Matty peels himself off his desk, abandoning his cereal.

Alarmed, I snag his arm before he can join the departing herd. "What the hell's going on? Why's Taylor summoning us to the boardroom?"

He stares down at me. "Holy shit. You don't know."

A chill of apprehension skitters down my spine. "Know? Know what?"

"Taylor's helming Project Tangra, Luce. Andy put her in charge."

The blood drains to my feet. "Taylor's my boss?" I rasp. "Is this some sort of sick office prank for my first day back? You're all in on it, aren't you? You, Spider, the girls, even Wolfe?"

He bursts out laughing. "Sorry, Luce, but this is comedy gold. Your face! But yeah, Taylor's running the show."

I'm too traumatized to speak.

Anybody else but her. I'd prefer to answer to Satan himself.

"Come on." He nudges me up out of my seat. "Didn't you figure it out from the emails?"

"No," I hiss. "Taylor's always been a bossy pain in the neck. I just thought she was being... well, her."

Is this the memory my brain has been shielding me from? It all makes sense now.

"Has the last year been a living hell?" I whimper.

"Pretty much," he deadpans.

I wait for the punchline, but it never comes.

He shrugs. "I thought Andy was tough with his Turkish buffet ban. Now he's hands-off, and Taylor's in charge, she barely lets me take a whiz."

"Did we ever think about quitting?"

"Come on, you know we're both too set in our ways to do that."

We edge into the cramped boardroom.

I'm relieved all the seats are taken so I can hide at the back, propping up against the wall with Matty in front of me. Boardrooms make me claustrophobic, and I turn into a gibbering wreck when I have to speak.

With thirty of us packed like sardines, I attract a few curious stares. Some crane their necks to gawk at the woman with no memories.

If this were a comic, I'd be Captain Confusion.

Taylor struts to the head of the table, smoothing out her suit jacket.

"Lucy." She smiles at me, her voice dripping with a sweetness that sets my teeth on edge. "We really can't express how wonderful it is to have you back. Feeling better, I hope?"

"Like a million bucks," I mutter, forcing a tight smile.

"That's just great." Her hands clasp over her chest like she's auditioning for a soap opera. "On behalf of management, rest assured, we're here to hold your hand through your recovery journey."

"So you're the boss now." The words escape my lips as a whimper. This must be some sort of twisted nightmare. Any minute now, I'll wake up in a hospital bed.

She grins momentarily before reining herself in. No doubt, she's reveling in the horror flashing across my face. "Oh dear, you *have* forgotten a few things. Yes, I'm leading the project."

Just like Taylor can't hide her delight, I can't hide my dismay. I try for nonchalance but end up pulling off an awkward grimace-smile.

Of all the rotten luck, having Taylor as the boss ranks alongside memory loss. Possibly worse.

I try to focus as she speaks—we're in the first sprint of Phase Two and I'm excited, but it's bittersweet because no matter how hard I work or how much I love the project, I'll still have to answer to Taylor.

I wonder, how long did it take for me to swallow this bitter pill the first time?

Just when I think this meeting can't get any worse, my neck prickles. Without even turning around, I can feel his presence. That scent.

Taylor breaks off mid-sentence, her eyes darting to the door.

"Don't mind me," a smooth, deep voice sounds from behind me, stirring the energy of the room. Everyone instinctively sits up straighter.

Tension tightens my muscles as I turn slowly, meeting his gaze. I wish now I hadn't chosen a spot in the back.

He leans against the wall.

"We were just discussing the retrospective, sir," Taylor stammers, clearly thrown off by his presence.

"Do continue," he orders, his eyes latching onto mine for an unsettling moment before he diverts his attention to the terrified team at the front. "I'm interested to hear about the team's challenges."

Whirling back around, I try to focus on Taylor, nerves buzzing. Now I'm on high alert, acutely aware of every inch of space between us. If I took one step back, we'd practically be spooning. His breath would be on my skin.

I'm supposed to be listening intently to hit the ground running, but all I can think about is how if

I moved my hand back, I'd be touching Mr. Wolfe's dick.

Ever since he growled out a threat to fire me on the spot, I've fantasized about what it would sound like when he comes. I bet it's primal and fierce. In my most secret fantasies (which I would never admit to anyone), Wolfe commands everyone to leave the office, then gives me a spanking for drawing that wolf caricature before delivering a proper punishment with his big angry cock.

The guy hates me and my mind goes *there*?

While Taylor finds her voice again my ears flame. They reveal all my dirty thoughts. I bet he's staring at them wondering what health issue is causing them to glow so.

He's really invested in this project if he's come to listen in on this. We have retrospectives every fortnight, low-level, nitty-gritty discussions.

On rare occasions, board members will sit in on some meetings to show us that they're apparently one of us, especially when we're pulling twelve-hour days to meet a deadline.

But the difference between us, the minions, and them, the Rolexed-up Suits, is a few billion dollars, give or take. They don't have to lift a finger except to pat us on the head to tell us we're doing a good job.

As Taylor circles the room for updates, I'm startled when she lands on me. "Do you have anything to say, Lucy? Anything that you'd like to contribute? I don't want you feeling left out."

Is that a joke?

I eye her skeptically. We're supposed to say what went well and what didn't go so well since the last meeting.

Let's see. Went well: lovely view of the Empire State Building from my hospital window. Slept in every day.

Not well: fell down stairs, brain turned to mush, I was doped up for an entire week, found out that my neighbor is a blow-up sex doll, I have a roomie named after an arachnid, oh, and this one time in the hospital, I nearly shit myself when I didn't get out of bed on time.

"No, Taylor. Nothing to add."

It's Matty's turn.

"What's the status of the new barcode design?" Taylor inquires, crossing her arms.

He doesn't respond. He's asleep with his eyes open.

Taylor snaps her fingers in his direction and I jab my finger into his back.

He pushes himself off the wall, shaking himself out of his stupor. "Oh, uh... we have our third user experience session tomorrow with Lucy's new designs. We're down to two possibilities that we're testing."

"We have to release it in seven days." Taylor's lips thin out and her eyes narrow to slits. "Seven days."

"Can we push it back?" Matty asks, a hint of panic in his voice. "Luce could do with a bit more time to play catch-up."

She turns her attention to me, hiding her annoyance with a smile. "If you could jog your memory by Tuesday, that would be perfect, Lucy."

Again, is that a joke? What happened to the sisterhood of women-in-IT, Taylor?

My brows knit together. "Let me just upgrade my brain RAM then. Maybe that'll help."

Laughter ripples through the room, probably at me rather than with me.

Cringing, I sink further against the wall. That's got to be the geekiest IT joke I've ever managed to drop.

"Taylor," Wolfe's deep voice booms from behind me, making me sweat instantly. "Lucy's been through a lot. Our staff's needs are more important than the deadline. Push it back."

Taylor looks surprised, almost offended. "Of course, sir," she says, her tone hesitant. "But... The casinos… They're waiting. We've already sent out company-wide notifications—they're all geared up."

"Let me worry about that."

Taylor nods quickly. "Of course."

I stand rooted to the spot, each shallow breath a struggle. The heat snakes its way from my ears to my neck. I know it's his glare that's causing the fire. I want nothing more than to shrink away into nothingness.

Slowly, I swivel to meet Wolfe's dark eyes. "Thank you," I say quietly.

His lips give the faintest quirk before he nods, acknowledging my gratitude.

"Like I said, Lucy," he says, his tone measured and steady, yet there's a slight clench in his jaw. "Your well-being is my chief concern."

It is?

The statement hangs heavily between us, charged with an intensity that feels exclusive to us, oblivious to the other thirty occupants of the room.

My gaze drops to his lips. Full, manly lips in rough, sexy stubble. They part just a fraction, seemingly in response.

I quickly refocus on Taylor before my shaky legs give out completely.

What the hell was that? Was Wolfe being... nice to me?

Maybe he feels sorry for me because I fell down the stairs, or he's concerned I'll sue the company.

I guess he is a man made of real living DNA but it's hard to see past the cold-hearted boss who cares only for his bottom line. You don't become a billionaire casino mogul without being some degree of an asshole.

But he has to have some human feelings under that power suit.

And unless my senses are playing tricks on me, he's edging closer.

The heat that originated in my ears is now trickling down, settling in places it has no business being. When he innocently clears his throat, I have to clamp my legs together to force down a wave of tingly excitement.

Taylor's voice fades into white noise. She might as well be speaking Klingon.

"Lucy," comes that rich, deep voice from behind me, right as Taylor's wrapping up.

Crap.

I swivel, half-hoping I misheard.

No such luck. Wolfe stands behind me, fixing me with his intense glower. "Could you stick around for a moment?"

His request reverberates around the room, loud and clear.

"Sure," I respond with feigned nonchalance.

Suddenly, the IT team collectively decides to move in slow motion. Matty, the usual front-runner for the door, is now grappling with the concept of walking.

Wolfe releases a sigh laced with obvious irritation, like he's gearing up to tear them a new one.

And then, as the last one shuffles out, it's just him and me. Alone.

A nervous knot forms in my stomach, making it difficult to swallow. Now what?

"Are you managing all right, being back at work?" he asks, his voice dipping lower.

"Absolutely! I'm thrilled to be back." I decide to go on the defensive. "I think you've got the wrong impression of me."

He raises an eyebrow. "And what impression do you think I have of you?"

I think of the stupid Daredevil figurine on my desk.

"Well, if I were to hazard a guess... it would be someone who isn't taking her job seriously."

His stare darkens, something burning beneath the surface. "You're way off."

What the hell does that mean?

My pulse starts running a marathon as an invisible force field of tension seems to spring up around us. It's electric. Suffocating.

Wolfe opens his mouth to speak again, but an abrupt knock on the glass stops him. My eyes flick up to see Killian Quinn giving Wolfe the stink-eye. I've never been so grateful to see the company's other grumpy co-founder.

Wolfe shoots him a curt nod, then releases a deep sigh. "I need to go, Lucy."

"Sure," I reply quickly, seizing the opportunity to put some distance between Wolfe and myself and rush out of the boardroom.

For the next half hour, I struggle to take a decent breath.

TEN

JP

I drag myself into the boardroom to join my business partners, Killian and Connor, my exhaustion embedded in every muscle. Lucy coming back to the office yesterday left me sleepless the entire night.

"You look like you went ten rounds with Tyson in his prime," Killian quips, eyeing me up and down. The guy never misses a beat.

Coincidentally, the championships are being held in our flagship casino this weekend. And as owner, I should be overseeing the whole production.

"Do I," I grumble, tossing my Armani jacket on the table, rolling up my sleeves, and collapsing into the plush leather chair. "Couldn't sleep for shit last night."

Concern flickers across Killian's sharp features. "Everything okay, buddy?"

"Just great," I respond, my voice a steady rumble. Bullshit alert: level ten.

The truth? I spent the previous day watching Lucy navigate her first day back at work. An amnesiac Lucy, oblivious of me and the intense history we share. Then nightfall brought a staring contest with the ceiling, the gears in my brain grinding as I wrestled with this seemingly impossible conundrum. The proverbial rock and hard place had nothing on amnesiac Lucy.

"Need another vacation?" Killian's query hangs in the tension-laden air, the underlying implication leaving a sour taste in my mouth.

Ha. Some vacation. Most people don't know that my so-called "R&R" was an intense detox retreat, instead of cocktails and bikini-clad women in Maui. But Killian and Connor knew because I'd been on the brink of complete self-destruction. I'd only been back a couple of days when Lucy's accident happened.

"I'm good," I grind out, fighting to keep the weariness from seeping into my voice. "If I need a breather, I'll sound the alarm."

"Okay, man," Connor says. "Just let us know. I know how working with Killian can tip anyone over the edge."

Killian glares at him.

"Without sounding like a broken record, what I really need"—I exhale heavily—"is to detach myself from the casino industry." And maybe join a monastery. Perhaps even take up herding yaks in the Himalayas, where I can't hurt anyone else.

But they already know that. I let the pent-up sigh escape.

Since the inception of the Quinn & Wolfe empire, I've been spearheading the casino operation. Casinos weren't just my business, they were my drug, my adrenaline, my whole goddamn life.

But now, I need an exit.

Vegas is a merciless beast, sucking you dry under the guise of a good time. All it left was the grime, the gritty bits, and a silhouette of the man I wanted to be.

I guess I thrived in the casino business because, at heart, I was a "well-managed" gambler. I was the guy who could shrug off losing a million on a Friday and make it back by the time the eggs benedict was served at Saturday brunch.

I'm the workaholic who clawed his way out of the grime and hopelessness of trailer park life. The gambler with an eye for business. But I'm also an introvert at heart, lacking charisma. I needed to lure the whales into our casinos, keep the gaming commissions off our backs, and have politicians eating from the palm of my hand. I needed to radiate charm that wasn't in my nature. And a few lines of the finest "Bolivian marching powder" usually did the trick.

No, Manhattan is better for my state of mind.

"Did we bait Tony Astion from Royal Casinos into an interview?" I ask.

"Tony's not cut out for this," Connor cuts in. "JP, you're the guy. You're the only one we trust with the casinos. Nobody knows the Vegas scene better. You've got the connections, the influence, the contacts into the mob, the feds, the high rollers."

"Why, thank you, Connor," I respond, my voice heavy with irony. "Always good to remember I have a veritable directory of unsavory characters at my fingertips." This conversation has been on repeat for the past two months. "I'm not disappearing. I'm stepping back. And ideally, not living in Vegas."

"You're getting ahead of yourself," Killian intervenes. "Fifteen years in the business, and now you want us to switch gears and start a damn hippie commune?"

What I'm actually trying to start is a wellness retreat branch of Quinn & Wolfe. My jaw tightens.

Without the Quinn brothers onboard, this could become a one-man uphill battle. "If I can make it rain in a casino, I can sure as hell get people to chill out in a spa."

A year ago, the idea of meditation and green juice would've had me doubling over. But after everything, maybe that kind of peace is exactly what I need.

"Just as long as you're not aiming to create some sort of 'Let's chant together, drink matcha, and find our inner peace' kind of place," Connor chuckles, cracking himself up. "If we're swapping roulette wheels for yoga mats, JP, we're gonna need to have a little chat."

"Maybe a bit of meditation would do your sarcastic ass some good," I counter, rolling my eyes.

Connor shoots me a knowing smirk. "This smells like a midlife crisis. Must be something in the water. Killian just had his."

"And what was my midlife crisis?" Killian fires back, eyes narrowing.

"Hooking up with the nanny."

"Clodagh is not a hook-up," Killian growls. "And watch your words, or my actual midlife crisis might involve me introducing your face to my fist."

Ah, Killian had to pick the Irish nanny, as if he

was auditioning for some heartwarming Hallmark movie. The arrogant tycoon, suddenly finding himself head over heels in love with the vivacious, fiery Irish nanny. Although Clodagh doesn't seem like the typical nanny.

"But Killian's downward dog is on point," Connor chortles, pressing his brother's buttons. While Killian's off playing Mr. Darcy with his Irish nanny, Connor, in contrast, is on an entirely different trajectory with most of the models in Manhattan. "His delightful yoga instructor, Clodagh, has schooled him well. You've already got your first customer, JP."

"All right, enough," I mutter, rubbing my temples. The weight of these incessant conversations is starting to weigh down on me. All I seem to do these days is try to convince people that I'm trying to take my life on a different course.

Killian looks at me, his teasing smirk fading to a more serious expression. "JP, we're in your corner. Rehab, yoga, fucking crystal healing, you name it. But let's not forget the backbone of Quinn & Wolfe: nightlife, luxury hotels, and casinos. Not *Eat Pray Love* retreats."

"We had a deal," I remind him, annoyance creeping into my voice. "We test one. I can make it profitable."

"Look, JP," Connor says, voice uncharacteristically gentle, "I get you're passionate about this, but don't let emotion cloud your judgment here. You know that's dangerous."

And I do know. One bad business decision fueled by emotions sank me once already. Long before the Quinn & Wolfe hotel empire was even a glint in our entrepreneurial eyes. I clung onto my first motel, long after it had become a sinking ship.

But the irony is, Connor's wrong—emotion is always part of my business, I just didn't see it.

"One wellness retreat," Killian concedes after a heavy pause, pushing away from the table and standing up. "But you promised you'd get Tangra over the line before we find someone else to run the casinos."

"And I will." My voice is firm, resolute. Because, hell or high water, I'm determined to carve out a new path—one that doesn't involve drowning myself in neon lights and empty debauchery. One where, perhaps, I might stand a chance at earning Lucy's forgiveness.

Implementing Project Tangra nationwide will elevate us to new heights. It's the most important project in the works right now, with a projected 15 percent revenue increase.

The gamblers want to be able to throw around

their money, without the hassle of counting bills and chips. And we're here to provide that service.

I need to get Tangra across the line before I can step back. I never go back on my word. We have some of the games cashless—but not all yet.

Killian paces toward the floor-to-ceiling windows. "This sudden urge for a yoga retreat... Has it got something to do with a certain blue-eyed member of the IT department?"

He turns to stare at me intently. As subtle as a sledgehammer to the face.

I meet his gaze evenly. "It's about business —expanding our portfolio, seeking new revenue streams. And it's about me choosing a different lifestyle."

And hopefully, that lifestyle comes with a side of Lucy.

"And how is she?"

"She's resilient, as always. Most employees would stay away as long as possible, milk the sick pay." I clear my throat, emotions making it tough. "But I'm keeping my distance. Since she doesn't remember me, it's not like I can barge back into her life, as much as I'd like to."

He nods. "Do we have to worry about a lawsuit on our hands?"

"Why?"

"Why? You fuck an employee, and she falls down the stairs. Don't ask me why, JP."

My fists clench involuntarily at his words. "We don't have to worry about a lawsuit. It was an accident."

Connor grunts, clearly not convinced. "Accidents tend to have a nasty habit of becoming lawsuits. Especially when they involve a billionaire, a spiraling staircase, and a lover's quarrel."

I bristle. Salt, meet wound. I have no desire to dredge up the events of that night at the Plaza Hotel, to untangle the ugly, twisted mess it was.

"You know there's a rumor going around that you pushed her down the stairs," Connor says, his casual tone making the words hit harder.

I snap to attention. "Are you fucking kidding me?"

He chuckles, lifting his hands in mock surrender. "I'm just the messenger. Seems like the marketing gals have an insatiable appetite for gossip."

"And why are they sharing it with you, of all people?" My voice takes on a hard edge.

A smirk stretches across his face. "Guess I'm just more approachable than you two."

I pinch the bridge of my nose, a headache

brewing. "Jesus Christ."

The last thing I need is for Lucy to catch wind of these ridiculous rumors.

I'm no angel, but to suggest I'd push her down the stairs? That's a new low, even for the office gossipmongers. Usually, I would shrug off the slander—let the corporate hyenas feast on the bones of my reputation. But with Lucy... this isn't just about me anymore.

Connor chuckles. "I told them you didn't do it. My theory is she passed out from an overdose of your aftershave."

I feel a prickling heat crawl up my neck. Maybe I've been overzealous in trying to make myself appealing to Lucy again. She's always loved this particular scent.

Second day into Lucy's return to work, and I'm already on damage control. Instead of buying roses and planning candle-lit dinners, I'm swatting off rumors of attempted homicide.

As if I don't already have enough buried scandals to deal with.

A sinking realization claws at my gut as the weight of Connor's words settles over me. I've got one hell of a battle on my hands—a battle against time, rumors, and my own damned knack for self-destruction. And the clock is ticking.

ELEVEN

Lucy

I've officially survived nearly two full days back at work after my accident, and while my memory is still MIA, at least the stares and whispers have dialed back. For now, I'm just focusing on catching up and proving to everyone—despite Wolfe's unexpected leniency—that I haven't forgotten how to do my job.

I'm so intent on responding to emails that I don't notice my legs have gone numb until Angry Andy walks by.

"Andy," I call, causing him to pause. "Thanks for visiting me in the hospital. It was really nice of you."

He grunts in response, hating emotional exchanges.

I smile. I nearly rolled off the bed when Mom told me my boss visited.

"How's your memory?"

"Still on vacation," I sing-song, humor is the best coping mechanism when you can't remember your own life.

"All right then," Andy says, starting to back away. "Let me know if you need anything. You know, for the memory situation."

My lips quirk. Like what? An ergonomic mouse won't help me now.

"Actually, speak to Helen from HR." He nods quickly and scurries down the aisle.

I watch him disappear, and my gaze collides with Wolfe's through his transparent office. I practically jump out of my skin. *Get a grip, you've lost your memory, not your sanity.*

Gritting my teeth, I redirect my attention back to my screen.

Wolfe is an enigma.

He's so difficult to read; his words were shockingly gentle toward me in the meeting yesterday despite the fact I obviously annoy him. But it's more than that—there's something unnerving about him that makes me think he's got his eye on me.

Am I imagining things?

What makes a guy like Wolfe tick? What secret stories do those brooding, dark eyes hold?

Unable to resist, I sneak another peek at the

handsome scary man through the glass.

His lips move as he talks on the phone, but his frown is fixed on me.

A flash of emotion ignites in his eyes— loathing? No, it's softer, like regret. But then it's gone, and his expression hardens into its usual unreadable mask.

Matty's stupid joke about Wolfe pushing me that night bursts into my mind, stirring an uneasy feeling in my gut. I don't actually believe that, but what *did* happen? I tossed and turned for hours last night racking my brain. No one saw me fall and I have no memory of it myself. Not knowing feels like it's going to kill me, but I can hardly march into Wolfe's office and ask him outright.

I force my attention back to my screen just as something smacks into my head—the office dunce cap.

"Really, Matty?" I snap, praying Wolfe didn't just see that. I snatch the chicken hat Matty tossed at me, narrowing my eyes at him.

He just smirks back. "What? You definitely earned it today."

"You're supposed to be nice to me. I'm in a fragile fucking state of mind here," I moan indignantly. "And I don't think it's recommended by the doctors in my fancy clinic to throw things at amnesia patients."

"Just getting you back in the groove." His smile doesn't waver. "I've been tossing that hat your way all year."

I shoot him a look. Apparently, it takes more than a silk blouse to get a little respect around here.

Getting back to the job at hand, I go through the contents of my desk drawer, hunting for the wireframe mockups I need. Thank God I'm a neat freak.

An image tumbles out alongside them: a photograph of me at a comic convention. It's one of those booth photos.

A spasm jolts through me and I hastily cough to cover it up, my heart racing. There I am, in all my Miss Nova glory. And there *he* is.

The man with the sexy briefs…?

Daredevil.

Who are you, Daredevil?

My thoughts race uncontrollably as I stare at the image, my first piece of concrete evidence that he exists. The men's briefs I found in my bedroom could've been a purchase I made, but this photograph is an entirely different story.

He's tall, donning a mask that shrouds his eyes and nose in mystery. His arm is wrapped protectively around me. I'm sporting a big, infectious grin, cosmic blue lipstick, and eyeliner drawn into starry cat-eyes. I'm gazing up at this masked man in a blue and red bodysuit like he's the living embodiment of all my filthy fantasies come to life.

Was I really that happy?

It looks like there's well over six feet of pure rock-hard muscle stuffed into that suit. And is that reinforced padding in his leather crotch or is he just thrilled to see me? Hopefully, I got to find out. Did I show him my sexy Miss Nova outfit? I hope he liked it.

Maybe it's just someone who works there...

No, it's him—my mystery man. My vagina's spidey senses are tingling.

I felt something for this man.

Remember, Lucy, you have to remember.

What did we share, whoever you are behind that mask? Will I ever know your true identity?

The background looks like that comic convention in Manhattan I usually attend. The one happening again this weekend. My pulse quickens at the realization.

I must've liked him if I put a reminder on my desk. I'm losing my goddamn mind.

"Matty." I pull my chair over to him,

interrupting whatever he's doing, which is easy to do. "Hey, I gotta ask you something and I need you to not mess with me."

He grins. "I can't guarantee that."

"Seriously." I scoot my chair closer. "Did I or do I have a boyfriend?"

"A guy? Nah. You would've told me."

I show him the photo, but he shrugs.

"Could be anyone, Luce. You always have those guys posing with you. It's like your nerdy version of Chippendales."

"No," I insist, glaring at the photo. "Mom, Priya, and Libby said I was seeing someone for a few months. So I didn't tell you anything at all?"

He shrugs again. "Not a thing."

Weird. Why wouldn't I tell Matty if I was seeing someone?

Then again, women are wired differently to men. I think we talk more about dates than men do. I can barely keep up with Matty's rotation of casual dates. And I doubt he can either.

"But if I'm seeing someone, why haven't they come forward yet?"

He pauses to think for a second. "Maybe he's out of town for work and has no clue. Or I guess it's possible he was gonna end things with you anyway, and this just makes that easier for him."

"*Matty.*"

"I dunno, Luce. Who the hell knows? I'm a simple guy. I'd come forward."

Maybe Matty's right. Is this what my brain's blocking out? Did I get dumped or ghosted by Daredevil?

"Matty," Brody murmurs from the adjacent desk. "Check out boss man's office."

We follow his line of sight.

JP is in his office talking to Helen from HR. With her long, flowing hair and a figure and face to die for, she looks like she belongs in the dictionary beside the word "stunning."

Something weird twists in my stomach as Wolfe leans across the desk, closing the gap between them.

I glance around the office. The guys have stopped typing, too busy trying to put their tongues back in their mouths from leering at Helen.

Watching them through the glass, it's easy to see why women fantasize about him. Who wouldn't fantasize about being the one special woman to accomplish the impossible—to break through that tough exterior, get him to relax that chiseled jawline, or even have him get down on one knee?

Heck, even to make the man crack a *smile*.

Lying in bed this morning, I'm ashamed to admit I entertained that foolish fantasy.

That Wolfe finds me attractive, instead of my usual lineup of weirdos.

That an experienced, successful, *sexy* guy like Wolfe looks at me how he looks at Helen.

That he sees me as more than another idiot on the IT team with a habit of doodling giant penises on printouts. That he could find me witty, charming, an equal. That he might respect me. And want to tear my clothes off to reprimand me over that cartoon of his furry likeness.

I mentally kick myself for being such a moron. This is Wolfe we're talking about. The day that man cracks a heartfelt smile over *me*, the four horsemen will ride, aliens will reveal themselves, the earth will spin in reverse, and Mom will finally get the hang of WhatsApp.

An exaggerated throat clearing interrupts my thoughts.

Swiveling around, I find Dwayne looming over my desk.

"Hi, Dwayne." As if my day couldn't get any worse.

"Hello, Lucy," he responds solemnly, eyes fixated on me while he runs his hands along the length of his tie. Both actions are equally unsettling. "So you really can't remember anything from this year, then?"

Christ, how many more times am I going to get asked this? Should I carry a sign?

"That's right."

"Interesting." He nods slowly, apparently mulling it over. "I've been doing some reading on your condition."

Oh, here we go.

"You'll require monitoring."

My brows jump to my hairline. "Excuse me?"

"As you are aware, besides being the data protection officer, I'm also the appointed health and safety watchdog for this floor."

"Uh-huh," I drawl, glancing at Matty, who's now all perked ears. "And what exactly do you mean by 'monitoring'?"

"I'll be observing to ensure you follow safety protocol."

Now the entire floor has hit pause on their tasks to eavesdrop.

"I'm not a convict on day release," I say through gritted teeth.

Dwayne slides his glasses up his nose, giving me a look that conveys he will not tolerate any defiance. "Safety is paramount. It's for your own good. And considering your recent head injury, it's only prudent for me to assess your workspace for potential hazards."

I snort out a laugh. "What, like dangerous staplers?"

His lips form a thin line. "I take my job seriously. I suggest you do too. Now, if you'll excuse me..." He looks at me expectantly.

Grunting, I heave myself up. "Fine then—let's get this over with."

Matty leans back in his chair, beaming as Dwayne starts his inspection. "Have you considered making Luce wear a helmet around the office? You know, to avoid any further head injury?"

"In case I get hit by a flying stapler?" I add sarcastically.

Dwayne pauses mid-inspection, and peeks out from under my desk. "It's not beyond the realms of possibility. I did see Matty throw a chicken hat at you."

As Dwayne fusses around my desk, tingles spread up my spine. I feel eyes on me from a corner office. Call it woman's instinct.

Cautiously, my eyes drift toward the corner office, and there it is: the zing of connection.

My instincts are on point.

I meet Wolfe's gaze through his window. Helen's gone. Wolfe's pacing like a caged animal, phone in hand. But his eyes? Glued to me. Not quite a smile, more an intense *I'm watching you.*

Christ, what do I do?

Andy did say networking was key. I lift a hand, giving Wolfe a friendly wave and my most casual "How's it going, boss!" face.

"Lucy, what on earth are you doing?" Taylor's voice nearly makes me jump out of my skin. She's approaching to her desk, arms laden with a mountain of paperwork. "Stop waving at Mr. Wolfe like you're in a parade."

"He was staring right at me!"

She gives me an incredulous look. "He's *obviously* looking at the stats board behind you, genius."

"Oh." I glance over my shoulder at the board showing our progress. Well, shit. That makes more sense. My face burns.

"Remember your last run-in with Mr. Wolfe? We thought you were going to get fired."

I gape at her, freaked. "Nooo. Memory loss, remember?"

She rolls her eyes, heaving a sigh. "Just... stay clear of him, okay?"

Goosebumps spread over my skin. If I can't

remember, it didn't happen. Right?

TWELVE

JP

I look at Lucy through the glass wall of my office. She's eyeing me like I'm some kind of psychopath. Probably because I've been staring at her. I haven't spoken to her all day, not since our little chat after the meeting yesterday.

If there's a God, they have a sick sense of humor. What's the lesson here, pal? That I don't get to be happy?

In the weeks leading up to Lucy's accident, I'd been walking the razor-thin edge of redemption, trying to scrub clean the stains of my past. All my attempts to be a better man. Yet, now, it all seems in vain.

I spot Killian striding toward my office.

These past few days he's attempted to be nice, in his own twisted way. Maybe it's the influence of Clodagh, his new flame. Maybe love is finally softening that stony heart of his, making him friendly.

Friends. Buddies. Are those terms I can use for Killian and Connor?

We have a mutual understanding, a well-oiled machine when it comes to business. We built this billion-dollar empire together, each of us with our designated roles. I handle the nightlife and casinos, while the Quinn brothers spearhead the hotel chains.

They know enough of my dirty laundry to hang me out to dry if they ever decide to turn their backs.

But would Killian prioritize my well-being, my desires, over the company's bottom line? Would Connor risk his stocks plummeting to save my ass from a public scandal?

I've never had to test the theory.

Until recently, I echoed their sentiment. A few months back, the company was all that mattered. My identity. My purpose.

I never considered putting in the effort to make friends. Who needs to chase friends when you're the biggest whale in the sea?

The magic of a two-billion-dollar bank account is that it works like a fucking magnet. It pulls people in, bends them to your will. I never had to bend over backward to please anyone.

But staring at Lucy now, I understand the emptiness of that power.

Killian barges into my office without waiting for an invitation, just like his entitlement always allows.

"Killian," I acknowledge.

His eyebrows arch as he pulls out an unmarked envelope, tossing it onto my desk. "I'm going to cut you some slack given your circumstances, but this"—he gestures toward the envelope—"this needs to be fixed. Now."

I open it up and my guts shred. Fuck. Inside, glossy images glare up at me, stark reminders of the night when I screwed up royally. The night that turned Lucy against me, the beginning of the end.

I was so blitzed I didn't even notice someone snapping shots.

"I'm handling it," I say in a low voice.

"It's worse than this. There's a video."

"Have you seen it?"

"Yes. Have you?"

"Yes." A heavy sigh escapes my lips. The tabloids already sent it over to me for comment. Now I'm doing everything in my power to tie them up in legalities and prevent that damn video from seeing the light of day.

Killian snorts. "We run a business empire, not

a back-alley racket. You handle the casinos, the clubs, and that does afford you certain... liberties. But this?" He jabs the envelope with enough force to dent the mahogany beneath it. "This is a PR ticking time bomb. We're one headline away from our shares crashing and the gaming commission revoking our licenses."

His words send a cold shiver down my spine, but there's a bigger dread gnawing at me. The one he doesn't see. The one he doesn't care about. If the story leaks, Lucy will be gone for good. My second chance at mending things with her will be snuffed out.

"I'm aware." I force the words out through gritted teeth.

"And it's not just about the media," Killian continues, ignoring my interruption. "Our employees see you as a leader, a role model. What happens when they see this?"

I drop my head into my hands, my mind reeling. "I've got the best lawyers working on it," I assure him, my hands muffling my words. I look up, my gaze hardening. "It's under control."

He raises a skeptical brow. "You sure about that?"

"As sure as I can be," I reply, my tone steadier than I feel.

It's a well-practiced routine, a front of confidence carefully constructed and maintained over the years. But the cracks are showing now.

"All right, then," Killian finally grunts. "Just... fix this shit, yeah?"

I nod, watching as he strides out of the office. I catch my reflection in the glass window behind him—the dark eyes, the tense lines around the mouth, the look of a man being crushed under the weight of his own sins.

How did I end up here? At the top of the world, surrounded by wealth and power, yet feeling so fucking empty.

Lucy was my ray of sunshine. But I let my demons consume me, and in the process, I lost her.

In that elevator ride, it took every ounce of restraint not to pull her close and make her mine again. I'm walking on thin ice, perpetually caught between what I want to say and what I can say.

"I am my own worst enemy," I mutter to myself.

My phone rings, jolting me from my thoughts.

"Hey, big bro." The cheery lilt in Maggie's voice is a jarring contrast to my own turmoil.

"Maggie."

"Wow. You sound worse than I expected. I take it you haven't made any progress with Lucy then?"

Maggie, my closest confidant, my little sister, knows about Lucy. But she isn't privy to the whole brutal truth behind why Lucy and I fell apart. I'm too ashamed.

"I don't know how much longer I can do this." My voice wavers, breaking the facade I've been maintaining for far too long. "Acting like she's just another employee... it's killing me."

Maggie's response is brimming with empathy. "I know this is tough on you, JP."

The admission rips a tortured growl from my throat. "I'm on edge, Maggie."

"Just... don't do anything rash, okay?"

A pang of guilt hits me. Now I've worried my little sister.

She knows about my demons but never sees them.

I always shield her, keeping her away from my dark side. Ever since we lost our parents and I took on the role of Maggie's guardian at nineteen, it's been my responsibility to protect her from everything. And even though she's now in her thirties, only four years younger than me, I still treat her like my little sister.

"I can only imagine what you're going through," Maggie offers. "But remember, Lucy needs space and time to heal. Just be patient."

"Patience? That's not one of my strengths if you haven't noticed."

She doesn't back down. "Feeling sorry for yourself won't help. You need to keep your focus on Lucy. She needs you, even if she's blind to it right now."

I let out a dry chuckle. The irony is overwhelming. This situation is more nerve-racking than death, if that's even possible. Death, at least, makes sense.

But this? This is a torment designed specifically for me. Grief for the living and breathing, yet utterly unreachable. A woman who walks, talks, breathes but doesn't remember.

"She's completely blocked me out. She doesn't want to remember us."

"Now listen here, you grump, that's ridiculous. I've seen the two of you together. Lucy cares for you deeply."

That was before I fucked it all up.

As I steal a glance at Lucy, her furrowed brow and intense focus stirs something within me. She's in the zone, her dark brown hair cascading over her shoulders, laser-focused on the task at hand. Her smile, a rare treat, is worth any gamble I've ever taken.

She's gorgeous, not in that obvious pin-up girl

way, but it's the kind that sets my heart pounding.

There's an unpretentiousness about her. Would she have bailed on me like my ex-wife did when my first company went belly up?

Instincts tell me otherwise.

Instincts tell me Lucy would stick by me even if my empire crumbled overnight. And in this volatile market, you can never be too cocky.

I'm lucky enough to know the woman behind that stunning face, even if she doesn't remember what's behind mine.

She once looked at me with a fire in those baby blues that made me willing to hand over my kingdom. Now all I see is wariness.

A long, uncomfortable silence hangs on Maggie's end of the line. "So what do the docs advise?"

"Gradual reintroduction," I reply, my eyes never leaving Lucy. "Let her rediscover her memories at her own pace. Problem is she looks at me like I'm some kind of monster."

"Killian told me everyone at the office is terrified of you. The Big Bad Wolf," she jokes.

I respond with a grunt, devoid of any humor.

From the corner of my eye, I see Lucy having a heated conversation with the data protection guy. He places a sign on her desk and she counters by trying to return it.

Maggie's voice is all sympathy. "Just hang in there. Give her time, she'll start to feel something. Let the treatment do its thing."

Easier said than done. I've built a life, a fortune, an empire on my impatience, on my drive for results, and now the same tenacity grates against the reality of my situation. It's like being at the casino table, with the house having all the odds.

"Her memories are still there, JP," she continues, hating silence. "They're locked away, yes, but they're there. I know they'll come back. I just know."

"Maggie, don't presume to fucking know," I snap with a biting tone. She's trying to help in her usual, optimistic Maggie way. She's always been the one to see the silver lining, even when we were kids. When our parents passed, when my first business venture tanked, when my ex walked out on me, she always had faith.

"Sorry. I'm just... I'm so fucking unsure right now. I'm drowning here. I don't know how to navigate this." I let out a harsh sigh. "I'm going to have to step this up. Create a situation where she has to be around me."

"Like work meetings and having lunch

together?" she asks excitedly.

"No."

That wouldn't be enough. Too slow. Too damn slow.

I run a hand roughly through my hair. "I don't know. I gotta think this through."

"Remember, JP, I'm here for you. You'll get Lucy back. I know it."

"Thanks, Mags. Tell the kiddos their favorite uncle misses them."

Without a clear strategy in mind, I hang up and cross the expanse of the open office floor plan. As I near Lucy's desk, my protective instincts kick in when I hear the tension in her voice.

Her fists are firmly placed on her hips as she squares up against Data Guy. "Just listen to me, Dwayne—seriously, put that thing away!"

I suppress a smirk. She's ready to explode on him.

"What's the issue here?" I demand.

They swivel toward me, obviously taken aback by my abrupt entrance.

I snatch the sign from Dwayne's hand and glance at it. The words on it make my blood boil: Lucy has amnesia. Please be patient and handle with care.

"What the hell is this?"

His mouth opens and closes. "I'm the Health and Safety Officer, Mr. Wolfe," he stammers. "We're supposed to highlight potential risks in the office."

My nostrils flare. "Lucy is not a risk," I snap, casting the sign onto a nearby desk. "Get rid of this."

I shake my head in disbelief. We hire some strange people around here.

The immediate silence in the office is deafening.

Lucy and Data Guy look frozen, as though deciding whether it's safe to bolt.

"Can I get rid of this sign on my desk, too?" Lucy's blond friend, Matty, pipes up.

I read the blue note taped to his workstation: *This desk has been declared a safety hazard by the Health and Safety Officer.*

Against my will, I let out a deep, rumbling laugh. Jesus Christ, this department.

"Yes, if you get rid of those cereal boxes."

Turning to Lucy, I lower my voice and say, "could you come to my office, please?"

She looks up at me with those captivating baby blues and I swear she can see the wildness burning behind my gaze. The memories of her body writhing beneath me flood back like a tidal wave; her breathy moans as I tasted her orgasm.

I almost let slip a term of endearment, stopping just in time.

"Of course, Mr. Wolfe."

I motion for her to lead the way. As she somewhat awkwardly heads down the aisle, I find it hard to look away.

Can't she see how utterly undone I am?

I close the office door with a click, sealing us off.

THIRTEEN

JP

Lucy stands uneasily, gazing around like it's her first time in here.

I motion toward the chair facing the large mahogany desk. "Make yourself comfortable." Though at this point, hell freezing over might make her more comfortable than being trapped in here with me.

She perches herself on the edge, her fingers rising instinctively to her necklace, her personal anxiety bead. It was a gift from her old man. Right now, she clings to it like a crucifix warding off the beast across from her.

"If that pendant had a pulse, Lucy, it'd be gasping for breath right about now," I joke.

Her gaze flickers to me, her expression a cool mask that can't quite hide the tinge of surprise. The humor doesn't land, but her hand drops from the necklace. Small victories, I guess. No one ever said I was a comedian.

The tension radiating between us would be laughable except it's tearing my insides to shreds.

An uncontrollable urge to seize her and hold her close courses through every vein in my body.

But instead, I maintain my distance, choosing to prop myself against the front of my desk, within her direct line of sight. "How was your return to work?"

"Fine, thanks," she shoots back, her smile strained, her body rigid. She looks like she's sitting on a fucking cactus. "The team's been great and we've got everything documented, so I'm catching up quick," she goes on. "It's like starting a new project, you know? You just need to hit the ground running."

"I'm glad to hear that." My voice drops down low as I lean in closer, catching the sweet scent of her perfume—jasmine and something else, her own natural fragrance. It's testing what little self-control I've got left.

"I want you to know that I'm here for you," I say, striving to keep my tone as gentle as I can. "You need anything, anything at all—work related or personal, you just say the word."

She pulls back like I threatened to bite her. If she grips those armrests any harder, she's going to tear holes right through the leather. "Thank you, Mr. Wolfe, that's very kind. But I'm confident I won't need to bother you."

The "Mr. Wolfe" stings. Every time.

"Lucy, you could never be a bother." I study her, trying like hell to figure out what's really going on in that head of hers. "How's life treating you outside these walls? Family being supportive?"

Her expression shuts down. "Yes, everything's fine, thanks for your concern."

An unexpected thud, courtesy of the window cleaner, provides a distraction. Lucy's attention snaps toward the sound, her body stiffening as if she's contemplating a dramatic exit through the glass.

Am I that unbearable to her? Her every move screams of her desperate wish to be anywhere but here. With me.

"Why does talking to me make you so uncomfortable?" I ask gruffly, regretting the words as soon as they escape my mouth.

She bristles. "I'm not uncomfortable. I'm just... this job is crucial to me and you wield a lot of power over my future. Networking isn't my strong suit."

"I see. Is this what we're doing, then? Networking?" My words are heavy with sarcasm, and I grit my teeth to stop any further outbursts.

Do you remember what we did on this desk late at night, Lucy?

Her mind might not right now, but her body fucking does. It remembers a time when she was writhing and moaning beneath me, full to the brim with my want.

What would she do if I fell to my knees and begged for a taste of her?

Probably scream the building down and get security storming in.

She bites her lower lip, visibly uneasy, and scuffs the toe of her sneaker against the carpet. Would it matter if I told her I purchased those sneakers for her? She goes through them every three months like clockwork, replacing each worn-out pair with the exact same style.

Her voice is soft when she speaks again. "I'm not sure what we're doing here; you haven't told me why you called me in."

She glances briefly at my lips before her eyes flicker back to meet mine.

A pulse of desire jolts through me, a sharp reminder of how long it's been since we've been close. It's been weeks. So many agonizing weeks since I felt the heat of her skin against mine, since I've been able to breathe her in.

"I wanted to see how you're holding up," I say, forcing my tone level. "You took a nasty tumble at the company event, ended up in the hospital. I care about my crew, contrary to popular belief."

She nods, though I can sense her skepticism. Her beautiful eyes stare into mine, full of queries she can't quite piece together. "I heard you were present at the Plaza when I... took a plunge?"

I stiffen, my pulse pounding. Just the mention of that night sets me on edge.

Jesus Christ, what do I say here? I need to approach this delicately, ease my way back into her life. This is not the time to stir up old wounds, not when she's still mentally fragile.

I force my features into a mask of composure. "That's right. I was there."

Her brows bunch together, carving little lines into her forehead. "Can you tell me what happened? I'm trying to piece it all together."

I search for the right words, for a version of the story that won't leave her completely dumbfounded and unhinged. "We were having a conversation, and then you turned to leave. Unfortunately, those high heels betrayed you, and you took a tumble on the stairs."

I watch her face for any spark of remembrance of our heated exchange but it's blank.

"Typical me. A disaster in heels. I should come with a health and safety warning, like Dwayne suggested." Her self-deprecating chuckle only ratchets up my guilt.

"No need for embarrassment," I counter, a little too swiftly. "You gave us a hell of a scare though. You were unconscious in the ambulance."

I fight to keep my voice level. "It was hours before you woke up at the hospital."

She gapes at me. "You *stayed* with me? At the hospital?"

Stayed with her? I practically haunted those hospital hallways, waiting anxiously for any sign that she'd wake up. "Yes, I did."

She recoils, a soft "oh" slipping past her lips. "That's really decent of you."

If only she knew the half of it, the full story of that night. She wouldn't be singing my praises, that's for sure.

I give a dry, humorless laugh. "Contrary to the rumors, Lucy, I'm not quite the monster they make me out to be. Did you honestly think I'd just leave you concussed at the bottom of the stairs?"

"Yeah, but I know some managers who would have passed that on to HR," she quips, a smile tugging at the corners of her mouth. "I'm sorry if I ruined your night."

"I do a perfectly fine job of ruining things on my own," I say tightly. My night, and everything that matters.

Her eyes soften, curiosity replacing the confusion. "What were we talking about... before I took a nosedive?"

My pulse spikes.

"Nothing important." I've got a poker face that could bluff the devil himself; it's one of the reasons I'm a fantastic gambler. But using it on her leaves a bad taste. "And for the record, if you've been hearing the ludicrous office chatter, I didn't give you a shove."

She chuckles lightly. "I wouldn't be in this room if I believed a word of that."

"Good to know you don't believe everything you hear about me."

"It's all good, of course."

"Of course," I echo, my voice dripping with sarcasm. I lock eyes with her. "So, tell me, Lucy, what *do* you believe about me?"

Her reaction is priceless. A visible gulp, her eyes wide as saucers. "About *you*?"

"That's right."

"Like, what do I know about you?" She takes a moment, letting out a slow breath. "Well, you're the co-founder of our company, obviously. And you're the sponsor for Project Tangra."

The basics. The public knowledge.

"Anything more?" I prod, a hint of a smile playing at the corner of my mouth.

"And you started the hotel group years ago after meeting Killian Quinn. You guys started your first hotel at the time in Queens..." She pauses, looking at me as if trying to gauge if she's passed some sort of test. "You're a, ah, very successful businessman and... eh, a great role model. I'm not sure this is what you're after, Mr. Wolfe?"

"I'm not asking for my biography. I want to know what you—Lucy—personally know about me."

She squirms in her seat, swallowing audibly. "I know we've had a few, eh, interactions before, but I hope we can start on a clean slate. I'll work on my professional filter."

A clean slate? She might as well have slapped me. A clean slate means she doesn't remember a goddamn thing.

A flush of color tinges her cheeks as she blurts, "I'm sorry for speaking out of turn that day in the meeting a few months back."

A surge of hope flares up inside me. "You remember?"

"Yes?" she squeaks out.

I can hardly breathe. "Are you being straight with me right now? You actually recall what happened?"

"No?" Her voice rises even higher. Her eyebrows knit together, eyes darting around as if looking for an escape. "What answer would make you less mad?"

I let out a groan, pinching the bridge of my nose. "The truth."

"Matty filled me in."

Fuck's sake.

But I'm not letting her off the hook. "What about our last encounter? What do you remember about that?"

Her eyes widen, searching for an acceptable response.

"Relax. I'm not setting a trap. Give it to me straight."

"It was the day you came to talk about Project Tangra. You weren't exactly my biggest fan that day."

My lips curve into a smirk as I lean closer to her. "When I caught you with the caricature."

She groans, blushing furiously. "God, this is so weird. I don't know if I said this already, but I'm really sorry about that. Matty mentioned that there were no consequences, so thank you for being lenient."

I chuckle lightly, but I'm too frustrated for it to have any real humor. "I assure you a silly doodle wouldn't be enough to scare me away, Lucy."

"You seemed pretty irate at the time."

"I was." I smirk. "Your department frustrated me."

"And it doesn't anymore?"

"Oh, it still does."

She grimaces and nods. "Well, I apologize for anything out of line I've done this past year."

"Forget anything you've heard. Your performance on the project has been nothing short of outstanding."

She exhales a noticeable sigh of relief. "That's so good to know."

"Since then, we've become more acquainted. You're welcome to call me JP, as you used to."

A line appears between her eyebrows, one I've traced innumerable times. "Oh... kay. Um, JP."

Something glimmers in her eyes as my name slips from her lips. A spark that could ignite memories if properly stoked.

Come on, Lucy.

I watch the gears turning in her mind. She crosses and uncrosses her legs, her movements restless and filled with tension.

A memory. There's one lurking around there.

I know it's there.

Come on, throw me a bone here.

Remember, sweetheart, you need to remember.

She absently smooths her blouse. "Are you now based in New York? The guys mentioned you've been around a lot lately."

I sigh and force a half-smile. "I've had more reasons to be in New York recently. So, yes, my time is divided between here and Vegas."

Wherever you are, that's where I need to be. Even if it's Antarctica.

Her gaze meets mine, a whisper of curiosity showing through. But it vanishes as quickly as it appeared, replaced by a polite nod. Like she's talking about the weather. She doesn't care. She doesn't remember.

Whatever I thought I saw before is gone.

A frustrated growl slips past my lips before I can cage it, and she visibly flinches.

I quickly regain my composure and take a deep breath, not wanting to scare her any further.

"JP, sir," she says in an unnaturally formal tone. "Thank you for this meeting. Umm... is there anything else you need from me?"

Looking at her face, devoid of any trace of recognition or warmth, hits me like a sledgehammer. I never imagined a world where Lucy and I would be... what are we now? Superior and subordinate? It's a bitter pill to swallow.

"How are you working on getting your damn memories back?" The words burst out, a cocktail of pent-up frustration and desperation making my voice harsher than I intended. I regret the words the moment they leave my lips.

She startles, blinking before gathering herself and squaring her shoulders. "With all due respect, sir, I'm getting really tired of being asked about that. I'm doing everything the doctors and therapists tell me. Counseling, coaching... I don't know what else I'm supposed to do."

"You're right, I apologize," I say, attempting to take the edge off my gruff tone. I'm acting like a class-A jerk. "That was out of line."

Now I need her to leave before I completely lose my shit. "We're done here. You can leave." If she stays, I might say or do something even more regrettable.

She nods, then rises and walks out.

Watching her leave feels like my heart is being put through a shredder.

I handled that like a jackass. A certified, bona fide jackass. Maggie would've torn me a new one.

I let my eyes drift to the liquor cabinet, its

polished surface reflecting back my drained eyes. Is it too early for a stiff one? Or maybe something a little stronger. I'm sure there's a bit of powder stashed somewhere in this office.

It's tempting. I can almost taste it, the familiar burn in my nostrils.

But I'm a changed man, I kicked that habit, swore off that life. No, what I need isn't in a bottle or a powdery line.

What I need is a plan. A damn good one, and fast.

◆ ◆ ◆

A quarter-hour later, I stride out of my office onto the open floor plan.

"Taylor," I say, my voice cutting through the office chatter. "Round everyone up and meet me in boardroom five."

Startled, Taylor quickly recovers and gets the team moving.

One by one, they shuffle in, casting curious glances my way. As they settle into their seats, I position myself at the head of the table. Their low chatter dies down instantly, replaced by an anxious silence.

"I gave you all an extension," I begin, my gaze

surveying the room, "but time isn't something we should waste." My voice hardens, the tension in the room ratcheting up a notch. "You've gotten complacent since knocking Phase One out of the park. The ideas I'm seeing now are weak. They lack vision. Guts. We need to step it up."

I pause, letting the weight of my words hang in the air before adding the kicker. "So, we're going all in. No exceptions. We're holding a one-week hackathon starting in two weeks. I know we usually hold these events in Vegas, but this time we're switching it up."

A sense of unrest ripples through the room. I ignore it, continuing, "We'll be meeting at my vacation home near Bear Mountain State Park."

The room falls deadly silent, some clearly disappointed we're not heading to Sin City, others wishing they weren't heading anywhere at all.

My eyes lock with Lucy's, the one person whose reaction I'm truly interested in.

I soften my tone. "Lucy, if you'd rather not come, I understand. Say the word. But I'll make sure you have everything you need."

The multitude of emotions playing across her face twists my gut, but she gives a resolute nod.

It's a strange disconnect considering the countless hours we spent at that place, the cabin she once called her "sanctuary." Maybe I'm arrogant, but I know she loves it there. Nestled in the Hudson Highlands, surrounded by rolling hills, it's breathtakingly beautiful.

Taking her back there might kickstart some memories for her. Ideally, reignite her feelings for me.

Plus, I know her therapy schedule for next week; I've been keeping tabs on her progress.

If she'd just let me buy that damn apartment of hers, she'd have her own sanctuary every night. She would be free.

Instead, her pride won't let her accept my help, so she continues to reside above some grimy sex shop with a clown who goes by the name Spider. His security check revealed his real name is William.

A few of the team shift uncomfortably in their seats. One guy clears his throat so violently he might be choking. Am I being an asshole, demanding they drop everything for work? Probably. But the pay is generous enough for them to endure the occasional inconvenience.

No one dares to object. No one says they can't attend.

Hackathons are tough. The name is misleading to people outside the business—it started with hackers and grew to be a wider practice for IT departments. The basic principle is to lock talented techies and creatives in a room until they generate the needed solutions.

It sounds cruel but they thrive on the challenge. This is their playground. This is where they shine.

"No problem, JP," Taylor shrills. Annoying as hell, but the woman gets shit done. "This sounds like an excellent plan. Could you share the objectives so we can ensure we meet them for you?"

My gaze stays locked on Lucy as I answer their questions.

The urge to have her in my place again, to imprint myself on her memory in every way possible, overwhelms me. I have to force myself to look away before I embarrass her.

Is it worse to be forgotten or to be hated?

That's the million-dollar question. If Lucy doesn't remember me, there's the possibility of a fresh start. Erase the past, start from scratch. I don't want Lucy to remember how much I hurt her.

The catch? That's like living with a ticking time bomb, knowing she'll find out eventually. An invisible noose around my neck. But maybe, just maybe, I can make her fall in love with me again before she discovers the truth.

A fresh start. A do-over. Not many people get one of those.

FOURTEEN

Lucy

Wolfe towers over me, his voice taking on a menacing rumble. "Let me ask you something, Lucy. Do you enjoy playing dress up?"

I stare at him, struck dumb. Every drop of blood in my body rushes to my face. Did the head honcho of Quinn & Wolfe really just ask me that?

"Are you referring to Comic Con?" I choke out.

"I think we both know what I'm really talking about here," he growls. The room seems to shrink as he grows larger in my view, his head soaring upward until it hovers near the ceiling, the same size as my get-well-balloon head.

This fucking man. I can't handle him.

I bolt from his office out onto the floor.

Brenda from marketing stares at me in horror. There are gasps from all around. Why is everyone gawking at me?

I look down. Oh my God. I'm wearing the Miss

Nova outfit with the nipple holes. I try to cover my bits but the damage is done. They've seen everything.

They've stopped working completely to stare at me. Phones ring off the hook, ignored.

I'm frozen in place, bits out, while I scream wordlessly at them to answer the goddamn phones. But not a squeak emerges.

Wait... hold up.

It's my alarm.

I awake with a start, sheets twisted and drenched. Oh, thank goodness. Just another bizarre dream.

About Wolfe, no less. Interesting.

I can't stop dwelling on that odd run-in with him yesterday. His words were kind of sweet, but his face? Might as well have been chiseled from granite. At least I know now he didn't push me.

The man is an enigma and talking to him fills me with anxiety. Chatting with people I know is fine with this amnesia malarkey, but my clearest memory of Wolfe is him threatening to fire me.

It sounds like he doesn't hate me anymore, yet there's something about me that gets under his skin. His jaw tightening yesterday was a dead giveaway.

I drag myself out of bed, the image of phantom

nipples on display still haunting me. At least I can reassure myself that my day cannot possibly be worse than this nightmare.

Or so I hope.

◆ ◆ ◆

Three hours later and I'm starting to find my rhythm again.

Matty and I have been engrossed in user flows and designs, bringing a rare slice of normalcy back into my confusing life.

People think designing a button is simple. That's what the rest of the company sees us as—the button factory.

Sure, we just arbitrarily choose a color, slap on some Comic Sans, and stick whatever content we like on it, right? Who cares about button placement and picking the right hue?

Certainly not us designers. It's not like we spend hours agonizing over every single pixel. Because heaven forbid if they have to deal with a poorly placed button or a user journey from hell.

"We're finished." I beam at Matty. "We're ready to showcase."

He eases back, yawning and tousling his messy hair. "About time. Most I've done all week."

I bite back an eye roll. Technically I did 80 percent of it.

"No more shop talk, please. I swear, if we discuss one more thing about work, I'm going to book a vacation on the spot," he grumbles. "Speaking of which..." He takes out his phone. With a few swipes, he shows me a photo of a luxurious swimming pool, with him grinning in the center. "Ring any bells?"

I peer at the image, straining for a jolt of recollection. "Is that... Wolfe's place?"

"Yup. It's like the Playboy Mansion. The guy's got the whole nine yards. It's a bummer he's taking us to the back-ass of nowhere this time. The Vegas ones were wild. Honestly, I'm gutted."

"Wow. That's one hell of a pool." I lean in for a closer look. "So, we've been to this place before?"

He nods. "Four times."

"*Four?*"

"The last one was brutal—twenty hours straight with no breaks. But then Wolfe said we could hang around and live it up in the villa after. Man, that place is massive. I don't even know how many rooms there are."

More images of Wolfe's pristine white mansion fill the screen as Matty swipes through.

"Talk about living in style." I stare at the

pictures. "Does he live there all by himself?"

"Seems so." Matty shrugs. "Though, if gossip carries any truth, Wolfe's hardly ever solitary."

"Meaning?"

"Well, let's just say our buddy Wolfe likes to let his hair down. A lot. The girls in marketing love to dish about his wild, um, 'social gatherings' every weekend."

My jaw slackens. "Seriously?"

"Allegedly." He grins conspiratorially. "Legal's up at all hours just to keep the rumors from making headlines. Can't say I blame him though. If I had that villa, it'd be sex party central too. I mean, where's my invite?"

It's as if I've swallowed a stone.

For a silly, fleeting moment inside Mr. Wolfe's office, I let myself entertain the notion that his interest in me was... well, more than professional.

Get a grip, Lucy.

I turn my attention back to the sprawling villa, blown away by the space *one guy* has. It's all glass, secluded up on a hilltop with a view of Vegas sparkling below. The pool looks as big as Central Park.

"His world is a universe apart from ours. By the sounds of it, he has homes all over the country." I sigh. Batman versus the mere mortals of Gotham.

How unreasonable for him to demand everyone drop what they're doing and follow his wishes at a moment's notice? He says jump and we're scrambling for a pogo stick.

I stare at the photo of Wolfe's lounge area, frowning. It looks like we commandeered it for the hackathon. There's a huge whiteboard littered with Post-it notes and a group photo of us. It's so weird to think I've been here before.

I've got a silly grin on my face. What was I thinking?

Seeing myself somewhere I can't remember gives me chills. It feels like I'm staring at a doppelgänger. Something about this photo makes me sad. Just like the Daredevil one. Maybe because I've got a real smile, not a pose-for-the-camera one. These pics look like proof of a new bit of my life. A bit that's come and gone.

And maybe I'll never remember why I was happy.

It's fine. I'll move on

It's times like this when I remember my doc's advice about living life in bite-sized chunks and moving forward one step at a time.

Today's mission: survive the work day and get in touch with that real estate agent to plot out my next steps.

Tomorrow's task: Convincing Spider my apartment's not a B&B and I'm no laundry fairy. Every time he hoists a leg to scratch his butt on my couch, I grit my teeth and imagine my mortgage shrinking by the second.

I turn to Matty, swallowing hard. "I need to get my life together and sort my financial mess; I checked last night and my mortgage payments are sky-high. No wonder I have a Spider. Was I out of my mind with worry every day before the accident?"

He thinks for a minute. "It's probably worse now since it's all hitting at once. Before, you sort of got used to it gradually. But yeah, the weeks before your accident you seemed really on edge, like everything was piling up. I kinda thought you were pissed at me since we barely talked. You even snapped at me a couple times."

Knowing I was stressed then adds to my stress now.

"Sorry," I say, embarrassed. "I guess the whole apartment drama had me overwhelmed."

He grins. "It's cool. I had it coming."

"Wish me luck, I'm calling my real estate guy now." With a heavy sigh, I stand from my desk and find a quiet spot in the office to make the call. The last time I remember talking to this guy was about twelve months ago.

Just when I think he's not going to answer, a voice booms down the line. "Dave Watson."

"Hi, Dave. It's Lucy Walsh."

"Ah, Miss Walsh," he says without missing a beat, though I can tell he's trying to place me. "A pleasure to hear from you. How are you?"

I give him the shortened version of events. "Great. I have a little... bump on my head."

"That's terrible," he replies in a well-rehearsed tone. I suspect I could have told him I had a head transplant and I would have received the same response. "What can I do for you?" There's a not-so-subtle hint of impatience in his voice.

"Just wanted to check in on how we're doing with selling my apartment?"

The emails have been scarily quiet lately and for the last few, Dave hadn't even responded.

"Sure, sure. Been some interest trickling in here and there. I'm sure we'll get a buyer before long."

The "zero fucks given" tone makes my stomach lurch.

I grit my teeth, remembering back to when I first met him. The guy bragged he could sell water to a water park. I remember that smug smile of his as he preened his tie like it was yesterday.

Now, I'm starting to think he couldn't sell an umbrella to someone caught in a monsoon.

I grip the phone tighter. "Will there be any viewings this week?"

"Leave it to me."

Is that a yes or a no?

"But you told me you'd have an offer for me within three days of it being listed!"

There's an uncomfortably long pause. "Market's a bit sluggish right now—your... um... unique business downstairs might make it a touch trickier to move. Maybe knock the asking price down a tad more... knocking off seventy should do it."

I almost drop the phone. "*Seventy*? Seventy thousand dollars?"

"Maybe make it ninety to be on the safe side."

"Ninety." I choke on the word as people shoot me curious glances. I might be sick. "But that's way below what I bought it for. I may as well give it away for free."

"Yeah, that's unfortunate," he says. Is he even listening to me? "Listen, I gotta run. We'll schedule more viewings ASAP. Speak soon, Miss Walsh."

I'm left with a dial tone in my ear and the weight of what's happening floods my gut.

I'm in deep shit.

Every penny of my savings went into this "smart investment." Real estate in Manhattan never loses value, they say—but one blow-up doll has tanked everything.

Soon I'll be in that window myself with Roxy, a "Buy Me" sign round my neck.

Or maybe I'll take up a second job, like becoming an Uber driver at night, since apparently, I can drive now.

Is life mocking me? All of the money Dad left me, all my savings were poured into that place. I can almost hear Mom's voice telling me I'm foolish to put so much into it, but I thought Dad would have been proud. And now? It's all gone.

I feel like a child, stumbling around in her mom's oversized high heels, attempting to play the adult without the slightest notion of how to go about it.

It takes me a minute to realize I'm crying, until one of the techies looks at me in horror and uncomfortably asks, "Are you okay?"

"Yeah," I mumble, because that's what he wants to hear.

He flees the scene, relieved to escape the hysterical woman. I take a deep breath and try to compose myself.

As soon as he's out of view, I let out a loud sob.

I can't believe I'm crying like this at work. How did I let myself get to this point?

An obnoxious cough cuts through the air, startling me out of my tears. I glance up to see Dwayne eyeing me as if this is the first time he's seen tears.

For fuck's sake.

He leans in and awkwardly pats me on the back. "There, there."

I shrug him off, mortified. "I'm fine," I sniffle.

"Do you want me to call HR?"

I shake my head and almost laugh. What good can they do?

"Okay." He stands there, staring.

I wipe my nose on my sleeve in the classiest way. "Really, Dwayne. I'm good."

Now take a hike.

He nods awkwardly and whips out his notebook. "I'll log this as an 'incident' anyway. For health and safety."

My jaw drops and all of my emotions come vomiting out.

"Are you for fucking real?" I roar. "I find out I can't sell my home and have to live above a six-foot sex doll forever with a guy called Spider and you want to add me to your stupid health and safety register? God, I'm going to strangle you."

The entire area falls eerily silent. Everyone stares at me wide-eyed, fingers frozen mid-type.

I take a deep breath, every muscle in my body tensing.

"Lucy," says a deep rumbling voice. I tilt my head to find JP Wolfe's piercing stare from the doorway of his office. "In my office, please."

Oh God, this is it, isn't it? I've messed up so badly this time. Is he going to fire me?

The silence shatters with Dwayne's loud teeth-sucking.

"So I'll log this as a... um... let's see... as workplace stress, and note that HR may need to be consulted if incidents escalate. Yes. That should cover everything properly."

I mentally give him the middle finger but I stumble, heart pounding, toward the unknown fate that awaits me with the Big Bad Wolf.

FIFTEEN

JP

She walks into my office with the eagerness of someone facing the firing squad. Even worse than the last time, and I didn't think that was physically possible.

"Mr. Wolfe," she rushes to say as I close the door behind us. "I apologize for the scene out there. It was completely out of line."

I close the space between us in two swift strides. "I told you to call me JP."

"JP. Got it." She looks like she's about to flee. Christ, this is hard for me to take.

A knock interrupts us, and Amanda peeks her head in. "The sales team is waiting in boardroom six, boss."

"Cancel it," I order, not taking my eyes off Lucy. Right now, I need to focus on the woman in front of me.

"Of course, sir," Amanda responds before

quietly slipping away.

Lucy's rooted to the spot, cautiously eyeing me.

I slide my hands into my pockets to keep from pulling her into my personal space. "Now, what was that all about? Why'd you get so upset?"

She tucks a strand of hair behind her ear, her gaze flicking to the team that's ogling us through the window. "He caught me at a bad moment. I just got off a call that left me... rattled."

"What was the call about?"

"Personal stuff. Not work related. I shouldn't have let it affect me here."

"I can help you."

Her eyes snap back to mine, wide with alarm. "No... sir. JP. It's fine. It's my issue, and I shouldn't have let it spill into work."

I rake a hand through my hair, fighting to keep my composure. This is torture, not being able to comfort her. "I can't help if you don't talk to me."

Not that she's exactly jumping at my offer.

"It's just a real estate headache," she spills out quickly. "My apartment's difficult to sell. I shouldn't have made the call at work."

I heave a deep sigh. Ah, the apartment. Perhaps now I can step in, like I wanted to before her memory loss. Now I can fix this mess without her knowing I'm pulling the strings.

"Don't stress, we'll get it sorted. We'll arrange a financial plan for you."

"What? Oh God, I couldn't ask…" She trails off, gnawing on her lip. "Well, actually… I guess talking to financial services couldn't hurt. Thank you." Her head hangs in shame and I hate it.

"Good. Now, I'm taking you home."

Her eyes widen like I just suggested we skydive off the Empire State Building. Naked. "Huh?"

"I'm taking you home," I repeat. "Amanda will get your stuff."

Flabbergasted, she anxiously massages her neck and edges toward the door. "Sorry for the drama, but there's no need to send me packing."

"I'm not sending you anywhere. I'm taking you home. And it's not open for discussion." Ideally to my place, but she's not ready for that yet. "You've had enough for today, Lucy. I'm not going to watch you cry at work." I grab my wallet and keys.

She stares at me, completely blindsided. She opens her mouth to object, but quickly reconsiders when she catches my no-nonsense look.

I flash her a grin, hoping to quell her nerves. "Look, I can't have an employee threatening to kill another in the office."

"Bad for PR?"

"Just a touch. Let's go," I say gently, motioning to the door, hoping for more enthusiasm.

"I live in Washington Heights. It's a bit out of the way."

"It's fine. I need to check on one of our hotels up north." Lies.

She silently follows me to the elevator.

I tell Amanda to grab Lucy's stuff from her desk.

We enter the empty elevator and I hit the button to descend.

Slowly, I swivel to face her, locking my gaze with her anxious, searching eyes.

"Is this your way of personally handing me my pink slip? You think I'm so messed up I can't handle my responsibilities?"

The words catch me off guard. I retaliate, my voice rougher than I would have liked, the words resonating in the small, enclosed space. "Don't be ridiculous," I growl out. "Lucy, for God's sake, what kind of man do you think I am? That's not what this is about. Not at all."

She eyes me warily. "I saw you axe five guys in sales. They didn't see it coming either."

I tug a hand through my hair, exasperated. "That's not what this is. You're clearly stressed, and I just want to make sure you're in a place where you can relax."

"But why the personal chauffeur service?" she fires back, her voice catching slightly.

"Because I want to."

Her chin lifts in that defiant way I know so well. "You always get your way, don't you?"

A wry smile tugs at my mouth. "99 percent of the time."

"And the 1 percent you don't?"

"Accepting defeat doesn't sit well with me."

I take a step forward, closing the gap between us. For a moment we just stare at each other.

Her eyes widen, lips parting. And right now, I want nothing more than to feel those lips crush beneath my own.

I'm close enough to touch her now. Another step, and I'll be close enough to hoist her up in the air and wrap her legs around me. My cock strains in my trousers. Damn, this is too hard for me to control.

The doors slide open and with great effort, I restrain the urge. I clear my throat gruffly. "This way."

I guide her to my Aston Martin, opening the passenger door for her. There's a moment when she hesitates, like she suspects I'm setting a trap.

Finally, she slides into the leather seat, eyes

roving over the luxurious interior like she's never been in here before.

I casually loosen my tie and chuck it in the glove box. Judging by her wide-eyed stare, you'd think I just put on a strip show rather than discarding a simple strip of fabric.

Suppressing a grin, I watch as she wrestles with the seat belt, scowling when the buckle refuses to cooperate.

Leaning in, my hand finds hers on the buckle, gently pushing it aside. Her breath catches in her throat as she turns toward me, our proximity suddenly making the car feel much smaller.

Our eyes lock, dangerously close now. I can see all the sweet little details that make up Lucy—the flutter of her eyelashes, the light freckles dusting her cheeks, and that small scar on her nose from her fall at my villa. I bandaged her up, kissing the cut to "make it better." Now it's just another mark she sees but no longer feels the history of.

Instead, there's a new scar, a constant reminder of our forgotten life together.

She's stopped blinking. Breathing too, it seems.

"Relax," I murmur, my voice low and intimate. I trace the belt down to where it disappears beneath her. My breath ghosts over her cheek, eliciting a visible shiver. "I promise I don't bite."

At least, not unless provoked.

Being this close without touching her tests every ounce of my restraint. Although every part of me longs to pull her close, I resist the temptation. Instead, in a rough voice, I ask, "You good?"

"Mm-hmm," she breathes.

"Excellent." My lips stretch into a smirk. "Your scar is healing well."

"My clinic is pretty high-end," she quips breathily. "They can work miracles."

I know they can. I'm paying for it.

Breaking our eye contact, I start up the engine.

Lucy jabs the button to roll down the electric window. "Mind if I get some air in here?"

My smirk widens as I press down on the accelerator and drive out onto Sixth Avenue. "Not at all."

We cruise down Sixth in charged silence, the sounds and smells drifting through her open window. I'm glad I strapped her in, part of me wonders if she's planning to jump out of the moving car.

An angry honk makes her jump. Damn, she's jumpy. That's a hard pill to swallow. She used to feel safe with me. Used to have her knees up in a lotus position, completely relaxed.

Now, she's all rigid and tense.

I catch her sneaking sidelong glances at me when she thinks I'm not looking, trying to figure out my next play. If only I knew what was going on in that head of hers.

"I assumed a busy man like yourself would have his own driver," she says.

"I like my privacy. Driving gives me space to think."

She reaches out to turn on the radio, but her hand freezes over the button. "Oh, sorry," she murmurs, her frown deepening. "I don't know why I did that."

My heart kicks into high gear. I know why.

"It's okay." I chuckle softly, flicking through the settings until my phone connects with the car's audio system.

The obnoxious bubblegum pop music that blasts through the speakers makes me wince. I hurriedly turn down the volume before my eardrums start to bleed.

I glance at her quickly to gauge her reaction. That ridiculous song on my phone is her fault.

Her lips twitch. "Didn't figure you for a K-pop fan."

More like an unwilling hostage to your questionable taste in music.

"I'm not. It's an assault on my eardrums and sanity. What kind of guy did you take me for?"

"The kind who listens to something more intense." She glances over shyly. "Let's see… what would a casino mogul listen to? The *Game of Thrones* theme on loop, to get you in a conquering state of mind."

I chuckle. "Definitely not. Despite the fun mental image of me ruling a corporate Westeros, I'll have to disappoint."

"That's funny." She smirks, and like a pathetic guy, I feel happy that I made her smile. It feels like a victory, small yet significant in the grand battle of bringing her back to me. "All right, how about something more inspirational. Chanting monks?"

"Just regular old rock works for me."

"I can see that about you. Old school kind of guy."

My heart thumps heavily in my chest. I have to physically clamp my hands to the wheel to keep myself from brushing that lock of hair behind her ear.

We stop at a red light and I pivot toward her.

Her gaze darts to me. "Seriously, I live near the rough end of Washington Heights. A car like this is asking to be jacked. You can drop me anywhere, here even."

My jaw clenches, annoyed. We've barely covered three blocks. "I'm more than capable of handling myself. I'm taking you all the way home."

Her eyes pop open. "I mean no disrespect but don't you have important CEO-y stuff to attend to?"

"Right now, this is the most important CEO thing I have to do."

"Playing chauffeur for an employee? Isn't this drive worth like thousands of dollars of your time or something?"

She wriggles in her seat, the movement causing her blouse to pull taut against her chest and reveal a glimpse of cobalt lace. A familiar ache stirs inside me. I bought that set for her. Memories of removing it from her body inundate my mind.

"I needed to clear my head," I murmur, tapping my fingers on the steering wheel.

"You mean, JP Wolfe's version of downtime is... driving?" she questions incredulously.

"Whatever it takes to keep me out of trouble," I reply, unable to shake the thought of how different this conversation would be if Lucy remembered how much trouble I can get into.

She laughs. "It seems I can drive now. Can't remember when or how I learned."

A slight smile tugs at my lips. She had indeed

taken the wheel of this car a couple of times.

"Driving in Manhattan doesn't feel like fun to me." She shifts in her seat, glancing out the window before turning to face me again. "Which do you prefer, New York or Vegas?" Her voice trails off as she sighs dejectedly. "The crazy thing is I don't remember even being to Vegas for the hackathons. Like, how do you forget Sin City of all places?"

"New York," I respond, my gaze locked onto the road ahead.

Her eyebrows arch in surprise. "Really? New York? I thought you'd be the last man to ever leave Vegas."

I chuckle darkly, the sound hollow even to my ears. I thought so too. "Vegas wore me down. I'm trying to move on to the next chapter of my life." I glance at her, her curious gaze meeting mine.

"That's... surprising." Lucy turns her head, studying me with newfound interest.

"I haven't exactly broadcasted this yet, but we're planning to branch out into wellness retreats under the Quinn & Wolfe banner."

Silence engulfs us.

"Wellness retreats?" she asks, smiling. "Really?"

I affirm with a nod, a ghost of a smile on my

face. "Yes, really."

"Wow. That's... quite a pivot from casinos."

"Yup. That's the plan."

"Do you know much about wellness?"

I chuckle. "Enough to know I need it."

She falls silent, absorbing my words. "So what's the unique selling point for these wellness centers? Burnout recovery for high rollers?" She smirks.

"Something like that. Burnt-out bastards like myself who have been looking in the wrong places for happiness," I explain. "It's a business venture that echoes my personal wants. I need to put some distance between me and the madness of Vegas."

Her eyes flicker in surprise. "But you're the owner. Can't you delegate the casino operations?"

"I could. But the temptation will always be there, lurking. It's better if I step away entirely. Truth be told, I'm craving a quieter life now." I flex my grip on the wheel, my arms taut under the fabric of my shirt. "This is off the record, Lucy. Not many at the company are privy to this plan."

She stares at me, her eyes wide, her mind ticking. "My lips are sealed. I don't think anyone would believe me, anyway. So, what got you into wellness?"

"I went to a retreat. As an apology to someone

special," I admit, feeling too close to dangerous territory. "It wasn't something I thought I would have liked, but I ended up having the best sleep of my life."

Her eyes flutter wider in surprise, but all she utters is a soft "huh" as she turns her gaze back to the passing cityscape.

"So I was on point about the chanting monks, huh?" she questions after a beat, a playful glint in her eyes.

"Quite possibly."

"That's pretty cool. I think I'd prefer that to casinos, if I was going for a weekend away. I don't think I could ever feel at home in a place like Vegas."

I know, baby.

"But really, it's not about the place," I say, my eyes burning into hers, not missing the slight hitch of her breath. "It's about who I'm with. The city doesn't matter if I have the right person in my arms."

She hesitates, biting her lower lip, as if wrestling with a question. "You're seeing someone?"

Shit. Cornered.

I clench my jaw, pressing the accelerator. "Things are... complicated."

"Oh."

The car comes to a halt at an intersection and I steal a glance at her, noticing the flicker of emotion in her eyes. Jealousy? Difficult to say.

She looks caught off guard, her lip still captive between her teeth.

I decide not to push her any further for now.

"Listen, about the hackathon," I say. "If it's too much, say the word and you're off the hook. I want you there, but not at the cost of your comfort."

"No, it's fine. I need to get back to work, back to my routine. The sooner I return to my normal life, the better... and apparently that includes hackathons at one of your mansions."

My lips curve into a tight smile. "Indeed, it does."

"I'm surprised you're okay with it. Having your employees invade your personal space."

"Some intrusions are more welcome than others."

I glance over to see her brows furrow.

Silence settles between us until a reckless idiot weaves into our lane. I jam the brakes as she gasps, her hands instinctively clutching the seatbelt. The sudden stop causes the glove compartment to burst open, spilling its guts at her feet.

"Sorry about that. You all right?" I question,

the irritation at the other driver manifesting as a growl in my voice.

My peripheral vision catches a pale blue envelope with a handwritten "JP" scrawled on the front. A jolt runs through me. The letter. Damn, I had completely forgotten it was tucked away in there. Should have incinerated it when I had the chance.

Moving quickly, I snatch the documents off the floor, shoving them back into the glove box with a bit more force than necessary. The last thing I need is for her to see that letter.

Her eyes flash with surprise and a hint of annoyance. "I wasn't planning on reading them."

"Uh-huh," I grunt out, feeling unnerved.

I let off the brake, my tense grip on the wheel slowly loosening as the GPS tells me to take the next left.

"Just drop me off by the CVS Pharmacy," she instructs.

I frown. We're a block from her street. "You live on this street?"

"A few doors down," she says breezily. "Here's fine."

Liar.

She doesn't want me to see the sex shop. She didn't want me to buy it either; this was one of our bigger disagreements.

Resigned, I sigh inwardly and ease the car into a vacant spot near the CVS. As I cut the engine, I can feel an odd tension hanging in the air.

"Thanks so much for the ride," she mumbles, scrabbling with the door handle like there's a fire under her ass.

"Hold on a second," I interject gruffly, exiting my side and coming around to open her door.

I reach out and take her hand to help her out, feeling an electric jolt at the touch. It lasts longer than it should, but I'm not complaining. I make my move. "You look like you could use some grub. I know a killer Eritrean joint not too far from here. What do you say, care to tag along?"

Her eyebrows shoot up. "You know that place? I'm practically a regular. How'd you find out about it?"

"A friend introduced me to it. So what do you say?" I try to keep my tone casual, but there's a hint of hopefulness I can't quite conceal.

She chews on her lip, clearly torn. "I can't. I have plans a little later with friends. But thanks for the offer."

The rejection stings a bit more than I'd like to admit.

She gives me a look that's half amusement,

half bewilderment. "I wouldn't have pegged you for a plastic-chairs-and-box-wine kind of guy."

I mirror her smirk, leaning toward her, enough to make her breath hitch. "Making assumptions about me again, are we?"

"Perhaps. I would chalk you up as more of a caviar-for-breakfast, champagne-sipping, Michelin-star man. I mean, Quinn & Wolfe isn't exactly known for its modesty."

I nod, playing along with her teasing. "While I concoct my wicked corporate schemes and the *Game of Thrones* soundtrack plays in the background."

"Exactly like that." Her smile fades into something a little more awkward. "Well... thanks again, JP."

"Wait," I interject as she's about to scurry off. I hadn't planned to do this yet, but on an impulse, I fish out a key from my wallet, offering it to her. "This is for an apartment you can stay in if you don't feel safe here. I'll email you the address when I get back in the car."

Her eyes nearly pop out at the sight of the key.

"It's a company apartment closer to the office —it's yours whenever you need it." Looks like I'm a liar too, but I'll spook her if I say it's one of my personal apartments.

She looks totally thrown, her mouth opening and closing in a struggle to voice her thoughts.

"No need to say anything. Just take the key."

"Thanks." She stares between me and the key like I've handed her literal gold. "I don't know what to say."

I grunt dismissively, wishing she wouldn't be so flustered by my supposed acts of kindness. "It's fine."

Her breath hitches, eyes locked on mine. The silence between us stretches, the air crackling with an electric tension. I know she feels this too.

"Lucy," I murmur, gazing down at her. "Look, it might not seem like it right now but you're doing just fine. You're a strong, resilient woman."

She responds with a dismissive laugh. "Not sure I agree with you right now."

She's always been stronger than she gives herself credit for. "Trust me, the way you're handling this? It's pretty damn admirable."

I force myself to step back before I do something stupid like kiss her. "I should go. Get some rest and don't stay out too late tonight."

She nods. "Thanks, again. I really appreciate everything. Okay... bye then."

I watch her walk at the pace of a snail down the street, knowing there is no way she can get inside any of these apartments.

"Lucy," I call out, my voice carrying over the noise of the crowded street, and she turns.

"I'm looking forward to spending time with you in Bear Mountain," I say, smiling as her cheeks redden.

She gives me a soft smile back, and for the first time since this nightmare began, despite my crushing fear of the moment she'll uncover the truth about my past actions, I allow myself a sliver of hope.

SIXTEEN

Lucy

The door slams behind me and I collapse against it, heart jackhammering.

What. The. Fuck.

Did I hallucinate Nice Wolfe back there?

I need an ice bath now to shock that ride out of my system. I wonder if Wolfe is going to include those in his fancy wellness retreats.

I couldn't tell if his piercing gaze was because I was writhing around on those leather seats or if the tension was all in my depraved imagination.

"Hello?" I shout into the empty space.

Silence. Fantastic. It looks like Spider is off doing his nude modeling.

I let out a long breath, resting my head against the door. I don't think I can handle any more interactions with Wolfe in confined spaces. The guy blows hot and cold too violently. One moment he's all charm, the next he's eyeing me like I'm a postal thief trying to pilfer his precious mail.

He's the most sexual man I've ever encountered, even when he's not doing anything particularly sexy. When his hands tightened around the steering wheel, my lady parts imagined them tightening around my ass. They screamed *Take me with your big man hands!*

Perhaps I should've told him I live in another state just to extend the ride.

"Get a grip, you horny woman," I say out loud, staggering toward the sink to get water.

For a wild moment back there, I thought he was actually going to kiss me when he helped me out of the car. Were it not for the fact that he's JP Wolfe, I'd dare say he was *flirting* with me.

"He said I'm strong and resilient," I mutter to myself, a strange lump forming in my throat. Is this really how he sees me? Or is this another one of his strategies?

Clearly, this memory loss has turned me into an emotional fool.

"Don't use this sink. It's blocked." I read the hand-made sign taped over the sink. Sure enough, it's clogged with unidentified gunk. Ugh. What does he expect to happen, that the plumbing fairies are going to flutter in and fix this?

Dumbass moron.

There's nothing like cleaning out a greasy sink to dampen a dose of arousal.

Should I consider Wolfe's offer to move out? No, if I leave Spider Boy alone for too long, my apartment will be condemned.

With a sigh, I grab the rubber gloves. When did I become such a pushover? How did I end up here, unclogging my own sink from the mess that my unwanted roommate left behind? If Wolfe—no, JP —could see the "resilient woman" now, he might rethink that assessment.

"We got you a mocktail." Libby waves a neon-colored, umbrella-topped drink at me as I perch on the bar stool. At least our local bar is the same. This cheese and wine bar has been our usual haunt for years, despite the ten thousand other options for bars in New York.

"Oh, goodie." I dump my purse onto the table and take a skeptical sip of the virgin margarita. Doc's orders, no alcohol for now. If only I could convince my body that kale smoothies are preferable. "Hope you got a ton of cheese to make up for the gaping wine-shaped hole in my life."

"Coming right up," Libby giggles.

Priya, typing furiously with one hand and barely glancing up from her screen, takes a sip of her gin martini.

"Make her stop working," Libby whines. "Her furious typing's making me jittery. Look at her! It's like she's got six hands."

"This defamation case is giving me a headache," Priya mutters, pausing to massage her temples. She snaps her laptop shut with a resigned sigh. "Sorry, Luce. It's your first night out post-amnesia and here I am, treating it like any other night. How are you holding up?"

I choke down more sugary sadness. "I'm okay. Survived my first few days back at work."

"I can't wrap my head around it," Libby muses, her face scrunched in genuine bewilderment. "I can't imagine how it would be. Erasing everything..."

"Yeah, it's pretty awful," I admit, forcing a grim smile onto my face. I search for a good comparison. "Imagine the worst hangover ever. You wake up and your night is a black void. But there are these people around you who weren't drinking, constantly poking you with a 'don't you remember what you did?' stick. And it puts the fear of God in you, like did you tell someone to fuck off, or shit your pants, or commit a felony, or something?

ROSA LUCAS

Because the way they are looking at you—it must be horrendous. And that's not even close."

Their shocked expressions say it all.

Priya finally manages a low "Jesus."

I tell them through gritted teeth that real estate Dave wants me to knock ninety thousand off my apartment.

Priya's hand covers mine. "Just hold out. Sex shops are probably more transient than other businesses. Don't do anything yet. Next year, there'll be a nice little cake shop there peddling cupcakes and overpriced coffee."

I stab my glass with my straw. "That's got to be the end of the nasty surprises, right? Sex shop, Spider. Taylor."

"Mmm," Priya sounds off, exchanging a loaded glance with Libby.

"What's that *Mmm* supposed to mean?" My incredulous stare bounces between them. "That's it, right? End of story?"

She stalls a moment, then: "Yeah... sure."

"Yeah... sure?" My voice squeaks with barely restrained panic. "Priya, there's more, isn't there?"

She swaps another look with Libby, who's now downing her wine. "That's probably the worst of it."

Probably?

I take another gulp of my drink to calm my nerves. Where's this cheese when I need it?

Libby breaks the silence. "Whatever happens, we'll be here for you." She rests a hand on my arm.

"Thanks," I reply with a feeble smile. "I'd be screwed without you two. Mom is a disaster. But she's agreed to go to the therapy sessions, even though she hates traveling to New York."

Priya's eyebrow arches, interest in her eyes. "How are the sessions going?"

I shrug, absentmindedly twisting my bangs into a makeshift unicorn horn. "Okay, I guess? It's not like I have any point of reference. We're doing CBT techniques. No miracle cure though. It's on me to fix me, which is scary."

"At least they let you out tonight," Libby chimes in, her eyes wide. "I was worried they wouldn't."

I can't help but roll my eyes. "Who are *they*, Libby? Did you expect me to be chained up in a straitjacket at home? I'm not Hannibal Lecter. I'm still perfectly capable of going out with my friends."

Her eyes bulge. "I just... I don't know anyone else with amnesia! You only hear about it in the movies. *Groundhog Day*!"

"Please, no. That poor bastard was stuck on

repeat. This is more like *Overboard*, except instead of a yacht and a ruggedly handsome carpenter, I've got a sex shop and Spider."

"*Overboard*. I love it." I see Libby's mind ticking away. "Oh my God, I could get you on *Page 12*! This is some *Days of Our Lives* level drama. Readers would eat it up."

I shudder. The last thing I need is to be turned into clickbait fodder in Libby's trashy tabloid. "I can imagine what they'd cook up. *Who the f**k is Lucy? A memoir*. Except in your tabloid, I'd be in my underwear for no logical reason. Not happening, Lib."

Libby's shoulders sag.

"Anyway," I continue, "speaking of me being allowed out into the wild... there's a comic convention happening this weekend..."

"Shit," Priya hisses.

"You're not trying to find this random guy in a rubber suit, are you?" Libby groans. "That's just crazy. One photo does not mean this guy is your soulmate."

"I know that," I snap back, prickling at her words. "But I've got a gut feeling. And since my head isn't working properly, I'm relying on my gut. Besides, my doc said I should get back to normal life and this is my normal. I go every year." I smile innocently at them. "So... you're coming, right? Because you're my 'loving and supportive' friends?"

Priya narrows her eyes. "You owe us big time, lady."

I grin, all fake sweetness. Memory loss has some advantages.

"And one more favor," I continue, while I'm on a roll. "Can you both join a therapy session online in three days? I'll send the details later."

"Sure we can," Priya supplies with a shrug, followed by a nod from Libby. "Honestly, this healthcare service is phenomenal. Even friends are involved."

"Apparently, it's part of my work's insurance package."

Priya looks up, her wine halfway to her mouth. "Impressive. Maybe Wolfe and the Quinn brothers aren't the assholes we thought."

"Actually..." I pause, swirling my straw in my drink. "Wolfe gave me a ride home today."

Their eyes nearly pop out of their heads.

"*JP Wolfe?*" Priya parrots, like she misheard. "For real? But why?"

I shrug. "I'm not sure. He made me go to his office after I had a meltdown at Dwayne. I thought I was going to be fired or something, but instead, he insisted on driving me home."

"Hold up." Priya's eyebrows reach for her hairline. "You're saying that Wolfe actually put his own billionaire butt in a car seat and drove you himself?"

"Uh-huh."

They look so stunned, it's almost insulting.

"That's so weird." Libby wrinkles her nose. "Why would *he* want to drive *you* home?"

"Cheers, Lib, way to make me feel special."

"He's the big boss. I'm just saying it like it is."

I sigh, pushing down that pesky pang of disappointment in my chest. "Okay, fine, maybe you have a point. He's not even *my* boss. There's a whole corporate ladder between us. It's amazing he even knows my name."

"Holy cow," Priya gasps, her mouth hanging open. "He's totally trying to fuck you."

I nearly spit out my drink. "What? No, he's not! There are plenty of other options at the office, trust me."

"Doesn't mean he wasn't hitting on you." She smirks. "Maybe he's got a thing for amnesiacs."

The words of protest die on my lips. I'm not the best at figuring out what men are thinking.

Was Wolfe hitting on me? That voice of his. It was sinfully sexy. His words felt as if they were tickling my clit.

But then, why on earth would he?

What did he say about his relationship status? "I asked him if he was seeing anyone and he was pretty evasive."

"Men like him always are. He's probably hiding a wife and ten kids."

An odd feeling bubbles inside me. The idea of him being off the market bothers me more than I care to admit. It's ridiculous, I know, but a small part of me wants him to be available.

Stupid.

I'm ashamed to say I did a little cyber-sleuthing before meeting the girls. Internet searches brought up pictures of him with beautiful, classy women but it was hard to tell if they were girlfriends.

"He asked me if I wanted to get a bite to eat," I tell them, avoiding eye contact.

"Like on a *date*?" Libby shrieks so forcefully, I feel a gust on my face.

I snort. "Hardly. I think he was hungry, and I was conveniently in his vicinity. No, I'm the opposite of his type," I say dismissively.

Priya nods, giving me a once-over. "True... you're probably not his type. Gorgeous but too geeky for someone like Wolfe."

"You don't have to be so quick to agree with me." I scowl and look at Libby for support but she just gives me an apologetic shrug.

The nagging voice in my head, a pesky, persistent guest, pops up again... What if JP *had* made a move in the car?

A surge of excitement zaps through me. An image of me blowing him in his Aston Martin as he drives down Sixth Avenue flashes through my head.

Jesus, why did I go *there*?

I smirk to myself and shake off the silly thoughts.

Priya lifts a perfectly sculpted eyebrow at me. "Please tell me you at least got some good gossip while trapped in the car with him."

I think back to what he said about wellness retreats. That was a surprise. He seems like the type of man to scoff at wellness stuff. I can't picture him in the downward dog position.

In fact, he seemed uptight even talking about it, which was a bit of a juxtaposition. Shifting in his seat and clearing his throat, as if loving wellness retreats carries shame like frequenting BDSM clubs.

But I can't tell the girls that.

"Well, you won't believe this, but he's actually

into K-pop," I say, unable to suppress a laugh. "I caught him listening to one of my favorite girl groups on the way home."

Priya looks revolted. "No way. My respect for him just plummeted."

Libby frowns. "He doesn't seem like the type of person who'd dance around to K-pop."

No, he does not.

He looks more like a guy who would be into that Nine Inch Nails song about fucking like animals.

Our long-awaited cheese arrives.

"Lucy." The waitress places a hand on my shoulder, concern etched on her face. "It's good to see you again—I've been worried about you. You feeling better now?"

"Yes, thanks. I'm great now," I stammer, not sure if I should know this woman's name.

"That's good to hear. You look after yourself." She smiles and gives my arm a reassuring pat before moving along.

I turn back to the girls. "How did she know about the accident?"

They glance at each other, a tinge of unease on their faces—a recurring expression these days.

Priya breaks the silence. "That was about what happened a couple of weeks ago. You had a little...

cry... here."

My fingers freeze around my glass. "I did what? Why? Was I drunk?"

"We don't know, Luce. Truth be told..." She pauses to draw in a deep breath. "Before the accident, you seemed distant. You started crying out of nowhere a few times."

"What?" I stare at her like she's talking in tongues. "Over the apartment not selling?"

She shrugs, looking lost. "You wouldn't tell us."

"Why the hell didn't you force it out of me? Pinned me down and hounded me until I spilled?"

Priya gapes. "We tried! We asked, begged even. You kept saying you'd tell us when you were ready."

"Oh God." I groan. "Was it related to Daredevil? He must have dumped me. Maybe it's a blessing I can't remember."

"Maybe."

I take another gulp of my drink to calm my nerves. The idea of a hidden secret, something so monumental it made me bawl in a bar, shakes me to my core.

She gnaws her lip, eyeing me anxiously. "The doc said to start small and work up slow, so... I really hope we're doing this right."

A knot forms in my throat. "So it's not about Taylor being my boss, a sex doll, Spider, or the apartment?"

They both squirm.

"We're not sure."

I gawk at them, mind racing. The noises of the bar fade away as my heart pounds in my chest.

There's something... even worse?

SEVENTEEN

Lucy

"This latex is giving me a yeast infection, I swear to God," Libby grumbles, adjusting her skintight suit. "Why couldn't we just wear activewear?"

I try not to laugh as we move through the busy convention center. With my expert body paint skills, they both look badass, though they won't admit it. Libby rocks a black catsuit, while Priya confidently embodies Poison Ivy, her curves concealed under vines and leaves topped with a fiery red wig.

What a great Saturday. Getting them here was a miracle thanks to the amnesia card. If my memory returns, I might continue pretending it hasn't, as it's a great way to get favors. Surviving my first week back at work makes this fun outing feel well-deserved.

Sometimes I meet up with other comic fanatics, but my comic bestie is in L.A. and can't make it to these events.

As for my outfit, I chose a more modest version of Miss Nova, minus the provocative cleavage and groin windows. Wearing a metallic blue bodysuit dotted with shimmering stars and a glowing crescent moon emblem, thigh-high solar flare boots, bold supernova blue lipstick, I feel both sexy and badass.

"We can't show up in gym clothes while everyone else is in full cosplay," I remark. "Go big or go home."

"Or go to a normal bar dressed like regular New Yorkers," Priya mocks, but I ignore her.

The exhibition hall pulses with infectious energy. It's an explosion of colors and creatures. Every superhero, mutant, villain, robot, ninja, and spy seems to have gathered.

A Stormtrooper clumsily steps on my toes, while a Viking breezes past us, his fake shield clattering against the floor.

I navigate the girls through the crowd, with Libby adjusting her clothing every couple of seconds to deal with ungracious wedgies.

But I breathe it in, feeling content. Spidey's webbing. Cowboy hats. Power rangers. Catwoman's leather catsuit. The Joker's green hair and purple suit.

Memory or not, this feels like home. I'm wrapped up in that comforting sense of belonging, amidst people who passionately channel their inner hero—or villain.

The crowd parts, making way for a Dalek from Doctor Who, shrieking "Exterminate!" in an electronically distorted rasp. I know I've got a big goofy smile on my face.

A Pikachu struts by us in stilettos and a mini skirt, its plump, furry behind wiggling seductively.

"Is that the yellow thing from Pokémon?" Libby mutters, blinking rapidly. "I feel like I just dropped acid."

I smirk at her, watching discomfort shift to reluctant intrigue.

A formidable Kratos from *God of War* muscles his way past us, two plastic axes slung over his shoulders.

Priya ogles his bare chest appreciatively. "Would not say no to that one."

"So, what now?" Libby asks, eyeing the Jessica Rabbit sashaying past. "Do I have to get into character or something?"

I smile. "You can if you want. Or you can-soak in the atmosphere."

The sight of a well-defined ass encased in

shimmering red and blue material sends my pulse skittering. Daredevil. The Lev Gleason kind.

But disappointment crashes through me. It's not him.

"Let's go find the bar," I suggest, scanning for the nearest one.

Libby's face lights up. "They serve alcohol? This just got a lot more appealing."

We order beers at the bar. It's my first taste of alcohol since the accident, so I go for something weak. As we sip our drinks, the atmosphere begins to mellow the girls.

"It's kind of empowering, really," Libby muses, her eyes gleaming. "Hidden behind a mask, you could be anyone, do *anything*."

"Not quite anything, Lib." I chuckle. "Let's remember this isn't some masked swinger's party."

As an Elastic Man saunters by, Priya recoils, her face contorting. "Please God, tell me that's not the same pervert as last time."

"I doubt it," I reply. "There must be hundreds of Elastic Men here." Like Daredevils.

Another Daredevil passes by, and I almost jump out of my skin. He's tall. Sturdy. But it's not him. My pulse spikes with each familiar red and blue suit until hope dwindles to nothing.

Daredevils are everywhere, both the Matt Murdock variety and the Bart Hill, teasing and taunting me. Duplicates all around, making my search for one unknown man feel futile.

This mission, searching for a guy whose face I couldn't even recognize in a lineup, is becoming my comic version of Where's Waldo.

I take a swig of my beer as we meander through the throngs of people and stalls.

"How did your clinic session go this morning?" Libby asks.

My jaw tightens. It was the first joint session with Mom, which is probably why I've chosen to drink now.

"I think I left in a worse state than when I went in," I mutter. "She just has a knack for winding me up. She's constantly nitpicking."

I gulp down more beer, the memory still bothering me. The girls appear uneasy.

"I did notice that," Priya says. "But she's probably just not good at dealing with stress like this. Most moms don't need to deal with amnesiac daughters."

I grunt in response, not wanting it to spoil my mood. This is my happy place, a comic convention.

For sixty adrenaline-fueled minutes, I scour the crowd, my body tense with anticipation at each glimpse of a Daredevil. My pulse races, spikes, and crashes every single time, when I realize it's not him.

Whoever the hell he is. Since I haven't seen him in real life, I'm clutching at straws. In the photo, he looks tall and solid, a good head above me, but for all I know, he could have been standing on a soapbox. I'm idolizing this nameless, faceless Daredevil.

By the time The Death-Defying Daredevil #360 strolls by in his glossy red and blue suit, I barely spare him a glance. The girls' energy is also fading, despite the beer fuel.

"Luce," Priya voices the obvious. "We've looped this place five times. Isn't it time to give up looking for him?"

"Yeah, I suppose." My shoulders slump.

She's right. Disappointment settles in, sour in my gut. There is no Daredevil here for me. It's all just a fantasy conjured up by my stupid, overactive imagination from a single photo. Pathetic.

"Come on," Libby says. "Let's grab one last drink then hit the road. We'll go to your favorite Eritrean restaurant."

"Thanks, you guys," I mumble, threading my arms through theirs as we navigate the cosplayers toward the bar.

We snag three stools, squeezed among an assembly of Spider-Men.

Surveying the wild circus of spandex and fake swords, I feel a warm fuzziness—probably the beer. This beats a therapist's office any day; real-life dramas can't touch me here. Not the sex shop, Spider, Taylor, or that little thing called amnesia.

Plus, being Miss Nova does wonders for my confidence. I feel utterly content. Invincible, even.

"I'll do one last sweep, then we're done," I declare with newfound determination.

Priya narrows her eyes. "You said that an hour ago. But fine, one more, then we're seriously leaving."

"Promise," I say, my mind already plotting the path through the stalls.

With a grin, I slip into the crowd, pretending not to have a destination. But I know exactly where I'm headed.

My steps slow as I spot it—the erotic graphic novel booth. Obviously.

Daredevil's not here in the flesh, so paper and my imagination will have to suffice.

My fingers glide over the glossy illustrated covers. Why aren't more women into these? Real men are fine, but they can't compare to a billionaire superhero in a weaponized metal bodysuit.

A sly smile curves my lips as I scan the selection of cheeky titles. "The Incredible Bulk" elicits a chuckle, but it's not what I'm after today.

There! My breath catches at the sight of familiar red and blue. Lev Gleason's Daredevil in all his glory—every inch of that suit clinging to muscles honed for power, speed, and raw pleasure. There's a half-naked woman molded to his body, head thrown back in ecstasy like she's about to... blast off.

Sexy solo session material: acquired.

At least I know he'll be waiting for me later, between the pages, primed and ready to go. I wander, flipping through the explicit scenes featuring "me" and my fantasy lover, cheeks heating.

"Escaping the masses?" a deep, velvety voice rumbles behind me.

My heart stutters, then races into a frantic beat. It can't be. This isn't possible.

I spin around and freeze in disbelief. There, leaning against the wall, is Daredevil himself— watching me.

It's him. The real deal.

All lethal grace and coiled power, encased in a distinctive suit of deep red and vibrant blue metal, molded perfectly to every inch of muscle. A body made to lift me up and pin me in place... or crush me without effort. His face is completely obscured behind his iconic red and blue mask, but I can feel the intensity of his gaze raking over me like a physical touch.

He pushes off the wall, closing the distance between us in a few steps. My pulse skyrockets as he stops barely a foot away, looming over me, gazing down through the slit in his mask.

"Do I know you?" I somehow find my voice, though it comes out husky and low.

He tilts his head, considering. For a long moment, I don't think he's going to respond.

"Do you?" he finally counters in a gravelly tone.

"Don't toy with me," I warn, my voice wavering. "I'm in no state for mind games. Who are you, really?"

I stare up at him, my breaths coming quick and shallow.

He dips even closer and I sense the smirk beneath his mask. "Today, I'm just Daredevil." A pause lingers. "Seems you were having some... impure thoughts about me."

Caught off guard, my eyes flicker down to the page in front of me. There's Polly Photon, boldly straddling Death-Defying Devil in his blue and red suit.

Cheeks burning, I shut the comic book.

He takes another step closer until only inches separate us. The heat pouring off his body washes over me, smelling of spice and raw masculinity. My nerves are a live wire, body tingling with hyper-awareness of this stranger. Is this a dream? Has my far-fetched fantasy come to life?

"Listen," I stammer, "this is going to sound crazy, but I've lost my memory. Did we... did something happen between us?"

Silence falls. A silence so fraught with tension I can barely breathe. I feel his eyes on me, seeing all of me while I see nothing. I feel exposed. Vulnerable.

"Something incredible happened between us," he finally murmurs.

My grip tightens on the book. "But it ended?"

Another silence, fraught and foreboding. My nerves wind tighter with each second.

"You come here to escape, to pretend to be someone else for the day," he finally says. "Why not pretend with me? Step into Miss Nova's shoes, just for a moment. Experience the reality of your fantasy."

I stare up at him, pulse pounding. Jesus, this guy is evasive. "Do you like Miss Nova?"

"More than anyone else in the world," he replies, voice filled with dark promise.

I want to know if he's smiling under that mask.

My throat constricts. "What's so appealing about her?"

"There's a strength that's more than just physical in her," he responds, his voice low and guarded. "She confronts whatever comes her way - never backing down, always thinking on her feet. She can roll with the punches, take things in stride that would crush most people. What captivates me is her spirit. Her beautiful resilience."

His words hang between us, filled with unspoken meaning. I shake off the strange ache in my chest at his praise, warning bells clamoring in my mind.

"But she was hurt, wasn't she?" I whisper. "By Daredevil?"

Another unbearable loaded silence.

"Yes."

The ache in my chest blossoms into real pain. Real pain even though I don't understand its source. Memories buried deep surface, instinct warning me of impending danger. This man is a threat. He's inflicted pain before. He will again.

I take a shuddering breath and force the words out. "Why did you hurt me?"

"Because I destroy the good in my life," he says coarsely. "But I regret it. More than anything."

The room seems to sway around me. "I shouldn't... I shouldn't trust you."

"You should." It's said without hesitation. His sigh is audible even through the mask. "Do you want me to remove my mask?"

"Yes. No. God, I don't know. This is freaking me out."

"I don't want to distress you. I should leave, Lucy."

"Wait." I lift my chin in defiance, though my body trembles. I need proof that this isn't some twisted hallucination. It might be crazy, but I need to ask him to do this. "Show me what I've been missing. Kiss me."

Time passes with excruciating slowness. Is he going to reject me?

Then, his gloved hands move, raising his mask just enough to expose a tantalizing glimpse of his mouth—sensual lips, shadowed with the rough stubble on a rugged jaw.

"Close your eyes," he murmurs.

I do as I'm told and slowly close my eyes, feeling a surge of energy course through me as powerful arms lock around my waist and pull me to him. His tight suit presses against my body.

I'm shaking, actually physically shaking. Full-body rattle.

The darkness only heightens my senses. I hear the slight catch in his breath, then feel the brush of his lips on mine.

I open my mouth. An invitation.

He meets it with fervor, his lips claiming mine in a consuming kiss that steals my breath. Heat ignites within me, a longing spreading from my core.

His lips are heaven, soft and full but masculine and rough at the same time. They mold against mine with a perfect fit.

His rugged stubble scrapes against my skin, sparking an involuntary shiver that zips down my spine. He tastes of honey and mint, laced with an undercurrent of the untamed and the dangerous.

His strong arms wrap around me even tighter and I feel his growing erection press into my abdomen through the costume. No one has ever kissed me like this before.

I slide my hands up his body, feeling every muscle tense under my touch. I don't give a flying fuck that we are two people in full bodysuits, making an X-rated spectacle of ourselves in the middle of a comic convention.

He groans in response, his kiss becoming more

demanding. His grip around me tightens as if he's trying to restrain himself from giving in to temptation.

"Stop," he breathes, pulling away from our heated kiss with a shuddering exhale.

I open my eyes, desperation clawing inside me to see beyond that mask. Traces of my bright blue lipstick smear across his captivating mouth.

"I need to leave," he murmurs. His thumb drags across my lower lip, possessive and demanding.

Panic surges through me. "Will I see you again?" I gasp.

He goes silent, staring down at me from behind that expressionless mask. Time seems to stop, uncertainty crushing my heart.

After an agonizing eternity, he finally stirs. With a gentle yet firm grasp, he cups the back of my head and pulls me close. I freeze, pulse pounding wildly as his lips press against my forehead in a chaste kiss, disregarding the streaks of face paint.

"Go back to your friends now."

I can only stare as he turns and walks away without a backward glance, his formidable figure fading into the crowd.

On shaky legs, I make my way back to where

the girls are sitting, looking bored.

They eyeball me.

"Where the hell did you go?" Priya blurts, her nose crinkling in confusion. "And why is your face paint all messed up?"

For some unfathomable reason, I burst into tears.

EIGHTEEN

JP

Cold, air-conditioned gusts prick at my skin as I explode to the surface, lungs heaving for air after fifty relentless laps.

At 10 p.m. on a Saturday night, I'm the only one in the Olympic-sized pool at the bottom of my apartment complex. The silence is a godsend.

These nocturnal swims have become a sacred ritual, a necessary respite from the incessant madness that comes with helming Quinn & Wolfe and navigating its ceaseless torrent of responsibilities and expectations.

Water, they say, has healing powers. An ancient truth whispered through the ages. It's the purification in the holy Ganges, the rebirth of Christian baptisms. Water, ever fluid, eternally present, offers a cleansing of sorts.

Maybe I'm looking for some of that healing.

For a man who's carved out his existence in

the pulsing heart of Las Vegas, seeking tranquility in a simple swimming pool appears comically misguided.

As I hoist myself onto the tiled edge, my arms braced against the cool surface, a smirk creeps up my face. A year ago, the concept of parading around in a superhero suit for a woman's attention would've seemed ludicrous. But for Lucy, I've become a comic convention cosplayer, amid fucking stormtroopers, all for a chance to relive those intoxicating memories, just beyond her reach.

Lucy and I have done cosplay before, in fact after the last comic convention we went to, we fucked all over my apartment in those costumes. Those are memories I long to revisit, if only Lucy could recall.

The taste of her lips lingers on mine, even through fifty laps of chlorine.

Was that a bad move on my part?

I knew she'd be there. It wasn't a shot in the dark, it was an undeniable certainty. I know her routines, her habits, her hobbies... I know Lucy. I even knew the exact stall where I would find her.

And in my gut, I knew she was looking for me.

Now, I've probably thrown her into a tailspin. Her face looked crushed when I admitted that I'd hurt her. And it killed me all over again. I just couldn't lie. And now I'm walking a dangerous tightrope because if Lucy connects the faceless identity of the masked man with mine before I've had the chance to make amends, to show her the man I've become... well, then it's game over.

Shaking off the daunting thoughts, I push myself to my feet, water cascading off my chest as I grab a towel to dry myself off.

There's a loud knock on the glass window.

Damn it. My features twist involuntarily into a grimace. Lisa, the model from a couple floors down. A living, breathing embodiment of my past recklessness. She was there that horrible night I fucked up with Lucy.

She beckons at me, her lips curving into a come-hither smile from behind the glass.

She's dressed in a tiny dress, accentuating her curves in all the right places.

"Hi, JP," she coos, the glass door to the pool sliding open with a soft swoosh. Her gaze sweeps down, taking in my bare chest before locking onto mine. "So this is where you've been hiding? You nearly gave me a heart attack with those splashes."

"Careful," I advise in a low rumble, my gaze drawn to the stilettos that teeter dangerously on the pool deck. Who in their right mind would attempt pool tiles in heels?

"What are you doing down here all alone on a Saturday night?" She's all smiles, her voice thick with suggestion.

Is an explanation needed when I'm standing here in swim shorts?

"Do I need a reason to enjoy a quiet night?" I counter, my words edged with irritability as I secure the towel around my waist. I don't need any distractions tonight. Or fucking ever again.

She laughs, her eyes filled with amusement and a hint of skepticism.

"You? A quiet night? That's a new one," she teases.

She takes a step toward me, and I catch her arm, afraid she might stumble on the slick tiles.

"Care for some company later?" she asks, as her eyes rove over my chest once more. "I should be back around eleven."

Resisting the alluring tug of the past is no easy feat, especially when it's dressed in a tight red dress, practically knocking at my door at 10 p.m. on a Saturday night. There's a ghost of a man inside me who wants nothing more than to take her up on that offer.

I shake my head, keeping my face impassive. "I'm good," I say, my voice carrying a note of firm politeness.

There's a brief flash of annoyance in her eyes, quickly smothered as her smile makes a reappearance.

"You already have entertainment for the evening?"

I sigh, rolling with her assumption. "That's right." A blatant lie, but if it makes her leave, so be it.

She gives me a tight-lipped smile. "Enjoy your night."

I guide her toward the exit, ensuring she doesn't take a tumble, then dry off, grab my things, and head to my penthouse apartment.

As I crack open a beer, the liquid sliding down my throat, my eyes wander to the telescope mockingly sitting in the corner. When's the last time I actually used that thing—weeks ago, before Lucy left?

With a sigh, I walk over and peer through the lens, adjusting it until I can see across the city to Washington Heights. Is she home or is she out with her friends? The friends she never wanted to introduce me to, because she was too scared or ashamed to admit we were dating. It may have started as sex but it turned into a lot more, and that freaked her out.

When we were together, we'd be right here in this apartment, enjoying each other's company. I'd be experimenting with a new dish, to show her how far I've come with my cooking skills. Taking good care of my body is the primary focus now, my way of rebuilding myself from the inside out.

Coming to appreciate the little things—like swimming and cooking—is what makes me truly happy.

It only took me around forty years to get the memo.

Sinking into the plush sofa, I open my laptop, ready to delve into my plans for the first wellness retreat under the Quinn & Wolfe brand.

There's an email waiting for me from my lawyer marked "Urgent." I let out an irritated sigh. I despise seeing that word in my inbox.

I scan the message. It's an update on the video circulating of me that the tabloid rags are having a heyday with. "Cease and desist sent for invasion of privacy and defamation. They're backing off," it reads.

I exhale deeply, feeling the tension release from my shoulders. It's not just about protecting my reputation with Lucy. I may live an indulgent lifestyle behind closed doors, but I don't need my nephews knowing the sordid details. They see me as some sort of role model, and for their sake, I need to keep it that way.

I click open the file with the retreat plans.

Can I make this work? The Quinns are right, wellness retreats aren't in my blood. Not like casinos. But it feels possible now my lawyers have squashed the incriminating footage against me.

If it's Quinn & Wolfe on the billboard, it has to be top-notch, nothing less. I won't have our name sullied.

Guests will be whisked in by helicopters, escorted to extravagant villas decked out with personal saunas, massage rooms, and health bars. We'll have Michelin-star chefs dishing up organic glazed tofu sculptures and wheatgrass shots at our farm-to-table restaurant, grounds teeming with mineral pools, tennis courts, golf courses...

I'm even floating the idea of equine therapy. Apparently spending time with horses promotes emotional growth. If that's the case, I need a whole stud farm.

My sights are set on a large plot of land beyond the borders of New York. If Lucy's dreams and mine could weave into one, she'd be near her mom, close to her friends. A slice of city life, a dose of the countryside—the perfect cocktail. Sure, it'd take me further from Maggie and the kiddos in Arizona, but hey, I've got a private jet to make that journey. Besides, how many times did I brush her off in Vegas, too swamped to visit?

Maybe even one day, in the not-too-distant future, Lucy and I would have some babies of our own, cousins for Maggie's kids.

Like a goddamn tsunami, the memory of her at the comic convention crashes over me. The visual of her body pressed against me in that tight costume floods my mind, staring up at me with those beautiful blue eyes. They're not just eyes, they're tranquilizers for my fucking soul, melting away the stress.

It's the only image I could see through fifty heart-pounding laps of the pool. Her, in that skintight cosmic-blue leotard dotted with glittering stars, thigh-high solar flare boots, and those mesmerizing blue eyes. I might have beaten my own personal record in the pool tonight.

She looked sexy as hell. Even with her face smeared with blue lipstick like some deranged galactic warrior, she was far more alluring than Lisa in her thousand-dollar designer dress.

My cock is throbbing, thinking about the way she rubbed herself against me and kissed me like nothing else mattered in the world.

For five glorious minutes, I forget about our

past. I forget about her lost memories. I forget about the chaos of my life, about the chaos of Vegas. For five minutes, she was my only drug.

I know it's her biggest fantasy. The tall mysterious superhero who takes control of her. I know she's masturbating thinking of it. Maybe even right now. God, I fucking hope so. Playing with her clit while imagining the big guy in armor dragging her somewhere to peel off that dress.

I want her naked with her little soft pussy wet and begging for me. I want to see her pleasuring herself while she dreams about my big throbbing cock and the way I can fuck her like no man has before.

I want to fuck her in that costume. Again and again. I want to fuck her in every single costume she has. I want to see her on all fours begging me to fuck her as I slap that sexy ass hard.

I pull down my shorts and release my aching cock. What I wouldn't do to have her sitting on it right now. I can almost feel her tightness around my shaft as I imagine myself thrusting inside her with all my might.

I let out a groan as I fist my cock. I'm so fucking hard for this woman. My thick veins protrude from under the taut skin of my shaft where blood pumps with urgent need.

I want to feel her tight walls convulse around me as I ram my cock into her. I want to hear her throaty moans as I push her to the limits. I want to hear her scream my name over and over.

I want to fuck her hard and rough. I want to fuck her until she doesn't remember who she is or where she is. I want to fuck her until she can only remember me.

Until I'm certain that no matter what, it's a memory she can never forget, amnesia be damned.

I groan as a hot burst of cum shoots from my cock, hitting my bare stomach and leaving a trail of hot stickiness down the hairs of my abdomen.

I pull my shorts up, forcing myself to calm the hell down.

This morning I traveled back to Vegas. I'm back for the annual heavyweight championship fight weekend—the biggest event on the city's calendar, and I find it prudent to be on site.

Case in point, last year, the ripples of testosterone-fueled chaos necessitated the intervention of a small army of law enforcement. Give guys an excuse to cut loose in Sin City for a few days and suddenly it's the Wild West.

Leaving New York, where Lucy is, wasn't easy. But I have to admit, it feels good to be back on my home turf, immersed in the electric energy that only Vegas has. As much as I tell myself I need to get away, some part of me will always love this place.

I walk into the heart of the casino, my casino, the neon lights glittering like the constellations themselves. The joint's buzzing, heartbeat matching the city's pulse, filled with laughter, clinking glasses, the sweet hum of excitement, and the roar of a hundred conversations jostling for airtime.

The casino floor greets me with its symphony of sounds—the constant chiming of slots paying out, cheers and groans from the roulette tables, the slap of cards at blackjack tables, and the clatter of chips being stacked and sorted.

This place is all about money and oxygen— the two things I and the Quinns believe will make people happy.

Literally, there are bills sitting around everywhere like napkins and there's oxygen pumping from the vents, making everyone feel more alive than they should be.

My manager snakes his way through the throng toward me.

"Evening, JP," he greets me, extending a sheaf of papers. "We're sitting at $1.5 million in gaming revenue already."

"Not bad," I remark, lips curling in satisfaction. It's only 9 p.m., plenty of night left to keep those figures climbing.

"How's the foot traffic?" I ask.

"Over 5,000 through the doors so far," he replies. The place is packed, just how I like to see it.

"Any big winners I should know about?" I inquire, adjusting my cufflinks and glancing around at the sea of hopeful faces.

"Just one. Local guy, hit a $75,000 jackpot on the slots. We have it under control."

"Good job."

Cutting through the casino floor, heads turn, nods and winks thrown in my direction. The familiar hum of "Evening, JP," and the respectful "Good to see you, sir," form a chorus that tails me. It strokes my ego, and yeah, I won't deny, it feels good.

Every time I walk through here, I think of the first time I ever stepped foot in a place like this.

Twenty-one years old, green as grass at a bachelor party with barely enough change for a round of drinks. I remember placing my first bet, the way my heart hammered in my chest, the heady rush of adrenaline.

I spotted him then, a whale of a player, puffing on a cigar as if he owned the joint, a model draped on each arm, stacks of chips so high they blotted out his face. I craved that—that feeling of invincibility, of ruling the world.

It's what still draws me in, why I need to be in the thick of it. You can't put a price on that rush.

I used to think I owned Vegas. I thought I was the fucking king of Vegas.

Nights spent living it up, under the illusion I was simply "taking care of business."

Every pulsing, iridescent light in the city was under my control.

The casinos with their showgirls beckoning fools to come and spill their hard-earned dough on a dream; they were mine. I ran them, I dictated their odds, I reveled in their fucking riches.

The suckers at the tables? They were lining my pockets too. High-stakes players, starry-eyed tourists, doe-eyed play bunnies spending their sugar daddies' cash, they all danced to my tune.

Then there were the music idols. The pop sensations and rock legends fighting for residency at our theaters, while the masses flocked to the city to listen.

But the hard truth is, Vegas owns me. And

when the time comes, I hope I'm strong enough to walk away.

NINETEEN

Lucy

I've been floating in a weird bubble of hormones these past few days since the kiss with Daredevil—arousal and excitement mixed with fear and dread. My brain feels like it's going to leak out of my ears. Now, I've met Daredevil, he's left me with more questions than answers.

It's Tuesday now and as the days go on, I start to question my sanity. Did that happen or did I just end up locking lips with a life-sized Daredevil doll, like Roxy the sex doll?

The girls were freaked when I came back in a flood of tears. I only perked up when I got a mouthful of sautéed meat at the Eritrean restaurant.

I've been in a daze ever since. Lucy land. No visitors allowed, no matter how much Matty chucks that dunce hat at me, or how hard Taylor clicks her fingers in my face, or how intensely

Dwayne stares at me like I'm some sort of experiment, or how many annoying texts my mother sends, or how often Spider eats straight out of my jam saucepan.

Wolfe's presence has been noticeably absent in the office these past few days. Rumor has it he's taken off to Vegas.

Restless, I reach into my bedside drawer and pull out the photo of Daredevil. I trace my smiling eyes in the photo. How did he hurt me? Will I ever find out? Did he cheat on me, lure me into a false pretense? I replayed the conversation in my head a million times after the convention. I realized later he didn't even react when I said I lost my memory. So that's either bizarrely not a big deal to him or he already knew.

And he didn't come after me.

I toss the photo back in the drawer. Maybe I'll never discover the truth. Maybe it's best to let it go, photo included.

The front door slams shut with a bang. Brilliant. 1 a.m. and Spider's home and by the sounds of it, along with some poor woman he's lured back. It's his place too so I can't exactly ban him from bringing guests.

I throw off my duvet with a grunt—no hope of sleep now.

A thud, followed by a muffled crash and a burst of swearing comes from the other side of the wall. Spider's room.

A wave of dread washes over me. Seems like Lucy land isn't as impenetrable as I thought.

"Turn around," Spider commands the poor woman through the wall.

Oh God. I left my noise-canceling headphones in the living room.

More shuffling and grunting.

"Giddy up, baby."

Did I seriously just hear that? I'm going to need therapy for more than memory loss.

The sound of skin being slapped makes me bolt upright.

"That's it. You're a dirty little cowgirl."

Another smack reverberates through the wall and I bury my face in my pillow. I haven't heard sex slapping in so long and now I have to hear it on someone else's skin?

There's a chorus of low, long moans followed by high-pitched feminine shouts that make it crystal clear what they're doing in there right now.

"Yeehaw, baby!"

The headboard bangs against the wall, building tempo, along with unnatural grunts. It sounds like a donkey having sex. The grunts subside for a moment, and then he lets out a loud groan which makes me jump.

These sex noises make me want to join the Tibetan monks in abstinence.

Maybe this is what my subconscious was trying to protect me from: Spider's hoedowns.

My ears. My poor eardrums will never be clean again after this violation.

Okay, this is the last straw. I should march in there and give Spider a piece of my mind, but I'm too much of a chicken.

Out of the corner of my eye, I see the key JP gave me days ago. It seems to call to me now, an escape.

◆ ◆ ◆

An hour later, I find myself standing in the lobby of Manhattan's most opulent high-rise, armed with a hastily packed duffle bag.

When JP emailed the address last week, I didn't put two and two together that he was referring to this skyscraper. Ninety floors of steel and glass towering over Manhattan, built for billionaires and influencers whose only struggle is deciding which private island to visit next.

And here I am, looking like a lost backpacker

who took a wrong turn at Central Park.

Yet the whole battalion of security guards doesn't even blink as I march toward the elevators. One even tosses me a smug smirk. I bundle up in my coat to cover my braless condition. The cool night air has sent my nipples into a military salute. I hightailed it out in a cab before Spider could wrap up. I have a lot of new space in my head right now and I don't need to fill it with that.

As the glass elevator climbs higher and higher, so does my panic.

Quinn & Wolfe own properties scattered all over the city, and they're known for providing temporary accommodations for relocated employees—but here?

What kind of batshittery is this?

Stepping off the elevator on the eightieth floor, my heart is lodged firmly in my throat. This is a mistake; I don't belong in a place where the flower arrangements cost more than my apartment.

As I make my way across the glossy marble, my sneakers emit a mortifying squeak like mice being stepped on.

Taking a deep breath, I approach the unit number and fumble with the key, feeling more out of place than anywhere in my life.

The lock finally gives, and the door swings

open.

"Holy hell," I gasp, my eyes practically popping out of my skull as I peer into the apartment.

This is what New York money smells like. Chic, cream interiors, ceilings so high you'd need a megaphone to have a conversation, and a chandelier that looks like it's made of Swarovski crystals that could do serious damage if it decided to detach.

"Lucy."

The deep drawl makes me squeal. Whirling around, I suck in a sharp breath as JP saunters out from the apartment across the hall.

"Do you... live here?" I stammer, drinking in the sight of him.

Fuck. Me. Sideways.

I had this image in my head of him in a suit 24/7 like some type of CEO cyborg. I figured he probably bathed in his suits. Slept in the fucking things. Had special suit pajamas for bedtime and naughty time.

Oh no.

His chest is bare, a brilliant showcase of sexy bronzed muscles. Obscene.

And those sweatpants. Those scandalously low-hung sweatpants with that perfect V, practically begging my eyes downward, willing me to have an impromptu eye-fuck.

It's clear that there's a monster package tucked away in those sweatpants.

God, give me strength.

I can't unsee this. This sight is seared into my brain, forever and ever amen.

"Yeah, this is my place. What's going on?" He strides closer, towering over me as his eyes scan my face with concern and something else that sends shivers down my spine.

The hallway shrinks around us and my body seizes up under his gaze.

"Lucy? You okay? Why are you here at this hour?"

I clear my throat, trying to compose myself.

"I'm fine," I croak, desperately trying not to ogle his distractingly fit body. "Couldn't sleep. My roommate's being a nuisance so I thought I'd take up your offer and come here. I'm really sorry, I can't believe I woke you up. I had no idea you live in this building. I wouldn't have..."

"Hey." He lifts my chin with a finger, forcing my eyes to lock with his. I swear all the air is sucked right out of the hallway. "Don't worry about it. You didn't wake me. Couldn't sleep either." He pauses, an unreadable expression crossing his handsome features. "And believe me, I understand the torment of sleepless nights. Got a lot on my mind too."

This sudden display of vulnerability has my tongue working without a filter. "So that's the secret behind your constant scowl," I blurt out, immediately clapping a hand over my mouth. "Oh God, I didn't mean... Sleep deprivation. Blame it on that!"

To my surprise, a rich, deep chuckle echoes through the hallway. And holy hell does it sound good. A sexy rumble that wraps itself around me and makes my skin tingle.

My ovaries wave little white flags of surrender.

"That's part of it. There's more to it than that."

I want to ask what keeps JP Wolfe awake at night but can't find the courage.

He braces a hand against the doorframe, looming over me, all hard muscle and bare skin. Now I'm suddenly in dangerous proximity to his bare nipples.

Every woman wants to see what's under those low-slung sweatpants. Probably every woman in America.

C'mon Lucy, eyes up.

His eyes smolder with lust and something dangerous. A cocky grin curves his lips. The bastard knows exactly what kind of effect he has on me. "You're not the first to point out my apparent grumpiness."

"Somehow I doubt many employees actually say it to your face," I mutter.

"No." His dark eyes gleam with amusement. "Only those... close to me."

Heat creeps up my cheeks. Oops.

I hastily avert my gaze from that gorgeous chest.

"I thought you were in Vegas."

"I was. For twenty-four hours or so. I had some things to do. Now I'm back."

That, you are.

"This place," I stammer, my breath hitching. "Is it seriously for employees?"

He smirks down at me. "Something like that. Consider it yours for as long as you need."

My heart thumps erratically. "You didn't mention that you were going to be my neighbor across the hall."

He moves in closer, dark eyes devouring me like a man starved and I'm the only nourishment. His voice drops an octave. "Would you still have come if you knew?"

The air between us crackles. An urge to hurl myself into his arms hits me.

A slow, dangerous smile curves his lips as he

places his other hand by my head, caging me in. The rush of his closeness, combined with the heady aroma of his cologne, sends my senses into overdrive.

"Yes," I whisper, finally releasing my death grip on my bag.

"Good." His voice is low.

For the second time, I hold my breath, thinking he'll kiss me.

Instead, he says, "Everything you need is in the apartment—fresh towels, toiletries, the works. Don't lug anything here."

This is sweet, really. "This is too much. Hopefully, it's just for one night. I'll negotiate a peace treaty with my roommate tomorrow."

"No need."

He's about to say more when his jaw suddenly locks, the heat of his gaze devouring my chest.

Oh, fuck.

I forgot my coat is hanging open and my nipples are proudly on display through my tee. Begging for attention.

His eyes zero in on them, hardening with arousal, and my unruly nipples fire off a salute, openly defying me.

Damn it.

The male equivalent of a rogue semi, that's

how it feels.

Slyly, I yank my coat shut, causing his throat to do a weird little dance before he re-centers on my face.

Is Wolfe actually flustered by *me*? The thought pleases me more than it should.

"Stay here for however long you like—or move in permanently if you want."

Or at least till your nips calm down, his pretend voice growls in my head.

Is he serious? Me, living here? Right next to him?

"That's... uh... I mean... wow, I mean... incredibly generous but, um..." I stammer, tripping over my own words like a bumbling idiot. "I shouldn't... I mean... I couldn't possibly..."

He takes in my panicked expression, stepping back from the door like he's dealing with a spooked cat. "Don't stress about it. You don't need to make a decision now. But the offer stands, for whenever you're ready."

"That's"—my stomach flutters, the idea of being in close proximity to Wolfe altogether too much—"incredibly generous of you."

He offers a smile that doesn't quite reach his eyes, retreating to his own door. Like he's used to being held at arm's length even when extending a hand. "I have a kind side, believe it or not. Sometimes it's not obvious."

"Starting to see that," I whisper.

He's staring at me, eyes locked onto mine with an intensity that makes me squirm. For what, I don't have the faintest idea.

"Well, good night, JP," I say, my voice a pitch higher than normal. Damn nerves.

He speaks just as I'm about to close the door.

"Hold up," he rumbles, his voice deep and gravelly, halting my movement. "Seeing as sleep seems to be eluding both of us, would you like to come in?"

I practically choke on thin air.

"It's three in the morning," I whisper.

"I can read a clock," he drawls, his voice taking on this husky tone that doesn't exactly help my erratic pulse. "Didn't answer my question though. Do you want to come in?"

I swallow hard, eyes darting to his bare chest then back up to his intense gaze. Oh my—his sex-slapping sounds must be incredible.

Hell yes.

Someone call emergency services; I'm being assaulted by dangerous levels of horn. Send oxygen. Or a vibrator. Possibly both.

Hell to the yes. I could live out all my Daredevil

fantasies.

His throat muscles flex as he waits for my response.

Deep breaths. Rise above your baser urges. Think pure, calming thoughts. Cold showers. Nuns. Ulcers. Warts. Spider on the toilet.

"No," I whisper, so softly it's barely audible. "Sorry to disturb you."

Without another word I dash into the apartment—my heart racing with an insatiable need for something beyond a good night's sleep, and my head completely and utterly confused about how I feel about the Big Bad Wolf.

TWENTY

JP

"Pull yourself together," I grind out, stalking the kitchen like a caged beast. I'm so wired I could put my fist through the five-million-dollar Pierre-Auguste Renoir hanging in my foyer.

It's rare for me to get worked up like this. If my sister could see me now, she'd never let me live it down.

It's Monday, hackathon day one. I've kept my distance from Lucy since our encounter last week, though keeping my distance hasn't been easy. I was too forward the other night—I see that now. I shouldn't have invited her into my apartment. The moment I saw the apprehension in her eyes, I regretted it. I used to have that effect on her, back when we first met.

But I couldn't help myself. I had to be near her, it's been ages since I had my hands on her, felt her against me.

All I'm left with now is watching her, like some perverted peeping Tom. Watching her with her crew, watching her work, watching her wrestle with her demons, and wondering if my intrusion is only adding to her suffering.

Then I go home, drink too much scotch, wrap my fist around my poor aching cock, and pretend it's her.

But this is my chance to win Lucy over again. It's just a shame I had to invite Quinn & Wolfe's IT department along for the ride.

I'm hooked on my cell, eyes riveted on the tiny blip that's crawling up Bear Mountain. It's the transport vans, moments out now.

Lucy loved this place. The endless floor-to-ceiling windows offer stunning views of Bear Mountain State Park and the Hudson River below. She loved watching the sunrise over Dunderberg Mountain as the valley woke up, loved how the sunset lit up the room in a blaze of color.

Loved. Past-fucking-tense.

Everywhere I turn, I see reminders of us—mundane shit like cooking together, eating dinner in the lounge, watching TV on the sofa. I knew she had me by the balls when she made me don a superhero costume, chasing her giggling figure around the house.

And let's not forget the holy christening of every flat surface in this mansion. Sofas. Beds. Kitchen table. Pool deck.

Makes me realize the shit I took for granted when it was stripped away.

The electronic gates to the mansion creak open and I grip the marble counter so hard I can feel every vein in my arms popping out. I take a steadying breath, a silent mantra to keep my shit together.

The prattling voices and giddy laughter get louder as the IT army piles out of the vans.

I swing open the grand oak doors to the mansion, and the chattering ceases, everyone sending me shy, hesitant glances. I catch Lucy's "hello" mingling with the rest.

I beckon them in. "Make yourselves comfortable," I say, directing them into the kitchen. "Our private chef will have dinner out soon."

Their jaws practically hit the floor as they take in the grandeur of the living space with the glass walls showcasing an unobstructed panoramic view of the tranquil mountains.

"Mr. Wolfe," Taylor coos, "this place is phenomenal! This is a brilliant plan! I'm sure the team will accomplish great things here."

I see Lucy scanning the room, a blank look in her eyes. Even weeks after the accident, it's unnerving to see her not remember.

Come on, look at me. Make a connection. And there it is—our eyes lock, if only for a heartbeat, and it's like a shot of adrenaline right to the chest.

But then she quickly looks away, a blush creeping up her neck, hands fumbling with her collar.

"Same drill as Vegas," I announce, grabbing some bottles of beer and wine from the drinks cabinet. "Eat or drink anything in the fridge but all your meals will be prepared for you."

The room fills with cheers as they scatter around the lounge.

Matty, her blond wingman, makes a beeline for the drinks. "Don't mind if I do, boss."

Lucy trails with the geeky data guy on her heels.

"Fancy a glass of red?" I extend, offering a glass of her favorite—though I'm betting she doesn't recall that detail.

"Yes, please," she peeps, her smile making my gut flutter. "Just half a glass."

Watching her sip the wine, her lips tenderly enveloping the glass rim... sweet mother of God.

Dwayne breaks the moment. "You sure you

ROSA LUCAS

should be drinking, Lucy?"

She pulls back, her voice edgy. "A sip won't kill me, the doctor said so. Could you maybe stop monitoring my every move?"

Before Dwayne can respond, Taylor jumps in. "So, Mr. Wolfe, will we have the pleasure of your company tomorrow? We'd love your input but understand if you can't spare the time."

I leave the bar to join the group, positioning myself beside Lucy.

"Call me JP. And yes." Our arms lightly touch, an electric jolt ignites between us. "I'll be around. Checking in."

I shift my gaze back to the others. "The rooms are on the first two floors. The one at the top will need to be shared. If anyone's uncomfortable with that, I can arrange for accommodation in my hotel down the mountain."

Just like in my Vegas home, the team will be sleeping on five-thousand-dollar silk sheets, bathing in deep-soaking bathtubs designed for sheiks, and doing their business on top-tier, remote-controlled, butt-warming Japanese super toilets.

As Matty drapes an arm around Lucy's shoulders, a pang of jealousy slices through me. "We'll be roomies. That way, Luce can make sure I get up."

She seems unbothered, maybe even content, to share a room with him. That should be me by her side, sharing more than just a room.

"Are you sure about this, Lucy?" Taylor asks with an eyebrow raised. "Rooming with Matty will be hell."

He grins cheekily. "Hey, she's used to living above a brothel with a roommate named Spider. I'm a step up from that."

"Well, that is true." Taylor looks at her condescendingly. "I could never fathom why you chose to live in that area. And look at the outcome —I'm relieved I chose Brooklyn."

Lucy's jaw tightens, the conversation clearly stirring discomfort. "It was a charming bakery when I moved in, okay? How could I predict its transformation into a red-light district? But you live, you learn. I'll manage with Matty."

Her smile is a bit too strained, her eyes a bit too haunted. I can see through the act.

That's it. I'm buying that damn apartment, with or without her approval. I won't stand by while she struggles.

Our heated argument months ago still rings in my ears. She accused me of controlling her life, bitterness lacing each word.

My intentions had been fueled by concern, not control. But maybe I had been heavy-handed, my protective instincts manifesting as overbearing actions. Or was it her own stubborn pride that had heightened the friction between us?

She's fiercely independent, always wanting to carry her own weight. It's one of the things I love about her, but it's also the one thing that drove a wedge between us.

"I'm the one you should be pitying," Matty chimes in, grinning. "She'll be whimpering about Daredevil in her sleep and keeping me up all night."

"What?" Taylor asks, confused.

Lucy blushes, shooting Matty a sharp warning glare. "Nothing!"

I can't help but smirk, catching her eye. Good, let her think about our steamy moment, even if she's clueless that it was me behind the mask.

"So why the change of scene from Vegas this time?" a developer pipes up. I think his name is Tony.

"Because this hackathon," I begin, the edges of my lips curving up slightly, "is going to look a little different."

Their collective body language tightens up, like they're bracing for impact.

"Usually, you guys work like mad and party harder, but I'm suggesting a shift in tempo." With a gesture toward the door, I say, "follow me."

They look equal parts confused and terrified.

I take them to the garden, our footsteps crunching against the gravel.

"Holy shit," Matty lets out, his voice rippling through the evening air.

His reaction is a cue for the rest, a symphony of gasps and murmurs echoing around.

But I'm only interested in one reaction. I glance over at Lucy. She stands there, frozen, mouth slightly agape. "It's like a... paradise," she manages to get out.

I can't help but chuckle. "That's the idea."

They drink in the scenery. The cabanas, the trails, the lush foliage—all painstakingly designed to be a peaceful oasis. A labyrinth of hidden paths winds through the greenery, enhancing the tranquility.

But it's the infinity pool that really steals the show. Perfectly heated, it melts into the horizon, blending seamlessly with the mountain backdrop.

I'm not fooling myself here. I know well enough that a sprinkling of Zen design elements and a few shrubs don't equate to some sort of spiritual awakening. But I'm hopeful that Lucy sees it as a signal of my intentions. A sign that I want to make real changes, even if they start small.

I want to create a space for her to unwind and recharge. A place where, just maybe, her view of me might start to shift.

"There'll be yoga and meditation sessions at dawn and noon," I continue. "There's no need to slave around the clock. Manage your time—be productive when inspiration strikes, relax when needed. Use all the amenities at your disposal. Trust me, your productivity won't suffer, in fact, it might just enhance by the week's end. Some of my most radical ideas have emerged from moments of relaxation. It's a hard-earned lesson."

Matty, never one to hold his tongue, leans in to whisper to Lucy. "This is nothing like the last hackathons," he mutters, disbelief lacing his words. "I swear he's had a brain transplant."

A smirk pulls at the corners of my mouth.

True, previous hackathons were hosted at my Vegas mansion, a venue synonymous with the ethos of "work hard, play hard." In Vegas, I compensated grueling work with hedonistic nights on the strip, all financed by a limitless credit card.

"Tomorrow, we hit the ground running," I announce. "I want groundbreaking strategies that will render every other casino as appealing as a dingy, back-alley gambling den. But you'll only work for half the day. The other half, you can opt to relax here, or for the adventurous, I have a little something up my sleeve."

Their suspicion is palpable as they all exchange uneasy glances.

"Paddleboarding on Lake Welch. I can assure you, out there on the waters, your best creative ideas will surface."

Their stunned silence is a priceless picture.

My eyes find Lucy. "Lucy," I offer, my tone softening, "you're not obligated to join in, but I genuinely think it could be an effective stress-buster for you, given recent events."

As she considers my offer, I find myself holding my breath. Then, she graces me with a smile and a nod.

Jackpot. That's exactly what I need. A relaxed Lucy, open to spending time with me.

The image of Lucy, glowing under the sun in a swimsuit, revs up my anticipation. It's going to take every ounce of self-control to keep my cool around her.

TWENTY-ONE

Lucy

Matty has assured me that JP is in the throes of a midlife crisis. Regular men typically navigate this life stage with a cliché convertible (ideally with a much younger, barely clothed woman riding shotgun) or by becoming cycling-loving MAMILs (Middle-Aged Men in Lycra). But those are your average Joes.

Over an aggressively healthy breakfast—with enough kale and avocado to make a nutritionist weep with pride—we arrived at a mutual conclusion. JP, having savored a life seasoned with the indulgent excesses only billions can buy, now seems to crave the opposite. When you've spent decades living in obscene luxury, you eventually crave the mundane as a novelty.

And so, it's paddleboarding. And meditation, and yoga, and all the other pastimes typically found on the covers of wellness magazines. He's not going to find his midlife salvation in the roar of a red sports car engine because he's probably had a garage full of them for ten years. Maybe he thinks this newfound Zen will make him immortal or something.

I couldn't tell Matty that JP confided in me about his plans to start wellness retreats under the Quinn & Wolfe brand.

I have to admit, I'm feeling relaxed. I woke up feeling shockingly Zen this morning, even after a night of Matty's deafening snores. Maybe it was the lush bed. Or the lingering dreams of Daredevil...

Our brainstorming session on the beautiful lawn this morning was refreshing too. JP kept his distance and let us work. Working with the team was actually fun—everyone was relaxed and joking.

We're en route, winding our way through the rugged mountains to Lake Welch, and an unfamiliar calmness is seeping into me. It's a sensation I haven't felt in what seems like ages. I'm so tired of feeling adrift and confused, like I was born yesterday.

As the van rumbles on, I let my mind drift to Daredevil. With his music playing, Matty is oblivious to my daydreaming.

I need to put him out of my mind. He admitted

to hurting me somehow. How serious was it? Did he cheat? Were we even together? Maybe it was just a kiss at some convention before I caught him with a Jessica Rabbit. But it doesn't matter now. I pointblank asked if we'd meet again and he went silent. I have my answer.

Stealing a quick glance up front, I see JP talking with the driver. His T-shirt hugs his muscular frame in all the right places. I did some late-night "research" on him before bed—because I can't figure the guy out at all. He's 38, has one sister, and came from a working-class family. He was married in his twenties but it didn't seem to last long. From what I can see, he's been living the bachelor lifestyle in Vegas ever since.

His hand scrapes along his stubbled jaw as he chuckles at something the driver says. He seems to be in a really good mood today. I tear my gaze away before he catches me gawking. Ogling my unfairly hot boss is a one-way ticket to disaster.

As we step off the bus, the landscape around us feels so alive, almost as if it's breathing. Lake Welch stretches out before us, a large, shimmering body of water cradled by the mountains, mirroring the calm sky above.

We get changed into our swimwear, then with every muscle in my body tightened—ass clenched, stomach sucked in, chest thrust out—I venture out of the changing rooms. The gravel crunches under my feet announcing my presence.

Most of the team is already out on the beach, sunscreened up and ready to go. Even Dwayne is game for paddleboarding.

And then, there he is—JP, lounging casually by the lake, dressed in nothing but swim shorts. The evidence of his quick dip—wet hair slicked back, drops of water on his chiseled torso—sends an involuntary shiver up my spine. And it's not from the temperature.

His gaze latches onto me and he executes a lazy scan up my body. I respond by sucking my stomach so far in, I'm sure my spleen is now doubling as a lung.

He saunters over to me with a life jacket in hand. Part of me wishes I was wearing some medieval armor so my nipples wouldn't betray my excitement.

"How cold is the water?" I ask, fighting the urge to let my eyes wander to his chest.

"Cold. I'm not going to lie. But once you swim in cold water, you'll never want to swim in hot water again."

"I find that unlikely."

He gives me a lazy smile that feels deliciously

intimate. "You excited for it?"

"Yes, but I'm not very graceful. I took a tumble down the Plaza stairs, remember?"

"If you take a tumble here, you'll be fine, in fact, I imagine we'll all be in the water at some stage. But I'll be near anyway to make sure you're safe." His voice drops lower. "Can I help you with your life jacket?"

"Uh, sure."

As I slip my arms through, he pulls the jacket closed around me. His hand skims my stomach as he tightens it. He's so close I can smell the lake on him, a heady mix of fresh water and some cologne that should be rebranded as pure pheromones.

"There we go. How does that feel?"

His hand slips a little higher on the life jacket, brushing the underside of my breast. It might have been unintentional, but his touch sends a current straight through me.

"Great," I wheeze, voice as tight as the jacket.

"Ready?" His fingers linger on the strap of my life jacket, his touch leaving a trail of goose bumps on my skin.

"Uh-huh."

"Good. Do you know the secret to good paddleboarding?"

I shake my head. "No, what is it?"

His eyes hold mine. "It's about trust. Trust in your body, your balance, your instincts." His voice turns huskier. "Much like... trusting another person."

I blink, taken aback. This must be the midlife crisis talking. Paddleboarding seems to have a philosophical layer I hadn't anticipated.

The sun beats down as we make our way toward the glistening blue water. I can't resist sneaking glances at JP in those sinfully low-slung black swim trunks stretched taut across his sculpted ass. Between that charged kiss with Daredevil and now my hot boss sauntering around half-naked, I'm more wound up than a dog in heat. Pretty soon I'll be pathetically humping the nearest male leg just to get some relief.

Wading into the frigid lake, I gasp as the water envelops my legs. JP cuts a path ahead of us, his strong thighs slicing confidently through the water. We trail behind him like obedient ducklings.

We wade out until the water level reaches our thighs, the right depth for us to bravely stand on the boards. Some of us, born with a natural talent for balance, make it look easy. I'm not a complete novice, but let's just say I wouldn't pass the *Baywatch* tryouts. After a few shaky rises, I finally manage to stand, knees bent in a slight crouch.

"Keep your eyes on the horizon, not your feet," JP advises. "Your feet know what they're doing. Trust them."

Matty, on his board and on all fours, shoots JP a disgruntled look. "Easy for you to say," he grumbles, attempting yet again to stand and failing spectacularly. He's on his knees, clutching the sides of his board with a death grip, his tongue sticking out in concentration as he attempts to stand again. And again. Which is funny, because with his sun-kissed surfer hair, you'd think he'd have this down.

"Matty, you're supposed to stand on the board, not spoon it," I heckle, getting some decent laughs from the gang.

Taking my jab as a challenge, he lunges in my direction, his board jittering beneath him like a skittish pony.

I brandish my paddle in self-defense. "Watch it, man! Back off."

In an impressive finale to his performance, Matty goes overboard, his plunge into the lake resulting in a mini tidal wave that drenches me.

He resurfaces, his eyes bulging, gasping, "My trunks!"

Silence. Then from somewhere, a snort of

laughter. It spreads like wildfire.

"Fuck me, it's an ice bath!" Matty yells.

We're all in hysterics as we watch him try to immerse himself in the water to retrieve his trunks then jump back up again.

"You can reach them," I splutter through my giggles. "The water's nearly standing height."

"I'm going to die here. Ahhh."

"Easy there," JP soothes, paddling toward our damsel in distress. "Breathe, buddy."

But Matty's too busy being melodramatic. Screaming, he hoists himself back onto the board, and in doing so, presents us with a full-frontal view that no one signed up for. The laughter amplifies to deafening levels.

"Oh my God!" Taylor shrieks.

I shriek in mortified amusement, shielding my eyes too late. The image of Matty's crown jewels glinting in the sunlight is seared into my retinas. "Christ, Matty!" I yell between bouts of laughter. "There are things in life that cannot be unseen!"

"I'm cold!" he howls. "Normally, it's much more impressive than this, I swear!"

With a surprising suavity, JP dives off his board into the lake, presumably in a search and rescue mission for the lost trunks. The sight has me flushing despite myself. Who knew trunks retrieval could look so heroic?

Matty flattens himself on the board in a feeble attempt at modesty, mooning us with his hairy ass.

The sight sends us into fits of laughter, knocking each other off our boards like dominoes. I'm overcome with giggles and slip off my board, hitting the water with a resounding splash. Trust, indeed.

Water floods my mouth, quickly quenching the remnants of my laughter and replacing it with frantic thrashing.

Suddenly, I'm yanked upward by a powerful grip around my waist—a grip so secure it can only belong to one person. I break the surface, gasping and sputtering, my lungs burning. I retch up what feels like gallons of lake water.

From behind me, a low, commanding voice cuts through my coughs. "You okay?"

I finally stop spewing lake liquid from my face.

Blushing, I turn to thank him, my legs reacting without conscious thought. They swing around, accidentally finding a perch on his hips. Our bodies align in a startlingly intimate pose.

His eyes widen in surprise, but his arms hold firm around me, locking me in place. The laughter around us fades into a distant hum as we lock eyes, his hold never loosening.

"I..." I start, my cheeks flushing even brighter as I realize our compromising position. "I... um, thank you."

I am suddenly aware of the distinct shape of something firm pressing against the fabric of my bathing suit. Holy shit, is JP *semi-hard*? Over me? In this cold water? The whole thing feels like a miracle.

Luckily the others are too busy laughing at Matty or trying to get back on their own boards to see our intimate embrace.

His lips part as if he's going to say something, but he tightens his grip around my waist and now I can really feel his cock, hard against my swimsuit-clad pussy.

Oh my God. My pulse races and all logical thoughts vanish. I'm so turned on I would happily have sex right here in the lake in front of the team.

He watches me intently, his eyes never leaving mine. His pupils dilate and his breathing becomes shallow.

"Fuck," he groans roughly.

I can't help myself. My hips move of their own accord, pressing flush against the hardness of his arousal through the thin layers of fabric.

His fingers squeeze at the flesh of my ass,

massaging it roughly in a way that leaves no question of what he wants from me: he wants me to spread my legs wide open so that he can slide his

—

The thought crashes into a wall when I remember where we are: surrounded by teammates lounging on their boards and floating nearby.

I look up. Matty, in all his bare-assed bravery, is lodged between the two Tonys, who are practically brawling to knock him off his board again.

Among the chaos, one pair of watchful eyes is directed at us. Taylor.

JP sees it too. His features contort into surprise for a moment, as if he's forgotten that he's in the middle of a team gathering.

"Can you get on the board yourself?" he asks me roughly.

I give him a flustered nod. Then, pushing away from him in the water, I paddle awkwardly back toward my own board, my heart thumping in my chest.

JP slices through the water with powerful strokes, Matty's trunks clenched in one fist. I hadn't even noticed him retrieve them in the haze of adrenaline.

"My trunks!" Matty yells in relief as JP tosses

them onto his board.

As JP hoists himself onto his board, water streams down each chiseled muscle, tracing the path I desperately want my hands to follow. The chilly water may as well be a hot spring with the molten desire coursing through my veins.

TWENTY-TWO

JP

We paddleboarded for hours, until the cold air and water force us to head back. Despite their yearning for Vegas's buzzing nightlife, the team appeared genuinely entertained. Even Dwayne, typically buried in his data analysis, seemed to be having a good time. I'm glad to report no injuries under my supervision.

The exhaustion from the day's antics hit everyone hard on the bus ride back, as they fell asleep one by one.

Seeing Lucy so relaxed, her laughter echoing over the water, stirred something inside me. Our fleeting moment in the water had caused her to erect an invisible wall between us. She stayed just out of reach, yet close enough for me to revel in her radiant happiness.

I can't read her mind but for those precious hours, I got the feeling that she was able to momentarily push aside her amnesia and just enjoy herself.

Our eyes meet across the clattering dinner table, a brief flicker of a smile gracing her face before she's back to her conversation with Matty. I'm not oblivious to her strategic choice of seating, positioned at the furthest point from me.

From the bus ride back to the dance of cutlery at dinner, she's been deftly maintaining her distance, skirting around me with impeccable politeness—a silent foxtrot we've been perfecting since we hit home.

When she excuses herself to go to the bathroom and doesn't come back, I have the sinking feeling she's called it a night. Or expertly avoiding me. So I go on the hunt.

I find her one floor above, entranced by the mountain skyline, night's canvas scattered with lights from far-off homes. Of course she's here. This is her preferred lookout point in the mansion.

Upon seeing my reflection, she jumps and quickly pivots to face me.

"Sorry," I say, coming up to stand beside her. "Didn't mean to give you a scare."

She shuffles awkwardly, eyeing me up and down. "It's fine. It's your house, after all."

"Hey, I didn't get a chance to talk to you after

paddleboarding. Did you enjoy it?"

Her eyes light up. "Absolutely! It was so much fun. I can see why you'd want a vacation home out here by the stunning lake."

I nod. "Yeah, it's a nice escape from the city. I come up on weekends to get away."

"You were right, you know. I got quite a few killer design ideas out there on the water. More than I would have in the office. When Matty wasn't distracting me, that is." She laughs softly.

I smile. "It was nice seeing you so relaxed and happy."

"Thanks," she murmurs, thrown off balance.

"So about that little incident in the water... you wanna talk about it?"

Her eyes go wide and she gnaws at her lip. "You mean Matty's swim trunks catastrophe? It was so embarrassing."

I hold her gaze. "Let's not play games. We both know what I'm referring to."

She forces an innocent grin. "It must have been the sight of Matty's hairy bare derriere that got you all flustered."

I clench my jaw, the memory still fresh. The second her legs locked around me under the water, I lost all sense of time and place. I was transported back to our old life, when it was just the two of us at the lake together. It gave me hope.

"Enough evasion." I exhale deeply, a steadying sigh. "Are you intentionally avoiding me?"

"Avoid you? No way. I mean, yes? I don't know. I was just admiring your lovely glass house, not hiding or anything. Honestly, who could resist such a view?" She looks back out at the lake. "Your place... it's remarkable."

I let her slide with the change of topic. "I'm glad you think so."

"Are the walls made entirely of glass?"

I lean casually against the clear barrier. "Predominantly."

"You know our homes are like mirrors, reflecting who we are."

I crack a smile, intrigued. "Is that so? Then what's this place telling you about me?"

She studies the world beyond the glass with a cute, furrowed brow. "All this transparency could suggest you're an open book. That you have nothing to hide. But I get the feeling that's not quite right."

My pulse quickens a tad but I recover, smiling. "You're on to me. It's one-way glass."

She laughs. "Just like you then. You take in the world while remaining shrouded in mystery."

"I suppose that's one interpretation. What else

are you figuring out about me from my home?"

She tilts her head, considering. "Well, the greenery and view make it obvious, you're a man seeking solace in nature after years of living somewhere like Vegas. And the single piece of art in your hallway, which I think is an original, shows a man who values subtlety and simplicity. It probably costs more than my apartment, too."

"Very perceptive. I value quality over quantity, in every aspect of my life."

She grimaces. "Come to think of it, I'm not keen on this theory. When I think about my apartment..." She rubs her temples as if the mere mention of her living situation gives her a headache. "About that day you drove me home... I may have stretched the truth. My place isn't exactly next door to CVS."

I arch a brow, feigning surprise. "Oh really?"

She sighs. "Yeah, I live on top of Naughty Nonsense, that's an adult novelty store in case you're wondering, with Spider, a roommate who moonlights as a nude model. If I had to guess what it says about me, it's that I must be a masochist."

"Well, had I known you lived above Naughty Nonsense, I might've offered to drive you home sooner. Purely for investigative purposes, naturally."

"I'm game for a house swap anytime." She smirks but then her expression sobers.

Almost reflexively, I reach out, tilting her chin up to meet my eyes.

"Hey, being serious, I know you mask a lot of pain behind those jokes. As for your current living situation, I'm aware it's less than ideal. The company apartment is a better option. Next to me." A wisp of hair falls over her eyes. Familiarity makes me want to brush it aside, but I refrain. "And my door is always open."

She smirks. "That's what HR says."

"I don't mean it like HR."

I realize I've backed her against the glass when she hits it with a soft thud.

Her baby blues pierce me, equal parts fear and desire. Her eyes, oh those fucking eyes. For a few precious moments, they let my soul breathe.

I clench my jaw, trying to ignore the near-painful arousal that's building in me. She's close enough that I can see the pulse fluttering in her neck, sense the heat rolling off her body. And Christ, she smells as delicious as I remember.

"Your door is always open? Even at 3 a.m.?" She barely breathes out the words.

My intentions weren't to come on strong to her, but shit, with the way she's looking at me now, my desire to touch her is almost unbearable.

Lowering my head so our mouths are almost touching, I brush away a lock of hair from her face before dropping my voice to a husky whisper. "Especially at 3 a.m."

Her breath catches in her throat as she stares up at me, her chest rising and falling rapidly with each breath.

Her tongue darts out, wetting her lower lip, and my willpower frays further.

I can't help myself. I have to feel her. My fingertips trace her jawline, finding the spot just beneath her earlobe where her pulse flutters wildly.

She gives a tiny gasp as I lean in closer, allowing my breath to tickle her temple.

"Do you honestly think you can hide your attraction to me?" I say, my voice low. "I've noticed the way you look at me, the little smiles, the blushing when our eyes meet."

"Pretty confident, aren't you?" she breathes, trying to sound indifferent but failing.

"Confidence grounded in hard evidence."

Her eyes smolder, desire at war with reason. "Look, you're an attractive man, anybody with eyes can see that. But you also happen to be my boss, the same guy who signs off on my paycheck. It's... complicated."

I hold her gaze steady. "Let's shed the titles, the hierarchies for a moment. Right here, right now, it's just you and me. We're adults, capable of making our own decisions."

"Easy for you to say, Mr. Top-of-the-hierarchy, pick-and-choose-your-own-title guy." She rolls her eyes, her voice tinged with both humor and annoyance. "But those titles carry weight for me."

I give her a nod. "Fair enough. You're right, and I don't want to abuse that power. But know this— I've always protected those around me. And you, sweetheart, are far from an exception."

My fingertips slide under the shoulder straps of her tank top, tracing the curves of her collarbone.

She shivers, a flush blooming on her cheeks. "What are you doing?" she whispers, wide-eyed.

Arousal courses through me as I watch her nipples harden from just a light brush of my finger. "If you're uncomfortable, tell me to stop."

My hand strays beneath her top, and I'm met with the curves of her breasts, but she still doesn't pull away.

"Do you use this hands-on approach with all your staff?" she quips with false bravado.

I nip at her neck, enjoying her shivers. "Only

the special ones who need to be reminded of their place."

Her breaths come fast and shallow. "And where... is my place?"

"Right here," I murmur against her skin, "with me."

I grab her around the waist and pull her close, my hardened arousal against her softness.

The contact has her gasping.

Good. I need her to feel how hard I am for her.

Her body melts into mine. She's begging me to take her right here, right now against this wall, and I need nothing more than to quench my thirst for her.

"You drive me wild," I growl out between gritted teeth, pulling her even closer to me. "You know that?"

"Oh God... I shouldn't..."

I don't give her time to finish her protest. I fist my hand in her hair and seize her mouth with my own.

She gasps into the kiss, and then her hands grip my arms.

Weeks of pent-up arousal explode inside me and I pin her against the wall, wrapping one of her legs around mine, almost lifting her off the ground.

A roar builds in my chest as I taste her sweetness, breathing in her scent. She makes me so desperate for her that I can't think straight, obliterating my plan to take things slow.

I'm communicating every memory, every emotion of *us* in this kiss.

I want her to know, even if only for a fleeting moment, the depth of my feelings for her.

She clings to me hungrily, as if her body is thanking me for finally giving it what it's been wanting.

Her hands travel up to my shoulders before slipping around my neck.

This mouth, this body. *Her.* I've missed her so damn much.

"Sweetheart," I groan into her mouth, breaking away to trace a hot trail down her neck with my tongue. "Believe me now?"

She arches her back and pushes her curves against my body, hungry for more.

Her sensitive nipples are screaming for attention and I'm more than happy to provide it.

Fuck, that feels incredible.

She lets out a sharp gasp of pleasure as my palm covers her entire breast. Does she remember this feeling?

With one hand cradling her breast and the

other grabbing tightly to her waist, I thrust my hard cock against her core. I need to fuck her before I go out of my mind.

Just as I'm about to push my mouth lower to her chest, voices from down the hallway startle us.

Her body goes rigid.

I break the kiss with a growl, panting for air.

She recoils, her eyes widening as the weight of our actions seems to crash into her. "Shit," she stammers, withdrawing from my grasp.

"It's okay, Lucy."

But she isn't looking at me anymore; her eyes dart around the hallway.

"Wait," I call hoarsely, watching her run away. I'm left standing in the hallway, desperate to finish what we started.

TWENTY-THREE

Lucy

Oh. My. God.

I bolt toward the relative safety of the entertainment room, away from the sinful temptation.

There's no "undo" for this kind of mistake. Ctrl +Z won't save me now. Dry humping my boss was definitely not on the hackathon agenda.

What the actual hell was I thinking?

Did I seriously just lock lips with JP Wolfe?

In his hallway, no less. What if someone saw?

That kiss... I don't even have words. Obviously, I've kissed guys before, but this... this was something else. Something to rival the kiss with my masked superhero.

I take a slow breath outside the lounge where the team is chattering away, glasses clinking.

They'll know. I'm a mess. I got so wrapped up in what he was saying, gazing at the mountain lights like a doe-eyed fool that my legs were sliding open for him.

Sweetheart.

He called me sweetheart. Does he call everyone he kisses sweetheart?

Regrettably, the only available seat is a cozy spot wedged between Matty and Dwayne.

As I drop onto the couch, avoiding any and all eye contact, I feel Matty's eyes on me.

"You okay?" he asks.

I manage a fake smile, heart pounding a wild beat. Can he smell Wolfe on me? "Yep! Great. Just needed to freshen up."

"You're doing that bizarre twisty thing with your hair that makes it look like you're crafting a dick."

Immediately, my hand falls from my bangs. "I'm fine," I fire back defensively. "What are you guys talking about?"

I feel like I'm wearing a neon sign that blares JUST BEEN HORNY WITH THE BOSS.

My nipples could cut glass. They'll probably stay erect forever now, a permanent reminder of my foolish dalliance.

Miraculously, everyone seems to be engrossed in their own world, each lost in their drinks, their conversations, their phones, whatever. There'd be nothing left of me but a Lucy-shaped hole in the wall if anyone witnessed me with the boss.

"Okay," Brody, one of the coders, begins, pulling me out of my stupor. "We got some good ideas rolling today. I think as a reward it's time to hit a bar. You know there's a town just a few miles from here?"

Matty, cheeks dimpling, grins. "Hell, yeah. I need it after the day I've had."

Brody smirks. "We all need it after witnessing that catastrophe."

I barely listen to them chatter on.

Across from me, Taylor straightens up, suddenly all businesslike. "We've only gotten through day one. Let's not get ahead of ourselves, shall we? Work first, party later. We're not setting foot outside this place until we've hit our targets."

She earns herself filthy looks.

Despite my usual annoyance with her, I find myself nodding in agreement. Maybe it's just my state of stupor but she can't exactly be having a blast playing the team's nanny. Andy sure as hell didn't cut it.

"Taylor's got a point," I find myself saying, to a chorus of groans.

Taylor gives me a surprised, grateful half-smile. I nod back.

"Okay, fine," Matty grumbles, rolling his eyes dramatically. "No hitting the bars tonight. But we've got to take advantage of this place. Pool party, anyone?"

Pool party means adorning a bathing suit again. No, my nipples can't be out around JP, they won't behave. It'll be a nipple apocalypse. I'll barricade myself in my room instead, flick through some smut, and ride out this damn hormone surge.

Dwayne clears his throat and leans in, breath hitting my face.

I jerk back. "What?"

"Are you running a fever?" he asks, eyes narrowing suspiciously.

Just a bout of raging libido, that's all.

I shake my head, trying to play it cool. "No, no. I'm fine. Just a touch of an upset stomach."

My racing pulse gives away the real culprit.

Oh fuck, and there he stands, in all his cocky arrogant glory.

The big, bad Wolfe who tasted my vulnerabilities in one powerful, stunning bite.

I hate the instant visceral reaction I have to him—a tug-of-war between dread and wanting to rip his clothes off.

He slouches lazily against the doorframe, his

imposing six-three frame filling the space, and just like that, the room's got this electric charge.

"Everyone settled in?" he drawls, his voice a low, resonant hum. "Got what you need?"

His eyes pin me as he says it, and I feel like I'm center stage under a blinding spotlight.

The room echoes with a chorus of "yep" as if anyone could dare to say otherwise.

"Excellent. That's what I like to hear. Like I said, outside of work, take a dip in the pool, use the games room, spa, cinema room. Treat this place like it's yours for the week."

His eyes sparkle as he grins, a glint of amusement that sends my gaze diving to the carpet.

I find myself sinking even further into the couch, praying it could somehow swallow me up, and spit me out somewhere less embarrassing.

He saunters into the lounge like he owns the place, which to be fair, he does. He's barefoot, but again, his territory, his rules.

"Now let's talk business." He switches gears effortlessly from casual seducer to the hard-edged tycoon bastard in an instant. He launches into a series of questions about our progress today. And just like that, he's back in company owner mode, seemingly unaffected by our reckless bout of horniness in his hallway.

I wish I could recover as easily. It took me the best part of ten minutes to roll my tongue back into my mouth.

I have questions but I'm too flustered to ask. His demands are pretty high. He lures us into his world with paddleboarding and charm, only to land us with the weight of his grand ambitions. A cunning play, indeed.

"Understood," Taylor concedes in answer to his demands, her eyes imploring us to follow her lead.

She smiles tightly, but I notice the subtle twitch in her throat. Perhaps under the bravado, Taylor is more anxious than she lets us believe.

No woman is an island and all that.

Is she worried JP might have her for lunch if we don't deliver?

JP's phone buzzes, and he steps out to answer.

For a stupid second, I wonder if it's a woman on the other end, and an absurd wave of jealousy stings.

"Next he'll want casinos on Mars," Matty mutters under his breath, breaking the tense silence. "With robot dealers."

The room fills with stifled laughter and hushed whispers.

Taylor lets out a huff and scribbles on her notepad. She looks really drained. How had I missed that before? Then again, I've been so wrapped up in my own little world since leaving the hospital.

"What's the plan for tomorrow, Taylor?" I ask. "What time do you want us to start?"

She stops writing and blinks at me. "Oh, well... I guess if we're to stand a chance of matching his expectations, we'd better be up and running by 7 a.m. I'm going to do yoga first."

There's an intake of breath.

"You kidding?" Brody groans.

"I'm serious," she snaps.

"I'm with Taylor on this one," I say, ignoring Matty as he elbows me. "The earlier we start, the earlier we finish. It's just logic, guys. Matty, no partying tonight. Sorry, buddy."

The room echoes with theatrical groans.

Taylor smiles at me, and it feels... real.

Since when did I join Team Taylor?

JP conveniently disappears for the rest of the night, leaving me with a head full of doubts.

I make a decision right then: Regardless of

how mind-blowing it was, I have no intention of reenacting that hallway indiscretion. I can handle four more days in this pressure cooker. I just need to dive into work, not the ravenous jaws of the Big Bad Wolf.

Taking Taylor's advice, we decide to hit the sack early. But sleep doesn't come easy. It never does when my dreams choose to run wild.

I'm transported back to being a pint-sized version of myself in the garden of my childhood home, sprinting toward Buddy.

A menacing growl reverberates from Buddy's throat, but I choose to ignore it. In my childish belief, I'm convinced I can melt his anger and darkness with my touch.

In a display of misplaced bravery, my arm snakes through the picket fence.

Buddy's growl deepens, his once warm eyes are filled with something cold. As I reach out to touch him, Buddy snaps, his jaws closing around my little hand.

"No!" I scream.

It's sharp, a searing pain that travels from my arm and spreads through my entire body. I try to scream, but all that comes out is a squeak.

The barking grows louder, morphing into a bizarre, grating noise.

Then, just like that, the dream fades away, transitioning into the soft glow of the early morning light. It takes me a minute to realize I'm in one of the luxurious suites at JP's mansion, not caged in my nightmare.

I glance over to the source of the persistent noise.

Matty.

Sprawled across the bed like a starfish, his mouth hanging wide open as he snores loud enough to wake Tutankhamun.

He lets out a loud grunt and jolts in the bed as if invisible hands smacked him in his sleep.

I choke back laughter and check my phone. 4 a.m.

My God, what was that? I reach for the dream journal the clinic prescribed.

Ever since the accident, my dreams have taken a nightmarish detour, as if my subconscious refuses to let go of the stupid memory of an old dog from years ago.

Rubbing the sleep from my eyes, I glance at my unscathed arm, still feeling the phantom pain of Buddy's bite.

The picture of Daredevil slips from between the pages of my journal. My sexy solo sessions alternate between JP and the faceless Daredevil under his boomerang-shaped hat.

Two hot kisses in the space of weeks. I think the universe is helping me make up for lost time.

It feels silly bringing the photo here. I thought if I squint hard enough at it, the past would rush back to me.

The happy girl in the photo seems to be saying, *Be brave, we'll find our way back to each other!*

I need to connect the dots between me and her.

Because this person? She's a stranger to me.

Kissing my boss? That's not my style. I'm careful, cautious. My job is all that's keeping me vaguely sane right now—even with Taylor as boss woman.

But now, I've blurred the lines with JP Wolfe, turning into some stereotypical office joke. From what I've seen, these situations rarely end well for the women involved. Meanwhile, the men just carry on, respect intact.

As if I, Memoryless Woman, need any more confusion in my life.

For all I know, he's got a revolving door policy with the women in the office. Am I the flavor of the week? Would things have gone further if I hadn't bolted?

Does he regret it?

That kiss.

Hot as fuck.

No man has ever looked at me with such intensity before. He felt thick and heavy and fucking delicious between my legs.

My nipples are still hard, like his phantom fingers are still brushing over them.

I give Daredevil another lingering once-over. He's tall, ripped, just like JP. Imagine if it were actually him...

But that's just stupid. JP Wolfe wouldn't be caught dead at a comic convention.

Matty erupts with a snort so loud, everyone in the villa must hear it. The poor guy bolts upright with a startled expression.

I can't help cracking a smile. Well, there's my alarm clock—time to roll up my sleeves and show Taylor and JP Wolfe that I'm not completely useless.

Following a lavish breakfast delivered from one of JP's nearby hotels, we're huddled around a large table on the lawn. Taylor holds court at the top, next to the glaringly empty whiteboard.

I keep eyeing everyone, trying to work out if any of them caught our steamy little moment.

They all seem blissfully oblivious, engrossed in Post-its and half-demolished croissants.

What's the post-kiss protocol with Wolfe? Pretend it never happened?

"Earth to Lucy." Taylor clicks her fingers, shooting me a stink-eye. "Are you losing your memory again?"

"Sorry," I mutter, trying my best to look innocent. "Could you run that by me again? The heat's making my brain a little... gooey."

Dwayne stares at me. "I've been watching you and something's not right."

Oh God.

Taylor repeats her question, saving me from more scrutiny. But then, there's a shift. Like someone cranked up the voltage, and now the air is crackling with energy.

Uh-oh.

My fingers tighten around the cool glass of orange juice, nerves coming alive in my belly.

I throw a quick, terse reply at Taylor, trying to maintain a professional facade, but the truth is, I'm on edge.

Seriously on edge.

Everyone's heads turn.

I risk a peek, immediately regretting it.

Holy fucking hell. That's quite a sight.

Dressed down in snug jeans and a simple white T-shirt, he's less Wall Street tycoon, and more beach hunk on a photoshoot. This casual JP thing is a disaster; it's making him way too human.

"Morning," he announces with a megawatt smile, and the team responds like a well-rehearsed choir.

My breath catches as he strolls over. He looks so damn self-satisfied.

There are two options for him to sit.

My eyes land on the vacant chair beside me. Panic surges.

Please don't sit here, please don't sit here…

He strides past the other chair.

My silent prayers are left on read.

Don't, don't…

But he does, easing into the chair next to mine with that satisfied smirk.

He murmurs my name in that low rumble that sends shockwaves straight to my clit.

"JP," I squeak back, sounding like I've just swallowed a whole lemon, rind and all.

This is shaping up to be one long, sweat-drenched day.

"Matty was just about to share the user research findings," Taylor announces, addressing the unfairly handsome distraction to my left. "It's about what our top spenders expect from their cashless casino experience."

Matty, usually unflappable, visibly tightens in his seat. His eyes flick to JP. "We interviewed twenty top spenders. They love the idea but want to know their data will be secure with the large amounts they'd be transferring."

He takes a breath that might've sucked all the oxygen out of the air, then says, "They'd also love if we could expand the cashless experience beyond gambling to things like the spa and restaurants."

JP leans back, a hand casually resting on my chair. "Good to know. Let's look at how we can extend this to the rest of the resort amenities."

"Matty and Lucy will sketch out some designs to prototype and test," Taylor chimes in. "The hurdle might be getting the high rollers to spare their time."

I nod, already itching to get started.

"I'll handle that," JP says, his gaze sliding over each of us. "You just focus on pushing the boundaries of the possibilities."

As he speaks, his leg brushes against mine under the table. It's probably accidental, but my body jolts like I've been hit by a Taser.

"Moving on." Taylor scans her notes. "Wendy, what insights does the user research offer about low-income guests using the cashless casino wallet apps?"

Wendy adjusts her glasses, rifling through her notes. "Some are concerned about overspending without cash on hand. Many try it once, then ditch the wallet app altogether after that."

Matty grins wryly. "Yeah, it's like raiding the minibar your first night. You know you'll regret it, but in the moment, it seems like your best life choice."

I choke as my orange juice goes down the wrong pipe. Damn.

"Easy there." JP's low murmur skates down my spine, leaving a trail of goose bumps.

My face flames as I manage a nod.

The irony of it hits way too close to home, since kissing Wolfe was my version of polishing off the minibar—a deliciously bad idea that felt amazing at the time, but now, it's like I'm nursing the mother of all emotional hangovers.

And now, Wolfe is staring at me like he's ready for round two. His eyes say this isn't over between us... not by a long shot.

TWENTY-FOUR

Lucy

We worked diligently all day yesterday, making good progress. To my relief, JP was occupied with important mogul things like counting his billions and didn't spend all his time sitting beside me. But he did make his presence known, popping by to scrutinize our progress and fray my nerves further.

This morning, the third full day of hackathon, after another stupid dog dream that woke me up at the crack of dawn, I decide to attend yoga. Shockingly, half the team turns up. With the mountains as a beautiful backdrop, the unnaturally cheerful instructor guides us through poses on the lawn.

My eyes, however, are not on the mountains, nor the sunrise. Instead, I gawk at JP's cobra pose like a perv. For a man built like Superman, the control he has arching that gracefully powerful frame is obscene. The morning sun bounces off his gym-honed shoulders and arms, which are straining in the most sinfully delicious manner. His T-shirt creeps northward with each stretch, riding up just enough to reveal a tantalizing strip of abdomen that sends my ovaries into a tizzy.

The only thing that tames my raging hormones is the silent deadly fart that someone— I suspect Matty, since I dragged him to yoga—let out, making me want to be sick in my own mouth.

I know it isn't JP. His farts are probably really sexy. They'd come up as growls and leave behind an intoxicating blend of spearmint, tea tree musk, and a hint of rugged cedarwood.

By lunchtime I'm a nervous wreck. The yoga was supposed to be calming, but really it just left me needing a cold shower and a confessional. It's been two nights since I kissed JP, and any time I've seen him, he's acted totally normal. Meanwhile, I'm barely keeping it together. Since I can't talk to Priya or Libby, Matty will have to do. He'll probably give me crap, but I trust him.

I drag him away from the buffet, a chicken wing hanging from his mouth.

"Matty, I need you to be serious for once and promise not to breathe a word of what I'm about to say."

He raises an eyebrow, clearly not expecting anything juicy. My usual meltdowns are more *Oh no, I used the wrong font* than life-changing drama.

"Okay, so... I did something."

He waves the chicken wing at me impatiently. "Out with it."

"I, um, made out with Wolfe," I say through gritted teeth.

"Didn't hear a word of that."

I sigh, scanning the area warily, before I repeat my confession a little louder.

His jaw drops, chicken wing frozen mid-air. "Are you messing with me?"

"No," I hiss back at him. "I'm not just saying this for shits and giggles."

"*You?*"

"What's that supposed to mean, *me*? What, like I'm not good enough for Wolfe?"

"No, no, you're a catch, Luce." He shrugs, looking genuinely puzzled. "I just didn't see that coming."

I sigh. "Yeah, me neither. It's a massive fuck-up."

I watch as his expression morphs from surprise to interest and then to a grimace, as if he's tasted something sour. "How the hell did that happen? When?"

"Two nights ago. We were talking and..." How *did* it happen? "He made a move, and I got caught up in the moment. Forgot where I was. Who I was. Who *he* was."

He sucks air in through his teeth, leaving me hanging on the precipice of judgment. "Did you fuck him?"

"No way! It was totally PG. Wait, what age is that again? It was definitely eighteen and up. But nothing that would get us kicked out of a movie theater. We kissed," I confess, twirling my bangs again.

He rolls his eyes. "Yeah, I'm pretty sure that's not gonna get banned."

I cross my arms indignantly. "It was an insanely passionate kiss!"

The most passionate of my life, but I can't go down that mental rabbit hole right now. "But that's not the point. What do I do now? Act like it never happened or do I talk to him about it?" Anxiety gnaws at my lip. "I'm all over the place. I can't believe I let it happen."

"Just let it slide, Luce. You're not in the right place for a fling with Wolfe. Memory loss or no memory loss."

"Wait, what?!" I sputter, laughing. "You think

I'm planning to… with Wolfe? I'm not that dumb."

At least, I hope not.

"Good." He nods approvingly. "Don't you remember the first hackathon?"

"No! Why?"

"Oh shit, yeah. I forgot you forgot."

"What?" My eyes are saucers. "Spill it!"

"The guy wasn't short of female attention. He tried to keep it discreet—actually he didn't try that hard—he had at least two different women that week."

I swallow hard and try to respond. To say what? It's hardly breaking news.

"It was just a dumb mistake." I muster some bravado. "Forget I mentioned it."

Oh my God. I'm such a dumbass. Wolfe is only making moves because we're stuck in the middle of nowhere, and not in Vegas. Out of the hackathon crew, I'm the most viable option. Most of the team are guys, Wendy is just out of college and too busy thinking about *Game of Thrones*, and Taylor is already tethered to a boyfriend.

Would his gaze wander in my direction in Vegas if he was surrounded by those glamazons he's photographed next to at "events"? Not a chance.

My face must spell out shock because Matty's

brows knit together. "Luce, what were you thinking?"

I manage a smile. "That's the thing. I wasn't. How long can I play the amnesia card?"

"Oh, you can milk that for months."

I steal a glance at Wolfe.

He's out on the lawn, holding court with the team. The sunlight catches his chiseled jaw.

It's a face that commands attention, even when my brain is screaming, *Retreat, retreat!*

What the hell was I thinking? I'm not built for office romances, not with anyone, let alone with the man in charge.

Priya can pull it off. She had a thing with a guy at work, but she's able to neatly slot lust, work, and love into tidy compartments. It only got messy when she discovered the guy was also "compartmentalizing" another woman at work.

I'm not built for that kind of drama.

A guy like Wolfe will chew me up and spit me out, taking what he wants and leaving me to gather the remnants of my dignity.

Our eyes meet, and he smirks. Matty's words echo in my head, and I can only imagine the other hackathons. The audacity of the man. He thinks he can use me for the week. What a total bastard.

Heat rises in my cheeks and I turn away,

busying myself by smoothing out my bangs.

"Five minutes till we regroup!" Taylor calls out from the brainstorming area, her voice cutting through the chatter.

A smug smirk spreads across JP's face before he saunters into the mansion. I glare back, giving my best death stare.

That's the last time I get involved with Wolfe. I must stay professional, avoid Wolfe, and focus on the job. I'm not here to become tomorrow's gossip around the water cooler. Doesn't matter that we had a "moment" in the hall, getting tangled up with a ruthless guy like Wolfe, especially as my boss, would end in disaster.

JP

Following a string of calls to Vegas over lunch, I step onto the lawn to assess my team's progress. But Lucy's absence is glaring.

I find her in the kitchen, staring into the freezer as if she's expecting a frozen chicken to engage her in conversation.

"Lucy."

She whirls around, shutting the freezer with a slam. She shoots me a look that could freeze hell.

So we're doing this dance again? Two steps

forward, one step back.

"Hey," she mutters half-heartedly. "I was just grabbing some ice."

I move toward her, my gaze fixed on those captivating blue eyes that I woke up this morning thinking about. Her back hits the fridge as her arms fold defensively.

"Feels like there's some tension brewing between us," I say, my voice low and quiet. "Everything okay?"

"Everything's a million bucks," she snaps, sarcasm dripping from each word.

She's pissed. Why? I search her face. Have memories returned?

"Do you regret what happened between us?" I ask with calculated smoothness.

"Obviously," she fires back straightaway.

Her response is a kick in the teeth.

"That's not who I am," she goes on, eyes blazing. "Maybe I gave you the wrong impression. I don't normally... get involved with the boss."

I'm aware. You're exclusively mine.

I rake a hand through my hair. "Lucy, I understand you more than you give me credit for."

She squirms, her discomfort palpable. Clearly, she'd prefer the ground to swallow her whole than be in my company.

Panic swells inside me, tightening around my throat like a vice. The past two nights, ever since our kiss, I went to sleep with a smile for the first time in weeks. I thought she did too. I was so sure this was the beginning of something real between us again. It's painstakingly hard to be around her without crowding her.

Now, she glares at me as if she'd prefer dealing with the devil himself.

I draw a deep breath, scrutinizing her face. Did I misinterpret the signals? The kiss—it wasn't one-sided.

"If I misread the situation, I apologize. The last thing I want is to make you uncomfortable. But for full disclosure—I've been replaying that kiss, every damned second of it, since it happened."

She flinches, as though I've slapped her across the face, and then I realize I've been harboring a fool's hope. The kind of hope that our kiss might be a kind of revelation for her, a cinematic moment where she awakens to the truth of us.

"Look, JP, I'm not like that," she says firmly. "I don't screw around. And frankly, there's nothing you're after that I can offer."

She steps back, putting some distance between us, as she reaches for her forgotten lemonade on the counter.

Her inference irks me, and a frown tugs at my brows. "And what is it, exactly, that you think I'm after?"

"Isn't it glaringly obvious?"

"Humor me."

"A fling for the week." Her words are clipped, her chin lifting slightly in defiance. She's slotting me into the archetype of a playboy without a second thought. "Some light entertainment."

I blink. "Where the hell did that come from?"

She huffs out a breath, avoiding a response.

"Seems we're on different pages then," I say in a low voice, but she's already edging away, ready to bolt.

"Lucy," I call, my voice hard as she moves to leave the kitchen.

She stops, shoulders tensing. "Yes?"

"You forgot your ice," I shoot back.

With that, I stride past her, exiting the room, my throat choked with words unsaid and emotions unresolved, feeling uncharacteristically powerless.

The treadmill roars beneath me, my legs hammering out a relentless rhythm, sweat flinging off me in waves. I dial it back to a leisurely stroll, my lungs gulping in sweet relief when a text lights up my phone.

Damn it.

A big-shot airline tycoon's charity event is tonight. This guy fills up our hotels across the country with his crew, so I've got to show face. A night of mindless babbling, forcing grins, and women making passes at me.

Regrettably, I said yes. A grunt of annoyance slips out as I jab the treadmill's stop button, slinging a towel around my neck.

It's Thursday, the team leaves tomorrow. Tensions with Lucy are running high, like a wire stretched thin. I can't afford to waste a whole night at this charity gig, not when every ticking minute seems to rile up Lucy's impression of me.

Stripping off my soaked shorts, I trudge into the shower, the cold water a rough remedy on my fired-up skin.

All right then. Two problems, one fix.

Leaning against the wall, I watch as the team lays out its strategies. They're on point, hitting every mark.

Lucy's changed into a snug blue T-shirt, probably because of the heat. The fabric hugs her figure perfectly, my gaze lingering just a touch too long. Her hair's swept up into a messy ponytail, bangs hanging over her eyes.

When it's her turn to present, her nerves are palpable.

Alongside Matty, they present their design concepts on the whiteboard. Their ideas are robust, though the delivery could use some finesse.

Watching Lucy, I remember what drew me to her in the first place—her quick wit, and the way her eyes lit up when talking about her work. Being around her made me realize how little I laughed.

Her striking blue eyes are clouded with uncertainty, feet shuffling. She's never been a fan of public speaking, but she's holding her own. I can't pry my gaze off her, a fact she seems acutely aware of. But I'll be damned if I look away.

As she wraps up her presentation, her voice wavers. "Is this... okay? Is it what you want?" She glances in my direction, the question lingering in the air.

I meet her gaze. "It's exactly what I want."

Her cheeks flush a vivid scarlet, my words working like unseen kisses. I've never seen anything so fucking hot in my life.

I allow the moment to simmer, building the tension until it thrums, before eventually breaking eye contact.

Pushing away from the wall, I address the crew. "Impressive work, guys. These ideas are solid."

A communal sigh of relief follows; Taylor leads the pack with a relieved, "Thank you, Matty and Lucy."

Lucy visibly recoils from the praise, her issues with Taylor are no secret to me. But she needs to work on that.

I swear, sometimes this team could give a kindergarten class a run for their money. The sales and marketing crew understand the dynamics of healthy competition. But the IT team? They'd snicker at the sight of a well-pressed shirt. A year ago, I nearly gave them all the boot.

"There's a charity event I need to attend tonight in New York," I begin. "It's hosted by a big client, an airline tycoon. With that in mind, I want one of you to attend with me."

Lucy's gaze dives toward the safety of her notepad.

"I'm happy to represent the team, JP," Taylor chimes in, all smiles.

But I have other plans. "Actually, I've got Lucy in mind for this one."

Taylor's smile slams into a brick wall.

Lucy's head jerks up, eyes wide. She looks like I just asked her to attend a satanic ritual.

"What?" she blurts. "I can't go. I have designs to finalize."

My jaw sets, muscles straining. "I'm giving you a reprieve. The team won't work tonight. Plus, Andy thinks you need to work on networking. Here's your chance."

Her eyes flash. "I wasn't aware the partners got a say in our personal evaluations."

What's she playing at?

"In my company, everything falls under my purview," I reply sharply.

A tense silence descends over the room. No one dares speak or even glance our way.

Lucy's throat bobs as she swallows hard.

"Lucy," Taylor murmurs. "If JP needs you, you should go."

Lucy's jaw juts out. "I don't have anything appropriate to wear."

"That'll be taken care of," I assure her, crossing my arms over my chest. "I'll have a dress sent over."

"I really don't think I'm the right choice. Taylor should go."

"This isn't a negotiation, Lucy. Be ready by six thirty." The words snap from my mouth, sharper than I intended, but my patience is fraying at the edges.

Without another word, I stride off, leaving them in stunned silence. Somehow, I've made things worse. Now, that's a skill.

TWENTY-FIVE

Lucy

The rest of the day is swallowed by an excited flurry of activity, as Matty and I hone the edges of our designs. But looming over it all is Wolfe's infuriating demand for my company at his grand soiree tonight.

The idea of spending the entire night with that insufferable, arrogant guy? My heart's pounding like I've hoovered up a kilo of cocaine.

Taylor finally calls it quits, and the room bursts into cheers. It's five thirty. The clock's ticking, and I have a measly few hours to transform from hackathon-frump to charity-ball-babe.

We stand, our hands weighed down with Post-its and papers scribbled with our game plan for tomorrow.

The team's heading out for drinks on the lawn—that sounds far less anxiety-inducing than playing arm candy for Wolfe.

Why on earth does he want me there tonight? He could have any type of professional model he wanted. Leggy, skinny, curvy, blonde, brown, redhead...

Am I meant to be his assistant? Or maybe he just needs a cocktail caddy? I still don't have a clue what he expects of me tonight.

I can't see how I'm going to make scintillating talk with big shots. If conversation's what he's looking for, I can't relate to billionaire woes like which race car to buy next or the tribulations of being a CEO. Poor lambs.

This already has "monumentally bad fucking idea" written all over it in pulsing neon lights.

"I'll keep my distance from the bedroom." Matty flashes me a cheeky grin. "You must have critical feminine rituals to attend to, like shaving your legs."

"Hilarious," I shoot back, rolling my eyes as we head inside. But honestly, he's not wrong. I've got a mountain of primping to do.

"And try not to provoke the beast tonight, Luce. You should've just wagged your tail and said, 'Yes, sir, three bags full, sir.'"

"He just wants to show us who's in control," I snap, neatly piling the papers. I brush a strand of hair from my eyes. "The guy's a jerk. Taylor is the one who wants to go, not me."

His smirk widens. "Oh, don't you?"

I press my lips together, refusing to rise to his innuendos, but I can feel myself blushing. I should have kept my mouth shut about the kiss.

"I hate going to company events."

"It's a charity event, not a company event."

"Yeah, but I'm representing the company. I'll be on edge. What if I make a fool of myself in front of someone important, with Wolfe watching?"

"Sadly, princess"—Matty grins—"you'll have to suck it up. We're scoring fat bonuses this week; we're basically at the company's—and his—mercy. People go to these shindigs all the time. That's the game."

"But I work in the back-office! That's not my job."

"Taylor does it, though."

My eyes drift to Taylor, brows furrowed as she scribbles frantically in her notebook. I can't recall a moment when she was relaxed during this trip.

Maybe Matty's got a point. Maybe I should seize this as an opportunity to impress Wolfe by charming the hotel high rollers. He might see me as a diligent employee, not just a random makeout sesh in the hallway.

♦ ♦ ♦

When I open the bedroom door, there are three suspiciously fancy black boxes on my bed with a note on top. Definitely not your average Amazon delivery.

"Dress code: Black-tie," the note reads. "The dress, shoes, and necklace should fit. – JP."

What the hell? Does JP moonlight as a tailor or something? Or can he guesstimate my measurements by eyeballing me with those brooding eyes? That seems plausible, given his reputation. But how did he magic this up so quickly?

My hands shake slightly as I approach the largest box and... holy shit.

This is by far the most exquisite evening gown I've ever seen. Blue, the shade of royalty.

Delicately, I lift the dress and hold it against me. This is class on a whole new level, a serious upgrade from my usual "it has pockets" dress. Perfect cut, off-shoulder, cinched waist, gentle flare... so classy, so intimidating.

The second box unveils a pair of sleek, strappy high heels that could probably double as deadly weapons.

And in the third...

This necklace. My God, this necklace.

Please tell me those aren't actual diamonds.

I'm floored. All this for a work event?

This doesn't feel like the getup a graphic designer would don for an outing with her boss. What role am I playing tonight?

Does JP Wolfe want to have sex with me? Is this his way of seducing me, or does he just not want me to embarrass him because he's seen the leggings I've been wearing at hackathon?

Swallowing hard, I strip down and pull on my best pair of underwear. I packed hackathon-appropriate underwear, not thongs. No one wants a wedgie mid-design marathon.

I slip on the dress and wiggle into the killer heels, then navigate past Matty's laundry on the floor to get a full view in the bathroom mirror.

Wow. I look like a Hollywood starlet.

It fits. A little too well. It's like he had it custom-made for me. The thought sends shivers down my spine.

Panic washes over me as I smooth out the silky fabric of my dress.

Reaching for my toothbrush, I quickly scrub my teeth, scowling at my reflection. "Mirror,

mirror on the wall, who's the most out of place of them all?" I grumble, my words lost to the toothpaste.

Rhetorical question, obviously.

I rinse, spit, and examine my reflection, checking for rogue underarm hair, food in my teeth, or any other potential cause for humiliation.

Fucking hell, I look good. Call the emergency services, I'm coming in hot.

◆ ◆ ◆

About a half hour later, there's a knock at my bedroom door.

Ungracefully, I totter over, the skyscraper heels and me still signing a truce. I yank the door open and—holy crap. My jaw drops so hard it almost smacks the floor.

I knew he'd clean up nice, but I wasn't expecting *this.*

There he stands, a vision of masculine elegance. He's Bruce Wayne meets James Bond, with a touch of Darcy all wrapped up in a sinfully tailored black tuxedo. The razor-sharp lines of the jacket highlight his wide shoulders and hug his muscular arms in all the right places. His striking brown eyes stand out against his tanned complexion and artfully groomed stubble. Even in my sky-high heels, I'm no match for his towering height.

He should come with a public safety announcement: Do not make important life choices after viewing.

Those deep, brooding brown eyes meet mine, and bam! My heart rate goes haywire, hitting a solid ten on the panic scale.

"Lucy," he murmurs, a ghost of a smile gracing his lips. "You're nothing short of breathtaking." His gaze sweeps down, giving the twins a generous once-over before continuing its southbound journey. "You could stop traffic. Though, that seems to be a superpower you have, regardless of what you're wearing."

I make a weird gulping sound, somewhere between a squeak and a dying seal.

The way he's sizing me up, all caveman-like and unapologetically masculine, sends my stomach on a rollercoaster ride.

"What, you don't believe me?" he asks. "Every pair of eyes will be on you in that dress."

His nostrils flare, and I have no idea about his endgame tonight, but in this moment, my self-pep talk, Matty's pep talk, and all common sense make a grand exit.

All that matters is that this God in a tux keeps looking at me like I'm the belle of the ball.

"Not too shabby yourself," I mutter, aiming for casual and landing somewhere in the region of flustered.

Not too shabby? If only he knew my ovaries were forming a fan club in his honor, cheering at full volume.

Keep it cool, woman. Don't let him catch a whiff of your attraction.

He chuckles, a playful glint in his dark brown eyes. "Thank you. I do my best not to repel people with my hideousness."

I snort inelegantly. "Somehow I doubt you've repelled any woman of late."

His expression darkens. "You didn't exactly jump for joy when I asked you to come with me. But I'd like you to have a good evening."

I make a noncommittal sound as a weird fluttering sensation invades my chest. If I didn't know any better, it could be mistaken for hope.

I quash that feeling ruthlessly. "I feel like my neck should have its own security team. What if something happens to this necklace?" I grasp it nervously. "What if it falls off?" I'm pretty sure I'd notice, but you never know.

He shrugs it off. "Nothing will happen. It looks

beautiful on you, by the way."

"I'll put the outfit and necklace away as soon as this event is over."

"Sure," he says, though something about my comment seems to irritate him.

He offers his arm. "Shall we?"

Those eyes. That smile. Being under his spell like this is dangerous.

As we walk out together, his hand firm on my back, guiding me along, one thought loops through my mind on repeat: I'm screwed.

TWENTY-SIX

Lucy

Our car glides to a halt outside the outrageously opulent Quinn & Wolfe seven-star hotel in Midtown Manhattan. The sight of glamorous women congregating outside the entrance sets my nerves on edge. A wave of unease washes over me —I feel out of place here, even in my stunning dress.

"Hold on," JP interjects, his voice slicing through the air. His hand intercepts mine as it reaches for the door handle. "You've given me the silent treatment for seventy minutes. Your face is practically stuck to the window. Before we get out of this car, you need to talk to me."

All right, yeah, I've been giving him the cold shoulder. I've said more words to the driver.

"I have no idea what you're talking about," I retort, fidgeting with my dress strap. "I was enjoying the scenery."

He sighs, the sound echoing through the confines of the car. "Just say what's on your mind. Out with it."

"Nothing to out," I snap.

"Lucy." His voice is a husky drawl that sends a shiver down my spine. He might as well have been whispering sweet obscenities in my ear.

Insufferable man.

"Why did you kiss me?" I blurt.

His brown eyes shimmer with amusement. It's both maddening and captivating at the same time. "Because I wanted to. Was that not clear enough?"

"Are you using me this week because we're in the middle of nowhere and I'm handy?"

He sweeps his arm across the window, indicating the bustling Manhattan nightlife outside. "Take a look around. This is Manhattan, Lucy. I could've easily found a date for tonight. I wanted you here. When did I give you any other idea?"

"But..." I huff, frustrated. "You're charming and all, but Matty has been filling me in on the hackathons. You're a massive playboy."

His face hardens, amusement extinguished. "Lucy, my past is exactly that—the past. Right now, it's you that I'm here with, it's you that I respect. All I want is to be a gentleman and give you a night to remember. So can we let that go and enjoy the evening?"

"Fine," I grumble, "if you insist."

JP exits the car with the assertive stride of a man who owns every inch of this city. Without missing a beat, he circles the vehicle to open my door. Meanwhile, I'm concentrating on not passing out.

As if on cue, a swarm of paparazzi swoops in, their cameras trained on JP.

He reaches out a hand to help me out, but my rebellious dress doesn't afford much room for a smooth exit. I stumble out of the car, coming close to an intimate rendezvous with the tarmac before JP's sturdy hand catches me.

He pulls me in so close that I can feel his body heat through my dress, sparking a thrill of desire. Bad news, considering I had to go commando up top in this dress. As if my nipples needed any further encouragement.

"Thank you," I mutter, extricating myself from his hold.

I try not to trip over my own feet as he leads me up the grand stairwell. I spot at least three people I think are famous, maybe from one of those trashy reality TV shows.

JP's hand finds mine, slipping into my palm as

if he's done it a hundred times before. He's being recognized, I see the nods from corporate high-fliers, the obscenely rich, and the less discreet flirtations of C-list celebrities.

It's hard not to get swept up in the adrenaline and the magic of it all. The whole place is a sensory circus: lights flash and twinkle from all directions, bouncing off chandeliers, walls, the sparklers in the drinks, and, not to be outdone, the nipple tassels of feisty burlesque dancers.

It's like being at a modern *Great Gatsby* party.

"Have you been here before?" JP asks me, a playful smirk dancing across his lips.

I must look like a total tool with all my wide-eyed gawking.

"Nope, not that I recall," I say with a grin. "Remember, I'm IT? I'm usually locked away in the server room."

Or that's the joke, according to the rest of the company.

"Lucy, in that dress, you should never be locked away."

Oh God. I attempt to thank him but my tongue has swelled to five times its size.

We ascend another stairway, approaching the main ballroom. That's when the real stares begin.

"Do you come to these events often?" I ask,

desperate to ignore the unnerving sensation of eyes boring into us from all corners.

"Only if unavoidable," he responds smoothly, conjuring up two glittering glasses of champagne. "No escaping it tonight, I'm afraid. Do you want something else non-alcoholic?"

"This is fine." I accept the flute. "What's the cause for tonight's event?"

His demeanor shifts, a shadow flitting across his handsome features. "Bowel cancer. I provide substantial donations, but I tend to steer clear of the events."

I blink, thrown. "That's... that's what my dad died of."

"I know." He tightens his grip on my hand, a quiet show of support.

My mind spins. Did I actually tell JP how Dad died?

Seeing my confusion, JP frowns. "Lucy? Did I screw up?"

I plaster a smile on my face. "No! Not at all. It's nice to attend something like this. So what's my role here then?"

"You're here so I don't have to talk to anyone else."

"Like a bodyguard? You're a big guy, I don't believe you require any rescuing. You seem perfectly capable of handling yourself."

His playful smirk returns. "Even big guys could use a little saving from time to time."

His words, though light-hearted, carry a weight that sends a thrill of anticipation coursing through me.

Suddenly jittery, I fiddle with my necklace and swallow a mouthful of champagne, my eyes flitting around the room. I wish everyone would stop eyeballing us. The women are feasting their eyes on JP like he's the main course and I'm just a side dish they can't place. I wish I'd worn a sign: Not His Date, Just Staff!

Sensing my discomfort, JP's hand settles on my hip, drawing me closer. His body radiates warmth, and his breath tickles my ear. "Hey, relax."

"Sorry, it's just... This isn't my comfort zone," I confess, trying to swallow down my nerves. "I've never actually been to a black-tie gala before. I'm more at home with code and pixels, not swanking it up with billionaires."

"Swanking it up?" His eyes twinkle with amusement. "That's right, you're more of a Comic Con girl. Daredevil still your number one, huh?"

The champagne threatens to escape my nose. "God. So you did see the stupid action figure on my desk."

He shoots me a look, a slow, knowing smile playing on his lips. "Something like that."

"JP," a sultry voice coos from behind us.

We turn to find a skyscraper of a woman. Her striking blue eyes and dark hair remind me uncomfortably of myself—if I were the 2.0 version. As if someone downloaded me and then upgraded me with a Pro version in Photoshop.

She brazenly flutters her lashes at JP, completely sidelining me in the process.

"Pamela," JP responds, his voice rich and gravelly, not unwelcoming. "Nice to see you. This is Lucy." His arm tightens around my waist, a possessive move that makes my heart do a funny little jig.

I flash her a polite smile, trying to wriggle free from his grasp, but he's not having it.

Ignoring me, Pamela places a hand on JP's shoulder. "We haven't caught up in a while, have we? Since..." Her voice trails off, a sly smirk on her face.

Great. Now it's clear JP has not only met her before but likely seen her without clothes too.

"Is this your assistant?" she asks, shooting me a look that's half curious, half dismissive.

"Yes," I blurt out in unison with JP's resounding, "No."

"She's not an assistant," he growls, his grip around my waist tightening. "Lucy is... she's someone very important to the company."

I wince at the lie. This is getting weirder by the second. Does he really think calling me "important" will make me feel better about being dragged into this?

Pamela gives me a once-over, her calculating smile not slipping. "How nice."

"Excuse us, Pamela." JP's voice carries a finality that brooks no argument.

She saunters away with a nod that tells me this isn't over yet.

"You can chat with her privately," I suggest. "I'm a big girl, I can handle myself. Seriously, I'll be over at the bar."

Even if I'll loathe every goddamn second of it.

"I have zero interest in talking to her. I'm here to exchange pleasantries and move on."

My brow lifts at his defensiveness. Maybe he's so used to supermodels now, they're just routine.

"I guess this isn't quite as fun as Comic Con?" He smiles.

I scrunch my face in feigned thought. "Well, the costumes at Comic Con are ironically more breathable." I sneak a hand behind me, trying to subtly wrestle my silk dress from the vice-like grip of my butt cheeks. The perils of gowns like this: fab for photos, shit for maneuverability. "It's not that it's not nice here. It's just... overwhelming. I've glimpsed into your bizarre world."

"This isn't my world. This is something I have to do every now and then." He smiles. "Comic Con with you sounds infinitely more fun."

My brows shoot up my forehead. Is JP hiding a geeky side?

Before I can answer, a deep voice calls out from behind us. "Wolfe."

As we pivot to confront the interruption, JP's frame turns to granite, his fingers on my hip hardening. Oh, they clearly have history here.

"Derek," JP grudgingly acknowledges. "This is Lucy."

Derek sweeps a smarmy smile over me, the kind that makes me feel like I need a shower, triggering an odd sense of déjà vu. It's a feeling I can't shake. *Have I met him before?*

"Going incognito, are we, Wolfe?" Derek drawls with an undercurrent of mockery. "You've become a veritable ghost in Manhattan. We miss you."

"Taking a breather in the mountains this week." JP's reply is terse, his jaw set like he's chewing on stale food.

Derek leans in closer, his smirk creeping wider.

"Did you manage to clean up your little mess from that night?"

JP's hand involuntarily tightens around my waist. "It's handled."

Now my curiosity is piqued.

Nodding, Derek's gaze slides to me, a twinkle of curiosity in his eyes. "Good to know. Wouldn't want my lovely wife catching me on camera. And who might the enchanting Lucy be?"

"I'm just part of JP's tech team," I spit out, maybe a bit too quickly. There's something about Derek that sets off warning bells in my head, a disconcerting familiarity. It's as if I've seen him somewhere, crossed paths maybe.

"We should get moving," JP interrupts gruffly, not waiting for Derek's response.

Once we're safely out of Derek's earshot, I can't contain my curiosity. "Who was that?"

JP chugs his champagne. "Just some Wall Street jackass."

"Has he been in the Quinn & Wolfe offices before?" I ask.

JP's gaze sharpens on me, curiously unsettling. "No. Why?"

"Uh, no reason." I shrug, attempting nonchalance. There's no reason for me to know the guy. To be fair, he looks like every other Wall Street banker—slicked-back hair, a Rolex worth more than my annual salary, pinstripe suit, gleaming shoes.

I just can't help myself. "What was the mess you had to clean up, if you don't mind me asking?"

JP's face darkens. "Nothing. Business."

Right. Message received then. No more discussion about that.

"Here's Killian and Connor," he murmurs, his gaze drifting over my shoulder.

I turn to see the Quinn brothers approaching us. I can't handle the top three together. Did they see me dislodging my dress from my butt? They're approaching from that direction. I'm worse than Libby at the comic convention.

They both look unfairly gorgeous. I've only talked to them at company events. Never when my nipples were trussed in silk though.

As if on cue, JP's hand finds the small of my back, sending a ripple of goose bumps across my skin. "Killian, Connor. I believe you're acquainted with Lucy from our tech division?"

"Hi!" I squeak.

Their dual gaze flicks back and forth, sizing me up and down, then darting to JP. A spark of something unreadable ignites in Killian's eyes. "Hello, Lucy," he drawls.

"We're doing the hackathon for Tangra at my Bear Mountain villa this week. I thought I'd bring along one of the team to this." JP sounds mildly defensive.

"Lucy." Connor, the younger Quinn brother, flashes me a reassuring smile. "We met a few months back. I'm sorry to hear about your accident. How are you holding up?"

"Oh! Fine! Well, surviving, I guess."

"I trust the company's providing you all the necessary support. Should you face any issues, feel free to reach out to us."

"Thanks." I smile. "That's really kind of you."

Network, Lucy. This is your chance. Engage the big bosses with some sharp, insightful comments.

"I like your tuxes. You both look great."

For fuck's sake.

They chuckle.

Heat pricks my cheeks as I desperately try to retreat into the safety of my champagne flute.

"And you look beautiful." Connor grins at me. "How'd he rope you into this then?"

Looking at the three imposing figures, I raise my eyebrow, letting a small smile creep onto my lips. "Has anyone ever managed to say no to you three?"

A smirk tugs at the corners of Connor's mouth.

"Occasionally," Killian says. "But JP's a stubborn bastard, it's easier to just give him what he wants."

My eyes bulge. That's what I'm afraid of.

After a few agonizing minutes of conversation, JP suggests we move on. I've never been so relieved. We stop by a few more groups of executives and investment bankers exchanging small talk.

By the time we break free, my feet are aching, my cheeks are sore from all the strained smiling, and my nipples have been rubbed raw from accidental silk friction. Sexy.

A slow, sultry jazz tune begins to waft from the speakers, luring couples onto the dance floor.

"Dance with me," JP says in a low voice.

I vehemently shake my head. "God, no. I've got two left feet; remember how clumsy I was getting out of the car? Dancing is way worse."

He steps closer, a wicked grin spreading across his face. "Lucky for you, I'll be taking the lead."

He somehow manages to make that sound filthy.

A flurry of butterflies invades my stomach as he whispers into my ear, his warm breath fanning my skin. "Lucy, there's nothing I want more tonight than to feel you in my arms."

His tongue glides over his lips, like a wolf eyeing up a lamb chop, giving me a look that makes my downstairs clench.

Against my better judgment, I allow him to steer me onto the dance floor.

TWENTY-SEVEN

Lucy

My pulse races as JP possessively slides his hand into mine and leads me out, drawing the attention of onlookers.

He locks his intense gaze onto mine and pulls me close. He chuckles, his warm breath tickling my ear. "No need to look like you're facing the firing squad, Lucy. We're just dancing."

I try to play it cool, laughing it off, but inside, it's mayhem. Fight or flight. Or fuck.

Maybe all of the above.

My arms wrap around his neck, feeling his muscles tense underneath his shirt. God, that's a whole lot of man. Warm hard masculine muscle. Hard in all the right places.

For a second, I forget about the pain-inflicting stilts I've strapped to my feet.

His hands trace a path up and down my back, the heat from his touch penetrating my dress.

They finally settle on my hips, his fingers drawing intoxicating circles that send shivers down my spine.

Just a dance, my ass.

Try as I might to focus on the rhythm, our proximity makes it impossible. The press of his strong thighs against mine sends delicious tingles through me.

He lets out a deep, sedated sigh and smirks down at me, his gaze filled with heat.

This man knows *exactly* what he's doing to me.

I can feel it in the way his hands claim me, in the subtle pressure of his body against mine, teasing and tempting through our clothes.

"What's going on in that head of yours?" he asks.

I gnaw my lip, gathering the courage to be honest—minus the part where my body is screaming *Take me now, you gorgeous man!*

"I'm a bit on edge," I blurt out, my throat dry.

His eyes lock on mine. "Why?"

"Really? You have to ask?" I laugh breathlessly, acutely aware of the slow circles his fingers are tracing on my skin. "You're one of the most intense people I've ever met. And intense is an understatement."

His lips curl wider as he leans in, close enough

for me to nibble on if I so feel the urge. "Intensity is reserved for the things and people that matter..." His gaze flickers to my lips before returning to my eyes.

I bite back a shiver, keeping my facade calm. "Oh? And what qualifies as 'mattering' to a guy like you?"

His smile deepens as he guides me into a slow turn on the dance floor. "What matters most to me? My family, for one—my sister and nephews. The business I built from nothing. Loyal friends, though they're hard to come by." His hand trails a feather-light circle on my hip and I nearly miss his next words. "And beautiful women who can challenge me."

I force out a light laugh to cover my fluttering nerves. "Well, you're definitely surrounded by beautiful women tonight."

In one smooth, motion he spins me out then pulls me back in, my chest pressed to his. I inhale sharply as his next words brush against my neck, and I feel them all the way down to my underwear. "There's only one woman who has my undivided attention tonight. The one with the striking blue eyes who outshines everything else in the room. Trust me, no one else even comes close."

Oh, hell. That's dangerously sweet. I let out a

strangled chuckle.

"You know, you're not what I expected," I say, breathless.

He raises a brow, a glint in his eye. "Oh? And what were you expecting?"

"Honestly, I pegged you for all business, Mr. Cold and Unfeeling. Sleeping and showering in your suits. Only caring about that bottom line."

A low chuckle leaves him. "I assure you I do both of those things naked. But you're not wrong —I always have the bottom line in mind."

"But I suspect there's more to you than a tough exterior and profit margins. If I didn't know any better, I'd say you're a closet romantic."

His mouth quirks. "I'm intense about everything I do, be it business or love. When I'm in love, I'm all in. I worship my woman. She becomes the center of my world, and I give her everything I've got, every single day."

My heart's tap dancing now. Like Riverdance on speed. "I think I might need some examples. Ideally a demo."

He chuckles again. A deep sexy rumble that slides into my underwear.

"I'm afraid those would be inappropriate to share in present company. But if you're asking for a private demonstration…"

He spins me again, this time pulling me flush against him.

I gasp at the feel of his hard body, the evidence of his arousal pressed into my belly.

"Keep pushing, and you just might get one. Because if you were mine, I'd make you come all night long until you begged me to stop. Then I'd carry you into the shower and wash every inch of your body, making sure to tease and caress each curve until you're weak in my arms. I'd wash your hair before wrapping you in a T-shirt of mine, then hold you close until you drift asleep. Come morning, I'd still be holding you."

Holy shit. My face is burning hot now, and my ovaries are screaming at me to hump him right here on the dance floor.

"How does that sound to you, Lucy?"

My breath catches. The sane part of my brain is screaming "Abort mission!" while the rest of me has already checked into a hotel room upstairs, peeled off my dress, and is lying seductively on the bed.

He gives a low chuckle as we sway together. "A bit too much honesty for you, huh? I'll keep myself in check for now." His voice drops even lower. "But damn you look sexy when you blush."

His hands slide lower until they find the curve

of my backside as he pulls me tight against his body. That hard bulge is impossible to ignore.

I stifle a gasp, heat pooling in my core.

Then, with a growl that's pure animalistic lust, he breathes, "Don't worry, I won't bite too hard," into my ear.

My breath catches as he does just that—pushes away my hair and starts planting kisses on my neck.

A million warning bells ring. I should stop him. This is dangerous. We're in public. Everyone knows who JP is.

Instead, I arch into his touch, silently begging for more. I feel his stubble, his firm lips pressing against me, the tingles rushing through me like electricity.

My thighs clench together involuntarily as sensations run rampant throughout my body.

"Let's take a breather," he murmurs as he comes up again.

I nod, completely incapable of doing anything else but blindly following behind him as he leads me off the dancefloor, wondering if everyone can see his massive boner.

I follow him silently as we descend the winding staircase, my body thrumming in anticipation with every step.

What's his plan here?

"Mind your step," he warns gruffly, clasping my hand in his.

We reach the end of the staircase and he leads me down the corridor with the skill of someone who knows this place inside out, which shouldn't surprise me, since he does own it.

Are we going to have sex?

My heart skitters in my chest when he suddenly wheels around and yanks me into a tiny cloakroom. With one powerful shove, he slams the door shut behind us, plunging us into semi-darkness.

Caught off guard is the understatement of the year. I gulp in air and stumble back until I'm pinned against the wall by his thighs. His strong arms cage me, hands bracing on either side of my head.

In the dimmer light of the cloakroom, his chiseled features take on a dangerous edge.

His muscled thighs spread around mine so that I'm deliciously trapped in the V of his legs. His hands grip my wrists, pinning them above my head, as he roughly takes possession of my mouth with his own.

It's a hot, heated kiss filled with passion and possession and hunger, shattering me into a million pieces.

A feral rumble of approval rises from deep in his throat as it merges with mine—he's not just kissing me, he's *claiming* me. This man has complete control over me now, the power to do whatever he wants to me.

He breaks our kiss abruptly and I shiver under his intense gaze as he looks down at me, breathing heavily.

My body vibrates with excitement, my hands dying to break free to roam all over his body. I can barely contain my own arousal.

It's startling and scary... and fucking wild.

"Lucy," he growls, his jaw muscles tight enough to break. "I want to take it slow but I can't wait any longer. I need you so fucking badly."

God. His voice is pure sex.

His hard cock presses urgently against my core, begging for attention.

I struggle to break free of his grip as he holds my wrists above my head, looking down at me with an amused smirk. "What do you want?"

My throat trembles as I whisper hoarsely, "You. Please."

Just when I think he's going to make me suffer, he releases my hands.

Before I can stop myself, I reach for his length,

feeling the thickness of it through his pants.

A satisfied moan passes my lips when I feel his hardness fully in my grasp.

"Oh God," I stammer. He's all man. He's thick and hard and throbbing with need for me.

Holy.

Fucking.

Hell.

Is it possible to die from overdosing on arousal? My tombstone will read: "departed this world due to a fatal case of sexual tension," and I'll go out with my face stuck in a moan.

His hands come back up to brace the wall on either side of me and every muscle in his body tightens in response to my touch. His legs part further, an invitation to keep exploring. Delicious shivers dance down my spine as my hand clamps possessively over his cock. It's mine.

His breath is hot on my forehead. "Don't fight it," he rasps. "It feels right, baby."

Oh God. It does. So fucking right.

Every inch of me is screaming for more. My breaths are erratic, my face is flushed, and my core *throbs* with desire. I've never needed anything so much in my life.

"It's been too damn long," he growls in my ear.

Wait—since he had sex? His words bring me

out of my stupor long enough for my hand to drop from his erection.

With a swift move, his hands loosen the straps of my dress and it falls to my stomach, exposing my breasts to him.

His mouth comes down like a predator swooping in on its prey, and then latches onto my nipple, sending shocks of pleasure through me.

My hands come up to fist his hair as his tongue swirls over my sensitive nipple.

God, that feels so good.

My pussy clenches with need.

I squirm against him as he hikes up the hem of my dress until it's bunched around my waist and then his large hand slides into my panties.

Breathy moans escape me as he rubs circles around my wet slit. The sensation has me squirming like it's the first time I've ever been touched.

Am I really doing this in a closet?

My hips buck, but he holds me tight, pressing my body taut against his.

He pulses his fingers against my clit, and I feel heat and chills simultaneously up and down my body.

Fuck, yeah. I don't care where we are.

He pulls away from my breast and stands to his

full height, gazing down at me fiercely. "I need to see your face when you come."

Damn, I love this man's dominance.

My head rocks back against the wall as pleasure ripples through my core, his fingers working some ridiculous magic down there.

I'm drenched, so wet it's embarrassing.

"That's my girl," he husks in a low voice, his thumb delicately circling my clit and sending waves of pleasure coursing through my veins. "You're so wet for me, Lucy. So ready. You need this more than you know."

My breath quickens and my core feels like it's on fire from the tingly sensations created. He holds my chin firmly in place, making sure our eyes stay locked as I start to lose control.

If it weren't for his strong arms keeping me upright, my knees would have already buckled underneath me.

"Relax into me and let yourself go, baby."

"Oh please, oh please, oh please," I pant, as the waves hit. I fist his hair as my moans grow frantic. I need more. All of him.

"Eyes open," he commands. His smirk dares me to defy him, but I couldn't look away even if I wanted to.

My orgasm pounds through me, my entire

body shaking wildly in pure ecstasy. "Oh God!" I gasp, coming down off my high.

"Uh," I groan. I just let JP Wolfe, company owner, get me off.

He smirks, eyes gleaming with satisfaction. "You okay?"

"Yeah," I breathe, still dazed.

With surprising tenderness, he reaches down to straighten my dress. Then he lifts my hand, pressing a kiss into my palm, before guiding me out of the cloakroom.

As we make our grand exit, a few onlookers watch us with smirks plastered on their faces. I can almost hear their thoughts: *Well, we all know what they were up to in there.*

Feeling my cheeks burn, I quickly yank my hand from his grasp.

He blinks in surprise, the cool facade momentarily broken.

"Let's get out of here." A note of urgency creeps into his voice. "Let's go home."

Panic wars with desire. I need to regain logical decision-making before I do something I'll regret. Or don't regret nearly enough. This can't end well.

His gaze burns into mine as he lifts my chin. "Listen, I understand the storm brewing inside that beautiful, complicated mind of yours. But there's nothing for you to worry or feel guilt over, you understand?"

Then he looks down at me with those smoldering eyes of his, and suddenly nothing else matters.

TWENTY-EIGHT

JP

The drive back to the Bear Mountain villa feels like one of the longest trips of my life. Lucy and I attempt a light conversation with the driver in an effort to ignore the massive bulge in my tux pants.

I reach out and take her hand, coaxing it from its protective position in front of her chest, and place it onto my thigh. She doesn't pull away, but the rigidity in her fingers speaks volumes.

I didn't mean to savage her in that cloakroom like some horny teenager, but goddammit, something in me unhinges when she's nearby. I'm playing a dirty game because I know she wants me sexually.

I was drowning in my own sweat when that schmuck Derek swaggered over and began jabbing at me, sure that he was going to spill all the fucking beans. The last thing I need is Lucy hearing about my sordid exploits from that halfwit. It's got to come from me, and it's going to, sooner rather than later.

Upon reaching the villa, the distant chatter and laughter drifts from the garden—sounds like my liquor cabinet has been ransacked.

"Lucy," I start as she edges toward the door, looking ready to bolt, "are we good?"

She gives a nod, eyes fixated anywhere but on me.

"Will you stay with me tonight?" I ask. "Just sleep, if you don't want anything else. I want you close, that's all."

"I can't," she stammers, striding into the villa. "I should... I need to crash early. Matty and I, we have... work to do."

She backs away as she speaks, putting more distance between us with every word until she has literally left the kitchen. She's as freaked out as the first time we fell for each other.

I suppress the instinct to chase after her, knowing it'll only spook her more. Instead, I treat myself to a shot of scotch, letting it burn its way down. One step forward, two steps back. I'm an idiot. A lovesick, foolish idiot.

I take the bottle of scotch to bed.

Two fingers of scotch deep, I'm wide awake, zeroing in on the soft pitter-patter of hesitation by my bedroom door. The steps go away and come back again.

I toss the blankets away from me.

She lingers in front of the door without making another move for what feels like an eternity until I can't take it any longer. Wrenching open the door, I find her there, fiddling with the strap of her jersey dress. It drapes softly over her curves, as flattering as any ballgown.

"Hey," she says awkwardly.

"Hey yourself," I reply, unable to contain my smile.

Her eyes take a round trip from my boxers back up to my face, and my cock twinges at the attention.

"I didn't get back to you before." She shivers despite the warm evening.

"Back to me about what?" I play along.

"When you asked how your... scenario sounded." Her words hang in the air, her gaze locked on me as she takes a small step forward. "Well, it sounds exactly like what I need."

Her baby blues are the size of dinner plates, staring up at me with this raw vulnerability, and damn if it doesn't catch me right in the throat.

"Excellent." My voice drops a whole octave. "Because I've been wanting this for a long time."

I throw the door wide like I'm about to kick off the Super Bowl halftime show.

Lucy takes a tentative step inside, looking around like she's just set foot on a different planet.

"Wow." She comes in to stand in the middle of the room, scanning it awkwardly. "This is like my entire apartment, squished into one room. I should have known it would be the biggest bedroom in the house. Though I was half expecting a *50 Shades* dungeon."

I chuckle. She had a similar observation the first time she was here. My bedroom is minimalistic and practical. "How so?"

"Matty's dead certain you throw some crazy *Eyes Wide Shut* parties here."

Matty needs to learn to keep his trap shut.

"Not quite," I reply with a smirk. "Most of the time I'm here alone."

She roams around the room, taking in the minimalist decor, feigning bravado. "Look, I need to know that whatever happens, it won't blow up my career. Matty says I can blame any strange behavior on the amnesia, but..." Her voice falters. "I need to be sure."

"Relax," I say. "Your job is safe. You've got my word on it."

I grimace inwardly at the reminder of what I've already done. But in this context, when it comes to her job—I can promise, with absolute certainty, that I'll never jeopardize it.

She wanders toward my walk-in closet with the full-length mirror.

Following her, I stand behind her, towering over her smaller frame, our sizes a striking contrast in the glass.

Her gaze meets mine in the reflection, a potent mix of apprehension and anticipation dancing in her eyes.

I trail my fingers along the soft curves of her arms, sending shivers dancing across her skin.

The air between us is charged with a familiar electricity.

For a heartbeat, the world rights itself. It's Lucy and JP, as it should be. No forgotten memories, just the passion that once defined us.

I brush my fingertips along her neckline before planting light kisses all over her exposed skin.

"We'll do whatever you want. Whatever you're comfortable with," I whisper huskily into her ear as I tug at the strap of her dress. "No pressure."

Her breath catches as I gently unfasten the

straps of her dress from behind until it falls to the floor and she's standing in only her panties.

"That's the issue," she rasps. "I want to do everything."

"Fuck," I groan, my eyes skating over her body.

Feels like an eternity since I've seen her like this. I'm desperate for her, and I can already feel myself losing control.

For a moment, I just stare at her in the mirror, my eyes unashamedly exploring every inch of her body. Her slightly parted lips, her breasts rising and falling with each labored breath, her hard nipples begging to be touched. Her gorgeous toned thighs. Even the scrappy scar on her knee.

My cock throbs against her ass. She has no idea how much she turns me on.

She's a fucking goddess and she doesn't even realize it.

My goddess.

Turning crimson under my gaze, she tries desperately to breathe in deeply, to suck in her stomach.

"You're magnificent," I murmur into the nape of her neck as I cup her breasts possessively. My lips trace a path down to her collarbone, making her shiver.

"I must be lumpier than what you're used to.

Staring at a computer screen twelve hours a day isn't exactly a core workout, so if it's washboard abs you're after, you've got the wrong girl."

I give her an admonishing look in the mirror. "I've definitely got the right girl. Do you feel how much I want you? You're perfect; every inch of you."

Like a man deprived of sustenance, I greedily massage her breasts, savoring the feel of her warm skin against my palms.

She makes a soft mewling sound, her eyes in a daze with heat. Her chest heaves as she melts into me, all shyness gone. I feel her hard nipples against my palms.

Damn, those whimpers.

"Goddamn, baby," I growl, almost angry at how she makes me feel. "You have no idea how much you turn me on, do you? How much power you have over me."

My hand moves lower to her stomach, feeling the contracting muscles there before pushing past the waistband of her underwear. I groan when I make contact with her sweet, sexy, throbbing pussy.

"You're aching for this," I breathe against her ear.

Groaning, I push my finger against her

softness, feeling her pulsate beneath my touch. So ready for me she's throbbing, writhing against me. "I love making you feel this way."

I caress her swollen lips hungrily with my thumb before slipping it inside and exploring her inner depths.

A moan escapes as her head falls against my chest. "Damn, you're good at this, JP."

I am, because I know every inch of her body. I paid attention. I listened. I know exactly what she wants. But I won't let her come yet.

My fingers slip away from her panties and she stares at me in the reflection.

"Why'd you stop?" she whispers, looking insecure.

"I haven't," I reply with a chuckle, peppering kisses on her neck. "I'm just getting started."

My lips trace the curves of her body as I coax her underwear down her thighs, one agonizing inch at a time.

She trembles as I kneel before her and slowly pull each foot from her underwear until she's completely exposed to me.

She squirms and tries to close her legs from my view, but I don't let her.

"Do you understand how breathtakingly beautiful you are?" I ask on my knees, making eye contact with her.

A tiny, nonsensical laugh flees her lips and I resist the urge to smile.

"Oh my God. Stop it. You're making me nervous." Her face flushes with heat and she squirms, putting her hands on my shoulders as if to anchor herself. "Told you you're intense."

"And I told you I don't do things by half."

Before she can register what's happening, I stand and lift her off the ground by the waist, encircling her legs around me.

Her bare pussy grinds against my stomach. She moans as her clit brushes against my abdomen. Her hips buck but I hold her tight, walking her over to the bed.

Which is far, considering my bedroom is enormous.

I lay her down on the mattress, my hands lingering along her curves. I slowly and meticulously unfasten her stilettos, each click of the buckle echoing in the room.

"What a gentleman," she murmurs. "I like this service—my hot billionaire boss undressing me."

I crack a bittersweet smile. The truth is, she is accustomed to this kind of treatment, she just doesn't remember it.

"But I won't be a gentleman for long—enjoy it

while it lasts."

Her breathing speeds up as she looks up at me with wide, pleading eyes. "Oh, oh my God," she murmurs tentatively.

I smirk down at her. "Do you know what's coming?" I whisper huskily, leaning over her body until our skin is almost touching, but not quite.

She bites down on her lower lip like a sexy vixen. "I think I need to be enlightened."

"You're going to be screaming my name all night long, Lucy, because I'm about to make you come again and again until you beg me to stop. First with my tongue, then with my hard fucking cock, until you can't take any more."

My words cause her to gasp; laughter mixed in with shock. "Holy fuck... You have game."

I peel down my boxers to reveal my rock-hard erection, fisting my length and pumping once, twice, all the while gazing down at her through hooded eyes.

She sucks in sharply. "*That's* your dick? I knew it. I don't know whether I should be scared or turned on."

I chuckle as she arches her back on the bed, hands curled around the sheets, desperate for me to fuck her. Her soft pussy opens up for me as she shifts her legs higher and lifts her hips off the mattress, begging to be filled.

Christ. My eyes hungrily drink in her pussy and it takes all of my willpower not to thrust my cock into her right now.

Moving closer between her legs, I pull her body toward the edge of the bed.

With a growl, I wrap my hand around my aching cock, stroking along her drenched slit with the other. "You should be both, baby."

And she is both—I can tell by the way her gaze flickers between my face and my hand sliding across the length of my hardness.

Adrenaline courses through me as I fist my painfully hard cock.

"You okay, beautiful?" I chuckle.

"Ummm… I'm not sure." She nibbles her lip. "That thing's huge."

A smirk curls my lips. "Why do you make that sound like such a bad thing?"

"Because it looks like it could tear me apart."

"Don't worry; I'll take good care of you. I'll make sure you enjoy every second of this."

I rub the tip of my cock against her soaking wet pussy lips, teasing and torturing us both. I'm fucking desperate to be inside her. Desperate to feel her wet heat clench on my cock.

And Lucy needs it just as much as me.

Her face contorts in pleasure, her breaths fast and jagged as her hips writhe beneath me. She's so fucking hot and ready for me. She wants to come so badly. She'd come just from me rubbing myself against her, if I let her.

With great difficulty, I manage to keep myself in check.

"Wait," she pants, her legs tensing. "I need to think with my head instead of my... other parts. I'm on the pill, but when did you last have sex with that billion-dollar dick?"

I chuckle then freeze too as the question hangs in the air between us. We don't use condoms anymore. How do I answer this?

"It's been months since I was intimate with someone else. I'm clean."

Her eyes go wide. "Really?"

"Yes, absolutely. I wouldn't lie to you, Lucy."

She stares at me with those big blue eyes and pouty lips that make me want to please this woman more than I've ever wanted to do anything in my life. She wiggles again, angling herself up to meet my erection, but I keep her firmly in place.

"Good," she says, biting her bottom lip. "Because I can't wait to feel you inside me."

Those words almost put me over the edge. Not yet, though.

"Soon, baby, soon. First, I'm going to take care of you."

I drop to my knees and wrap her thighs around my shoulders.

Softly pressing kisses up her thigh, my eager mouth finds its way to her perfect clit.

She shivers and lets out a loud, heady moan. "Oh my god. You're really good at that."

I smile into her pussy. Of course I am, I know her body like the back of my hand.

She squirms as I savor her with my mouth. She's so close, I know by the way her legs tremble in my grasp, the way her pussy grinds against my mouth. Her little grunts and moans drive me fucking wild.

Her legs instinctively move to close around my head, but I keep them open with a gentle grip as I hungrily lick every inch of her tantalizing sweetness like a man obsessed.

"You taste amazing," I murmur between kisses. "Absolute perfection."

"I'm so close, keep going, oh God!"

And she is so, so fucking close.

Those whimpers.

I devour her with urgency. Faster. Harder.

"Oh God, oh God, oh God."

I hold her to me as she thrashes under me.

Her legs shudder until finally, an almighty moan rips from her throat as she climaxes against my tongue.

And damn, if this isn't the best sensation of my life.

TWENTY-NINE

Lucy

If he isn't the sexiest man on the planet, then kill me now.

I melt into the bed, utterly spent. "That was incredible," I say with a nervous laugh as my body continues to ride out the orgasm aftershocks.

JP stands at the edge of the bed, his dark eyes smoldering with lust as his rock-hard cock pulses in his fist. His gaze pierces into me, never wavering as he pumps himself slowly up and down.

"Tell me about it," he says throatily with a smirk that tells me I'm in trouble. "Nothing is better than feeling you come all over my mouth."

Another jittery giggle escapes me, but it comes out all wonky, like some bizarre animal mating call. Damn, this man is dirty. He was right when he said he doesn't do anything by half.

I stare up at him for a moment, my breath caught in my throat as I drink in his whole intimidating package—every sculpted muscle, each chiseled line, every powerful move of his hand around his shaft.

Watching this man pleasure himself is more arousing than anything I've ever seen. Fact.

"See what you do to me, Lucy?" he says in a low voice. "This is all for you."

God. As I squirm under his gaze, my toes curl so tight, I swear they're going to break.

I need to channel my inner Wonder Woman here, but instead, I'm a shivering mass of nerves and sweat.

He grabs hold of my legs, pushing them wider and wrapping them around his waist. He has me caged beneath him and, as if to prove it, his thick cock nudges at my entrance, teasing and taunting until the ache between my legs is unbearable.

"*Please*," I moan, my voice trembling with need.

My hips gyrate against his, pushing him closer and closer to my opening. His thick arousal throbs between us, the sensation sending shivers running down my body like a sexy stun gun.

Damn tease.

"You're dying for my cock, aren't you?" he says in a husky voice that makes goose bumps prickle along my skin.

"Yes! Yes!" I cry out. What a stupid question.

"Have you fantasized about this moment? How it would feel?"

"Yes," I reply, practically panting. It doesn't even sound like me.

"Have you touched yourself with thoughts of me?"

I squirm, my already hot cheeks reaching full boil. A, I'm too embarrassed to answer that, and B, my bedroom talk appears to be limited to "Yes."

"I won't give you what you want until you tell me the truth."

"Yes," I whisper.

"Yes, what?"

"Yes, I've touched myself and imagined it was you."

"Good girl. That's what I like to hear."

His lips curl into a wicked smirk, and just when I think he's going to finally give me what I want, he suddenly lifts me off the bed and flips me around so that I'm straddling him.

My legs spread around him and I gasp at the feel of his hard cock pressing against my wet entrance.

Holy hell. This is actually happening. I'm going to get fucked by JP Wolfe.

I tensely lower myself onto his cock,

whimpering as my core reacts to his size.

"Take all of me," he growls.

My senses go wild from the pleasure and pain until I finally relax, letting pleasure take over. His cock fills me completely and my inner muscles clench around him.

Thrills rush through my body, making me whimper in delight while he groans in unison. He's fucking huge.

His hands are tight on my hips, keeping himself steady as he fights against losing control.

"You're the boss now," he murmurs. "Show me how you like to fuck."

We both know that isn't true, but I'm willing to play along.

I slowly grind myself against him, savoring every second of the pleasure that pulsates through my body with each thrust. His gaze is intense as he watches me, his hands squeezing my hips as I take charge of the rhythm.

This man has the best cock ever. He might never get it back. We're tethered to each other forever now.

His grunts grow louder and hungrier as I ride him faster and harder.

His cheeks are flushed, eyes half-lidded, veins popping on his neck as he strains with pleasure.

I tilt my head back, letting out a moan of delight as I clench around him, feeling like I own him completely.

I'm never going to last. Listening to JP's sex noises is enough to make me come.

"You feel amazing inside me," I moan. "This is my favorite position."

"Is that so?" he says with a smirk that is quickly wiped off his face when I up my pace even more. He groans into my hair as I hit my sweet spot again and again.

Every thrust feels like it could be the last, each second more intense than the previous one. I know this will be the mother of all orgasms. A mind-blowing, earth-shattering experience that my poor vagina may never recover from.

"This angle," he grunts. "So fucking deep."

The intensity builds until finally, it's too much, crashing over us like a tidal wave of pleasure as I show him exactly how I like to fuck.

"Oh, fuck." He groans as my movements become more frantic.

I'm done for.

He lets out a final choked noise of pleasure as his body stiffens and he comes hard. I feel him swell and pulsate inside me, every sensation heightening my pleasure.

The look on his face. Something I never thought I'd see. It's too much.

My pussy tightens and quivers around his dick as the orgasm explodes through me. I moan so loudly I'm sure everyone on Bear Mountain heard.

For a moment, we remain like that, him still inside me and both of us struggling to catch our breath. This wasn't just good sex. This was unbelievable, earth-shattering, should-be-forbidden-in-some-states type of sex.

And the way he is looking at me right now? He couldn't agree more.

"Thank you, baby. That was incredible."

A nervous laugh bursts out of me. "You're probably used to great sex."

His fingers glide along my jaw, forcing me to meet his gaze once more. For a second, the confident businessman is gone, replaced by a man who suddenly seems years younger, eyes brimming with a vulnerability I never imagined he possessed. As if I have the power to wound him deeply. "Sex is only great with the right person."

My heart skips a beat as I realize what he's implying. Is he for real or just feeding me a rehearsed line to turn me into a puddle of simpering goo?

"Come on." He lifts me up off the bed. "Let me

take care of you and get you into the shower."

I giggle as he walks us both into the massive en suite and sets me down.

I don't have a clue what this thing between us is becoming, but I'll say this—I will never forget how he made me feel tonight.

A relaxed sigh escapes my lips as I place my face in the shower.

His hands roam over me as though afraid to leave an inch of skin untouched, like he's on a mission to scrub away every ache and worry.

How am I supposed to go back to my boring little life after this night of debauchery?

I needed this so badly.

"Me too."

My eyes fly open. Did I say that aloud?

When I bring my eyes up to meet his, he's grinning down at me.

"I just hope I didn't wake the whole building with my moaning," I joke, cheeks flaming at the memory.

"Relax. No one heard a thing. These walls are practically bombproof." His grin turns wicked. "Though your enthusiasm was duly noted."

I return a sheepish smile. Easy for him to say "relax."

"I can see you freaking out behind those beautiful blue eyes. We're doing nothing wrong here."

"Sorry. Overthinking's my second nature. You're the boss, in case you've forgotten."

"Do you trust me?"

His question gives me pause. Do I trust him? After all the stories I've heard? I'm not convinced he won't smash my heart to smithereens—therein lies the problem. For him, this is likely a seven-day fling.

To me, I know he's got inside my head now. And he can't find that out.

"Sure," I lie.

"Good. Will you spend the night with me, in my bed? I have unfinished promises to deliver on."

My eyes almost pop out of their sockets. The idea of waking up beside JP is... beyond amazing.

My fingers slide down his wet skin, exploring his shoulders, chest, and abdomen. I trail a slow path above his pubic line, and his stomach muscles twitch in response.

He's already getting hard again.

Ugh, the temptation.

"I can't," I groan as the hot water cascades over

us. "Matty will know if I'm not back in my room soon. And if I go MIA, Dwayne will probably have the SWAT team knocking at your door."

He exhales heavily, his breath mingling with the steam rising around us. "Okay, okay. But I want to see you again, in New York. Not just at work."

My heart goes full Usain Bolt. "You do?"

"Of course I do," he says with a smile, droplets clinging to his eyelashes.

"But why?"

"Why? Who asks 'why'?"

I return his jest with a serious look. "Honestly, JP. I'm not naive. You have it all. Billions, looks that would make a nun reconsider, and, of course, that big, beautiful dick. You could have any woman you want. I'm not saying I'm ugly," I tell him. "But I've got a healthy amount of self-awareness. There's a reason why I'm not America's next top model, and I'm fine with that."

"Hey, I don't want to hear you putting yourself down, sweetheart," he says, his tone serious. When I nod, he grins and adds, "So my wealth and my... 'assets' are my best qualities? And here I thought my charm might be a winning factor." He chuckles, the sound echoing around the shower.

Something about the sound makes me jolt.

It's a jolt when you knock your funny bone and

there's a white-hot flare shooting through your nerves. It's intense, startling, a strange mix of pain and surprise, and you don't quite know why you want to cry.

Was that even real? Did he just laugh or was that in my head?

"Lucy." JP is looking at me. "What is it?"

"What?" I gape at him. "Nothing."

That was weird, like déjà vu. Like I had with smarmy Derek this evening.

"You sure?"

"Just the champagne talking. I'm good." I give him a smile to reassure him. "And yes, your charm is pretty incredible too, except when you're being a slave driver with deadlines."

His demeanor changes, his gaze softening. His hand cradles my face, his thumb tracing my jaw. "You really don't get it, do you?" he murmurs.

"Get what?"

"I want you, Lucy. Just you."

Before I can react, he reels me in for a kiss that blows every other kiss I've ever had out of the water. It's the kind of kiss that changes things, that forever shakes up your world.

And in that electrifying moment, one terrifying truth crash-lands: I've fallen. Fallen hard and fast. And there's no safety net in sight.

THIRTY

Lucy

Here we go again. The familiar scene begins to play once again. I'm little Lucy, my childhood home a backdrop, fingers itching to stroke Buddy through the faded picket fence.

Buddy's dark, clouded eyes meet mine, and a ripple of unease courses through me. Uncertainty gnaws at me: will he greet me with a wagging tail or teeth bared?

His paws rake against the ground, like he's in some unseen agony. It's an unsettling echo of reality, a déjà vu I can't quite place.

I want to reach out to him, comfort him, but I'm scared of getting hurt.

Summoning my courage, I slide my fingers through the gaps in the fence. And just like that, Buddy becomes the good boy, succumbing to my touch, and I breathe easy. He whines and leans into my strokes.

But then Buddy's playful growl morphs into something out of a Stephen King novel.

And then, bam! The bite. Pain, like slamming my fingers in a car door, only worse. I open my mouth to scream, but all that emerges is a mousey squeak.

My tears, hot and salty, race down my cheeks. I should have trusted my instinct. He lured me in and gained my trust, only to throw it back in my face.

Then, as if someone flips a switch, the nightmarish world bleeds into soothing light.

There's the chilly kiss of the AC, the silk sheets on top of me, the familiar scent of JP's mansion.

I whip my head around, following the source of a guttural noise. Matty's sprawled out, his head hanging off the edge of the bed. I can already hear his incessant whining about his stiff neck in the morning.

My heart's still going a mile a minute as I sit up, wiping damp hair from my forehead.

I'm no shrink, but it feels like my subconscious is practically shouting at me.

Swinging my legs off the bed, I pull my dream journal from the bedside drawer. I scribble down the bizarre fragments of the dream. *What the actual hell is my brain trying to tell me?*

There's definitely a hidden note in there, a message tangled up in the madness. Some buried memory trying to claw its way out. Is it about Dad's death? Or is it some deep-seated bullshit about my inner child that Libby loves yammering on about?

Would waking up wrapped in JP's arms have changed anything about this bizarre dreamscape?

Dangerous thoughts. It took all the willpower in the world to leave his bedroom in the middle of the night to come back here.

It's the final day of the hackathon, so I really need to get my act together and focus on work.

I tiptoe across the room and gently reposition Matty's head back onto his pillow. He mutters incoherently but remains dead to the world.

This dream is like a cryptic crossword puzzle that I need to solve, but it makes absolutely zero sense. Maybe it's just some silly dream and means nothing at all. And maybe, I should stop looking for meaning in everything.

When the rest of the team eventually surfaces, the caterers are laying out a breakfast spread fit for a seven-star hotel, which is likely where it came from. The spread screams luxury, and a small part of me wonders: Is this how JP starts his day, or does he only break out the silver platter when he has an audience?

Meanwhile, my neon sign has been upgraded to JUST FUCKED THE BOSS.

"God, I feel like I've been run over by a truck," Matty groans, kneading his neck. His eyes narrow at me. "Lucy, did you use my neck as a pillow last night or what?"

I roll my eyes. "Actually, I was nice enough to put your drooling face back on the bed. So, you're welcome."

His eyes narrow further. "I didn't hear you come in last night."

With a saintly smile plastered on my face, I retort, "I stayed up reading downstairs for a bit. You were in dreamland, snoring your head off when I came up."

He gives me a look that calls bullshit, but then shrugs it off and proceeds to savage a croissant.

"How was the charity event, Lucy?" Taylor probes, forcing a smile that doesn't quite reach her eyes. She's clearly still salty about me going instead of her.

Oh Lord, flashbacks of JP and me in the cloakroom come flooding back. "Oh, you know, it was fine."

Her gaze is piercing. Oh my God, does she know? I can feel my ears burning.

Coughing awkwardly, I mumble, "Um... I'm... going to run it past JP about taking some time off for my clinic session this afternoon..."

"Honestly, he's not a monster. Of course he'll let you," Taylor says as she pours herself a glass of orange juice. "For the record, I think you're handling this remarkably. I don't think I could cope with amnesia like you are."

I'm floored. "Is that a compliment, Taylor? Are you feeling sick or something?"

Her lips tighten, clearly not appreciating my jab. "Maybe if you and Matty didn't provoke me so much, you might recognize when I'm being genuine."

My eyebrows rise. "Okay. Well... thanks."

I smile at her and walk away, mind churning. Is it really such a disaster that Taylor is the boss? She's meticulous, dedicated, and not afraid to get her hands dirty. Begrudgingly, I admit she's more suited for the role than Andy.

Maybe it's my own pride getting in the way of seeing that.

I glance over at Matty, who's laughing it up with Brody and the Tonys. Sure, he's fun, but maybe he's not the best influence on me. And I can't just keep going with the flow.

For so long, we've complained about Taylor, vilified her even. But maybe the real villain here is... me?

◆ ◆ ◆

All morning, we're immersed in the grand scheme to magically make every Quinn & Wolfe casino game and amenity cashless. This alpine retreat of a hackathon is proving to be quite the productivity booster. Even Matty has declared it decidedly less wild than the standard Vegas hackathons, with a hint of disappointment, I might add.

However, my mind is a hot mess, simmering with post-coital angst after last night. I can't stop replaying all my dirty moments in my mind, but now, as typical, paranoia has set in.

All morning my emotions have been spinning like they're stuck in a high-speed blender because of the stupid unsettling dog dream and last night's X-rated encounter with JP. My reaction feels too intense for someone who isn't my boyfriend.

JP didn't promise me anything. Just because a man says he wants you doesn't mean he wants to be exclusive. Guys can say the most spectacular things to get you into bed.

I had this issue with a guy I called Bumble Brad. After five dates I assumed exclusivity. He showered me with compliments, calling me an "amazing human being."

Meanwhile, he had a whole lineup of other "amazing" human beings for each night of the week. I was just Wednesday. I promptly resigned from the Miss Wednesday position.

But who was in the wrong there, him or me? He never said we were exclusive. I never asked if he was seeing other people.

Still, I didn't use protection with JP. What the hell was I thinking? The truth is, in the moment it just felt so intimate. So natural. I got caught up in how he made me feel.

"Get it together, you floozy," I mutter, dropping into my chair and adjusting the angle of my laptop screen. I massage my temples and take a deep breath to regain my sanity before hitting the call button.

The smiling digital face of Dr. Ramirez pops up on my screen. "Lucy, how are you doing today?"

"Honestly? I'm a bit of a mess," I admit, surrendering to a weary sigh. I slump back in my chair, fingers weaving through my hair. "Just another day in the life, I guess."

"Healing isn't a linear process. Don't be too harsh on yourself if progress seems slower than you'd like," she advises, her gaze carefully scrutinizing me. "What's troubling you today?"

I dive right in, gushing about my insane dream about the Jekyll and Hyde dog.

She takes a moment to chew on my dream saga. "Well, dreams can be quite mysterious," she muses, smiling at me. "Like an unsolved Rubik's Cube."

I squint back at her through the screen. A Rubik's Cube? Could she conjure up something a bit less metaphorical and a bit more helpful?

"Dreams," she continues, "often offer a glimpse into our subconscious, shedding light on worries or fears that we might not realize we're carrying."

"But what could the dog possibly signify?" I ask, frustration coloring my voice. "And more importantly, what am I supposed to do with it?"

"Perhaps the aggressive behavior of Buddy signifies a fear or anxiety you're currently wrestling with. It could represent an impending threat or stressor in your life against which you feel powerless."

"Could be anything then." I sigh, sinking further into my chair. "My apartment not selling for one."

"Let's simplify this," she says with an encouraging smile. "Tell me about the dream again, but explain it like you're talking to a nine-year-old kid."

"Buddy was a good dog one minute, a terrifying beast the next. And I didn't see it coming."

She nods. "This could be your mind's way of preparing you for something difficult you've been avoiding."

I bite my lip. "That's a bit unsettling, doc."

"Sometimes we have to confront the possibility of pain or stress that we've been avoiding. Our discussions, the strategies we are working on, are all aimed at making you stronger, more resilient. And they're preparing you to confront any distressing or traumatic experiences that may surface."

I shrug, feeling overwhelmed. "That's all well and good, doc, but I'm not sure what I'm supposed to do with that knowledge."

"I believe that once we initiate your hypnotherapy sessions, things will start to get clearer."

I release a long, heavy sigh.

Switching gears, she asks, "So Lucy, what else has been happening this week? The last time we spoke, you were prepping for a trip to Bear Mountain. Judging from that breathtaking view behind you, it looks like you're there."

"Yep. It really is spectacular here. So calm and peaceful. I'm just up to my neck in work." I feel my cheeks redden.

"Is there anything specific you'd like to share?"

I fucked the boss.

"No! Nothing."

"It helps to let it all out. And remember, what happens in therapy, stays in therapy."

God, it really is written all over my face. Do I have some jizz on it or something?

"Actually, I did something a bit reckless." I pause. "I had a moment with the boss." I clear my throat pointedly to indicate precisely what kind of moment we're talking about.

She nods slowly, contemplating this new information. She doesn't seem shocked. Should that offend me?

"How do you feel about him?"

I swallow hard. "I'm terrified. Terrified of getting hurt by someone like him."

"Have you shared your concerns with him? Have you discussed where you both stand?"

I shake my head vehemently. "No, absolutely not. It was just a one-time thing."

"Has anything similar happened before?"

"What? No! Absolutely not."

Except... I wouldn't remember if it had, would I?

I stare at Dr. Ramirez, a shiver of panic slithering down my spine. What if this wasn't the first time? What if something happened with JP before that I don't remember?

I hastily swat away the disturbing thought. That's ridiculous. Why wouldn't he tell me? No, this is a convenience thing for him, I'm right-place, right-time woman. The way JP acted in the elevator when I returned to work told me everything I needed to know.

And he has no reason to lie to me.

Right?

JP

Things are finally falling into place.

We've got solid results from the hackathon, a robust blueprint to transform the remaining casino amenities cashless.

I go through the data from the market research reports for the first wellness retreat. We're keeping it quiet until I can prove I can make it a success. The data confirms there's a market out there, I just have to execute it properly. I'm reviewing details with Killian and Connor later—another step toward my Vegas exit plan.

And then there's Lucy. She leaves Bear Mountain today, but she's let me back into her life. For the first time since her accident—hell, since our bitter breakup—I can taste the sweetness of happiness again.

I know I'm playing with fire by keeping our past from her. The deception eats at me, but I shove it aside. I tell myself this is for Lucy's benefit while she recovers. But if I'm honest, it's just as much for me. I miss her so damn much. I'll do anything to keep her close, even if it means lying to her.

I'm well aware I'm treading on dangerous ground. I've deliberately turned a blind eye to the colossal elephant in the room—our shared past that she doesn't remember. But eventually, the day will come when she uncovers our buried history and I'll have some serious explaining to do.

It's a risky gamble, getting involved again without coming clean. Lucy trusts me enough to open up and be vulnerable, and I'm deceiving her.

But I can't think about that now.

THIRTY-ONE

Lucy

I'm plunger-deep in Spider's toilet clog from hell; what a way to spend a Saturday afternoon. Since leaving Bear Mountain yesterday, I've been questioning if last week with JP was real or some kinky sex dream cooked up by my messed-up, amnesia-tortured mind.

If it was just a dream, then I'm all for it. It beats the recurring one I had again last night with Buddy the dog.

That's the end of that. Let's be honest. It was a temporary escape from reality, like when I indulged in that Daredevil roleplay at the comic convention.

Because the cold, hard truth is I'm a 27-year-old introverted graphic designer who, in some insane twist of fate, wound up in bed with her billionaire boss.

Now, back under the cold, judgmental glare

of my less-than-luxurious apartment, paranoia has dug its claws into me, flourishing in my insecurities.

What happens if word gets out that I had a fling with JP? I can't handle that kind of scandal.

I want to tell the girls so badly, but can I trust Libby with something like this? She's always begging for gossip about Wolfe and the Quinn brothers, and until last week I was a useless source on that. But now?

Now I know the size of his monster dick.

And I know if I told her that she couldn't tell anyone, she would have the best intentions not to gossip, but it might slip to a colleague when she's on one of their raucous team nights out. Not in a malicious way, she just doesn't remember what she's not allowed to tell when she's drunk. Drunk mouths speak sober thoughts, and all that.

I've been out with those media sharks before, tagging along with Libby, and those guys could get secrets out of a stone.

The jarring ringtone of my phone echoes through the tiny-ass bathroom, cutting into my downward spiral of thoughts.

I give the plunger a last shove with both hands and the blockage finally clears. Typical Spider.

Washing my hands, I grab my phone from

beside the sink before it rings off. The screen reads "Real Estate Jackass Dave."

"Hey, Dave. Any updates?" I ask, struggling not to sound desperate.

"Got something for you, Miss Walsh," he bellows over the line.

Don't get excited. He's probably trying to sell you a timeshare in a Florida swamp.

"Somebody's made an offer for your apartment. Full asking price."

I stare at the plunger in disbelief. "You're shitting me."

His laughter crackles over the line, nearly as incredulous as I feel. "Hand on heart, Miss Walsh. It's some company that wants it. I'll shoot you the details in an email."

Pulse thundering, I force out, "So, what's the catch?"

"Legit offer. They're ready to pay cash and wrap up the deal pronto."

Dear God, don't toy with me like this. I can't handle the crash after this high.

I sink down onto the closed lid of the toilet seat, my whole body trembling. "Are you sure this isn't a scam? How can I trust that this is for real?"

"They're a reputable investment company. Based in the Caymans."

"But why? Why do they want my apartment?"

Is it JP? No, that's an insane thought. One doesn't just sleep with someone and then buy their property.

Although, he is a billionaire.

Dave brushes it off. "Well, you know the drill. Real estate is usually a safe bet. They're probably expanding their portfolio."

Meaning he's got no fucking clue.

His sigh drifts through the phone. "Do you want the damn offer or not, sweetheart?"

"Yes! Yes!" I can barely get the words out. I just don't want them to change their minds. "Have they actually seen the apartment?"

"Doesn't matter. If they're stupid or rich enough to buy it without seeing it, we accept it."

I slam the end call button and burst out of the bathroom with a primal scream that wouldn't be out of place in Jurassic Park.

I break into a victory dance around the living room, all flailing limbs.

Spider pokes his head out of his room. "What's the party for?" he asks, deciding to join my dance despite the confusion, nearly taking out the coffee table.

In a fit of sheer exuberance, I find myself lunging at him, wrapping my arms around his neck.

"What's the party for?" he repeats, sounding somewhat muffled from my embrace.

"The place is sold!"

"What?"

I freeze. "Sorry, Spider. I'm selling the apartment."

"You sold... wait, WHAT?"

The penny drops and his face crumples. "Ah, shit," he hisses, storming back to his room.

Half an hour later, I'm still blinking at Dave's email, my eyes darting over the zeros again and again like some paranoid accountant. No matter how many times I read it, it still says full asking price.

I've already tried, and failed, to cyber-stalk this mysterious company intending to purchase my apartment for no good reason. Now all that's left to do is pray to the gods of real estate that this deal goes through quickly and without any snags.

Because with all the recent madness swarming around my life, it feels as though I'm a mere puppet in the hands of some higher power orchestrating my good days and bad ones for their own shits and giggles.

My phone springs to life, an unknown number setting my heart pounding against my ribs.

Because I already know who it is. Women's intuition.

"Lucy." JP's voice seeps like aural Viagra down the phone.

"H-hi," I squeak, realizing too late that I sound more like a schoolgirl than a woman of the world. I cough delicately, hoping to scrape together some scrap of sultry sophistication.

"I'm curious to know what you're up to."

I'd been knee-deep in bathroom grime; a task I'd abandoned midway when Dave called. But that's not exactly sexy banter material.

"Just unwinding a bit," I lie smoothly, getting to my feet to pace the kitchen. "What about you?"

"Thinking about you."

Oh, sweet mother of all... My pulse stutters, then picks up speed like an out-of-control vibrator. Pull yourself together, woman. Surely, you can manage some semblance of flirtation?

"I'd expect a billionaire casino mogul to have better things to do on Saturday," I quip playfully.

"Not this one."

"You might want to consider taking up a hobby. Knitting or something."

He chuckles huskily. "No need. I already know what I enjoy," he drawls, the hint of sexual undertones enough to stir my ovaries into a frenzy.

Silence hangs between us for a beat too long because my flirt game stinks.

I let out a snort that was supposed to be a sexy sound.

"I want to see you," he says, having the good manners to ignore my snort. "I'd like to take you out tonight. Or rather, I want to bring you in."

I stop pacing to lean against the wall. Holy shit, he's asking me on a date.

"I don't understand."

"Allow me the pleasure of cooking for you."

"You cook?"

"You sound shocked. I assure you; I have a few tricks up my culinary sleeve."

A flicker of caution flutters in my stomach. *Don't get excited*, it whispers. *An emotional attachment could be a slippery slope.*

"Lucy," he draws out my name like a dirty sexy promise. "Did I lose you?"

"N-no," I stutter, suddenly breathless.

"And?"

"And..." *And you're all I thought about last night, but I don't know what this is or where I stand and I'm too chicken-shit to ask, and I'm absolutely terrified of getting hurt.* "I don't know."

"What don't you know?"

"You must have more enticing options for a Saturday night than playing chef for me?"

"What kind of question is that? No, Lucy. Absolutely not."

"Okay," I whisper, my voice barely audible over the pounding of my heart. What the hell am I doing? But how does any sane woman refuse an invitation like that?

"Okay, I can expect you tonight?"

"Suppose I can pencil you in," I quip, finally finding my voice.

He lets out a low laugh again. "Good girl," he purrs, a single phrase that has me sliding slowly down the wall. "I'll send a car for you at seven. I'm looking forward to it."

The line goes dead, the arrogant bastard disconnecting before I can utter another word. Just as well. My tongue has apparently swallowed itself.

I slide the rest of the way down the wall, landing in a heap on my ass.

THIRTY-TWO

Lucy

How do you dress for a night in with a billionaire?

No clue. As it's apparently a home-cooked meal, I suspect he'd prefer something more *Girl next door* than *Dominatrix mistress*. So I spend the next few hours crafting an outfit that says "I'm chill but also up for anything, maybe even anal."

Right on cue, a car sent by JP arrives to whisk me away.

Nerves humming like a live wire, I tap lightly on his apartment door.

The door swings open, and I'm suddenly grappling with the urge to either dissolve into a puddle at his feet or race back to the elevator.

Tonight, he's dressed down in black sweatpants and a simple gray T-shirt, his feet tantalizingly bare.

That panty-dropping grin makes me shiver. In the six years of working at Quinn & Wolfe, I've never seen the man crack a smile. Now it's directed at me, dark and hungry.

My heart's a mess.

Do not overthink this.

"Hey," I say.

"Hey, yourself. You're stunning," he drawls, a hint of a growl underlying his words. His gaze languidly appraises my ensemble—a blue dress designed with a theme of "boho sexy casual chic" in mind—leaving me feeling utterly exposed.

I'm blushing, and barely through his front door.

Little does he know what's under this innocent frock. I might be dressed for a casual dinner, but underneath, it's all Agent Provocateur. I am plucked, preened, primped, and primed for whatever's to come. So hairless that my clit is rubbing against my underwear, raring to go.

He opens the door wider to let me in, but just as I'm about to slip past him, his hand lightly skims over my hip, halting my steps. Electricity zings up my spine from his touch.

"You're forgetting something."

My mind spins, then it hits me. Mortified, I slap a hand over my mouth. "I'm such a disgrace of a guest. I didn't bring any wine! Just because you're a billionaire doesn't mean I should abandon my manners." How embarrassing.

"No, darling, not that." A deep chuckle rumbles in his chest. "This."

Then, faster than my poor brain can compute, he yanks me into his steely embrace, landing a kiss on my lips so possessive, it robs me of breath. Oh, Jesus. We're getting down to the dirty already.

The man's kisses are lethal. My knees buckle under the onslaught of sensations but he holds me up effortlessly.

"Mmm, I've been wanting to do that all damn day," he murmurs against my lips.

"Hmmm," I manage back. I really need to brush up on my sexy talk. Maybe even enroll in a course.

Luckily, he doesn't seem that put off. His arousal presses against me through his sweatpants.

He groans into my mouth, hands roving over my backside with an urgency that would make even Christian Grey blush. "I should be a gentleman. Wine and dine you first." He winks, eyes glinting with mischief. "But just so you know, I plan to do a lot more of that later."

A thrill races through me as I imagine those plans in vivid detail. "I'm always up for skipping straight to dessert," I rasp.

"Patience, sweetheart." He chuckles, the sound reverberating through my entire body.

He releases me from his embrace and takes my hand, leading me through the hallway.

I tail his glorious ass into the giant kitchen/dining room combo. The place looks like it could be on the cover of *Billionaire Monthly*, all sleek lines and minimalism.

My eyes are drawn to the dining table, decorated with an amazing centerpiece of flowers.

"Did you do all this?" I stutter.

He gives a nonchalant shrug and a coy grin as he saunters over. "I'm not completely inept, Lucy. I know how to set a table."

"But it looks like you've put in so much effort." My palms are a hot and sweaty mess. Suddenly, the reality of JP going all out for me has me brimming with terror. And I didn't even think to bring a bottle of wine. Idiot.

He shrugs again, bracing his hands on the counter, caging me in. "It's just dinner."

Just dinner. As if anyone's ever put this much effort into feeding me. The cost of these flowers alone probably tops my monthly bills.

I let out a sound, hoping it sounds like "I need to have all your babies."

With that, he saunters off casually toward the

bar area, pours a small glass of wine—which is quickly becoming my favorite—and slides it over to me.

When he opens the oven, my eyes nearly pop out. He actually cooked.

"Fifteen more minutes," he says, a hint of a smile tugging at the corners of his mouth. "You like lobster tail and king crab?"

"Are you serious?" I peer into the oven, mouth watering at the smells. Take notes, Ramsay. "I've never tried lobster tail, but it looks freaking amazing."

"I have a feeling you'll love it."

Well, one can't deny the man's confidence. "Actually, I've got a deadly allergy to shellfish. Puff up like a balloon."

He quirks a brow.

"Kidding. I'm seriously impressed. Honestly, I didn't think you'd be able to cook. Why would you bother? You could easily hire someone to do it all."

He smiles, cracking open a beer. "Yes, but then I wouldn't be cooking for you."

I titter like a schoolgirl as he winks. Christ, get a hold of yourself.

"Don't worry," he says. "I've done this a few times. I won't be serving you up a plate of salmonella."

"Great. Amnesia's a handful as is."

He laughs. I like making him laugh.

Trying to play it cool, I take a sip of my wine and wander over to the giant wall of windows, peering down at the little ants of traffic below. No TV in here, not that he'd need one with this.

A telescope catches my eye. "Ooh, you've got a telescope! Mind if I have a peek?"

"Be my guest."

He steps up behind me, adjusting the telescope to my eye level, his chest sturdy against my back. "How's this angle?" he whispers, breath tickling on my neck.

Just right.

I eagerly put my eye to the lens, gasping at the details. My God, I can see everything. The intricacies of a couple lost in a passionate embrace in Central Park, the vibrant rush of shoppers bustling down the street, the everyday drama of people hailing cabs.

The world unfolds before me in vivid technicolor.

I tilt the scope north. "You can see all the way to Washington Heights from here! I can almost see my street!"

"That's right, you can." His lips blaze a path down my neck, sparking shivers that pool heat between my thighs.

"Hey." His breath falters as I grind back against him, desire pulsing in my veins. "You comfortable here with me? In my apartment?"

"Should I be worried?" I quip, my voice humming with veiled arousal. "You're not planning on going all *American Psycho* on me?"

His growl vibrates through my body, raking goose bumps across my skin. "No deflecting, Lucy. I'm asking how you really feel."

Jeez, the guy is intense.

My nails dig into the smooth wood of the telescope. Comfortable? Hardly. I feel off-kilter and nervous in the best way. And there's a healthy dash of fear of having my heart pulverized, plus a generous dollop of self-doubt stirred into this mix.

"The truth?" I lick my lips, catching his gaze in the reflection. "I'm not all the way there yet. I'd love to pull off a confident femme fatale vibe, but let's be real, you still kind of intimidate me."

He doesn't back away. His lips blaze a trail of fiery kisses down my neck, while his hands firmly hold onto my hips. "How can I help you relax?" he murmurs.

Thinking straight with those lips on my skin is challenging.

"This is my own problem," I confess,

vulnerability seeping into my voice. "But it's normal, right? I mean, you're this billionaire bossman, and I'm... doing okay. Have a job I like, my own place at this age, despite the crazy roommate and the unfortunate proximity to a brothel. Not on meth. I'm hanging in there. What I don't get is why you, out of everyone, would be interested."

"Aside from your obvious beauty and charm?" His palms slide higher, brushing the underside of my breasts. "You're refreshingly genuine, Lucy. You're real. You bring humor and light into my life without even trying."

There's a spike in my pulse but I try to laugh it off. "Well, now I feel the pressure to be on my A-game."

His eyes soften. "Just be yourself. That's all I want."

That, right there, is the sexiest thing a man has ever said to me. I stare at our reflection, my back arched into his solid body, and swallow hard.

Oh. We're ready for lift-off, Captain.

Need builds hot and insistent, screaming for release. I'm not sure I'll make it to the main course at this rate.

My eyes flicker to his lips in the reflection, wondering if they taste as good as his dinner. Only one way to find out.

I turn in his arms, fisting my hands in his shirt, and yank him down for a taste.

His mouth claims mine, hot and demanding, in a clash of lips and tongues that sets my senses ablaze.

The telescope forgotten, he walks me backward toward the table, thankfully not the part set for dinner.

"What are you—" My query dies as his strong hands grip my hips, hoisting me onto the table in one smooth move and pushing me down.

I gasp, the show of sexy caveman behavior making my downstairs clench.

His hand on my belly holds me in place. The sexiest restraint I've ever known.

My thighs spread instinctively, heels hooking around his waist to draw him closer.

Still not close enough.

I stare up at him, pulse hammering as his eyes rake over me. He looks ready to devour me whole.

Please do.

In one swift motion, he rips off his shirt, exposing his sculpted, lickable chest. His sweatpants and underwear are discarded on the floor until it's just him in his sexy naked glory, thick erection proudly pointing toward the sky.

The sight of him in all his manliness, hard in all the right places, lights me up like a life-sized erotic game of Operation.

"See what you do to me?" he rumbles, looking down at me with an intense gaze. "I can't wait until after dinner."

Then one hand is back on my stomach, bunching up the fabric of my dress, and the other fists his throbbing cock, roughly stroking up and down. My eyes can't decide between his face and his busy hand.

"We don't have to wait." My voice comes out raspy and low.

"You want this?" he taunts, smirking down at me.

"Is that a rhetorical question?"

"For your sassiness, sweetheart," he growls as his hand slides up my thigh. "You're going to get fucked really hard now."

Oh, boy.

My breath grows shallow as he slides my panties down my legs with excruciating slowness.

His hands wrap firmly around my thighs, dragging me toward the edge of the table. I let my eyes drift shut as he lines his cock up with my entrance. With a deep thrust, he buries himself inside me, sending shudders through both our bodies.

"Look at me," he says roughly.

I force my eyes open to meet his gaze as he slides inside of me fully again with one smooth motion. It feels... incredible.

He holds back for a second, giving my body time to adjust to him. He takes his time sliding out, until just the head of him is left inside me, and then slams back in again.

His hands grip my hips firmly as he takes control, thrusting in and out of me. I've never been fucked on a table before.

And I'm gone. Everything fades away—nothing matters except the sensation intensifying within me, making it hard to breathe.

I meet his gaze and it's wild, dark, hungry, demanding. He looks like a barbarian; grunting and pounding into me with no apology or remorse. And it's hot, so hot that I can barely breathe.

He moans my name, head thrown back, as he comes deep inside me.

Hearing my name on his lips sends me over the edge. Then I'm there, seeing stars behind my eyes as violent waves of pleasure take hold of me.

Nearly an hour in, he's proven he can whip up a mean seafood dinner.

When he asks about my day, I tell him about the bargain-bin shower curtains I bought for my apartment and my good news on the sale. In return, he talks about buying a hundred acres of land just outside New York for his first wellness retreat.

It's not really an even keel.

I have to admit, he's outdone himself with the dish.

"Look at you, Mr. Multitalented. Billionaire businessman, culinary king, and bedroom barbarian. That's one for the tombstone. Am I the luckiest girl or what?" I say, struggling to appear ladylike while ripping the lobster to shreds with my bare hands.

He smirks at me. "You should be a poet."

"I was quite proud of that alliteration."

"Care to explain the barbarian part?"

"All women secretly want a barbarian in bed. A guy who lets his primal needs take over in the bedroom. If we were in the prehistoric era, I'd be out doing prehistoric women stuff like foraging for berries; you'd see me in the field and just rip my loin cloth off right there in the middle of the grass.

And it would be hot and gross at the same time, since there was no toothpaste yet."

He quirks a brow. "So after all these years I finally find out what women want, huh?" His eyes gleam with amusement. "I'm happy to act out your fantasy anytime you want in Central Park."

"I can see the headlines now: Billionaire Business Mogul JP Wolfe Caught Humping Memoryless Woman on the Grass."

Something flashes in his eyes at that, like my comment struck a nerve. *Has* JP been caught humping someone in Central Park?

But then he smiles. "Maybe we'll just keep it away from prying eyes."

I try to spear a plump lobster chunk with my fork, but it slips out and skitters across my plate. "Slippery little devils," I mutter.

He watches me with amusement, lips curved in a smirk as I battle the defiant seafood.

"So," JP says, "have you thought about where you might move after the sale on your apartment closes?"

I nod, swallowing a bite of lobster.

"I plan to stay local, maybe find a quieter street," I respond, feeling a wave of relief wash over me. "Selling the apartment feels like a huge burden lifted. As much as I loved that apartment, ever since the sex shop slash brothel popped up downstairs, it's been a nonstop nightmare."

I feel my cheeks flush and I look down. "You must think I'm so silly."

"Lucy, I'd never think that way. Hell, in my twenties, I was just scraping by, climbing out of bankruptcy and getting out of a trainwreck of a marriage.

"Do you mind me asking what happened with your divorce? Or is that overstepping?"

"Not at all," he says, nonchalant. "She wasn't the right woman for me. We met young, around twenty. When times were good, we were good. When times got tough, she didn't want to stick around. Bankruptcy hit, and she left a few months later."

"Wow. I'm sorry."

"Don't be. It was a wake-up call I needed."

"Have you had any other serious relationships since?" I ask, nerves knotting my stomach.

He drags out a tortuous pause. "Not really."

My heart hammers in my chest, and I quickly take a sip of my drink.

"Is it that you don't want to be in a relationship?" I venture, feeling like I'm standing on a ledge. It's like I'm about to play Russian Roulette with my heart here.

His gaze intensifies, making me shift uncomfortably. "Quite the opposite, Lucy. But only with the right person."

His declaration charges the air, like a loose live wire. I seize my glass once more, my brain scrambling for some kind of response.

Pick me! my heart shrieks.

Ask him. Get him to lay out the blueprint for his perfect gal. Have him sketch a detailed portrait.

He clears his throat, shifting uneasily. "I haven't always been the kind of guy you could bring home to mom. I've made some poor decisions." His voice deepens, roughens. "Got caught up in the Vegas lifestyle, forgot what mattered." A grimace crosses his face, as if the admission is a physical blow. "But that's all in my past."

His words settle heavy in the silence. It's not exactly reassuring. I can only imagine the implications of the "Vegas lifestyle." Just what is he confessing to? Infidelity? Hookers? Sex parties? Criminal activities? Just how bad is it?

I swallow, my fingers tapping against the glass. "But you've changed now?"

"I won't pretend to be an angel." His gaze meets mine, unwavering. "I still have rough edges, but I've learned. I'm not the same man, not because my world changed, but because I did."

I wet my parched lips, unease creeping in. "Could you fall back? Into old habits?"

His eyes darken. "I've worked too hard to become the man I am now," he asserts, "Nothing and no one will derail that."

I smile back at him, but a shiver runs through me. I came here hoping to know him better, but his words sound more like a warning to stay away.

THIRTY-THREE

JP

Ecstasy and torment. I'm no stranger to the dichotomy. The highs that made me feel alive always came with gut-wrenching lows. Every taboo pleasure, every sinful indulgence was laid out before me like a feast, and I gorged myself. Yet, the more I indulged, the hollower I felt.

Now, I find those very feelings watching Lucy's gentle breathing, her chest rising and falling. The contours of her cheekbone under my finger, the sighs that ghost past her full lips—it's a fucking tableau.

Her eyes flutter with dreams I wish I could peek into. I could spend a lifetime watching her sleep, and wouldn't trade a second of it.

My love for her crept up on me. Unplanned. The unwanted proximity with her team led me to appreciate this quirky girl with her self-deprecating wit and down-to-earth modesty.

It was merely physical at first, no emotional attachment. I never sought any sort of sentimental connection.

Yet, as the saying goes, familiarity breeds fondness, and soon I found myself hopelessly hooked.

Now, I'm tangled in a complex web of half-truths and hidden facts. Not outright lies, but a calculated evasion of the whole truth. A nagging guilt persistently gnaws at me, posing the inevitable question: Would she be sharing my bed if the accident hadn't robbed her of her memory?

I got what I wished for—Lucy, back in my life, back in my bed. Trusting me. The doctors suggested reintroducing myself slowly, letting her hidden memories emerge on their own.

But damn, it feels like I'm handling a live grenade with the pin already pulled. Every decision is like skirting around a potential explosion. I hinted at my past, but conveniently left out the part where she was caught up in my personal mess.

Should I come clean now and brace for the fallout? With each moment we share, I can feel the impending disaster drawing near—the unavoidable day of reckoning. I'm terrified that when her memory comes back, she won't forgive me. Terrified of the possibility that she'll be gone forever.

A tiny whimper breaks my train of thought. Her eyes fly open, lingering dreams clouding them. She looks up at me, breath catching.

"Morning," I say, keeping my tone light, hoping to set her at ease.

"Morning." Her smile falters.

"Everything okay? You're not having second thoughts about staying over, are you?"

"No, no. Just... More strange dreams. Since the accident. They're coming every night now."

My stomach knots. "About what?"

She hesitates. "It's silly."

"Lucy." I tilt her chin up until our eyes lock, my tone gently insistent. "I want to know."

"It's too bizarre to even describe. There was this dog on my street called Buddy when I was a kid. I used to play with him, but one day he went crazy and got taken away. I don't know why. Now I'm dreaming about him turning into this evil dog and attacking me. I think it's my subconscious trying to deal with something. Or just fuck with me. I can't decide."

A self-conscious laugh escapes her. I try to keep my expression neutral. Christ, has her subconscious turned me into a rabid dog?

"Lucy." I rise, propping myself on my elbows to level our gazes. "I need you to know something. If you're ever scared, upset, or need someone, I'm here for you. You can come to me in tears or in a panic, doesn't matter the hour. Any time of day or night, I'm here."

She gives me a tentative smile. "Even if it's a dream about a dog?"

"Even if it's a dream about a possessed teddy bear. I don't care what it is."

My heart pounds as I look down at her lying next to me, her hair splayed across the pillow. This is my chance. She's in my bed, vulnerable and trusting.

I need to tell her the truth. To own up to my past. I'm striving to become a better man, someone worthy of her.

But the memory of her anger, the sharp words she hurled at me on the stairs of the Plaza Hotel, holds me back.

I lean in, pressing a kiss against her lips, but the usual assurance is gone. I'm unsteady, unsettled. I need more time.

"I've just realized something," she says, her fingers tracing abstract patterns on my chest. "I never asked you what JP stands for. John Paul, right?"

"That's right."

She smirks up at me. "Like the Pope?"

"Not exactly." I chuckle, moving hair from her face. "My grandfather was named Juan. It's a nod to him."

"Ooh, Spanish?" Her eyes glint with interest.

"Yes, indeed."

"Can you speak Spanish?"

"I can," I affirm, my thumb gently tracing her bottom lip, prompting her to part her lips ever so slightly.

"Say something for me then," she breathes.

I draw closer, my chest against hers, and murmur in her ear, "*Quiero pasar el resto de mi vida contigo.*"

"Wow. That was hot. What does it mean?"

"It means I want to spend the day with you," I murmur. In actuality, it means *I want to spend the rest of my life with you.*

She grins.

"So," I ask. "What do you say?"

She squirms under me. "I can't. I have a therapy session this afternoon."

I nod. "Okay. That's important. But let me at least make you breakfast first."

"Oh, my God. Dinner and breakfast? This is a great deal. What will you do for the rest of the day?"

Try not to lose my sanity worrying about what you might unearth in your session. "I'll go for a jog. Maybe a swim. Try to clear my head. But I'd like to pick you up from your therapy session. Bring you back to your place, or here, ideally."

"You don't have to… but it'd be nice to see you. You've been warned though, my therapist said this one could get pretty intense. You might walk in on me clucking like a chicken."

I force a smile despite the growing unease. Will this be the session that unravels everything? "I'll take my chances. Maybe I'll learn your 'safe' word in case you start trying to peck at me."

I cup her face, holding her gaze. "Are you worried about your session today?"

"No, why would I be worried about digging into the dark recesses of my psyche?" Her laugh is strained. "What could possibly go wrong?"

A million things, and not a damn one I can control. "Come on, Lucy. Open up to me."

"Yes." She sighs. "I'm terrified."

"That's why I'll be waiting outside the clinic."

And when she smiles at me like I'm the most important man in the world, I know it's going to be okay.

I just need a little more time.

THIRTY-FOUR

Lucy

Finally, life seems to be getting itself into order. True to his word, JP was waiting outside the clinic for me last Sunday. Since then, I've had two more mind-blowing nights with him at his penthouse apartment, survived two rounds of hypnotherapy, and those weird dreams about demon dog appear to be subsiding.

Date number one: Rewind to last Sunday. JP swoops me up post-therapy session—still no memories—then we went back to his place for a swim. The pool was more *I seem to have misplaced my yacht here* rather than *Oh look, I have a pool*. Then we went up to his penthouse and chilled out with a movie and takeout. Not exactly the fantasy date with a billionaire I imagined, but honestly, I loved it. Then he showed me his "downward dog" which involved me on all fours, so that was a nice surprise.

Date Two this week was like something you'd do after dating for months—basic but amazing. We strolled around Central Park, popped into my favorite comic shop, and grabbed hot dogs from a street cart. Then back to his for an advanced yoga session, namaste.

He wore a baseball cap out so people wouldn't recognize him, which I found stupidly hot. When he crept up behind me while I was reading a latest edition comic and gave me a gentle spoon and kissed my shoulder, it was the most romantic moment of my life, to date, on earth.

I know it's not equal—I'm going to his place all the time—but who's the winner there? If I brought him back to my apartment, I'd be scared of what surprises Spider might leave in the bathroom.

Work's been good too—we've made good progress on Project Tangra and I've managed to survive meetings with JP without screaming I'M FUCKING THE BOSS.

It's a beautiful Saturday morning in New York and Spider is moving out today, so I get my living space back until the apartment sale goes through. Freedom at last.

I've been scrolling through house porn on the internet all morning, but this time, I'll be vigorous in my checks.

I'm diving headfirst into what I like to call "therapy cleaning." There's something strangely calming about scrubbing away your problems, one dirty dish at a time.

Spider wanders into the kitchen area with a backpack and a guitar.

"Hey," I greet him, guilt seeping into my voice. I drop the sponge in the sink. "Sorry about this. Where will you go?"

"Nah, don't worry, it's for the best. I actually found some digs on Fifth Avenue. For free, no less." He grins, stuffing the last of his belongings into his bag.

I stare at him, mouth hanging open. "Seriously?"

"Some cool squatters are living there."

I shake my head. Wow. Well, to each their own. "Is that all you have?" I ask, nodding to his pitifully scant backpack.

He shrugs. "I travel light."

"Well, good luck then," I say. "Sure I'll see you around."

We clasp each other in the world's most awkward hug, then he heads for the door, slinging his guitar over his shoulder. The door clicks shut behind him and he's gone. Just like that. My toilet-clogging saucepan-abusing roommate is a past memory.

I let out the breath I've been holding since Spider moved in. No more overhearing his late-night rendezvous through the walls. No more strange smells wafting from the bathroom. No more digging his hardened food out of my Le Creuset. Just sweet freedom.

I flop onto the couch, enjoying the quiet, when my phone buzzes.

"Lucy," JP's husky baritone drawls, doing unspeakable things to my insides. "I have a surprise for you."

Instinctively, I pull my knees up to my chest, hugging them.

"A surprise?" I reply, feigning nonchalance while my insides twist into pretzels of curiosity and lust.

His chuckle is low and warm. "How do you feel about comic conventions?"

A startled laugh escapes me. "You're joking!"

Another chuckle, this one raising goose bumps on my skin. "We're heading to a comic convention in Boston. I got us tickets."

My mouth opens and closes like a goldfish. The word *No* stumbles out, even though I mean yes.

JP Wolfe, hot billionaire enigma, is taking me to a comic convention? "I... I hadn't pegged you as a comic enthusiast."

"I'm not. But you are. And I might even let you go all Miss Nova on me."

A grin spreads across my face. "Funny you should say that. I found a costume among my things from before I lost my memory, and it's quite something."

"That's a sight reserved for my eyes only, then," he shoots back, his tone dipping lower, darker, evoking images of him peeling that costume off me inch by inch.

"It's next week, right?"

"That's right. I can fly us there and back in a day, or we can stay overnight, whatever you prefer."

I suck in a breath. "I can't believe you're willing to go. Either way works for me."

"Then it's a date," he rumbles. "We'll make a night of it in Boston."

"Thank you so much," I say, feeling a lump forming in my throat. "This is awesome. Those tickets sell out really quickly. I haven't been to that one in years."

He chuckles, a low sound that warms me. "Well, you can repay me by coming upstate. I want to show you the site for the new wellness center, near Bear Mountain. We can stay at my place."

"I'd love that," I breathe, butterflies taking flight in my core. "So what are you up to tonight?" I ask. "If you're at a loose end, we could hang out. You know, only if you're not swamped with CEO-y stuff."

"I have some admin to attend to."

Disappointment sinks into me. "Oh, okay, no worries."

There's a brief pause before he speaks again. "Can I see you tomorrow night?"

My thighs clench involuntarily. "Yeah, tomorrow's good."

Lady-wank it is tonight, then.

"But I'll miss you tonight," he drawls in a deep voice. If the man ever goes bankrupt again, he'll make his billions back selling steamy audiobooks.

"You will?" I ask, my voice hitching.

"You have no idea. I gotta go, Lucy. See you."

My teeth catch my lower lip as a mixture of excitement and apprehension swirls inside me. I've been careful not to label anything between us, especially after our conversation where he hinted at being less than perfect in relationships. But this is skirting perilously close to boyfriend territory.

I grab my keys and head to Central Park to meet Priya, feeling like I might spontaneously combust if I don't unload onto someone soon.

"OK," I say as we meander through the park. "I have a confession, but you have to swear on your life not to breathe a word of this to Libby."

She looks curious. "Spit it out."

I tuck a loose strand of hair behind my ear, stalling. "I may have started seeing someone."

"What?" Priya exclaims loudly, clapping a hand over her mouth as a jogger shoots us a look. She grabs my arm. "Who?"

I lean in close like we're making some sketchy back-alley deal and whisper, "JP Wolfe."

She stares at me. The look on her face is hilarious and insulting all at once.

"JP fucking *Wolfe*?!" she yells. "Are you kidding me?"

"It just happened, in Bear Mountain. Don't lecture me, I know how stupid it is."

"Well damn." Priya holds up her hotdog in defense. "No judgment, just... damn."

"And please, Libby can't know because her vulture of a magazine will totally include it. I can just see the headline: Wolfe Slumming It With Regular Chick."

"So have you…?"

"Yes." I blush, unusually embarrassed. "And it's pretty hot."

Priya smirks, eyebrows raised. "Pretty hot?"

"Mind-blowing. Life-changing. Ruined me for other men. That better?"

Priya grins, clearly enjoying my discomfort. "I never thought you had it in you. A secret fling with JP Wolfe, this is the juiciest gossip I've heard in ages."

"And there's the problem." I sigh, fiddling with the sleeve of my coat. "I think I'm actually falling for the bastard. He even cooked me dinner last weekend."

"Wait, the guy cooked for you?" She blinks in surprise.

"Last Saturday night. I fibbed; I didn't go see the new *Spiderman*. I was with JP, having the night of my life."

The smile slips from Priya's face and she's quiet for a moment. "Please, be cautious around Wolfe."

I sigh, poking at the remains of my hot dog bun. "I get it."

Priya shakes her head, her dark eyes serious. "No, you really don't. There's… potentially some legal stuff going on with Wolfe right now. He's trying to keep it out of the press."

My stomach lurches. "Can you tell me what it is?"

"I can't. And you can't ask him either." Priya gives me a pointed look. "I'm telling you this because I love you and don't want you to get hurt. Just remember that there's always more beneath the surface with men like Wolfe."

Men like Wolfe. A brooding man with dark eyes and a short fuse who, by his own admittance, has made lots of mistakes.

I sink my teeth into the soft bun, the sweet tang of the ketchup mixing with the sharp onions and smoky hot dog. Stress eating.

Priya's right. My gut feeling was always there. But sometimes the heart wants what it wants, logic be damned.

I swallow my mouthful. "He asked me to go to a comic convention with him in Boston next week."

Priya stares at me for a beat before bursting into laughter. "A comic convention? The man must really like you to subject himself to that."

The absurd thought that has been pestering me ever since JP suggested the comic convention crawls to the surface, refusing to stay buried. "You're going to think I've lost it but what if JP is actually... Daredevil?"

"The guy you made out with at the comic convention?"

"Yeah." I instantly regret voicing my ridiculous theory.

Priya knits her brows together, her gaze clouding with concern. "You think something went down between the two of you before your accident? But why wouldn't he tell you?"

I gnaw on my lower lip, chest tight with anxiety. "It's a stretch, I know."

She smirks. "Like some Clark Kent double life thing? So Wolfe's strutting around in suits with a Daredevil costume underneath?"

"It feels like he does. But I dunno, it's not completely out of the realm of possibility. Now I know he's into me enough to take me to bed. Should I ask him or does that make me sound crazy?"

"Look, if he is your mystery man, tread lightly, Luce. Because that would mean he's lying to you for some reason. That's so manipulative."

"Like what?"

"Maybe something happened, like you found out he had a few women on the side and that's why you were upset. Now he's using your memory loss to reel you back in."

I think back to how he was the one with me

when I fell on the stairs at the Plaza.

I scoff, a pathetic attempt at bravado. "Please, I'm not that good in the sack that he'd go to such effort. It's hardly the highlight of his year. Plus, he seems pretty genuine. I don't think he'd play games like that."

Priya's expression remains skeptical. "Just watch yourself with him. These billionaire playboy types are usually total jerks."

I laugh. "Oh yeah? You know a ton of 'em?"

She grins. "A couple we've worked with, yeah."

We carry on with our casual stroll through the lush greens of Central Park, the weight on my chest feeling slightly lighter after sharing my ludicrous theory with Priya. But I'm still miles away from making heads or tails of any of this.

We part ways at the entrance.

"I've got a night out with the law crew," Priya says. "What're you up to tonight?"

"Spider's moving out, so I'll probably just curl up with a book." I smile. The simple life. My poor overwhelmed brain needs it.

"Not seeing your superhero?" Priya teases, a mischievous glint in her eye. "I can't believe you've been keeping this from me."

"No, he's busy tonight, doing admin stuff."

"Admin?" Priya scoffs. "What kind of

billionaire does admin on a Saturday night?"

I shrug, getting defensive. "He's pretty down-to-earth."

"Mm-hmm." Her tone says it all. Priya kisses me goodbye, throwing one last warning look over her shoulder.

I roll my eyes, feigning indifference.

As I stroll down Fifth Avenue, Priya's words swirl in my mind. A down-to-earth billionaire doing admin on a Saturday night? It does sound sketchy.

I suddenly remember I left my Kindle charger in the apartment I stayed in opposite JP's. I've been meaning to get it back, and I'll need it if I want to read tonight.

And spying on Mr. Billionaire is purely coincidental, obviously. I just can't run into him. The last thing I need is for him to think I've turned into a bunny boiler.

◆ ◆ ◆

An hour later, I'm creeping down the hallway past JP's place, my heartbeat pounding in my ears. There's the faint hum of his music playlist, a telltale sign he's home. A knot of anxious energy forms in my stomach.

Why did I think this was a good idea again? I should just leave the damn charger, to hell with needing it.

Mission: Retrieve the charger. Operation: Swift exit. Now that I'm here, I'm too chicken-shit to play private detective and snoop on what JP classifies as "admin."

I slide the key in, wincing as it clicks loudly in the silence. With bated breath, I creak the door open, expecting a dozen alarm bells to blare at any moment.

Nothing. I exhale and slip inside, gently closing it behind me. So far, so good.

For a moment, I'm dazzled by the view from the floor-to-ceiling windows. Manhattan stretches out before me, glittering like a sea of precious stones, stretching as far as the eye can see.

If this were my place, I could happily spend all weekend here, sipping tea and staring at the view. The questions plaguing me, the mysteries swirling around the man across the hall, they all seem distant for a second.

But reality soon snaps back—this isn't my home, and now that Spider is gone, I should hand JP back his key.

But first... I might as well read here for a while.

I get lost in my book for the better part of

an hour. Books are one thing I can rely on during memory loss because they don't hold back from me or lie to me. If only there was a book on my missing year.

It would be *365 Days MIA*, and it would be anything but a steamy romance.

The setting sun peeking through the towering skyscrapers snaps me back to the present.

Time to execute phase two.

I hastily gather my forgotten Kindle charger and the toiletries I left behind in my hurried departure that morning after I stayed here. The fear of running into JP had driven me out at dawn.

Then, cutting through the silence like a shard of glass, the elevator dings. There are only three apartments on this floor. Are they coming here? To JP?

Clutching my bag like a life raft, I edge to the door and listen, every nerve alert.

Footsteps come closer, louder.

A knock on JP's door. A pause. And then another knock, more assertive this time. I find myself holding my breath, my pulse racing a mile a minute.

"Hey." JP's voice filters through the door, deep and gruff. The sound of it makes my heart pound even harder.

Peering through the peephole, I see a sleek brunette, knocking on his door. If her front is half as sexy as her behind, she's totally hot. Pangs of hurt and jealousy stab at me.

JP lets her in without a second thought.

Admin my ass.

I move away from the peephole, not breathing in case they hear me, until his door closes with both of them on the other side.

Together.

Fuck.

A lead weight drops in my stomach. I slink back from the door, questions screaming in my mind. I don't want to think about who she is and what she's doing at his place on a Saturday night.

Looks like I've been relegated to Miss Sunday.

I want to believe there's an innocent explanation. That JP wouldn't deceive me.

He wouldn't, whispers a hopeful part of me.

But reality drowns out those naive hopes. One —JP said he was tied up in admin tonight. On a Saturday. Really? Even I don't deal with paperwork on weekends, and I'm not the one with a personal assistant.

And two—a glamorous brunette shows up while he's supposedly working.

My eyes fill with tears, threatening to overflow.

I retreat to the sofa, unable to leave yet. God forbid JP sees me.

But the knowledge that JP is next door with another woman sends a sharp, painful twist through my chest. What a fucking asshole.

The dazzling lights of Manhattan suddenly seem harsh and cold. A raw sob wrenches itself from my throat.

Somehow I have to pull myself together and escape unseen.

And then what? Confront him? "Hey, JP, funny thing! I was lurking outside your apartment and saw you with a gorgeous brunette after you lied about working..."

No, screw that.

That's it. I'm done with JP Wolfe.

THIRTY-FIVE

JP

I pace the kitchen, nerves pulled taut as a wire. Hours have crawled by since Lucy's vague text about an "unforeseen engagement." Radio silence since. She's left me on read, vanishing into the black hole of her phone.

This isn't like her. Lucy doesn't ghost—she's always shot straight, for better or worse. But each call that dumps to voicemail twists my guts.

If she won't come to me, I'll go to her.

I snatch my keys from the counter and head to the parking lot.

The drive is a blur of tense thoughts. I'm sure I shattered every speed limit in Manhattan. Thankfully, since it's Sunday, the traffic is quiet.

When I pull up outside her apartment, I ignore the ridiculous blow-up doll glaring from the shop window and scan her windows. No silhouette. Damn it.

Hard to know if she's even in. Only one way to find out.

I tap a message into my phone: **I'm outside your apartment.**

The typing dots taunt me, disappearing and reappearing.

A reply pops up: **Busy right now. Talk tomorrow?**

Like hell. I dial her number. Again.

The seconds stretch into a lifetime before I finally hear her voice trickling down the line.

"Lucy." I can't hide the relief in my voice. Or the annoyance.

"Hey." Her voice is light, but there's an undercurrent I can't place.

"Why the hell aren't you talking to me? Do you have any clue how worried I've been?" I grind my molars, willing calm I don't feel. "You can't just vanish."

"Sorry, crazy morning." She's lying. I hear it in every word. "Are you really outside? I'm not home."

"Where are you?"

"My mom's." Another lie.

"Can we meet?" I need to see her, need to fix whatever this is.

"No, I can't today. I have to do some things at

my mom's and I have the presentation tomorrow. Sorry."

"You'll knock me dead at the presentation. You always do, Lucy." Is that all it is—she's worrying about tomorrow? "Can I see you later this evening?"

"I'll be at Mom's until late tonight. Sorry. Maybe another time."

I draw a sharp breath, clutching the phone so tight my knuckles turn white. "What's happened? Did some memories come back?"

"No, nothing like that. I wish."

I breathe a slight sigh of relief. Maybe it's just cold feet.

"Dammit, I'm heading to your mom's. There's something going on. We need to sort this out face-to-face."

"No, don't." Fear laces her words.

"Help me understand what's happening here." I'm pleading now, dignity be damned.

A heavy sigh. "Just give me some space, OK? And please don't make this weird at work. I love my job."

And then she's gone. Disconnected. I'm left grappling with silence, my heart pounding a rhythm of frustration and concern.

THIRTY-SIX

Lucy

I trudge into work on Monday physically, mentally, and emotionally drained. I feel like I've been on a twenty-four-hour flight from hell.

I plop down at my desk and do what I do best —lose myself in work so I don't have to think about all the shit in my actual life. Because all that matters is that the high rollers can spend all their money lining Wolfe's pockets even further. I managed to avoid him all day yesterday. And I'll admit, I cried. More than once.

I'll have to confront him eventually but I'm not ready yet.

So engrossed in work, I barely notice Matty arriving and rattling his cereal box like maracas at a goddamn party.

"Hey," I mutter, only half paying attention.

"Hey, Luce," he returns loudly, settling in at his desk. "You gotta see this ridiculous thing I stumbled across last night—"

"Matty." Taylor's voice slices through his as she lands beside us. "You're twenty minutes late."

He gives her a nonchalant look. "Relax. I thought we didn't punch the clock around here. I put in the hours."

"Wasting half the day on YouTube isn't 'putting in hours,'" she snaps back, her patience clearly waning.

I turn to look at her. Taylor seems particularly irritated today.

Matty leans back, hands behind his head like he owns the place. "I finish by the deadline."

"Barely," she hisses.

"Lay off, dude. You might be the project Lead, but you're not the one signing my paycheck. Only Andy can lecture me about punctuality." Or lack thereof.

"Fine," she huffs. "I'll have Andy do it."

"Ah, come on," he protests.

"You compromise the whole project with your minimal effort," she lectures, towering over my desk and turning it into a war zone.

This is all I need, to be caught in the crossfire of their escalating fight.

"Hey, I work hard," he argues defensively.

Hmmm. Not sure I'd agree with that one.

Matty's a good User Researcher, and we work well together, but the guy has zero motivation.

"I finished the user research in time for Luce to do the designs; what's your problem?" he challenges. He turns to me. "Back me up, Luce."

Shit.

Taylor's glare bores into me, waiting.

I cave. "Yeah, he does."

"Because you work all hours to compensate!" she shrieks, throwing herself into her chair in a rage.

"Fuck's sake," Matty mutters, but rolls his eyes and goes back to YouTube. There's a cat playing a piano on the screen. I can tell the cat has a better work ethic than Matty.

I watch as Taylor abruptly stands from her desk and stomps off to the restroom, every step like she's stomping on Matty's balls. I can't help but feel a twinge of sympathy for her. As tough as Taylor tries to appear, Matty's jabs seem to be taking their toll.

I glance over at Matty. He doesn't even look up from his screen. It's become a running team joke that Matty's a slacker. But that's his role, right? We've all fallen into our roles in this absurd office play, and Matty has claimed the role of the jester. He's capable of delivering results when the situation calls for it, but those moments seem to be becoming less frequent.

Still, as Taylor walks away, something niggles at me. Sure, Matty's full of laughs and jokes, but even he admits he has the motivation of a tranquilized sloth.

Maybe Taylor has a point. Maybe I've been seeing Matty through rose-tinted glasses, conveniently overlooking his lazy tendencies.

The thought is interrupted by the sound of a cat hitting piano keys.

"Matty," I say sharply, startling him. "I don't want to stay late tonight. Come on, man, can you put a pause on the cat videos and finish the report?"

"You people are wound up today," he grumbles. "Chill, Luce. I'm nearly finished."

He isn't.

Matty chuckles at the piano cat, lost in the music.

A lump gathers in my throat as I scowl at him, wrestling with the urge to cry. When did I evolve into this spineless creature? Fixing the clogged sink after Spider, always carrying the lion's share of the workload so Matty doesn't have to? Was I always this way or did I deteriorate in the lost year?

Picking up the dunce-of-the-day hat, I launch it toward his head with a vehemence that would make a football player proud.

"Christ! That's a bit extreme!" he protests, rubbing his head.

"Matty," I hiss. "I'm not joking. I'm sick of doing the majority of the work. If you are a proper friend, you won't let me deal with all this by myself."

"Hey, don't guilt-trip me..." He tries to deflect, but his voice trails off as he catches my hardened expression. "All right, Luce. Sorry."

I breathe a sigh of relief as he finally diverts his attention to the user research report, although I notice his YouTube tab still winking at him from the corner of his second screen.

It's a start, at least.

Usually, I'd scoff at Taylor, dismissing her as the office tyrant. But something feels different today. I follow after her to the bathroom.

When I open the door, it's quiet. Did I imagine seeing her come in here? But then I hear it—a soft, sniffling sound.

Shit, she's crying? Matty and I always thought she was made of stone.

"Taylor?" I call out tentatively.

"What?" she snaps. I picture her glaring at me

from inside her stall. "I'll be out in a minute."

"I come in peace. Just checking in, I wanted to see if you're okay."

"Whatever, Lucy. Just get lost."

That's a burn. Not entirely unexpected though.

A part of me wants to turn on my heel, leave her to her own devices. But something, some newfound compassion, stops me in my tracks. I can be the better woman here.

I gently knock on her stall door. "I mean it. I'm not here to make fun or anything," I insist. "I'm trying to help."

There's a silence that seems to last forever. Then, the door swings open. She's standing there, not looking like she's been crying. But she has.

"What do you want?" she demands.

I shift, uncomfortable. "Listen, I know we've had our differences. I'm dealing with this memory loss issue, and I really don't need extra stress," I confess. "I thought, you know, maybe we could try to get along."

Her eyes narrow.

"I'm not trying to trick you," I add hastily, raising my hands in surrender.

"Suddenly, after six years of constant taunts, you're turning a new leaf?"

Her words hit me like a gut punch. Me? I'd

always seen her as the one throwing jabs, not the other way around.

"Taylor, you've always been the one with the sharp tongue. Constantly prodding me about my work, my lack of promotion, my outfits... pretty much anything."

She dismisses me with a scoff, checking her face in the mirror. "Any time I try to be friendly, I'm met with sarcasm. This team feels like a high school clique. It's all about banter and fitting in. And God forbid if you want to better yourself. All you and Matty do is laugh at me."

I fall silent, taken aback.

"I guess it escalated between us," I say quietly. "It's not me and Matty against you. Or the team against you. Or at least, it shouldn't be."

"It's not just about you two against me," she continues, "it's the whole suits vs. us narrative. We all have to work together in this company. But you and Matty act like you're somehow above the sales team."

"The IT department gets made fun of all the time," I retort, rolling my eyes. "How often does a sales guy tell me to 'Just make it pretty pronto'? They're dismissive."

"Maybe rise above it then? Not everyone's like that," she retorts, a faint smile playing on her lips. "Steve from marketing called you 'Wonder Woman,' remember?"

I give a small smile. "I've been tempted to make that my email signature."

She turns to me seriously. "You're a hard worker, Lucy, and your output is excellent, but you worry too much about blending in with the team. You don't even notice that Matty is holding you back. This is why you haven't been promoted."

I bristle, about to snap back, when her words hit home. A lump lodges itself in my throat.

Is she right?

I've been afraid to rock the boat, too busy trying to fit in, to make everyone like me. I've let Matty's antics slide too many times.

I nod. "Okay, maybe I have been a bit of a doormat when it comes to Matty."

Perhaps Angry Andy's right. This place is like the Wild fucking West.

"Anyway, what do you really want? A promotion? A leadership role? You know it comes with more responsibilities, right? Matty will never take that leap. But do you want to?"

Her question strikes a chord. The truth is I don't know what I want.

But I know one thing.

"I'd like us to start afresh," I say after a pause.

"Call a truce. Maybe we'll never be friends, but this relationship right now isn't a healthy dynamic. I'll support you as project Lead."

She smiles. "I'd like that a lot too. And hopefully, we can work out how to get you promoted if you do want to be Lead. And I'd like to be able to support you more with your memory loss. I think I've been on guard because I've always felt like when I try to be nice, it'll just get thrown back in my face."

"I probably would have," I admit.

We smile at each other awkwardly. Not quite friends, but not quite enemies.

Enough of this soppy shit with Taylor. I clear my throat awkwardly as we head out together.

As we approach our desks, I'm dismayed to find Dwayne lurking by my workspace.

He nudges his glasses higher. "Lucy, I understand amnesia must be difficult, but could you restrain the physical outbursts in the office?"

My jaw clenches. "What are you talking about?"

From his desk, Matty smirks and suppresses a laugh.

Dwayne shifts his weight from one foot to the other. "Violently throwing an object at Matty. Though given your recent penchant for heated disputes, I can't say it's entirely unexpected."

I stare daggers at him. "What disputes?"

"I don't want to have to write up another incident, but chucking things around the office is a health and safety violation."

"*Dwayne.*" I give him another withering look. "What did you mean by heated disputes? What the hell are you talking about?"

"Let's see, first there was your altercation with Mr. Wolfe. Then you threatened to strangle me. And now this outburst."

I freeze. "Altercation with Mr. Wolfe? The one where I supposedly challenged his deadlines?"

"Not the deadline dispute. The nasty confrontation at the Plaza." His eyes glint behind the lenses. "Right before your accident."

My stomach drops. "What are you talking about?" I ask slowly.

"The rather heated disagreement that took place at the top of the staircase."

"You saw me?"

"Yes. Arguing quite inappropriately at that."

JP and I were arguing at the top of the stairs at the Plaza? The same stairs that I fell down?

There's a bizarre sensation taking root in my stomach. My mind strains like an old TV set struggling to tune in to a forgotten station, static mingling with flickers of images.

A memory striving to claw its way to the surface.

My pulse thunders in my ears. JP never mentioned an argument. Only that I fell.

Dwayne goes on, relentless, "You stormed away, and that's when it happened. I heard rather than saw the fall."

Bile scorches my throat. That lying bastard. JP and I had a fight moments before I fell.

And he conveniently forgot to mention it.

THIRTY-SEVEN

Lucy

I sink into the plush sofa, its cushions embracing me. The clinic room is all soothing sage and dusty rose clearly meant to calm. But I'm immune to such psychological tricks, the pit of unease in my gut growing by the second.

I told Taylor I had to leave work early and called for an emergency session with Dr. Ramirez.

I clutch one of the velvet pillows like a security blanket. "Okay, Doc. I'm ready to revisit that night at the Plaza. I suspect some of my much-needed answers start there."

Her lips curl into a smile, a silent applause of support. "Okay. I agree, you're ready. You can do this. Remember, you're in control and I'm right here with you. And no matter what, you have the strength within you to face it and come out the other side stronger. Are you ready for that, Lucy?"

Am I?

I nod, sucking in a shuddering breath. The walls feel like they're closing in, tight as a corset two sizes too small.

A part of me wants to say to hell with it and stay in the safety of the present, keep the past locked away in the forgotten recesses of my mind, like a cringe-worthy drunken memory. If it's locked away, I don't have to deal with the fact that JP fucking lied to me.

But the stubborn, masochistic part of me knows this is the necessary next step toward healing. Even if it's agonizing.

Dr. Ramirez lounges in an armchair opposite me. It feels somewhat odd that she's upright while I lie sprawled out, in what feels like a pretty vulnerable position. I'd rather she lie down too so we're on an equal footing.

Not right beside me though. That'd be weird.

"Relax, close your eyes, breathe slow and deep." She drags out her words like HR Helen does. "Feel the tension leave your body with each exhale. Focus on the sound of my voice. Let your mind become void."

"That's the problem though, isn't it? It's already a void." I suck in a lungful of air and let it out. "Sorry, doc." Another breath fills my lungs. "Working on the whole *relaxing* thing."

"Breathe from your core. Put your hands on your stomach, feel it rise and fall."

I obey, squeezing my eyes shut. I focus on my breathing, trying to fool my jittery mind into believing we're sprawled on a sandy beach, not holed up in a therapist's office.

"Good," she soothes, her voice mingling with the new age music she insists aids relaxation. Her carefully posed questions about everyday trivialities lead me gently into a drowsy, dream-like state.

"Now, Lucy, we're back at the Plaza Hotel. Tell me what you can see."

My mind morphs into a private cinema, splashing vibrant visuals of the Plaza Hotel, a Quinn & Wolfe flagship hotel in SoHo. I see the opulent ballroom lit up by grand chandeliers. I hear tuxedos rustle, high heels clicking, champagne glasses tinkling. Coworkers laughing, taking advantage of the free drinks. I relay it all to the doctor.

"And how do you feel?" she asks.

I take in my surroundings.

Everyone is wearing expensive suits or formal workwear. I'm wearing a tight shift dress and stilettos I can hardly walk in. A chicken wing remains untouched in my hand. I'm too sick with nerves to eat it.

"I feel... anxious," I admit. The knot pulls tighter, filled with a nameless dread. I hate these work events. But this feels different. More sinister.

My throat clenches as the memory sharpens, and I want to move on the couch, but I feel like I'm trapped under a weighted blanket.

"I'm scared," I whisper to Dr. Ramirez, dimly aware of her hovering at the edge of my consciousness.

"It's okay." Her voice filters through, far-off yet somehow grounding. "You're safe."

And then, without warning, I'm there, in the thick of it.

I'm right there.

The ballroom explodes to life around me. I smell the heady mix of perfumes, taste the rich flavors of the catered food, and the laughter and light chatter are almost deafening. I see Matty, Taylor, the rest of the IT crowd, our whole marketing team, the annoying sales guys.

Matty struggles with his overly tight tie, looking as if he's on the verge of asphyxiation. Taylor laughs loudly beside me.

Tears sting my eyes. Matty asks if I'm okay, but I can't find the words to answer. Even Taylor's booming laughter fades into a worried hush.

I manage to croak that I need air and escape the suffocating ballroom.

My heart is shattered, but the reason eludes me. A missing puzzle piece my mind hides. I gasp uselessly as I weave through smiling faces trying to coax me to do shots. Their cheer grates. I don't belong.

Then I see him, JP Wolfe, at the top of the grand staircase. Arrogance personified.

His dark blue tailored tuxedo hugs every inch of his muscular frame. Our eyes lock, a storm churning inside me. Love and hate in equal measure.

I want to scream at him, hurl curses. I hate him. I love him. But I hate him more.

He crooks a finger, demanding my presence.

I want to flip him off and storm away. But I need to keep my cool. I'm trembling with rage, but I know what I have to do.

I reach into my bag and remove a pale blue envelope.

Each step amplifies my anxiety as I ascend toward him. But I won't let him see how much this is hurting me. He's dangerous. A threat to my sanity, my heart. Trusting him was a mistake I never should have made.

His eyes flicker with an unspoken emotion as

he begins to speak, his face hard. But I can't hear him. I strain to catch his words, but it's futile. I'm a ghost.

I scream at him, hurling poisonous words meant to wound. I want to hurt him as much as he hurt me.

Shock crosses his face as he reads the letter I shoved at him. Anger, pain, a hint of regret, but the soundtrack of our heated exchange remains muted. Maybe I don't want to hear it.

My hands shake with adrenaline. I jab a finger at his chest, unleashing a torrent of rage I can't comprehend. We stand toe to toe at the top of the sweeping stairs, oblivious to the ballroom below.

His eyes blaze, but behind the anger is a well of hurt I didn't know he could feel. He reaches for me. I recoil, the betrayal still bleeding and raw.

With one last look, I turn and flee down the marble steps. I have to get away from him.

Focused only on escape, I don't see it coming. My heel catches. Balance lost, arms flailing as the ground rushes up—

"Lucy," a voice calls, its gentle lilt replacing his voice. It's Dr. Ramirez, coaxing me back from the precipice of the memory.

I gasp, the room swimming into focus as pain stabs through my temples.

That confrontation had to be real. But can I even trust my own mind?

If it's real, why did JP lie? We weren't talking like a boss and employee; we were locked in all-out war. There's history here that he's not telling me. He shattered me that night.

He's the guy! the little irritating voice in my head screams. *He's the guy who hurt you. He's Daredevil!*

Did he push me in a fit of rage? Surely not, but… I don't trust him. Not anymore. Betrayal churns in my stomach like acid. He could have helped me regain my memories. Instead, he hid the truth.

JP tried to bury the truth of that night. What really happened at the Plaza Hotel?

THIRTY-EIGHT

Lucy

An hour later, my caffeine levels and nerves are both through the roof as Priya and I sit in a café across from the clinic.

She came to collect me. I must've been a blubbering, incoherent mess over the call.

I actually threw up my ham and cheese sandwich in the clinic toilet. Somehow I managed to pull myself together and lie to Dr. Ramirez, pretending I was fine. For a second, I thought she was going to force me into a straitjacket, just as Libby predicted.

I remember now. The blue envelope. I've seen it before. It's the letter that had JP turning all shades of awkward in the car when he drove me home. A car pulled in front of us and the contents of the glove box spewed open. He got flustered when it landed at my feet. I'd written it off as classified corporate mumbo-jumbo but now... now I can't ignore the knot of unease tightening in my gut.

That was the letter I gave him, one he clearly didn't want me to remember. The knot of dread in my gut twists painfully. JP has been lying to me, covering up something.

Knowing something traumatic happened, yet having no recollection... it's a disturbing, twisted state of mind. I can't find the proper words to describe it to Priya.

Reaching out to JP isn't an option. I can't trust him. The man is lying to me, covering something up. And that thought alone cuts deep.

Because even with all the anger brewing, my feelings for him lurk around, raw and tender as an open wound. If only I could rip them out. Easier said than done.

I let my fears tumble out, painting Priya the grim portrait of my hypnotherapy session. The retelling leaves me with a nauseating sense of dread.

"I got a recording of the session," I confess, my skin crawling just from the thought of it in my bag.

"Well, that's good," Priya says. "You can play it back, see what you've missed."

I shake my head, a shiver running down my spine. "It's not that simple. I can't just apply cold logic here. I'm scared of what I'll feel if I hear my own voice narrate those forgotten moments."

"Do you want me to listen for you?"

"Yes. No. God, I don't know." I shove the untouched coffee away, the bitter aroma suddenly too strong for my delicate gut. "Honestly, I'm in such a horrible mental state right now."

Priya pulls me into her soothing embrace as I try to mimic the breathing techniques from the clinic. In and out. Deep, slow.

Around us, the other café patrons seem so chill. I envy their peace.

"Do you have any idea what could be in that letter?" Priya asks gently.

I shake my head helplessly. "None. I've rummaged through every file on my laptop to find a soft copy. Found nothing."

Her eyes widen in alarm. "You don't think he could have deleted it?"

At her suggestion, my stomach coils unpleasantly. He has the access, the power to do so.

She chews on her lip, face etched with worry. "You don't think he could have hurt you on those stairs?"

"No." The denial comes quick, too quick. The thought twists my insides. Because a tiny part of me isn't sure what he's capable of. "I am fairly sure, though, that he's the one I was... seeing, in whatever twisted way, before the accident. The one who reduced me to a blubbering mess. That made me cry in the bar that time."

Her eyes practically bug out of her head. "But that means he's Daredevil? The guy you dry humped at the nerd convention?"

I manage a weak smile at her jab, despite my spiraling thoughts. "Possibly. Who the hell knows? I'm just grasping at straws right now. Second-guessing every element of my existence. But one thing's certain—JP Wolfe is a lying bastard."

She swallows hard, clutching my hand. "That scandal I mentioned, the one JP wanted to keep hush-hush... I think it's about to explode."

"Does it involve me?" A chill of dread slithers down my spine. "I'd know if it was about me, right?"

"I don't know details," she admits. "And even if I did, I couldn't disclose them."

I study her face, searching for any hint that she's holding something back, but her regret seems genuine. Not that I'd blame her for toeing the company line. This is her job she's risking.

"The letter..." I say slowly. "I saw it in his car. He panicked and snatched it away when it fell out. I'm dreading having to confront him about this."

She frowns thoughtfully. "Do you think a

confrontation is wise? He's lied to you before. What makes you think he'll be truthful now?"

Her question leaves me at a loss for words.

"Is there any way you could get ahold of the letter without him knowing?" she suggests gently. "That way you'd have the facts first before talking to him. You wouldn't be going in blind."

"So what should I do?" I ask.

"This is where you need to think strategically. Use your head, not your heart. Get close to him, get that letter."

"What do you expect me to do, seduce and swipe the keys?"

"Yes, that's exactly what you need to do. He's lied to you. Don't trust this bastard. You need to gain the upper hand here." She looks at her watch. "Go back to work, call a quick meeting with him, and get those keys."

I stare at her, my mind a whirlwind of emotions and strategies. Asking JP outright will probably yield more lies. But maybe it's time to stop being manipulated. It's time for me to know what went on in my own life.

My throat feels dry as I swallow. "He'll be furious if he finds out."

"True. What if there's something he's trying to keep quiet? Christ, what if he tries to silence you and there's another 'accident'?"

"He's not Tony Soprano, Priya," I scoff, but it rattles me. I may have been on the receiving end of JP's charm but I've seen his ruthless side. Through six years of Quinn & Wolfe, I've seen how many careers he's ended.

Could I really pull this off? Could I pretend everything is okay just to get the keys?

JP

The message from Lucy pops up on my screen: **Hey, are you free?**

Distracted by the incessant drone of the meeting, I tap a response: **Busy. But for you, I can spare a moment.**

Her reply lands in seconds: **No, don't worry about it. I know you're busy.**

After a frosty stretch, her sudden thaw is startling. I rise from my seat with a brisk dismissal for the room, ignoring the sea of questioning faces.

I message back: **Where are you? I'm en route.**

The ellipsis appears again before her response: **Near your boardroom, top floor, the little meeting room.**

I frown down at my phone screen, confused by her mixed signals. One minute she's cold, the next she's hot. If she were any other woman, I'd tell her where to go. But this is Lucy—and so I oblige.

She's perched on the table edge when I enter, knuckles white around her necklace. My gaze makes her shrink.

"Hi! Thanks for breaking away," she breathes.

Frustration edges into my tone. "You've been avoiding me, Lucy. My options were limited." I move closer. "What's the matter?"

"I just wanted to see you. I missed you." Her words are coupled with unexpected physical contact as she wraps her arms around my waist. "I'm sorry I've been moody."

Her proximity stirs something within me, but I push it down. "You're acting out of character. What's really going on?"

Her big blue eyes dart away from mine. "It's nothing, really! I just freaked out a bit about us. But I'm over it now, really."

I examine her. Her eyes scream fear, and her body language is all wrong. Years of navigating the calculated facades of high-stakes gamblers have made me an exceptional human polygraph.

She's lying. The thought kindles a flame of anger within me. I've got my own secrets, sure, but I can't stomach dishonesty aimed at me. It's part of my ego. The hypocrisy isn't lost on me.

As if to prevent me from questioning her any further, she grabs on to my waist and pulls me closer to her body before planting a passionate kiss on my lips.

Arousal courses through me when she moves her hands down my body and caresses my cock through my pants. Every ounce of resistance I had slips away and suddenly I'm pressing her against me.

"Right here?" I growl into her mouth, feeling myself swell in anticipation.

"Shh," she murmurs, swinging herself onto the table and wrapping her legs around my waist. Her hand squeezes around my cock, and thank God we aren't in one of the glass offices.

My grip tightens on her thighs as I trail kisses down to her neck and take in the scent of her perfume. "Damn it, Lucy," I say against her skin, "are you trying to make me come right here?"

I let out a deep, guttural groan as she continues to stimulate me. I can't take it anymore. Hell, I'm actually close to coming in my pants.

"Stop," I command, grabbing her wrists so she can't make me go over the edge. I quickly unfasten my zipper until I've released my throbbing cock from its confines.

She grips my hardening erection tightly in her

hand and slides up and down, sending waves of pleasure through me with each stroke. The blood pumps into my erection as precum drips out. Fuck. I'm so close. My hardened cock fills with heat, pulsing urgently.

Suddenly, she pulls away from me as if something's repulsed her.

What the fuck?

"Sorry," she exhales. "Okay, you're right, this is ridiculous. I should go."

"What the hell, Lucy?" I stare at her, breathing hard. "Why'd you get me worked up like that in the office? You get me all aroused and then just change your mind?"

"Sorry. Just lost my nerve." She jumps from the table and gently pushes me away. "I'll catch you later, JP."

"What? Wait."

I stare after her with an aching hard-on as she rushes from the room. Why do I feel like I've been played?

THIRTY-NINE

Lucy

I don't think I'm being dramatic when I say my heart feels like it's going to explode out of my ribcage. I step into the elevator, crammed with oblivious people headed to meetings, or coffee, or other mundane tasks. Not breaking into the company co-founder's car.

The ride down drags on for an eternity, people shuffling on and off at a glacial pace. I dig my nails into my palms to keep myself from shoving them out of the elevator just to speed things along.

Inhale. Exhale. Breathe.

The stolen keys burn a hole in my hand. How I managed to multi-task and get them from his back pocket was nothing short of a miracle. How can I return them undetected? What if he already knows? What if he's connected the dots, my seduction, the theft? Could the letter hold something so horrifying, I'll never be able to face him again? Or even worse—what if he wants me whacked? Okay, a bit extreme, but he could definitely fire me.

Stop it. You're spiraling.

The doors creak open at long last and I step out, feigning calm.

Except for one man, the garage is deserted. I saunter to a random car, acting out the charade of searching for non-existent keys in my bag. Just another woman going about her day, nothing suspicious here.

Come on, buddy, move it! Just get in your car and leave already!

At last, the man departs. The electronic doors lift, releasing a flood of blinding sunlight.

I brace myself, my breathing shaky as I inch toward the executive bay on unsteady legs. The gleaming collection of luxury toys—Rolls-Royces, Lamborghinis, Ferraris—seems to watch me with accusatory headlights.

There's a security guard at the entrance to the garage, not to mention the cameras that must be trained on this million-dollar fleet of automobiles. If anyone spots me on this bay, they'll know for sure I'm up to no good.

Crouching, I dash between the cars like I'm in a Quentin Tarantino movie until I reach JP's

Aston Martin. The guard can probably hear my thundering pulse by now. More likely than not, I'll vomit or lose control of my bladder before this heist even begins.

The Aston Martin chirps open, deafeningly loud.

I gently tug the passenger door and slide inside. I've never been so nervous in my life. My hands shake violently as I pop the glove box. What if it's not even here? It was weeks ago that I saw it.

The interior smells of leather and JP, a scent that sends a jolt of adrenaline racing through me. The glove compartment is a jumble of papers, sunglasses, tissues, and there—the edge of a pale blue envelope, my envelope. My hands shake as I reach for it, my stomach clenching in anticipation.

My heart thuds aggressively as I examine the name JP Wolfe, scrawled in my own handwriting. Why hadn't I recognized it as my handwriting before? I have no idea what awaits inside or why JP hid it from me.

A rap at the window makes me yelp.

Shit. It's Logan, the security guard. The one I didn't recognize on my first day back to work.

He peers in, motioning for me to step out.

I step out slowly, buying myself time to think. I paste a beaming smile on my face, a desperate attempt to mask the terror coursing through me. "Hi!"

"Everything okay, Lucy? Mr. Wolfe send you down here?" His brow furrows.

My smile wavers as I swallow back my fear. "Yes, absolutely! I just needed to grab something from his car."

He nods but his eyes stay fixed on me. He's not buying it. My poor poker face probably screams of guilt. Or nausea.

With an exaggerated show of nonchalance, I close the door and press the fob button to lock it. "Have to run. Meeting to attend."

Logan remains unmoved. "No problem, Lucy. But I'll need to confirm with Mr. Wolfe. It's standard procedure." He brings out his phone.

I barely keep my voice steady. "Of course! I'm in a hurry, though. Here, you can have the keys." I practically throw them at him. "Gotta run!"

And I do. Without waiting for his response, I break into a run, letter clenched in my death grip. If I'm trying to squash Logan's doubts, I'm not doing a very good job.

Where do I go now? I can't possibly read this at my desk. I take the stairs up to reception, swallowing air in hyperventilating gasps.

Breathe like the clinic taught you.

I dart into the restroom on the reception floor, my hands barely able to hold the letter steady. Should JP question me, I'll claim I dropped something during that car ride and was going to retrieve it.

Taking a shaky breath, I tear open the letter, a silent prayer on my lips. And then I read.

Mr. Wolfe,

This letter is to formally resign from my position as Senior Graphic Designer at Quinn & Wolfe, effective immediately.

While I have thoroughly enjoyed my time at your company, working under your 'leadership' has become unbearable.

Your dishonesty has made your presence insufferable. For my own well-being, I need to distance myself from you and everything you stand for.

I'm done. Finished.

Lucy Walsh.

I hunch over in the bathroom stall, dizzy and disoriented. Did I really resign?

The thought rattles in my brain as my anxiety spikes. The letter clutched in my hands is harsh, biting—nothing like my usual calm, professional tone. Clearly, I intended to make a point.

Something terrible must have happened to make me snap, to shred my composure and unleash such vitriol.

I hated JP. No, more than that—I loathed him enough to abandon the job I love. What could he have done to spark such fury in me?

The bitter truth hits my gut like a punch. He lied. He hurt me. And then he covered it up. Whatever it was, it held the power to drive me away from the company, and him, forever.

My fingers trace the harsh words in the letter as I read them again, sending a shiver up my spine. A locked memory strains against its chains, shrouded in a fog of dread and trauma, desperately struggling to break free from the clutches of amnesia.

JP's face appears, towering over me like an imposing statue at the top of the grand staircase in the Plaza. He looks every inch the polished executive in his sleek tuxedo, but I'm boiling with rage. The scene is hazy, blurred at the edges, just like those first days in the hospital.

But I can hear my voice echoing. I see the flash of pain in his eyes, the clench of his jaw. My heart shatters all over again, as if I'm reliving it in real time.

He broke me. I don't know how, or why, but I know he made me sob for days on end.

"You're not good for me. I can never trust you again," I spit, the hurt and disappointment radiating in my voice. The harsh words linger in the air.

"Don't do this, Lucy," he growls, his polished veneer giving way to desperation.

In a final act of defiance, I push the letter into his hand, giving him a big fuck you, then turn away.

I lose my footing and tumble headfirst down the staircase.

The memory fades, leaving a bitter aftertaste. With trembling hands, I fold the letter and tuck it back into its envelope.

I need to get out of here. Now.

By now, Logan will likely have contacted JP. He probably went back into his meeting with the executive board. Maybe he didn't answer his phone.

Yet, if that call was answered, JP would know for sure what I took, and he'll figure out I seduced him to steal his car keys.

I can't go back to my desk. I message Matty to get my things and bring them to me at reception, and to tell Taylor I'm not feeling well.

Navigating my way through the reception, I find a conveniently human-sized plant as the perfect ruse and pretend to be enthralled by my phone. I'll wait here for Matty. On second thought, I should have asked someone more efficient—like Taylor. Matty's probably turned back to his cat video already—although ever since I snapped at him, he has been trying.

His number—JP—makes my phone flash to life. Oh, fuck.

Anxiety strikes my chest. A sudden, intense shot. I want to drop the damn phone, fire it into the pot plant.

Around me, the world is in fast-forward. Heels clack-clack-clacking, phone calls punctuating the air, the ebb and flow of traffic to the cafeteria, and the routine humdrum of greetings at the reception. Their apparent normalcy only stokes the inferno of my rising panic.

The woman beside has a sickeningly sweet tone—until the call ends. "Insufferable prick," she hisses into the now-dead line.

And the giant phantom arrow that followed me on my first day back to the office is back, rudely jabbing my skull.

Then, like someone hit the pause button,

everything slows. Stops. People freeze in place like sophisticated androids, their systems abruptly switched off. The scene unfolds with an eerie stillness, reminiscent of a chilling *Black Mirror* episode.

Risking a look from behind my giant plant, I strain to see what has glued everyone's gaze. The massive screen behind the reception desk flickers with the sensationalism of a live news channel.

And prominently displayed on the screen is JP, slumped on a couch, eyes shut, his chest exposed. His arm hangs in a heavy drape over the couch's edge. I stifle a gasp, my hands flying up to cover my mouth.

Is he...?

Relief, sharp and brutal, courses through me as his head shifts ever so slightly. He's not dead, but the nightmare is far from over.

A naked woman comes into focus, sauntering into view, her ass filling the screen. She leans over him, attempting to rouse him, and his eyes flutter open—glazed and unfocused.

A visceral wave of nausea sweeps over me. So, not dead, just drugged out of his mind. Even better.

The camera zooms in to show his dilated pupils, drowned in a cocktail of narcotics. A thin sheen of sweat glistens on his face.

I fight back the urge to retch.

Before I can even process this, another naked woman saunters into view, just as the screen plunges into blackness.

Chaos erupts in the reception area, shattering the silence with a flurry of frantic activity. Receptionists scramble, coworkers murmur in hushed, agitated tones.

"What the absolute fuck?" An explosive, muffled curse detonates in the air beside me. Accusations fracture the silence, questions explode like grenades, ripping through the calm. The name "Wolfe" echoes around me like some morbid mantra.

I back up, stumbling into the plant, memories resurfacing with a vengeance.

His eyes. Those vacant, soulless eyes. Haunted me for days before the accident. How could I have forgotten them?

And just like that, I'm transported. I find myself standing at the threshold of JP's penthouse apartment, the night everything imploded coming back into sharp, heart-wrenching focus.

FORTY

A Few Weeks Before The Accident
Lucy

His door isn't fully closed. It's slightly ajar, and my heart races, syncing up with the pulsating bass vibrating through the door. Laughter and music, disembodied, seep out into the hallway, striking me like a sucker punch.

A party? Seriously? We're in the throes of an argument and he responds with a party? Seems like a *Fuck you* to me.

I'm here playing peacemaker, ready to say "I love you" and salvage whatever's left of us. Because I know I love this man, and if we don't sort things out, the hole in my heart will never be filled again. I'm here to say I'm ready to meet him halfway if he's willing to put the work in.

I won't deny I hurled some severe words at him. But his power doesn't entitle him to always get his way. He tried to steamroll me, buy out my apartment, and became irate when I put a stop to it. He can't whisper "I love you" and expect that to nullify his high-handed actions. I didn't mean to throw it back in his face though. I shouldn't have told him I wanted nothing to do with him, but he was being so arrogant, the words just vomited from my mouth.

With a dose of dread, I nudge the door open and step into JP's penthouse. It's filled with people, a chaotic whirl of music and laughter, the air ripe with expensive alcohol and, oddly, smoke. A surprise, given JP's aversion to it. He's allowing smoking here tonight?

I muster the remains of my nerve and call out over the noise, my voice barely audible, "Hi, is JP around?"

Everyone in the hallway ignores me. I scuff a sneaker across the floor, feeling like shit as I eye the sharp-suited men and women dressed in sexy dresses. I'm nothing to them.

While I've been at home, agonizing and stewing over our fight, JP's been here, living it up. All the angst about telling him I couldn't date him anymore because I can't stomach the heartache of playing second fiddle to his extravagant lifestyle— it all feels pretty futile now. I regretted the words as soon as they came out of my mouth. My heart was literally screaming at me to shut up.

I tap a guy on the shoulder in the middle of a group of suits. They have Wall Street written all over them.

"Is JP here?" I shout.

He smirks at me and responds with a nod. I hate that smirk. He motions toward the epicenter of the chaos—the living room.

The noise grows louder as I move further in, each unfamiliar face, each intrusive burst of laughter, increasing the knot of apprehension in my stomach.

My stomach clenches with anxiety. It screams, urges, *Turn away. Go home. This isn't worth it.*

But do I listen? Of course not.

A guy tries to strike up a conversation but I brush him off. A woman sashays past me to the bathroom looking like a supermodel. She leaves behind a cloud of expensive perfume and questions.

Finally, I make it into the living room, and it's a scene straight out of a wild movie. Bodies writhing to the music, people laughing and shouting. There are so many people everywhere. The whole room looks like it's on coke and a million other drugs. Are these people his friends?

What's this, a fucking orgy he's having? Underwear and bras have gone optional for some people. Jesus.

Like a sickening punch to the gut, I see him —JP. He's sprawled across his plush leather couch, the couch where we cuddled so many nights, his eyes shuttered against the world, oblivious to the ongoing chaos.

A naked woman saunters over to him.

I feel the ground beneath me wobble.

"Don't you dare touch him!" I scream inside my head. She tilts her head upward, making me wonder if my silent cry leaked out. But no, she disregards my existence and drapes herself over him, trying to stir him from his stupor.

His eyes flutter open—hazy, unfocused.

His gaze lifts, meets mine, and I feel my soul crumble. It's the indifference that shatters me. It's like he's seeing through me, and it cuts me like a knife. I'm a ghost at his party.

His lids lower again, shutting me out.

The woman's fingers playfully dance along JP's chest. Her voice, laced with sultry promise, cuts through the din. "Come on, JP, you're missing all the fun."

He stirs as she playfully slaps his face. He opens his eyes and stares at her, then moves his focus back to me. Once again, it's like he's looking straight through me. Like I'm an unwelcome stranger in his debauched playground.

I stand there in shock.

He lied. He promised that he'd stopped. That I could trust him. He swore he'd chosen me. He had me convinced—this ordinary, plain Lucy—that I was enough. That I was his world.

But I was never enough.

I'm just dependable old Lucy, foolish enough to think a man like him could love me.

Plain little Lucy, not quite enough to get promoted. Lucy-the-doormat, Lucy-the-yes-woman, always bending over backward for everyone—Mom, Andy, Matty, Spider, Dave the real estate jerk.

It started as sex. Raw, primal, unforgettable sex.

And that's when he presented me with the finest version of himself, the facade. He reeled me in gradually, exposing a gentle, nurturing side. He stripped away the layers of his moody exterior, showing me something unique, a side I was convinced nobody else had glimpsed.

The flawless boyfriend act. Sweet, caring, intoxicating. The dinners, the comic conventions, the shared evenings, weekends, stolen moments in the office that made me lower my guard. He made me trust him, and I let him into my heart.

Then the curtain lifted on his clandestine double life.

A night in my arms, followed by a night in the grip of his high. JP Wolfe, the billionaire playboy with an inclination for snorting lines of white and whatever else suited his whims. Not quite an addict, but close enough to fracture our budding relationship.

At first, when it was just sex, I looked the other way. Who was I to dictate his lifestyle?

But it started to gnaw at me. So he swore he was changing. That he fell into this lifestyle when he moved to Vegas at twenty-one. That he was going to prove it to me and stay away from drugs, the party lifestyle and all that comes with it.

I believed him. Like a doormat.

Now his gaze meets mine, empty and cold. He looks like he's been hitting the powder harder than Scarface.

I choke out his name, a plea, a final effort to reach him in his narcotic haze. "JP," I whisper, hoarse. "Get up."

He stirs, stumbles up from the couch, and staggers toward me with a disturbing cockiness.

My gaze desperately searches his features for

any remnants of the man who once made me feel special.

But there's nothing.

I'm just plain Lucy, boring Lucy, not sparkly or exciting enough to hold JP's interest.

Without saying a word, he grazes a finger slowly down my cheek, smiles, then saunters off toward the bathroom.

My heart shatters into a million pieces. The sob I've been choking on finally escapes, a feral cry marking my defeat.

I'm done. Enough of this crap. I pivot and stride out, angrily wiping the tears off my face. But I won't shed any more over that bastard again. I'm worth more, even if he can't see it. More than this circus, more than him. I have to be.

The party can rage on without me, and JP Wolfe can go to hell.

FORTY-ONE

Present Day

JP

Amanda, my assistant, couldn't bluff her way out of a paper bag, let alone a poker game. I once tried teaching her the art of the game, but poker's not all about the nuts and bolts. It's a performance, a dance where you shroud your raw emotions beneath a poker face of stone-cold stoicism.

One look at Amanda's face now, and I can tell —the floodgates are open. The secret I've hidden away like a monster in the closet has been let loose.

"Mr. Wolfe," she stammers, her voice barely audible, hovering in the doorway like she's on the brink of a precipice. "The internet... you need to see it."

"The internet? You're going to have to be more specific," Killian jests. His smirk widens, only for it to fade when he catches my gaze.

Connor throws a glance my way.

"You're trending," Amanda says as she stares at me, horrified.

Exhaling deeply, I turn on the boardroom screen and web-search my own name. I'm trending nationwide, above geopolitical conflict, economic collapse, and some celebrity scandal.

Billionaire Playboy's Wild Drug-Fueled Parties Exposed! screams the headlines.

As expected, the provocative tabloid-style headlines shout from the top, with the more measured pieces hidden away below, unnoticed and unread.

"Click on it," Killian barks.

I comply, watching my life unravel in millions of pixels across the country. A deadly silence fills the room, only broken by the distant echoes of laughter on the screen.

The video that I've been so desperately trying to hide has been viewed over a million times, according to the number in the corner of the screen. The lawyers had said it was dealt with.

But it's not the judgment of the world that worries me. It's the judgment of four people—Mags, my two nephews, and Lucy.

"Goddammit, JP!" Killian explodes, his face crimson. "Our license is on the line here! I thought you said it was handled."

Connor, usually the wisecracking guy, is speechless. Amanda stands frozen at the door. The poor girl looks like she's been sentenced to death.

A tsunami of dread crashes over me, a cold reminder of the magnitude of my screw-up. The casino industry, a fortress of iron-clad rules and regulations, doesn't take kindly to renegades. Killian's right—this scandal could cost us our license.

I'm hit by a wave of self-loathing as I gaze at the screen. I've been the worst kind of jerk. Not only have I gambled with my business and fortune, but also the Quinns' future. Now everything we worked for could come crashing down because of my stupidity.

But the real knife in my gut, the one thing that showcases my selfishness more than anything else, is that all I can think about is Lucy. I know how she'll react because I've been here before. I've faced this torment once, and here I am, gearing up for round two.

I may just have found my biggest fear in life: being forced to relive the same damn mistakes.

I imagine her face crumbling as she learns the truth. That thought is the real blow, the gut punch that leaves me winded.

"Leave us, Amanda." Killian's voice cuts through the heavy air. She nods, but before she leaves, she drops one more bomb.

"Just one more thing, Mr. Wolfe," she squeaks. "Security called. They wanted to know if Lucy Walsh from IT was authorized to access your car."

She doesn't wait for an answer, scurrying out of the room and leaving me with my head in my hands. The laughter on the screen dies, replaced by an eerie silence. Killian must have paused it.

As Killian breathes in deeply, I raise my eyes to meet his. His gaze is filled with such raw fury, it's palpable. He's a breath away from breaking my nose.

The image on the screen freezes, capturing my glazed eyes. A mirror to my shame, my ego. I can only think about the damage I've done, the trust I've broken. And Lucy... Lucy...

Why would Lucy want access to my car? Has she found the letter? Fuck, does she know everything?

"I have to leave," I announce abruptly, standing from my chair.

"What?" Killian is on his feet, his eyes blazing.

"I'll talk to the lawyers and get ahead of this," I say, grabbing my phone and shoving it into my pocket. "But first I need to see Lucy. I know I don't deserve it, but I'm begging for your trust. I'll make the hard choices to protect us and this company."

Ignoring Killian's protests, I step out of the boardroom, my mind reeling and my heartbeat pounding in my ears.

The mutters and wide-eyed stares in the elevator, the hushed whispers of the IT department—they don't register. They are nothing more than background noise, a ripple in my deafening inner turmoil.

"Where's Lucy?" My voice comes out more as a command than a question as I stride toward Taylor's desk.

"She wasn't feeling well, she's heading home. Matty just went down to the lobby with her stuff," Taylor replies, her eyes wide.

"Thanks," I growl, barely pausing in my march toward the elevator. The weight in my gut grows heavier, drenched in regret and self-loathing. I botched this. I played my cards all wrong, should have taken the time to tell Lucy privately, away from the prying eyes of media vultures. I thought I had more fucking time.

I find some solace in the thought that none of this reflects badly on Lucy. No one knows we were together, exactly as she wanted it.

The elevator ride down feels like a descent

into purgatory. The car is packed with people, their faces a blur, their breaths seemingly held in anticipation of my impending breakdown. When the doors slide open, I storm out toward reception, a man on a mission.

Outside the reception, I catch a fleeting glimpse of Lucy disappearing, her bag slung low over her shoulder. A visceral ache ricochets through my chest as I beeline toward the entrance.

Several members of my executive board try to intercept me in the reception, but I barge on, seeing nothing but Lucy. She's just a fading silhouette now, swallowed by the city streets.

"Lucy!" I bellow, my voice cracking with desperation.

She halts in her tracks, spinning around to face me. Her face hardens as our eyes meet. Before I can say another word, she's marching away again.

Ignoring the sting of rejection, I bridge the gap between us and seize her arm.

"Lucy, please. Stop." My voice is a hoarse whisper, barely audible over New York's sounds.

"Get off me!" she hisses, tearing her arm away from me and casting me a look of pure disgust.

"Can we please go somewhere private to talk about this?"

"Go fuck yourself."

The harshness of her words slices through me, but I push on. "I just want you to hear me out, please."

"Hear you out?" she scoffs, jabbing a finger into my chest. "I never want to hear your voice ever again."

Her blue eyes blaze with resentment.

Panic surges through me as I struggle to maintain my composure. "Stop. Don't do this on the street. Lucy, I... I love you." The words tumble out, raw and ragged and desperately sincere.

She throws her arms out wide. "Love me? You're incapable of loving anyone other than yourself."

"You're wrong," I respond, my breaths coming in harsh bursts. "The only thing I love about myself is my love for you."

She blinks, taken aback, as I stumble over my words. "I... I mean it. I've despised myself for so long. You were the only part of me that felt good."

"I'm done hearing your lies. How could you trick me? How could you win me back, seduce me, earn my trust when this whole time I already left you once?" she snaps back, her voice choked with anger and pain. Her accusations hammer down on me, relentless.

I lift my hands defensively, shaking my head

in desperation. "That wasn't my intention. The doctors said I should wait. I just wanted you to see who I am now, before all that old stuff came up again."

Her chest heaves with emotion, her voice rising in anger. "Why the hell would I want to do that? I told myself I wouldn't go back, and you manipulated me into doing just that. Who does that? How dare you?"

"I'm not the same man, Lucy. I've changed. I gave up everything for you—the drugs, the lifestyle. I'm giving up the casinos. I'm ready to start fresh, in New York. All for you."

It's true—this isn't just empty bullshit. For longer than I care to admit, I've been questioning the direction of my life. Staring down the barrel at 40, facing my own mortality, I realized I needed meaning in my insane, hedonistic life.

But it wasn't until I started developing real feelings for Lucy that the stakes became clear. She represented something meaningful, something worth fighting for. But it wasn't an overnight flip.

Her words, however, cut me off, cold and bitter. "I remember, JP. I remember the night at your stupid party when you treated me like shit and broke my heart, and I remember the night at the Plaza when I gave you my resignation."

"I screwed up. No excuses. I messed up that night at my apartment. You broke it off with me, you kept going hot and cold. One minute you were in, the next you wanted nothing to do with me. I chose to forget the pain of our fight through pills and coke. But I regret it more than any decision in my life."

"You didn't look like you gave a shit. You walked straight past me like I was nobody."

A bitter truth. "I was high, Lucy. A pitiful excuse, I know. I won't ever forgive myself for it."

"How many women did you fuck that night?"

"No," I fire back, the sting of her accusation hitting hard. "I was in a bad place, yes, but I would never—do you hear me, *never* betray you like that. You have my word. That night, after our argument, it tore me up inside."

"Words. Just empty words." She turns away from me.

"They're not empty, Lucy. I'm leaving Vegas, my past life, everything, for you. I'm working to build a new future with you. I went to rehab, got a sponsor. I'm doing everything I can to become the man you deserve."

She whirls back around, her face a picture of disbelief. "Bullshit. This was all a lie. We were together, separated, and you kept it from me? I can't even wrap my head around this."

"Lucy, you had amnesia. The doctors suggested a slow reintroduction. I wanted you to know the person I've become, to understand my growth before confronting my past mistakes. I'm sorry I didn't tell you earlier. I just... I was scared. Please, baby."

With every word, I feel like I'm stripping my heart of its protective layers, laying it bare on the cold concrete. It's hers to trample on, to accept, to dismiss.

"Don't *baby* me. You don't fucking love me."

"I do. I've never been more sure of anything in my life." My voice drops to a hoarse whisper. "And it wasn't easy seeing the woman I love forget our past."

Her lips press together tightly as if she's afraid to speak.

"Lucy, you're my catalyst for change. You're the reason I've managed to turn my life around. I don't give a fuck what any one of the twelve million people who watch that video think. All I care about is you. All I think about is you."

She retaliates with a push to my chest. "Absolute bullshit. It was all a lie."

"It was never a lie! My life in Vegas was the lie! The pills, the parties, the drugs, that was the lie!

I'm willing to give up everything here. I'll never enter a casino again in my life if that's what you want. Just tell me what you want me to do and I'll do it. No questions."

Her hardened facade cracks for a moment. She's on the verge of tears, her lower lip quivering.

"Do you want me to get on my knees?" I ask in a low voice, a voice I barely recognize as my own, stripped of its command. "Because I will."

Her silence hangs heavy between us.

I drop to my knees on the cold, unyielding sidewalk, reaching for her hand. "Lucy, please see it from my point of view. You forgot me. I almost stormed into your hospital room to tell you everything from the start, but the doctor held me back. She warned it could traumatize you further. I was told to reintroduce myself gently. When I asked you as Daredevil if you wanted to see behind the mask and you declined, I took it as a sign you weren't ready. Was I supposed to lead with the part of me you hated? The shitshow chapters of our story? I wanted to show you I was a man worthy of your love."

She pulls back. "People in love don't lie to each other."

Even from my low position, I can see the startled faces of passersby turning toward the commotion, but I couldn't give a flying fuck.

"Well, most people in love don't have to deal with one of them forgetting everything," I retort, weariness seeping into my voice.

She glares down at me. "So this is my fault now?"

I look up at her, my gaze unwavering.

"No, I'm not fucking saying it's your fault." I exhale heavily. "Lucy, please. Don't give up on us."

She jerks her hand away as if she's been burned, walking backward until she bumps into someone on the sidewalk. Tears shine in her eyes even as her face hardens. "Stay away from me," she whispers. "That's all I want."

As she turns to leave, the murmurs and laughter reminds me we have an audience, and that I'm still in my kneeling position. But I barely notice the flashing cameras. The only thing I see is Lucy slipping away for good, taking my damaged heart with her.

FORTY-TWO

Lucy

If I thought the pain and fear of amnesia was bad, a broken heart has nothing on a broken mind. I'd gladly wipe my mind blank all over again than endure this relentless, gut-wrenching heartache another second.

Roxy, the nymphomaniacal sex doll, Spider, the human hurricane of mess, and Dave, the truly pathetic real estate agent, all look like saints in comparison to what JP has done to me.

I remember his words at the charity ball: *When I'm in love, I'm all in. I worship my woman. She becomes the center of my world, and I give her everything I've got, every single day.*

But I was never enough to be his center.

In an alternate universe, JP Wolfe would have remained a cold, arrogant boss who casually threatened my job. That would've been better than owning this heap of tragic memories with him, especially the ones where he turns my heart into a soggy doormat.

The memories keep clawing their way to the surface, each one more agonizing than the last. That God-awful night in his apartment, where I found him wasted out of his mind, surrounded by overpaid bankers, power-suit executives, and half-naked hangers-on.

Now I know why that smarmy creep at the charity gala set off alarms. I'd seen him before—the night of JP's coke-fueled party. He gave me that same smarmy look when I asked where JP was. No wonder JP tensed up seeing him again.

JP looked right through me that night. Like I was nothing. Invisible. Worthless. I may as well have been a houseplant.

Every time the memory resurfaces, I feel sick. I can't help but imagine what happened after I left. I can't halt the tormenting images of JP and one of the women in his bedroom. Why wouldn't he give in? It's unrealistic to believe he resisted. The thought of them together, his hands on her skin, his mouth on hers—it shatters me inside.

There's a special corner in hell for that JP. I hate that I know that side of him.

But I hate more that I saw the man within—the alluring enigma who let me glimpse his damaged soul. The one I fell hard for despite all the red flags and alarm bells.

I wish I could rip that JP from my memory, cut him out of my splintered heart.

Naturally, the office gossip machine is in overdrive with the latest about me and JP, ever since photos spilled out onto social media. The pictures of us fighting on the street haven't quite reached the tabloid gold standard set by JP's video masterpiece. Why would it? JP Wolfe in a public brawl with an average Jane doesn't exactly scream "page-turner" like him coked out of his mind.

Unless, of course, you work at Quinn & Wolfe.

Apparently, the marketing department, the pulsating heart of our rumor factory, is having an absolute field day.

I hold my pillow tighter, nausea stirring in my gut. For years at Quinn & Wolfe, I was a pro at fading into the background, camouflaged among photocopiers and whiteboards. Terrified of stumbling over my words or tripping on my heels, I shied away from the execs.

But now, look at me, the dazzling star of the fucking gossip freak show.

I can't go back to work. My love life is swirling down the toilet and my career's itching to take the same nosedive. It's an impressively catastrophic clusterfuck I've managed here.

The only silver lining to this cloud of shit is finding out who's truly in your corner.

Priya and Libby are playing hooky to make sure I'm not alone in my misery. I didn't sleep a wink last night, not since the fight on the street with JP yesterday. I half-expected him to go full-on battering ram and charging at my door in the middle of the night. But the anticipated assault never came, leaving me, if I'm being honest, disappointed.

Matty and Taylor have both been messaging support. Matty even promises he'll work hard to keep us on top of things while I'm busy "nursing a fever."

I've used my time at home efficiently, at least, and done a little more digging into who bought my apartment. Okay, most of the sleuthing credit goes to Priya.

No surprise, it was him. JP.

I told real estate Dave to decline the offer and he spat so strongly down the phone, I nearly felt the spray from over a mile away.

The guy thinks I'm off my rocker. He gave me a not-so-heartfelt farewell and basically suggested I take a long walk off a Chelsea Pier.

"This will all blow over," Libby says with

forced conviction from my recliner chair. "By next week, the office will be too engrossed in a new scandal!"

Priya nods, a master of cool. "Yep, it's not like you were caught having sex in the washrooms."

I sniff. "Actually, two guys in sales were caught having sex."

"With each other?"

"No." I shake my head. "One guy got a warning because he let a random woman into the building after a date and slept with her in the office."

"See?" Priya's brows rise. "Your office thrives on scandal! All you did was have a dispute with the boss. In fact, you might look like a badass."

"No, people think it's more. Matty told me."

Libby nods knowingly. "It's because he got on his knees. That didn't help."

No, it did not. I nearly lost it when he did that.

A heavy sigh slips past my lips as I turn my gaze to the window. We've been marooned in my living room all day, sipping tea and binging on the fabricated drama of reality TV wives to distract me.

But regardless of how many perfectly coiffed, surgically enhanced wives I gawk at, JP's face haunts me. His declaration of love was convincing, but his actions suggest a master of deceit. How can

I believe he didn't have sex that night? How do I know he won't treat me like shit again? Lie to me, go behind my back, betray me...

Priya says logistically he probably didn't sleep with anyone. If he was that far gone, he wouldn't have been able to get it up. It's not much of a comfort.

"You should have told us earlier, Luce. About you and JP the first time around," Priya murmurs, casting a contemplative look my way. "I think even Libby could have managed to keep it to herself."

"Hey!" Libby hurls a pillow toward Priya, defending her honor. "It's not like I don't try! I'm a good friend."

"I know you are." I lean over and rub her arm. "You're here, aren't you? Prioritizing me? I've had so much shit going on and you girls have really come through for me." I feel my eyes welling for the billionth time since yesterday. "Lesson learned here—be more trusting in people and myself. I think I didn't tell you all about it because I was afraid you'd think less of me. I'm pretty sure it started as no-strings sex. But if I opened up to you, then there would have been no mystery when I took a swan dive down the Plaza stairs."

"So, for future reference—"

The shrill buzzing of the doorbell interrupts

Priya mid-sentence. I nearly decorate my couch with my now trembling cup of tea.

We freeze, exchanging panicked looks. It buzzes again, more insistent.

"Are you expecting something from Amazon?" Libby asks, her voice barely above a whisper.

I shake my head, adrenaline spiking. I cast a nervous glance toward the half-open window. Shit.

On a shared impulse, we sneak out of our seats. Then we drop to our knees, crawling toward the window, reminiscent of my mom hiding from Jehovah's Witnesses when they used to show up at the door.

"You look," I mouth to Priya.

She peers out cautiously. Her eyes widen as she drops down again, mouthing, "It's him."

My heart hammers against my ribs. He can probably hear it through the window.

"I can see you hiding," JP calls out from the street. Shit. Busted.

Like three bobblehead dolls, we raise our heads in unison.

Just the sight of him triggers a wave of sadness. His tousled hair, his weary eyes, his worn-out jeans and rumpled blue tee.

His gaze lands on the three of us. "Hello,

ladies." He addresses Priya and Libby. "Luce never wanted this introduction to happen." He sighs. "I'm sorry it isn't under better circumstances. This isn't the way I pictured it."

Despite the hurt, curiosity compels me. "Why didn't I want them to meet you? Besides the glaring fact that you're a lying psycho?"

His lips twist in a melancholy smile. "For a long time, you were embarrassed. You downplayed our office fling. Never believed it was serious."

"Clearly you didn't either," I retort, my temper flaring as I push the window open wider. "What are you doing here?"

"Can I come up? We need to talk."

"No. Say what you want from there."

Frustration flashes across his face, but he swallows it down. He runs a hand through his tousled hair and a pang of longing hits me. I wish that was my hand. "Just hear me out. Please."

I fold my arms. "You've got five minutes. From down there."

His face darkens, agitated. "Seriously, from the street, Lucy?"

My eyes narrow.

"Okay." He runs a hand through his hair again as if he's flustered. His gaze finds mine, locking me in with that familiar formidable intensity that both frightens and excites me.

"I'm not the best at heartfelt speeches, but there are things you need to know. I'm flawed, yes. But I tried with us, Lucy. You only remember our darkest moments, it seems. But I have all our memories locked away and I can tell you we have some amazing ones. Real, beautiful memories that show we're worth fighting for."

"Ahhh," Priya swoons beside me. I elbow her harshly.

"We had the best life, full of laughter, love, and simplicity. You gave me the foundation of happiness that I was always looking for. You were the one who I went to the wellness retreat with. Bear Mountain wasn't our first time paddleboarding. You're good at it for a reason." His face softens as if he's remembering something.

"But you held back. You didn't take that leap of faith. You refused to fully let me in, kept your friends and your mother at a distance from me." His voice breaks a little, the words heavy with emotion. "But I wanted all that. I wanted you to let me in. I wanted to meet Priya and Libby. I wanted to take you and your mom to Captain's Crab for your birthday. I wanted to take you to garden centers with your mom. I wanted to go to comic conventions with you. That's the only thing you let me do—because I was wearing a mask."

"You're my Daredevil," I say, the words slipping out.

"Of course I'm Daredevil. If you want me to parade around in a damn rubber suit all day I'll oblige."

His declaration earns him bemused glances from folks wandering the street.

"I got that action figure for you on your desk, to remind you of me while I was in Vegas, but without raising suspicions." The regret is thick in his smile.

"You bought that action figure?" I say breathlessly.

"Yes."

Priya's swooning escalates, much to my annoyance. I make a futile attempt to push her away from the window.

My eyes well up traitorously. This is too much.

No, you fool. Hold it together. He manipulated you. Remember his dead gaze when he walked past you like you were nothing?

"Luce," he demands, locking me in a gaze that steals my breath. "I'm asking you to take a leap of faith for me now. I will do everything in my power to prove that I deserve it. We'll live wherever you want. Hell, even this apartment, above the sex shop, I don't care. I'll never step foot in a casino again if you say the word. Never take another drug. Never make another bet. I'm not the man I was that awful night. I fought tooth and nail to prove it before your accident, and I won't stop until you believe."

His words hang in the air, stirring a cocktail of emotions in me.

"Are you an addict?" I demand bluntly, shouting down to him.

He stares up at me. "You really want to hash this out here on the street?"

I stay silent, arms folded. It's my way or the highway.

"No." He sighs. "I don't physically need drugs or alcohol every day. But sometimes I overindulge and go overboard when I'm stressed. No one reined me in, including myself. But those days are behind me now."

"Bullshit," I snap, another painful memory flashing through my mind. "You're nothing but a big liar. I saw the woman at your apartment the other night. Admin, my ass. How stupid do you think I am?"

Confusion crosses his face. "What are you talking about?"

"Saturday night," I state flatly.

"Saturday..." He frowns. "That's my therapist. I couldn't tell you until you knew everything."

"Therapy? On a Saturday night? That's almost as believable as admin."

"I pay enough that I can do it whenever I want."

Skepticism narrows my eyes. "Why should I believe that?"

"You can meet her yourself, ask anything you want." He gazes up solemnly. "I have nothing left to hide from you."

"Why would I believe that you'll stick around? That you won't go back to your old ways next time you're in Vegas?"

His sigh seeps with desperation. "Believe me, Luce, I'll stick around."

I scowl down at him, my heart pounding with uncertainty. "You're the pain my subconscious warned me about. You're the stupid dog, Buddy."

"I guess I am."

More weird looks from passersby.

"How can I be sure you never had sex that night at your party?" I demand.

"You'll have to trust me. No matter how messed up I was, I never betrayed you like that." His jaw clenches, voice dropping an octave. "So get this straight—I've never wanted another woman since I had you."

I snort and roll my eyes, even as his words pierce my chest.

His eyes darken with intensity, like a switch has flipped. "You clearly don't care enough to fight for us. The truth is you don't want to meet me halfway. You want to lose yourself in comics and live in Lucy fairyland because that's easier than actually doing the hard stuff with me. We could have an incredible life together—it would be raw, challenging, exhilarating. Not some fairytale bullshit. But it would be a lot more satisfying and exciting than living apart."

He runs a hand through his hair, looking genuinely anguished. "This isn't easy for me either, Lucy. I'm not some emotionless fucking robot. You wiped me from your heart and memories like I was nothing. Even when you hated me after that night at my place, the party... at least you still cared deeply. Your pain meant I still mattered. Then you woke up in the hospital and I meant nothing to you." He takes a breath. "I'm laying my heart on the line. Asking you point blank—do you want me?"

"No," I sob, tears betraying my facade.

He nods slowly, jaw clenched. "If you don't want me, I can't force you. But know you have my heart." His eyes blaze. "What you do with it is up to you now."

The metallic glint of the saucepan catches my attention too late. I hadn't noticed Libby's disappearance.

As if in slow motion, the water propels from the saucepan out of the open window and lands all over JP's face and chest, drenching him.

My hand flies to my mouth as Priya and I gasp.

"Libby!" I screech.

"He deserved it!" she shoots back.

JP doesn't flinch, doesn't retaliate. Just stands there, water dripping down his muscular frame.

Slowly, he wipes his face, piercing my soul with one final fiery look. Then he turns and strides down the street without a glance back.

I watch him disappear as my heart shatters once more, scattering to the Manhattan breeze.

FORTY-THREE

Lucy

For about forty-eight tedious, exhausting hours, things are pretty mundane apart from one decidedly non-mundane detail—a dread-cloud, monstrous and dark, like a gloomy stalker refusing to get the hint.

It takes hold in every tiny bit of me, rooting itself down into a tight, knotty mess that seems to have replaced my stomach. Food, for all intents and purposes, might as well be cardboard.

My fingers seem to have a mind of their own, relentlessly pulling up those social media pictures of JP on his knees in front of me in the street. It doesn't matter where I am—slicing onions in the kitchen, strolling in the park, sipping my coffee at the café, or even, God help me, while sitting on the toilet. Waking up at stupid o'clock in the night to peep at them, as if maybe they'll vanish in a puff of virtual smoke. Then when I've had enough of those, I watch the video that publicly shamed JP over and over again.

It's a compulsion. A full-blown addiction. Every few minutes, my fingers betray me, clicking on the photo, each time feeling the sharp sting of anxiety. I feel more stripped and vulnerable than if I had strutted into the office in my racy Miss Nova getup with the eye-popping cutouts.

The camera's interest was fixated on JP's disgrace more than on my own existence in the frame. I take a peculiar comfort in that. I don't want my fifteen minutes. The idea turns my stomach.

Ding, ding, ding. The messages from Taylor, Matty, and some of the office lot continue to stream in. Their concern seems genuine, but I can practically hear the gossip cranking into high gear back at HQ. I'm haunted by imagined chatter from sales and marketing and finance and all the other teams... and especially, oh especially, from IT.

Taylor called and told me to take some days off. She said if there's anyone who can cash in their sick leave, it's the Memoryless Woman.

Angry Andy, apparently, is not feeling as charitable. We have the presentation to the directors in two days for a significant Project Tangra milestone, and he's having kittens that I'm playing truant.

I've been working from home, keeping Taylor in the loop. I'm not about to leave Project Tangra in the lurch, or the team. And Matty, good old Matty, is making a heroic stab at getting his shit together and manning the fort until I come back to the office.

Maybe it takes not doing your best all the time for people to appreciate your best.

I'm trying my damned best to shove JP out of my head. The memory of him, drenched, haunts me. He looked so destroyed.

I pick up books, but the words are just squiggles on a page. I drag myself to the coffee shop two blocks down, but the coffee might as well be dishwater. I waffle into the comic store, but the panels and speech bubbles might as well be hieroglyphs.

Heartbreak is a fucking minefield.

I scrub the bath with vigor in an attempt to scour away my anxiety and pain.

When I see Mom's name light up the phone, I let out an audible groan. She's the last voice I need to hear. But I can't ghost her indefinitely.

"Hi, Mom."

"Lucy."

I wince. Christ, that tone.

"Mrs. Mills down the street has just sent me some links. Lucy, why on earth are you squabbling with your boss in public? What the hell has gotten into you?"

"Hold on," I drawl. "You see a picture of my boss groveling at my feet and you automatically assume *I'm* to blame?"

"It's not exactly professional. You need to consider the fallout of your actions."

My eyes nearly pop out of their sockets. Something inside me breaks, like a ten-year-old dam. She's hit a nerve. Just the right mix of words, tone, and timing has tipped me over the edge I've been teetering on for years.

"You know what, I've had enough of this. You're either in my corner or you're not. I can't do this right now. Call me when you're ready to play the role of a supportive mother instead of pumping venom into my life. As if I don't have enough crap to handle."

I slam the phone down, my heart pounding as I slump next to the bath. Mom's name pops up on the screen again but I mute it. I'm physically trembling.

No wonder I'm all tangled up about what people think, trying to outwork myself at the office. I've endured her sniping, backhanded comments for years. Ever since she figured out that Dad was sometimes a bit of an asshole—sorry, dead dad—and maybe she hadn't quite bagged Prince Charming after all.

I take a deep breath and rest my head against the bath. It's time I sort my shit out.

◆ ◆ ◆

As usual, the neon arrow follows me into reception, no longer pointing at the Memoryless Woman, but the Memoryless Woman Who Had A Thing With The Boss.

People who usually wouldn't give me the time of day now stop and stare. All eyes turn to me, judging, dissecting. I force a bright smile as my heels click-clack conspicuously across the floor.

Not that I think heels make me a better creative or anything, but why shouldn't I wear them if I want to? I'm a woman on the edge, so if any of these nosy bastards say the wrong thing, they'll be getting a spiky heel up their crack.

"Hi, Abigail," I call out loudly across the reception and wave.

Her eyes nearly make a break for it out of her skull before she plasters on a smile and waves me over, no doubt looking for gossip.

"Can't stop, sorry!" I yell as I nearly crash into Logan the security guard. "So sorry for breaking into Mr. Wolfe's car. Hope I didn't get you in trouble or anything?"

Logan looks startled. "No, no trouble. I was just worried about you." How sweet.

"You're too kind." I give a wave and stride toward the elevator.

The elevator bay is packed, but suddenly everyone is tripping over themselves to make room for me in their carriage.

Just as the elevator doors are about to close, a polished black shoe wedges in.

My heart leaps out of my chest, does a little somersault, and lands with a splat on the elevator floor.

Of course it's him—JP fucking Wolfe.

You could hear a pin drop as all eyes volley between us, the tense elevator now a living tennis match. I wish I could melt into the floor and disappear. I give JP a tight smile and stare desperately at the closing doors.

Despite his suave exterior, dark circles under his eyes betray exhaustion. Part of me aches to run my hands through his hair, to hold him, to kiss him. The mere sight of him makes my body ache.

As we ascend, I agonize over how to play this.

Shit, is he getting off on my floor?

The doors open and everyone deferentially steps back to let the boss exit first.

I consider riding this thing to the top just to avoid him, but that's too obvious.

So I follow him out, pulse quickening as those penetrating eyes find mine. Unfairly handsome in his tailored suit, he waits for me.

"Lucy," he rumbles in a deep baritone, his gaze seeking answers. "How are you holding up?"

"Spectacular," I snap sarcastically through a tight smile.

He acknowledges my tone with a sad half-smile and inhales deeply, drawing my attention to his broad chest and the heart beating underneath. A swell of emotion chokes me.

I wish he'd stop looking at me like that.

"Things are going to change around here," he says. "I'll do whatever it takes to make you comfortable at work."

My throat constricts. Is this his way of saying he's done fighting for us?

I don't know what he's getting at, but it doesn't matter now. I'm taking control of my own destiny, starting with the Project Tangra presentation.

"It's fine, really," I manage to choke out, forcing myself to hold his gaze. "Look, I'm sorry for Libby chucking a saucepan of water over you."

He lets out a soft chuckle. "It's not the worst thing that's happened to me lately."

I make a noncommittal grunt, too choked up to quip anything in return. "I gotta run."

"Hold on." He pulls a white envelope from his jacket pocket. "I want you to have this. Look at it when you're alone."

I accept the envelope, hoping my trembling hands aren't too noticeable. What is this? A severance package?

Before he can see the moisture pooling in my eyes, I turn and walk away. My heart feels like it's being stomped by my own stilettos.

I make my way through the open office plan to my desk, bracing myself. I'm half expecting a "Congrats on banging the boss!'" balloon waiting for me.

But everyone just stops and stares with needle-prick eyes as I pass. Even the hardcore coders halt their typing. This is worse than when I first came back with amnesia.

To my shock, Matty is already at his desk, working diligently.

"Matty! Look at you, a new man," I say.

"Yeah, don't get used to it," he snorts. "Tried the whole 'responsible adult' thing, but turns out

I'm still a lazy asshole. You'll have to pick up at least 60 percent of my slack as usual."

I laugh for the first time in days. I'll take 60 percent over his normal 90.

Then they descend—my colleagues swarming in with their endless questions. From the mundane to the outright outrageous.

"So what's the deal with you and Wolfe then?"

"You two an item now or what?"

"I heard he's being indicted for smuggling drugs. That legit?"

"Think he'll give us a budget bump?"

"Is it true Wolfe's in the mafia?"

"Can you sweet talk him into extending the deadline?"

In the commotion, Matty leaps up, rolls up his sleeves, and does a perfect impression of Andy, sniffing his pits theatrically. "All right, people, show's over! We've got actual work to do here."

Reluctantly, the crowd around my desk disperses.

I dip my chin and smile, while inside, my heart shrivels like a sad little raisin. I put on a mask, keeping my head high and my heels steady. But the truth? I'm barely holding it together.

I race to the bathroom, JP's letter in my white-knuckled grip. Hands shaking, I tear it open.

Photographs spill out—snapshots of a life erased from memory. My breath catches as I stagger back against the cubicle wall.

There we are, paddleboarding at Bear Mountain, so happy and carefree. A selfie of us nestled between towering trees, his strong arms around me. A picture of us on his mansion's viewing deck, the mountains as our backdrop. Him kissing me as I laugh.

Candid shots he's taken of me when I wasn't looking. One of us lounging on his couch. One where we're fumbling to kiss while taking a selfie.

And there's a note in his scrawl: "These are my memories. JP."

I sink to the floor, photographs scattered around me like memories I'll never get back.

Two hours later, we're presenting the final grand Tangra solution to the terrifying Quinns and the rest of the vulture suit circus.

Taylor's at the helm, with Angry Andy—God love him—bouncing out of his seat, offering his pearls of irrelevance at the worst moments.

Killian Quinn, in a rare occurrence, smiles at me. He knows everything. Of course he knows.

JP, though, is conspicuously absent. A pang of disappointment twinges within me. Despite still feeling utterly betrayed by the man, I want him to witness me in action, maybe beam with a bit of pride. Ugh.

With sweaty pits and knocking knees, we lay out our game plan to drag all those other casinos into the cashless era, one agonizing milestone at a time. I can feel my blouse gluing itself to my back with sweat.

The suits, they're not letting us off easy. It's an eternal tug-of-war between the creative peasants and the corporate overlords.

"Your rollout plan is sluggish," Killian drones in his trademark monotone. We counter, warning of the potential risks in rushing.

"Shave off a month," cuts in Connor Quinn. And back we fire, loaded with data, numbers, and a dollop of despair.

Meanwhile, Andy perches eagerly, ready to be a yes-man to their every inane whim.

When Killian Quinn finally breaks the tension, praising our efforts and calling it a day, there's a communal exhale of relief. We survived the lions' den this time.

"Lucy," Killian commands as everyone else shuffles out. "A word, please. The rest of you are dismissed."

Great. Just great.

They shoot me pitying looks, relieved it's not them left alone with the executioner. Even Andy doesn't look happy as he exits.

It's just Killian and me now, the silence heavy and ominous. I swallow hard, my fingers fidgeting unconsciously with my bangs.

"I'll be direct," he begins. "I'm aware of what transpired between you and JP. Not all the details, but enough."

I swallow hard, mouth dry.

"If you feel you can no longer work here comfortably, we will make sure you are taken care of. Rewarded generously."

My palms turn clammy. Is JP trying to get rid of me?

"Are you saying my job is in jeopardy?" I ask, struggling to keep my voice even.

"Not at all," he says. "Simply that if you wish to leave, we will ensure a smooth transition."

I force a tight smile. "I'll think about it."

He's not done. "JP wants you to feel comfortable here. If that's no longer possible, we'll make your exit a painless one. One that sets you up."

A buyout. They want to toss cash at me to

disappear quietly.

JP wants me gone. That's what he was alluding to when he said things would change.

The realization lands like a blow. He's done fighting for me—for us. Now he just wants the "problem" eliminated.

"Where is JP now?" I ask breathily.

"He's in Vegas. Had business to attend to."

Vegas. I knew it. His pretty words were nothing but bullshit in the end.

I make my escape on wobbly legs. As soon as I'm out of sight, I slump against the wall, dizzy with anxiety.

This is why I have to do what I'm planning quickly. I need to prove that I'm valued here or it's years' worth of work down the toilet.

I stride down the aisle toward Andy's seat.

"Andy," I say, the artificial calmness in my voice contrasting the riot of nerves within me. "Can I borrow you for a moment?"

He scowls but waves me into an empty office. "If this is about the situation between you and Mr. Wolfe, HR can help."

"Oh, it's not," I assure him, pulling out my self-evaluation from my bag—that wretched document we all fill with a billion performance markers thanks to HR Helen. "Actually, it's about this. See, I feel like I've downplayed myself the past few years. But the proof is here that I consistently exceed expectations. I'm operating at Lead level, and with the presentation today, I hope you agree I'm ready for promotion."

I flash him a dazzling smile.

Andy grunts, noncommittal as ever. "We'll reassess at performance reviews."

Still smiling, I go in for the kill. "Here's the thing. I feel my contributions have been undervalued here for a while. So if I'm not promoted by the end of the month, I'm handing in my notice."

His eyes bulge out. "You'll what?"

"I've loved my six years here, but if there's no room for growth, then it's time for me to move on. You understand, right? Opportunities abound elsewhere... Solaris International Hotels & Resorts, for instance, have a rather appealing vacancy in their IT team..."

He inhales sharply, nostrils flaring like he's trying to suck in the room.

And for the first time since that horrible video of JP surfaced, I feel a smidge of hope.

FORTY-FOUR

Lucy

Five days later, I get the email that I'm being promoted. My eyes dance over the email on my phone. So the winning recipe was 30 percent talent, 30 percent hard work, and 30 percent backbone.

Good thing I don't work in accounts. Apparently, my math is a bit off.

"What's got you smiling?" Priya asks, leading me to her spare room.

I share the news of my promotion, my plan paying off. She envelopes me in a warm hug. "See? Life's not so bad."

I force a smile, but it's brittle and false. Sure, life's looking up, but deep down, I'm shattered. My nights are filled with insomnia as thoughts of JP invade my mind. He's the first thing I think about when I wake up. I haven't seen him since the day outside the elevator.

He's back in Vegas. The ever-chatty office gossip asserts that he's there for good. Matty managed to glean a bit of information about JP's location from a girl in marketing. The word is, JP has been a steady fixture in the casinos every evening. Ruling his empire.

Priya pirouettes in the center of the room like a kid. "Well, what do you think?"

I take it in—modest but homey. Only a bed for now, but I can already picture my possessions scattered about. A breeze drifts in through the open window.

"It's perfect," I say, and I mean it.

She pulls me into another hug. "Welcome to your new home, roomie."

Yesterday, I tackled the apartment issue head-on. Deciding to put it up for rent. Turns out there's at least a rental market for living above a sex shop. The rent's enough to cover the mortgage until I conjure a permanent fix. For the time being, I'm shacking up with Priya, an arrangement I'm genuinely thrilled about. If I survived living with Spider, I can handle living with my best friend.

Priya squeezes my shoulder and tells me she'll give me "space," and thank fuck for that because I've needed nothing but space lately.

With a heaviness I can't shake, I collapse

onto the bed and begin to unzip my bag. Amid the everyday detritus—my phone, keys, wallet, an absurd number of coffee receipts—lies my secret torment, the pieces of the past I can't bring myself to abandon. The photos JP gave me. Our shared moments, frozen in glossy 4x6 rectangles. For days, I've been this way, masochistically thumbing through them, only to hastily shove them back into the safety of my bag.

The one on top is like a punch to the gut. Central Park. A selfie with his strong arm wrapped around me, my lips pressed to his scratchy cheek. He's wearing a baseball cap and he looks so handsome. There's a picnic basket in the background. I look undeniably smitten, the proverbial cat that got the cream.

I don't know why this photo hits me the hardest.

My eyes well up, the happiness in our faces too stark a contrast to my current reality. I turn it over.

Here's to new beginnings. New beginnings without JP. My throat tightens painfully.

Central Park has a way of tricking you into thinking you've escaped the city. Strolling along the curving pathways, it's all trees and blooms as far as the eye can see. But then the Manhattan skyline peeks through the greenery, an ever-present reminder that you're still in the concrete jungle. One of them is JP's apartment building, jerking up into the skyline like an arrogant cock.

I tell myself that I'm just out for an innocent stroll, and I almost believe the lie.

Feet with a mind of their own take over. It's not like I know where I'm going, except I do.

The Untermyer Fountain, with its iconic bronze figures forever suspended in a watery waltz. It's unmistakably visible in the background of the photo.

An unsettling knot forms in my stomach, pulling tighter as I near the section of grass that lines up with our picture. The exact spot where our bodies had apparently once lain entwined.

Now, it's just me.

I ease myself onto the grass, its blades jabbing into my skin like tiny reminders of reality. I yank the photo from my pocket, holding on to it like I'm Rose gripping that dang Heart of the Ocean in *Titanic*.

As I look at my beaming face in the photo, my heart doesn't just clench; it trips over itself.

With a heavy sigh, I lie back, letting the grass

cushion my body. I hold the photo above me, the sunlight filtering through the glossy print.

Slowly, I shut my eyes, the photo clutched in my fist. The park's bustle recedes to a low hum, like the world's got its volume down, and suddenly, I'm right back there.

Back in that moment.

JP's sprawled on the blanket, the sun gleaming off that perfectly sculpted jawline hidden beneath a layer of infuriatingly sexy stubble. I sit cross-legged beside him, absentmindedly picking at blades of grass, resisting the urge to run my hands over his broad chest. I'm horny just looking at him. God, I'm always horny these days.

"I'll be in Vegas all next week for work," he drawls, eyes closed from under his baseball hat.

My shoulders slump. "The whole week?"

One gorgeous brown eye opens, piercing me. "Come with me. Work from the Vegas office."

I shake my head with a wry laugh. "Oh, yeah. Let me tell Angry Andy that I'm jetting off to Vegas on a sudden whim."

He raises a brow, both eyes now fixed on me. "Have you forgotten who owns the company?"

"I can't play that card. You know that." I flick a piece of grass at him.

He intercepts my hand, suddenly serious. "Why not, Luce? Isn't it time you started telling people about us?"

My eyes widen. "Why would I do that?"

He hoists himself onto his elbows, a scowl etched into his handsome features. "Why? You're asking why? Are you planning on keeping me your dirty little secret forever?"

My heart flutters traitorously. I look away. "Yes? We both know I'm just using you for sex and status."

A heavy sigh leaves his lips. "Look at me," he says, his voice a soothing, deep baritone that has my eyes meeting his. "I need a serious answer."

"I just... I didn't think you were the forever type." I lower my gaze, finding a sudden interest in the grass beneath us.

His fingers cradle my chin, tilting my face upward. "I'd like to stick around, if you'll let me."

"Yeah?" I breathe.

"Absolutely." His thumb traces a path over my bottom lip. "I have no intention of letting you go."

I can't stop the giddy smile spreading across my face. "I think I might like that."

"So does that mean you'll come clean about us?"

I shuffle. "The last thing I need is to be the hot gossip in the IT department."

"The same guys who have a shrine to Sheldon

Cooper? Why the fuck do you care? I'm not sure half of them would even be interested."

"Of course I care!"

He wraps an arm around me, pulling me on top of his firm, gorgeous body. "We can handle this, Lucy. I'll make sure nothing looks bad on you."

"You can do a lot but you can't do that. You can't control people's judgments and snide remarks."

"No," he agrees. His grip on my hips tightens possessively. "But I can shift your perspective on handling it. And I can sure as hell fire anyone who messes with you."

I smack his chest playfully, laughing. "I hope you're joking!"

His expression grows serious, eyes darkening. "Nothing I say is a joke right now. Come on, Lucy, you've met Maggie and my nephews. Isn't it time you started telling some people?"

Suddenly he rolls, pinning me beneath him against the picnic blanket. He gazes down at me, his muscular frame pressing against my softer curves. His face is just inches from mine, his minty breath warm against my skin. "And it's time you let me tell people you're mine," he murmurs.

I bite my lip nervously. "I'm just scared... in case it ends and then everyone knows I slept with the boss."

He brushes a strand of hair from my face, his eyes

tender. "That won't happen."

My breath catches. "How can you be so sure?"

He holds my gaze. "Because I love you. I'm all in, Lucy. I'll do whatever it takes to make this work."

My pulse spikes. "You... you love me?"

"I do," he murmurs, his brown eyes fixed on me. "I'm not expecting you to say it back yet. Just know I'm in this for the long haul."

His eyes bore into me with such intensity I swear he's staring into the depths of my secrets.

Overcome with emotion, I knock off his baseball cap so I can run my fingers through his silky locks. He comes down to press his lips against mine. My hands roam urgently over the muscular planes of his back, pulling him closer. His body presses harder against mine.

We melt into each other, our kisses growing more heated, more consuming. I wrap myself around him, craving no space between us. Hands roaming everywhere like we have eight of them. Breathing ragged.

This is it. This is the kiss I've been waiting for. A kiss that tastes undeniably of love.

FORTY-FIVE

JP

"JP, this isn't something you're obligated to do," Killian protests, spinning in his chair to fix his penetrating gaze on me.

"Or to be precise," Connor interjects, heaving a tired sigh, "we'd prefer if you didn't. Our gaming license is locked down. How you managed that with the gaming commission is beyond me."

His tone, laced with a hint of begrudging respect, brings a fleeting smile to my face. Being aware of who the top dogs' mistresses are comes in handy, as does subtly hinting I may gather them all for a soiree.

"There are zero logical reasons for you to step down," Killian argues, his voice bouncing off the sleek, minimalist walls of our executive boardroom. The one with the twenty-foot window overlooking the Manhattan skyline. I'll miss this view, that's for sure. "This is your company. You built it with us. Without you, we wouldn't be taking in more money than any other casinos in the country."

His argument hits home. The logical, ambitious part of my brain is screaming bloody murder, pleading with me to cling to this empire I've shed sweat, tears, and blood for. Turning my back on it feels like amputating a limb. As I was mentoring my enthusiastic successor this week, it all surged back—the thrill of the casino floor, the electric buzz in the air, the dizzying wave of power that washed over me whenever I walked through those doors. I've spent more time on those casino floors than in my own home.

Maybe she's a lost cause. Maybe this grand gesture is me pissing my legacy away on a love doomed to fail. It wouldn't be the first time I lost it all on a bad bet.

"I have to do this," I reply, my voice calm but firm. Because this is the only way to show Lucy I'm in this for real. Vegas has been my lover, my life, for the longest time. But Lucy needs to see that she's taken that place now, whether she accepts it or not.

Sure, the wellness resorts are little more than a pipe dream at the moment. A billionaire playboy like me might keep Vegas buzzing, but no sane person is going to look for peace and detox at a wellness center run by a casino mogul playboy.

But I can't keep running the casinos. Not if I hope to convince Lucy of my sincerity.

We're just about to kick off our monthly staff-wide assembly, and I have a rather significant disclosure to make.

Just then, Killian's PA, a young woman who always appears on edge around us, knocks and enters. "Sorry to intrude. The staff is assembled."

"Are the video links to the other branches ready?" I ask.

She nods, her voice filled with nervous energy. "The staff here is congregated in the Grand Conference Hall."

No turning back now.

I return the nod and we stride toward the hall, the only space vast enough in the entire structure to accommodate the throng of employees waiting for the impending news.

As I walk onto the stage, the sea of faces looking up, expectant and curious, is overwhelming. Killian initiates with company news and sales forecasts, but the air of anticipation is undeniable. They're all waiting for me. I can't see Lucy among them—I don't even know if she's here.

My mind flashes back to her image, glaring out the window at me, rejecting me. Maybe I've lost faith in the prospect of her forgiveness, of her changing her mind about me. But at the very least, I need to prove to her that I'm serious about steering my life toward a new horizon.

"And now, JP would like to share a few thoughts," Killian announces over the microphone. He turns to me, his face a mask of devastation.

I step forward, feeling the weight of every eye on me. "Afternoon. I'll cut to the chase here. You've all caught that footage of my slip-up. I let you down. The man you saw isn't the leader I've aimed to be. For over a decade, I've lived and breathed Vegas and our casinos, but in the process, I've hurt people I care about deeply. I've lost sight of the man I want to be. With that said, I'm stepping down from Quinn & Wolfe, effective immediately."

A collective gasp ripples through the conference hall. Wide eyes, gaping mouths—the shock is palpable, sweeping over the room like a wave.

I force a smile, struggling for normalcy. But inside, the war rages on. Vegas has been my whole world for so long. The ambitious wolf in me howls in outrage at stepping aside.

But the man willing to change for Lucy stands resolute.

"Let me assure you, your jobs are secure, and our casinos will remain at the top. Tony Astion from Royal Casinos will take the reins of the casinos and clubs. As for me, I intend to focus on a new chapter in my life, one that hopefully brings about growth, understanding, and a commitment to becoming a better person. Someone that the people I love will deem worthy to take a leap of faith in. Someone deserving of trust, respect... and love."

Never in my years in charge have the staff heard me bare my soul like this. I can see the shock, the disbelief, the bewilderment on their faces. It would be comical if my heart wasn't pounding inside my chest.

The silence that follows is deafening. I offer up a silent plea. *Lucy, wherever you are, hear me. Understand this is for you. Every word, every heartbeat, it's all for you. I am ready to change, ready to evolve into the man you deserve.*

All for you, Lucy. Just for you.

Deafening silence follows. Then a lone fool starts clapping before stopping abruptly, realizing no one is joining in.

I make my exit from the stage, leaving the

stunned crowd in Connor's capable hands.

Killian corners me in the deserted hallway, his eyes reflecting a medley of disappointment and reluctant acceptance.

"What now?" His voice is gravelly, matching the turmoil in his eyes.

I force a smile, attempting to inject some normalcy into the situation. "I'm heading to Phoenix, going to spend time with Maggie and the boys. I'll spend some time at Bear Mountain after that."

Killian nods, a small smile playing on his lips. "That sounds right. What's all this worth if we can't enjoy it with the people who matter?"

And lord knows, I have so few left of those.

I slap him on the back and tell him I'll see him soon.

I leave him in the silent hallway, my mind swirling with mixed emotions. Heading back to my office, the usually buzzing HQ is eerily quiet, a ghost town—the fallout of my resignation still hanging heavy in the air.

It's too late for regrets now. I've rolled the dice, gone all in... for her. Even if it's all for nothing in the end.

FORTY-SIX

Lucy

He resigned... he actually resigned.

I walk back to the IT floor in a daze, the team trailing behind me. A hush has fallen over the office after that shocking mic-drop of a speech.

"Are you okay?" Taylor asks gently as we return to our desks. All eyes are on me, but no one speaks up, not even Matty.

I'm stunned. I'm in shock. My brain's stopped working. Error 404: Cannot Process This Shit.

"I'm fine," I reply with a weak smile.

He's leaving for good. You'll never see him again, a voice inside me wails.

That week he went to Vegas, he must have been handing over his duties, preparing for his departure. I thought it was because he'd moved on. I thought he'd gone back to business as usual, completely giving up on us after a saucepan of water was dunked over him outside Naughty

Nonsense.

I wish I could remember his words during the speech. I was just too frozen in the moment to think straight.

When I get to my desk, I find a delivery waiting for me. I open it up to reveal a glossy graphic novel, and my pulse quickens. What the hell?

"You all right, Luce?" Matty asks.

I must look alarmed, clutching the comic with my mouth hanging open. "Yeah, fine. Just grabbing a coffee," I mumble.

I hurry down the aisle, trying not to draw attention.

Quinn & Wolfe have little "relaxation nooks" on each floor filled with beanbags, plants, and a coffee machine—although I've never seen anyone actually sit in a beanbag chair.

I enter the coffee area, finding it deserted.

I stare down at the graphic novel in my hands, my pulse thundering in my ears. The glossy pages shine under the flickering fluorescent lights of the office's relaxation nook. This is a custom story— Miss Nova and Daredevil don't exist together in comics.

I sink into a plush beanbag chair, hardly aware of the world around me as I turn to the first page.

The pages leap out, bold blues and reds and the

occasional flash of flesh.

Nora Allcott, bug-eyed in jeans and a checkered shirt, gazes at the stars through a telescope. She looks just like me, but with superpowers and way better boobs.

A cosmic storm strikes, transforming her into Miss Nova, defender of the galaxy.

I keep reading. A two-page spread fills my vision with bursting stars—supernovas blast from Nova's hands as she manipulates gravity.

I turn the page with trembling fingers to see the brooding, tortured figure of the "Golden Age Daredevil", in his blue and red suit, lurking in the shadows of a dark city. Ripped, obviously.

JP's eyes—God, his eyes—pin me with that intense stare. Eyes that seem to follow me as I turn the page.

He tries to be a hero, but a demonic rage threatens to consume him, leaving only violence and instability in its wake.

And Miss Nova comes to rescue him from himself. Daredevil slowly falls in love with Miss Nova, who brings light into his dark world. He buys a telescope to share her passion for stars.

As I continue reading, a gasp escapes my lips. There before me is an image of myself and JP, recreated in stunning comic book art. JP stands behind me, his hand on my shoulder as I peer into a telescope under a sparkling night sky. It looks so real. Is this from a photo?

The pages slip through my fingers faster now, showing Daredevil falling for the cosmic heroine Miss Nova. Fantasy combined with our love story. Scenes of our passion play out on the pages—kissing in the office, strolling in the park, at his apartment. At my apartment... Did that happen? The details are true to life but with quirky cosmo editions. The casino in Vegas has stars in the ceiling. We are on a floating ship flying across Bear Mountain, looking down at it.

Christ alive, he's even penned an explicit scene. Nova and Devil going at it. Rutting on a spaceship above the city.

A speech bubble appears on the next page between them: "My dearest Nova, you are the center of my universe. Without your light, I am lost in darkness."

But his rage returns.

The smooth pages slip through my fingers faster now. Sensing Daredevil's demons, Miss Nova pulls away, the pain evident in her blue eyes. In desperation, he commits a vague crime that pushes her further away. There's blood all over the Q&W building.

Tortured by losing her, Daredevil tries to make amends. I read the speech bubble. "My Miss Nova, you are my superpower—you brought the galaxy into my life. Without you, I have no strength."

I turn the page. As they kiss in the final panel, the speech bubble reads, "With you by my side, I can conquer any demon."

The End.

I close the graphic novel, pulse still pounding.

FORTY-SEVEN

JP

Stepping into the elevator, the mirror-finished steel doors closing feels like the end of a chapter.

"Wait," a female voice echoes, and a stiletto wedges in the gap, halting the closure.

Adrenaline fires inside me as I look up. "Lucy."

Her gaze locks on mine, blue eyes burning with purpose. She jams the button on the panel, shutting us in together.

"Remember the elevator ride we shared my first day back at work?" Her words come out rushed and breathless. "It felt like that ride lasted forever. I hope this one will too. There are some things I need to say to you."

I watch the nervous flutter of her hands. The urge to reach out and touch her is overwhelming, but I keep my fists clenched and stay still.

Someone approaches outside, but she slams the button again, shutting them out. Shutting us in.

My voice comes out low and gravelly. "Were you there? Did you hear my announcement?"

She nods slowly, eyes wide. "I heard every word. I can't believe it's true. You're really stepping down?"

"Needed to make a statement." I advance a step closer, the distance between us shrinking. "Actions over words."

"That you did." Her breath hitches, and she swallows audibly. "You created a graphic novel for me?"

A smile tugs at the corners of my mouth. "I had some help with the technical stuff. But the emotions and detail—all me. Could've worked on the plot a bit more. I now have a newfound respect for the intricacies of graphic design." I let out a chuckle.

"Nova's Light?" She smiles. "Who'd dream of coupling Miss Nova with Daredevil?"

"You know what they say about opposites." I meet her gaze directly. "Did you like it?"

"It's incredible. Beyond cool. It's... it's outstanding. And really sexy."

"I'm glad you approve." I pause, my eyes fixed on hers. "I wanted you to have a reminder of me—even if you didn't want me."

She takes a tentative step closer, close enough to touch. "In case I forget again?"

"If that were to happen... I don't think my heart could bear the brunt."

"Is that why you went back to Vegas? To hand over your responsibilities?" She looks at me with a glimmer of weariness.

"Yes. That's the only reason."

She hesitates, her gaze searching mine.

"Is that all you wanted to say to me, Lucy?" I murmur.

"No. I want to meet you halfway too," she says. "I'm ready to take that leap of faith."

Hope flares within me. "Yeah? You sure?"

"Yes. You said you love me. Do you mean it?"

I step closer, backing her against the elevator wall. Tracing a finger along her jawline, I tilt her chin up to meet my gaze. "I mean it."

Her breaths come faster as she melts under my touch. "Do you promise to talk to me if you ever relapse? I've realized I can't just expect you to be perfect. I have to try to support you." Vulnerability clouds her eyes.

"No more secrets between us," I tell her firmly.

"All right. The thing is"—she takes a deep breath—"I've never said this before... but I think I love you too."

This makes everything worth it.

I chuckle. "You think?" I raise a brow.

"I know," she says decisively.

I press her body against mine, ready to kiss her senseless. She's everything I've been searching for, and I will never let her go again.

"Wait." She pulls back slightly. "I have to know. Have I already told you this before? That I love you?"

"No." I smile down at her in amusement. "We're making new memories now."

I grab her and crash her lips to mine.

The moment our lips touch, it's a whirlwind of sensations—her taste, sweet as honey, the softness of her lips.

My hands find their way into her hair, gently grabbing a fistful. Her hands follow suit, fingers wrapping around my strands before pulling me so close that no air can slip between us.

Our kiss deepens, our bodies flush against each other as though an electric current binds us together. Our hands are everywhere, tracing a path of desperate yearning.

The walls of the elevator become our anchor as we stumble, panting and groaning and laughing breathlessly into each other's mouths at the absurdity and sheer intensity of the moment.

This small, confined space suddenly feels like our own personal wellness retreat—where past mistakes have no hold on us, and our future is a blank canvas, ready to be filled.

It's chaotic, intense, fucking beautiful.

"JP," Lucy laughs against my mouth, "if we keep going like this, we'll end up breaking this elevator."

With a smirk, I pull back just enough to look into her eyes. "Well, sweetheart, there are worse ways and places to get stuck, don't you think?"

FORTY-EIGHT

One Week Later

Lucy

Lying in my hammock, I close my eyes and turn my face toward the sunset. Its remaining light dances over Bear Mountain's rugged terrain, offering a tranquility that should be bottled up and sold.

A smile tugs at my lips as I take a deep breath, the crisp, pine-scented air filling my lungs. It's beautiful out here. The peace is palpable. After all the recent chaos, this serenity feels good. Really good.

Today, JP and I hiked, then spent the afternoon reading in his garden. Tomorrow's plan is paddleboarding. Just two normal people, on a normal vacation, stepping off the grid for a week.

We agreed to vanish from the world, just for a bit.

Escape was a necessity with all the media mayhem. JP made a public announcement about stepping down from Quinn & Wolfe, his stint in rehab, and the dated video that's been circulating. Now he's a hot topic in the meme community.

The transition was bound to be daunting—for both of us. JP, the former helm of America's biggest casino empire, is now caught in the crosshairs of uncertainty, with a stretch of leisure time yawning at him. But, as his mentor has emphasized, this hiatus is an essential part of his journey.

We're not exactly a classic couple, me with my botched memory, and him, the reformed bad boy trying to keep his nose clean. It's less Cinderella, more twisted Grimm tale, but in this chaos, we're scrabbling to find our happily ever after.

Matty and Taylor told me that the rumors are spreading like wildfire around the office about me and JP.

Of course, Matty relayed it in his unfiltered, no-nonsense manner, while Taylor applied a more empathetic filter. I've jumped from being office wallpaper, to the Memoryless Woman, to the Memoryless Woman caught in a street-side confrontation with Wolfe. And, quite honestly, it scares the shit out of me.

Living in the spotlight isn't my vibe. But if I'm

going to figure out what's between me and JP, I guess I'll have to suck it up.

In JP's book, we've been an item for months. To me, he's a thrilling new chapter. This relationship skew, courtesy of the accident and my amnesia, isn't going to resolve overnight. His memories of us aren't mine. But when we're together, playing at domestic bliss, I can't deny the connection. It's there, buried deep. I can feel it resonating in my bones. That sizzle. That affection. That love. It's in my gut. And yeah, the ovaries are feeling it too.

JP rises from the jacuzzi, every muscle of his magnificent body glistening, completely naked. Saying he's sculpted like a Greek god might be cliché, but he's a walking, dripping cliché. His thick cock protrudes proudly from its nest of groomed coarse pubic hair, like a mighty oak tree.

It's the most beautiful penis I've ever seen, even more so than anything I've seen on my ethical porn website.

"Hey!" I squeal, shivering as icy rivulets pelt down on me from his body. "That's freaking freezing."

He dips, pressing his lips to mine, and my hands defy all known self-restraint, frisking over the moisture-glossed landscape of his torso.

"Dinner in an hour," he breathes huskily

against my mouth. "Sound good?"

"Sure." I grin, feeling like eating is definitely not what I want to be doing right now. "Whatcha cooking tonight?"

"That spicy beef stew from your favorite Eritrean joint."

"Dang." I think of the dish I always order from the cozy little place near my apartment. He's confident, I'll give him that. "Pretty ambitious of you."

Apparently, I've tasted his lobster dinner that we had on our first date, like, a dozen times.

"Found some time today. Skimmed through the recipe."

"That's real sweet of you. You sure you wanna take on that challenge?"

"Absolutely. And no, you've never tried this one." His grin is infectious. "Not my version, at least."

He saunters off, giving me a view of that glorious ass. Two firm mounds of steel.

He told me that he wants to fill our relationship with countless fresh memories, even if it's just something as simple as dinner. Not that the spicy beef stew is simple. And for all his thoughtfulness, it's not exactly a meal that screams "pre-coital appetizer." Spicy Eritrean cuisine turns me into a human balloon.

And yet, despite our newly minted pact of honesty and transparency, I reckon that particular nugget of information can remain my little secret.

Bits of the past are tiptoeing back into my mind, albeit wearing fuzzy socks. As JP steered us up the mountain road, an echo of me, cross-legged and cackling while we quibbled over the superiority of rock over pop, materialized. Submerged in the bath together, as I reached for the bubble bath, I was hit by a splash of déjà vu.

Even the other day, as Libby spun around to ask if I wanted a cup of coffee, I was sideswiped by the oddest sensation of been-there-done-that. Obviously, we have, many times. The memories are trivial. But to me, they're precious breadcrumbs on the path back to myself.

They might never fully return, and I'm learning to be okay with that. Perhaps everyone's memories get a little mixed up and distorted over time. After all, what we remember is just how we saw things from our own point of view.

My phone buzzes on the table and I let out a groan, not wanting to leave the cocoon of the hammock. JP saunters over, snatches the phone, and casually scans the caller ID before handing it to me.

"It's your mom," he says.

I exhale heavily, not having spoken to her since our argument. Even responding to her texts feels like an epic feat.

JP raises an eyebrow. "She's still your mom. You should talk to her."

"Fine," I grumble as JP gently lifts me up so he can slide into the hammock behind me. I feel the hammock dip and sway as he settles in. I lean back into the warmth of his chest, enveloped in his embrace as his strong arms wrap snugly around my waist. He plants a soft kiss on my bare shoulder.

"Hi, Mom," I say, striving for a sunny cheerfulness. The hammock begins to sway gently as JP initiates a rhythmic motion.

"Lucy, I've been calling for days! Why haven't you answered?"

"I've had a lot going on," I mutter.

"I know, I just... I didn't like how we left things. I thought maybe I could come into the city and take you to dinner?"

I pause, surprised. She never suggests coming to Manhattan.

"If this is about lecturing me again..."

"No, no," she cuts in. "I want to spend time together."

JP's hold on me tightens, his body a wall of comfort behind me. His voice is a low rumble near my ear. "Tell her we'll swing by after Bear Mountain." One of his hands trails up to sweep my hair aside, baring my neck for him to kiss.

"Who's that?" Mom questions sharply.

"Tell her you're bringing your boyfriend," JP says, louder this time.

Caught off guard, I tilt my head to meet his gaze, finding a smirk playing on his lips.

"That's JP, my boyfriend," I say. "He'll be joining me."

"JP... JP Wolfe?" she screeches so hard I wince. "Your boss in that God-awful photo?"

JP shifts behind me.

"Yes, that JP. Got an issue with that?" I retort, irritated by her tone.

She fumbles for a moment. "No! No issue at all. I... I just want you to be happy, Lucy. I feel that maybe I haven't been supportive enough." There's an awkward pause. "So, I'll be seeing both of you soon then?"

"Give us a few days, Mom. We'll let you know our schedule," I promise before ending the call. I lean my head back against JP's broad, naked chest with a sigh.

A soft chuckle escapes him. "Finally, I get to

meet your mom. You've already met my sister and my nephews, after all."

I tense slightly. "I have?" More people from my life I'm supposed to know but can't remember.

"You did. And they're crazy about you. Just like I am."

"They won't if they think you stepped down from the company because of me. You don't need to do this. We can make it work without you giving up your job." I swear we've had this debate more times than I've blinked in the last few days.

"Listen. This isn't about them or the company or the whole damn world, it's about me. And you. For the next six months, my only job description is 'be a kickass boyfriend to Lucy Walsh.' Everything else can take a backseat."

"Unless you're planning to double up as my cleaner and chef, I'm not sure that's a full-time job," I challenge, half in jest, half desperately hoping he might. "What exactly does a 'kickass boyfriend' do all day? Should I be worried you'll reorganize my closet?"

He responds with unyielding conviction. "Whatever it is you need, I'm on it."

Jesus.

"Turn around," JP commands gruffly. "I need to look at your gorgeous face."

Impatiently, he lifts me up and flips me over so I'm perched on top of him in the hammock. We both nearly fall off as it wobbles from side to side.

"JP! Go easy!" I laugh as my thighs slide down on either side of him. Wow. He's throbbing hard already.

His voice drops to a husky murmur, his warm breath sending a shiver racing down my spine. "I love you, Lucy Walsh."

"I love you too, JP Wolfe," I manage to reply, my heart pounding. Our hammock sways lazily beneath us.

Our words hang thickly in the mountain air as he draws me close. His thumb grazes my bottom lip before his mouth claims mine in a slow, deep kiss that steals my breath. I clutch at him urgently, weeks of tension and worry spilling out of me.

He slides my thong to the side and his thick erection looms eagerly against my slick opening. His experienced fingers press rhythmically against my clit as he grabs my hips firmly with the other hand.

"Let me in," he commands gruffly, and I squirm slightly at his size. He slowly pushes himself into me until every inch of him is seated.

"God, that feels amazing," he groans, and his fingertips continue to work their magic on my sensitive areas as his other hand holds me firmly in place allowing him to drive deeper into me.

A wave of pleasure courses through me as I feel him pulse and swell within me. His fingers continue their magical work on my clit while his other hand holds me firmly in place, allowing him to drive into me with maximum effect.

"This angle," he grunts. "So deep. It's driving me insane."

Cursing, he thrusts into the deepest parts of me again and again with a ferocity that sends the hammock swinging wildly around us.

His face contorts in pleasure as his breathing intensifies and he grunts louder and harder with each movement, coming closer and closer to his climax.

"Lucy," he groans as he comes hard inside me.

I'm done for. My body trembles uncontrollably the moment my orgasm hits me. My spine sends a wave of electricity outward as I quiver around him.

"I'm the luckiest man alive." He grins lazily up at me before capturing my mouth in another passionate kiss.

In that kiss, nothing else matters—not the office rumors, the media circus, my missing memories. With the fervor of his lips against mine, the urgent pressure of his body, I know we can make this work.

We are the only two people in the world right now. Okay, maybe just the mountain. And I never want this feeling to end.

EPILOGUE

Nine Months Later

JP

The view from the terrace of the Bear Mountain Wellness Retreat is stunning—the lake mirrors the vibrant sunset, a palette of orange and pink. The first under the Quinn & Wolfe brand. It's a universe apart from the frenzied, glittering streets of Vegas I once called home. Out here, I feel calm and at peace.

This weekend is a big milestone for the retreat as our first guests arrive—VIPs and popular bloggers eager to experience what we offer. The staff—yogis, wellness coaches, spa therapists, waiters, chefs—they've been busting their asses to get this place polished up and running smoothly. You can see the excitement on their faces, but you can also tell they're nervous as hell.

Lucy and I are staying nearby at my place in the mountains. I'll be living here until this operation's making money like clockwork. She has to head back to the city on weekdays for her job at the firm, which isn't ideal for me, selfish bastard that I am. I miss her like crazy when she's not with me.

She's still renting her apartment and living with her friend Priya. I've asked her to move in with me, but I'm not pushing it too hard. I understand she's not quite ready to take that leap. A half-week with Lucy is better than a Lucy-less existence.

Thankfully, the gossip rags have moved on to new scandals, which means there's less heat and eyes on Lucy at work. That's all I ever cared about—keeping her safe and away from the spotlight.

Connor joins me on the terrace, handing me a beer. "You sold this place well, Wolfe. It's trending and we haven't even opened the doors. The press is eating up your whole spiritual reinvention thing. They're calling it 'Wolfe's Redemption.'"

I roll my eyes and take a long swig of my beer, the cold liquid hitting the spot. Beer's my only vice these days. "Billionaire bad boy goes Zen, builds wellness retreat to find enlightenment," I say drily. "Not my favorite PR angle."

But it was my only way to salvage the situation, and my plans.

"Exactly how hands-on are you planning to be?" Connor grins. "Will you be teaching yoga yourself?"

I shoot him a dry look. "Clearly you want this place to fail."

The terrace door slides open, and there she is— my personal sunbeam. My calm in the chaos. Vegas looks like a sad, soggy fry in comparison.

It's been a few days since I've seen Lucy and those striking blue eyes of hers. Her hair, all glossy chestnut waves, falls over her shoulders as she walks toward us, that radiant smile lighting up the whole damn terrace.

"Hey," is how she greets us, her smile infectious.

Connor greets her then makes himself scarce, no doubt reading my thoughts, which are currently R-rated and laser-focused on getting Lucy out of that T-shirt dress.

I pull her in close, a reminder of how much I've missed her. "Hey, baby," I murmur, unable to contain the affection in my voice. "I've missed you so much."

She wraps her arms around me, hugging me tight. "Is everything ready for the weekend?"

I nod, trying not to lose myself in those eyes. "How was your week at work, IT goddess?"

She grins. "Oh, just the usual, shifting buttons around on the screen like you corporate suits assume we do."

"I never thought that." Well, maybe once or twice... Truth is, I never used to get why we had so many people on the IT team. "And I'm in a T-shirt, if you haven't noticed."

She tugs at my shirt. "I noticed. You look hot."

I pull her in for a heated kiss.

"Wait," she groans playfully, pulling back just enough to catch her breath. "I have one more hour of coursework to do before I can spend time with you."

I let out a dramatic groan, my eyes still locked on hers. "Seriously, Lucy? On a Friday night? Can't you do it tomorrow?"

Lucy chuckles, her fingers tracing my jawline. "As much as I'd love to, JP, you know I have to finish this. It's the last assignment, and then I'm all yours."

I groan. "Fine."

A few months back, Lucy began a course on comic graphic design. Her creative streak, paired with her passion, makes her a natural. She's been toying with the idea of becoming a comic book artist, perhaps as a side gig, but I see her potential to soar high. Her artwork is enchanting, and her eyes sparkle with passion whenever she talks about it.

"The place looks incredible, JP. I'm so proud of you."

"I couldn't have done it without you by my side," I tell her, meaning every word. "I love you, Lucy."

"I know," she teases, her smile reaching her eyes. "And I love you too."

Standing there, the dying sun casting long shadows of gold on the wellness retreat, I look down at Lucy. Her body fits perfectly in mine, as though we were molded for each other. I can't help but feel a surge of gratitude. It's a powerful feeling, swelling inside me, making my chest feel tight.

We've had our share of fuck-ups, sure, and there's no telling what's waiting for us down the road, but this moment, right here with her, feels like hitting the jackpot.

One Year Later

Lucy

Caught up in the vibrant whirlwind of the comic

convention, my pulse syncs with the throbbing energy that buzzes through the crowd. Dressed in the radiant blue-and-gold uniform of Miss Nova, complete with thigh-high solar flare boots and a supernova symbol emblazoned across my chest, I'm a shining stellar spectacle amongst a sea of technicolor superheroes and eccentric villains.

From behind, a deep voice, rich and resonant, rumbles into my ear. "Your costume—it's pretty fierce."

Spinning around, I come face-to-face with the "Death-Defying 'Devil". The crimson and blue leather of his suit clings to his muscular form, accentuating every contour of his body. His gloved finger reaches out, playing with the ends of my jet-black wig.

"Do you come here often?" he questions, his voice layered with teasing undertones that send a thrill running along my spine, causing the faux fur trim of my costume to flutter slightly.

Damn, he still gets me every time.

Even though I now live with the man, my stomach still flips with butterflies when he's in *and* out of costume.

Arching a flirty smile, I quip, "Only when I'm not occupied with fighting crime and looking drop-dead fabulous. Figured I'd see what the fuss was about. Heard a certain devilishly handsome masked man might be present."

His mask-covered eyes narrow slightly in interest. "Is that so?" His teasing voice reverberates through the air. "In this case, it appears you've found your masked man. Now what are you going to do with him?"

"Hmm, decisions, decisions..." My grin morphs into a smirk. "That depends—does the suit come off, or are you just trying to entice a woman through that tiny mouth slit?"

His laughter, rich and warm, resonates through his metallic suit. My heart threatens to jump out of my chest. This is the best comic convention ever and way better than any of my adult graphic novel scenes.

"How about a tour?" I purr, trailing a claw down his chiseled chest. "I could use a strong, capable man to guide me through this labyrinth."

Unexpectedly, he shakes his head. "Afraid I can't."

What's this curveball? This isn't in the script.

"Why not?" My playful guise slips, replaced by genuine bewilderment.

"Because I'm on the hunt for my wife here."

I blink rapidly. "Daredevil isn't married, though."

"He's looking to change that."

And then, he does the unthinkable. Daredevil, in his striking crimson suit, gets down on one knee. His striking figure against the bustling convention backdrop stirs a ripple of surprise, the lively chatter giving way to a collective gasp. The focus of the crowd swings toward us, all eyes riveted on the scene unfolding.

A small box emerges from his suit. As he cracks it open, the twinkling gem nestled inside outshines the cosplay weaponry around us. It's not some prop ring, it's a diamond ring—a real one. The air in my lungs seizes. Am I hallucinating from the heat of the costume?

"Lucy Walsh," he says, his voice echoing in the suddenly quiet area, "will you do me the honor of being my wife?"

My vision blurs with emotion as I stare, astonished. I manage a choked-out "yes", and the crowd detonates into applause. Daredevil rises, sweeping me into his arms. An elated shriek escapes me as he sweeps me off my feet, his hands gripping my backside.

"This is the most absurdly romantic proposal ever!" I exclaim, laughter and tears mingling.

In one smooth motion, he rips off his mask and crushes his mouth to mine.

I break away, beaming at him.

"Quiero pasar el resto de mi vida contigo," I attempt in my abysmal Spanish accent. I only recently discovered the meaning behind those words - *I want to spend the rest of my life with you.*

Among the superheroes and fantasy characters, on this day, I found my real-life hero.

THE END

ABOUT ROSA

I'm Rosa, a contemporary romance author based in the UK. My stories revolve around strong and sassy heroines, who are paired with alpha heroes, creating a blend of steamy and humorous moments.

My characters are far from perfect; they have genuine flaws and insecurities that make them relatable and human. I love incorporating certain tropes into my work, such as billionaire alphas, age gap romances, workplace romances, enemies-to-lovers, and grumpy sunshine characters.

ALSO BY ROSA

Have you met the grumpy London misters yet? Each one in the series is a standalone, dual-point-of-view romantic comedy with heat, banter and a happy ending.

The London Mister Series

Taming Mr. Walker: An Enemies to Lovers Age Gap Romance

Resisting Mr. Kane: An Age Gap Office Romance

Fighting Mr. Knight: A Billionaire Office Romance

Made in the USA
Middletown, DE
21 October 2023

41201398R10318